# FORGOTTEN MURDER

# FORGOTTEN MURDER

## Dolores Gordon-Smith

This first world edition published 2018
in Great Britain and 2019 in the USA by
SEVERN HOUSE PUBLISHERS LTD of
Eardley House, 4 Uxbridge Street, London W8 7SY.
Trade paperback edition first published
in Great Britain and the USA 2019 by
SEVERN HOUSE PUBLISHERS LTD.

British Library Cataloguing in Publication Data
*A CIP catalogue record for this title is available from the British Library.*

ISBN-13: 978-0-7278-8846-4 (cased)
ISBN-13: 978-1-84751-970-2 (trade paper)
ISBN-13: 978-1-4483-0180-5 (e-book)

This is a work of fiction. Names, characters, places and incidents
are either the product of the author's imagination or are used fictitiously.
Except where actual historical events and characters are being described
for the storyline of this novel, all situations in this publication are
fictitious and any resemblance to actual persons, living or dead,
business establishments, events or locales is purely coincidental.

*All Severn House titles are printed on acid-free paper.*

Severn House Publishers support the Forest Stewardship Council™ [FSC™],
the leading international forest certification organisation.
All our titles that are printed on FSC certified paper carry the FSC logo.

Typeset by Palimpsest Book Production Ltd.,
Falkirk, Stirlingshire, Scotland.
Printed and bound in Great Britain by
TJ International, Padstow, Cornwall.

*Dedicated to the 'real' Jenny.*
*With love.*

# ONE

Jack Haldean looked over the breakfast table at his wife. He repeated the last two words to himself. His wife. It seemed incredible that Elizabeth Lucy Haldean, *née* Wingate – Betty – should actually be here, with him, not at a night club or restaurant or for a few stolen hours in the park, but here, at breakfast in their own house, eating toast and marmalade and drinking tea.

Where to live had been a thorny problem. Betty had some money of her own, but even their joint funds weren't inexhaustible and flats – at least, affordable flats – in London were hard to find. They had spent quite a lot of time searching the parts of the city where they fancied living before Jack's landlady, Mrs Pettycure, had come up with the perfect solution.

The lodger on the ground floor, Mrs Kenworthy, was vacating her rooms to live with her sister in Bournemouth. Would Major Haldean and his bride care to take over her rooms in addition to his own? What's more, her maid, Kathleen Quinn, would be willing to oblige. That would give them a whole half of the house, with a separate entrance and a garden.

Major Haldean and his bride-to-be could hardly believe their luck.

So here he was. At breakfast in his own house, looking out onto his own garden, with his own wife.

They had had an exhilarating honeymoon in Italy – the tablecloth was an Italian souvenir bought on the Rialto – but the sheer everydayness of seeing Betty crunching toast gave him a little jolt of nearly painful joy. Life wasn't a holiday, however much fun that had been. Life was, amazingly enough, this deep contentment of tea, toast, breakfast and Betty.

Betty; clever and kind; light brown hair, blue eyes and freckles. She didn't care for her freckles but he thought they were adorable.

Betty stopped crunching toast and slowly turned to look at

him. 'Whatever are you staring at me like that for, Jack? Have I got marmalade on my chin?'

He laughed apologetically. 'I'm sorry, sweetheart. I was just thinking how nice it is being here, with you.'

Her eyes sparkled and, pushing her chair back, she came to stand behind him. She put her hands on his shoulders and dropped a kiss on the top of his head.

'Don't get marmalade in my hair,' he murmured, covering one of her hands with his.

'I can eat without getting it everywhere,' she said, pressing her thumbs into his shoulders. 'You ought to know that by now. What are you doing today?'

Jack wriggled back his chair and smiled up at her. That was great, too. That someone should really care what he did with his day.

'You look,' she said suspiciously, 'very pleased with yourself.'

'It was a very nice breakfast,' he said with a grin. 'And I'm enjoying the company.'

She dropped another kiss on his hair. 'Well? What are you doing today?'

'I've told Archie Keyne I'll see him at the magazine office at eleven. That should take up most of the day. After that,' he said, doing his best to look doleful, 'because my wife is heartless, I'm cast back to my lonely bachelor existence.'

Betty gave a crack of laughter. 'Heartless, indeed! Jack, it's one evening only, a girls' night in. You'd be bored to death listening to Jenny Langton and me chattering about Doris Beckett and Eileen Padstow and do you remember what Miss Fitzwilliam said to Winnie McKenna when she found her trying to sneak a white mouse into the dormitory and so on.'

'I could listen avidly, take notes, and start a new career writing schoolgirl fiction.'

'Stick to detective stories, darling. They're much more your thing.'

Jack squeezed her hand. 'If you say so. I'll go and play snooker at the club. The evening belongs to you and Jenny Langton.'

With one eye on the clock, Jennifer Langton checked her appearance critically in the mirror inside the open wardrobe door. The new two-piece, light-grey suit had caused some heart searching. The advert in Marshall and Snelgrove's catalogue – the catalogue had been the cause of much study – described the dove grey, stockinette jumper suit as 'useful and becoming' and also as 'inexpensive'.

Well, Marshall and Snelgrove might think that five guineas for a dress was inexpensive but five guineas was a sizable chunk of money. It was the best part of nearly a fortnight's wages but, thought Jenny, adjusting the wardrobe mirror to make the most of the light from the window, she just had to look smart at work. She had plans for work and couldn't afford to look anything but smart.

Not only that, but she was meeting her old friend, Betty, that evening and that was certainly worth making an effort for.

She and Betty had been in the same house and the same dormitory at school. Would she be the same? Marriage did change some people, she knew. In a way, although she'd happily agreed to the suggestion of a girls' night in, Jenny was sorry not to be meeting Betty's new husband. She'd seen him at the wedding, of course, but that wasn't the same as meeting him properly. Especially, thought Jenny, giving the grey suit a final nod of approval, as the husband was Jack Haldean, the detective story writer.

*The Secret of the Second Shroud* (author Jack Haldean) lay on her bedside table and it was responsible for her going to sleep at least half an hour later than usual last night.

But still, thought Jenny, picking up her coat, Jack Haldean or not, she was really looking forward to this evening.

Mr Gilbert Lee, senior partner of Wilson and Lee, house agents, Stowfleet, Surrey, stirred his tea as he read the *Daily Mail*. The article that had caught his eye was, as so many articles in the newspapers seemed to be nowadays, about the Modern Girl and the need for an up-to-date employer to recognise her capabilities. It really was extraordinary just how many articles on the same theme he had read recently. Not that Gilbert Lee, who had been married for twenty-three years, had ever doubted a woman's capability, modern or not.

He was up-to-date he thought, with a degree of satisfaction.

He had to be. Stowfleet had grown out of all recognition from the village in which his grandfather had founded the firm sixty-five years ago. In a wave of pre-war building, London had first lapped, then encircled the village, so that although, as he was keen to point out to prospective clients, Stowfleet retained its village atmosphere, it had all the conveniences of actually being (more or less) in London.

How much more or less depended, of course, on the customer. To those who hankered after rustic charm, he pointed out the old-world shops in the high street, the ancient pubs, the duck pond and the village common. To those who wanted a faster pace of life, he emphasised the excellence, speed and frequency of the railway up to the City. Yes, it was all about finding out what the customer wanted and letting them have it. If these chappies who wrote this stuff in the papers about up-to-date employers and the Modern Girl ever talked to him, he'd be able to show them how a modern firm worked.

Why, only six weeks ago, conscious he was breaking new ground, he had employed Miss Jennifer Langton, and a nice, hardworking girl she was turning out to be.

If Mr Lee had a rather more suspicious nature, he would've realised the number of articles he'd read about the Modern Girl had increased substantially six weeks ago.

Jenny Langton knew that simply working hard and being pleasant, polite and punctual wasn't enough. She'd noticed how Mr Lee invariably picked up the topmost of the daily newspapers as he walked through the outer office when he arrived, to read with his morning cup of tea.

As she was in the office a good half hour before Mr Lee, it was a simple matter to flick through the papers and leave the topmost one turned down, not at the property pages, but on any article on the Modern Girl she came across. Wilson and Lee were a decent firm and Mr Lee a likable man but, Jenny had quickly decided, needed their attitudes bringing up to date.

Jenny, whose grey suit had drawn an appreciative stare from Albert, the office boy, glanced up from her typewriter into Gilbert Lee's office, saw him absorbed in the newspaper, and turned away with a satisfied smile.

One of these days – surely it would be soon? – Mr Lee would

cotton onto the idea that she – the only girl, modern or otherwise, in the office – was capable of doing far more than taking calls and typing up particulars of houses.

The telephone shrilled beside her. Jenny, with her best telephone manner, answered the call, professionalism turning to friendliness as she recognised the caller. 'Mrs McKenzie? Mr McKenzie's not well? Oh, I'm sorry to hear that. Yes, Mr Lee is here. I'll just put you through.'

And if Mr McKenzie was ill, that would scupper up the morning's timetable, thought Jenny as she transferred the call. Robert McKenzie, a senior in the firm, had a viewing that morning.

Gilbert Lee was also sorry to hear Bob McKenzie was ill. Mrs McKenzie was apologetic but firm. Her husband had hardly slept last night and was now sneezing and coughing in bed. Yes, they had called the doctor. And yes, it was probably nothing more than a bad cold, but even so, Bob couldn't possibly come into the office today.

It was, thought Gilbert Lee, very inconvenient, as he hung up the telephone with a sigh. He pulled the ledger of appointments towards him and glanced down the list. Stephens and Whittaker were both tied up with viewings, Connor was engaged with Boxted, the solicitors, which left, he thought glumly, old Southwick. His heart sank.

McKenzie should have visited Saunder's Green that morning to take down the particulars. Saunder's Green? He couldn't call the house to mind, but he was sure he'd heard something about it. What the dickens was it? Something his wife had said?

He drummed his fingers on the desk, chasing the memory. That was it! Saunder's Green was supposed to be haunted. Mr Lee snorted dismissively. That sort of nonsense could do a lot of harm to a property's reputation.

Saunder's Green, thought Mr Lee, visualising its location, could be a very desirable property, even though it probably needed bringing up to date. It was certainly in a first-class spot. It was just a pity he had to send Southwick.

Ernest Southwick was excellent with figures but he lacked imagination. McKenzie would have done it justice and, perhaps, even more than justice.

Southwick could take down the particulars of Buckingham Palace and make it sound about as exciting as a gas works. Yes, all the measurements would be correct, but a house was more than measurements with so many bedrooms, so many reception rooms, rent or purchase price so much, rates, water, electricity and gas ditto. A prospective client started with the particulars and that was the first step to being *sold* the property. They had to be made to imagine what it would be like to live in the house, to be given a vision of a rosy future that could be theirs if they made the house their home.

Still, it couldn't be helped. Mr Lee got up from his desk and, crossing the room to the outer office, opened the door. Southwick was there, bent over a file and, seated behind her typewriter, was the new girl, Miss Langton. She looked up and smiled. Jenny had a very nice smile.

He was just about to call Southwick's name when he paused. What about Miss Langton? She was smart and enthusiastic. An up-to-date employer, he thought, unconsciously echoing what he had just read in the *Daily Mail*, needed to recognise the Modern Girl's capability.

Why not give her a chance? If she did a good job, he might even let her show any prospective tenants around. And that, he thought, with the *Daily Mail* article in mind, would show any clients that they were dealing with a thoroughly up-to-date firm.

He cleared his throat. 'Miss Langton?' he called. 'Could I have a word?'

Jenny Langton closed the door of Wilson and Lee behind her, bubbling with excitement. It had worked! She had wondered how Mr Southwick would take it when she, gathering her coat and hat, had told him she was going out to view a property. If he was going to sulk, that might make office life difficult. To her relief he merely said that he was glad to be staying indoors. It might be September but the wind was chilly.

Still grinning to herself, she looked around to cross the road – and stopped dead.

There was a man, a man in a black coat and trilby hat, in the shadow of the tree across the road. Jenny drew her breath in, then, with sudden determination, stepped off the pavement to cross the road.

The man turned and walked quickly away.

Jenny drew back. She could hardly chase after him, but he'd been there. Again.

She'd seen him before. She'd first seen him when she was very young. She'd seen him at home in Yorkshire, she'd seen him at school in Surrey, and now here he was, in Stowfleet. The man never did anything but watch, but he was *there.*

He had never approached her and never attempted to speak. Sometimes it would be a couple of years between sightings but she knew it was the same man.

Her mother had thought she was imagining things. Mum had been a very practical, down-to-earth sort of person, who had no time for silly fancies, as she put it. Yes, Jenny very well might see a man, but it was ridiculous to suppose that it was the same man.

Jenny shook herself. The Watcher was gone and she had a job to do. Perhaps Mum had been right. Maybe it was nothing more than coincidence and imagination. She didn't really believe it, but whatever the truth, she couldn't allow herself to be distracted, not now.

Very consciously, she fixed her mind on Saunder's Green. She wanted to get this right. She needed to make a success of her job. Very literally, she couldn't afford not to.

Her mother had died five months ago. Dad, a doctor, had died eight years previously. Her two brothers, Martin and Eric, were following in Dad's footsteps and that, in a way, was the problem.

Jenny was very proud of her brothers. Eric, two years younger than her, was studying medicine at Leeds. Martin, who was eight years older, had qualified as a doctor some time ago. Four months ago he'd had the opportunity to buy a partnership in a good practice in Leeds. The trouble was that the cost of the partnership was just over £1,500.

Once that had been paid, together with the expense of Eric at university, there was precious little left of Dad's money. Martin had promised to make it up to her in the future, which was all very well – Martin certainly would keep his word – but she had to live in the here and now.

So Jenny had to earn her own living, but doing what?

She'd had a good education at Rotherdean, Mum's old school in Surrey, but she wasn't *trained* for anything. Rotherdean expected its pupils to be good wives and mothers in whatever corner of the world their husbands saw fit to live. Marriage, not work, was their expected destiny.

Jenny had grown up with stories of doughty daughters of Empire doing their bit amongst fire, flood and famine. Elementary nursing had played a part there. Rotherdean had taught her how to manage a house, both at home and abroad, instruct servants, supervise the cooking and presentation of dishes from bandicoot (stewed in milk) to hash bogurrah (mutton with ginger) how to greet an Indian Native Prince and what to say to an Arab chieftain's first wife. In addition, she was taught French, Latin, fine needlework, botany, the piano and had been instructed in watercolours.

That was all well and good and doubtless useful to the right woman in the right place, but none of it added up to a job. At a pinch, Rotherdean admitted that occasionally a pupil might be employed as a governess, but Jenny loathed the thought.

No; she didn't want to be a governess but she did have to work. She spent some of her small reserve of money on learning to type. That was bound to be useful. Martin wanted her to take a job in Leeds, but she'd set her sights on London.

Mum had been a Londoner and always talked about London very fondly. Jenny had managed to find a room in a decent boarding-house in Catton Street off Southampton Row, and then set about finding a job. She had never thought about being a house agent but the advert in the *Evening Standard* had leapt out at her. The idea of Stowfleet being a village was, to her Yorkshire-bred senses, almost laughable, but at least she wasn't hemmed in by endless streets. There was open space in Stowfleet. Mum would've liked it.

Mum. It would be nice to have been able to tell Mum where she was and what she was doing and how, after only a few weeks, she had made the longed-for jump from behind the office desk. Apart from anything else, the sensation of being outside in the sunshine, even if the wind was chilly, instead of being inside made her feel as if she'd been given the next best thing to a holiday.

She arrived at the gate to Saunder's Green. She opened her handbag, checking the note from the office. The house was untenanted, but the housekeeper was a Mrs Offord. Jenny took a moment to gather her impressions.

Saunder's Green was one of a series of houses built on a slope that ran up to half an acre or so of shrubby grass that was all that remained of the green. At a guess, Saunder's Green had come first and the other houses accumulated around it, so that it was now part of a suburban square.

It was a substantial detached house – could it be described as 'manageable'? thought Jenny, in the language of Wilson and Lee – separated from the road by a reasonably sized front garden with a driveway leading to what was obviously the later addition of a garage.

How old was it? Victorian, about 1880 or so, at a guess. Brick-built with a red-tiled roof, it seemed to Jenny to exude stability and comfort. It would, Jenny thought, who had studied Wilson and Lee's 'To be Let' or 'Sold' properties closely, sell for anything up to £850, depending on the condition inside.

Not that, as Mr Wilson had told her, Saunder's Green was for sale. It was to be let only, but with a value of about £850, that meant the rent should be about one pound, ten shillings a week. She guessed Mr McKenzie would verify the figures, but if she'd got them right, that would be another feather in her cap.

She opened the gate and walked down the flower-bordered path to the front door. The date 1882 was carved into the stone lintel above the door. She'd been right about the age.

The door was opened by a plump, comfortable-looking, older woman, evidently Mrs Offord.

'You're from the house agents?' she said. 'Mr Lee telephoned to say to expect you. Miss Langton, is it? Come in, do,' she said, leading her through the lobby into the hall. 'Let me take your things, Miss.'

She opened the cupboard in the hall, hung up Jenny's coat and hat, and turned round with a smile. 'I must say, I was surprised that it was a . . .' She broke off and quickly summed up the grey suit and Jenny's apparent social status. 'A lady who was coming. Mind you, ladies do all sorts of jobs nowadays, don't they, Miss?'

'We have to,' said Jenny, with a smile, entering the hall. 'However, I enjoy what I do very much. I love looking round houses.'

Now, why had she said that? The truth was that although she had the usual amount of curiosity, she had no particular affinity with houses as such. A job was a job and she was determined to do her best, but this house was something special.

The hall was exactly *right,* so much what a proper hallway should be. An imposing staircase led up to the upper floor, lit by a coloured glass window at the turn of the stairs, throwing patches of rich amber and blue light onto the brass-rod separated stairs. It was all just as it should be, even to the carved wooden pineapple on the newel post of the banister.

'What a lovely house!' she exclaimed.

Mrs Offord smiled at her genuine pleasure. 'It's nice to hear you say so, Miss. I do like to keep it nice, even though I say so myself. Mind you, there's plenty of work for me and Mavis, the housemaid. I daresay she'd be willing to stay on if that was desired. She's in the village at the moment, but I know I can speak for her.'

That was worth knowing. Finding the staff to run a large house like this was the big difficulty in letting these older houses. They had been built in the secure knowledge there was an endless stream of girls willing to go into domestic service. That was before the war and long before what was called the servant problem had arisen. Servants nowadays wanted rather better wages and an array of labour-saving devices that would have shocked the original tenants of Saunder's Green.

'Would you stay on, Mrs Offord?' asked Jenny.

Mrs Offord's face fell. 'I can't say as I would, Miss. I've only stayed on to oblige, like. I was looking to retire, when the new tenant comes.'

That really might be a problem. There were quite a few Victorian houses on Wilson and Lee's books, no matter what the papers said about a shortage of housing. The staff to run them simply couldn't be found or afforded.

'If a family was here,' said Mrs Offord, unconsciously echoing Jenny's thoughts, 'there'd have to be more staff, of course.'

'Was there a family here?' asked Jenny. She felt oddly moved that Saunder's Green, with its coloured window and polished oak bannisters, should be left unloved. The house needed a family. A happy family in a happy house.

'What, with children, you mean, Miss?' Mrs Offord shook her head. 'I've not known a family here, Miss. Not in my time, and I've been here twelve years and more. No, it was Colonel and Mrs Trenchard that had it, and after the Colonel passed away, Mrs Trenchard kept it on, even though it was really too big for her. For the last couple of years she couldn't manage the stairs, poor soul, so it's all untouched upstairs. Not that I've neglected the cleaning, of course.'

'No, of course not,' agreed Jenny. 'I can see it's been very well kept.' She looked around the hall and gave a little sigh of satisfaction. 'I don't know what it is, but it feels a welcoming place, somehow.'

Mrs Offord was obviously pleased. 'It's funny you should say that, Miss, but I've always felt that, too. I've always found it a very welcoming house, despite what some say.'

'What do they say?' asked Jenny. If it was a question of drains, draughts, a leaky roof or awkward neighbours, she'd better know.

Mrs Offord seemed flustered. 'It's nothing, really, Miss. Perhaps I shouldn't have mentioned it. I daresay you'll think it's a lot of nonsense and silly tales.'

Jenny was intrigued. 'What is?'

Mrs Offord took a deep breath. 'I hardly like to say, Miss, but there are those who say it's *haunted*. I know what it sounds like,' she added, bridling at Jenny's sceptical look. 'I must say I've never seen anything myself, but Mrs Trenchard, she saw something and, of course, the tale got around, as it would. Mrs Trenchard,' she added, as if suspicious Jenny was going to argue the point, 'was as honest as the day was long.'

She was obviously so sincere, Jenny moderated her scepticism. She didn't believe her, but the last thing she wanted to do was put the housekeeper's back up.

'That must've been very upsetting for her,' she said diplomatically.

'Oh, she wasn't frightened, Miss. It's not something to be scared of. Mrs Trenchard said as how it was a lady in blue. That's all. Just a lady in blue. She saw her a few times. Out in the garden, it was. It was always in the garden and always in the afternoon. Mrs Trenchard said she'd see her just like it might be out of the corner of your eye and then gone. The lady in blue doesn't mean any harm but she's there.'

Jenny decided not to add the ghost, scary or not, to her notes. In her opinion, Saunder's Green House would be difficult enough to let as it was, without telling any prospective tenant an afternoon in the garden would be disturbed by visitors from beyond the veil. 'That's very interesting,' she said, hoping that was enough of a placatory comment.

Mrs Offord shook her head. 'I can see as how you don't believe me, Miss, but I know what I was told. But as I say, she does stay in the garden.' She shook herself, as if to draw a line under the conversation. 'Never mind about that. You've come to be shown over the house. Shall we start with the kitchen?'

Jenny followed Mrs Offord through the green baize door off the hall, noting measurements. A good-sized kitchen, fifteen foot by twelve, with a vast old-fashioned range, which led on to Mrs Offord's sitting-room, where she did the household mending. Not that, as Mrs Offord said, there had been much with just poor Mrs Trenchard to look after. A scullery (eleven foot by seven) coal store and larder completed what Wilson and Lee would undoubtedly call the domestic offices.

Once more in the hall, Mrs Offord led the way upstairs. 'We'd better start at the top of the house, Miss, and work down,' she said, as she wheezed her way up the attic stairs. 'Not that I ever comes up here much.'

The dusty attics (two rooms, twenty-three foot by twenty) were, to Jenny's eyes, exactly like any other attics with a collection of old boxes and trunks.

She was about to go downstairs when a box, a white-painted ottoman with a cushioned seat and a wooden back, caught her eye. It would be perfect for toys. Dollies, skittles and a jack-in-the-box that would make her jump.

'I like the ottoman,' said Jenny. 'It needs repainting and upholstering but it's a nice thing. I suppose it's empty?'

She lifted the lid. It wasn't empty. A jumble of Victorian dolls with porcelain faces stared out at her and there, on top, was a small box with a clasped lid. She slipped back the clasp and, with a tinny whistle, out came the papier mâché clown's head of the jack-in-the box.

Jenny started back. For a fraction of a second, she was very small and the jack-in-the-box was very large. The clown's face, with its sinister painted smile, rocked on the cloth-covered spring. Jenny gulped, squeezed it back into the box, fastened the clasp and shut the lid of the ottoman.

'There now,' said Mrs Offord in surprise. 'I wonder how Mrs Trenchard came to have such a thing? I never knew it was there and that's a fact. What a face! It'd scare a child, that would.'

Yes, it certainly would, agreed Jenny to herself.

'Shall we go downstairs?' she asked. For some reason the sight of the old toys had rattled her.

First the Watcher and now the jack-in-the-box. She got a firm grip on her nerves. Maybe Mum had been right about the Watcher. Maybe she really was making a mountain out of a molehill. Maybe, as Mum had said, there was no Watcher, just a man – different men – who she happened to see from time to time. Maybe; but she didn't really believe it and she hadn't liked the jack-in-the-box.

Once on the first floor, she consciously resumed the mantle of house agent. A bathroom with a magnificent Victorian bath, a separate lavatory on a dark-stained oak step, various cupboards and four good-sized bedrooms were all noted down. Everything needed painting, but nothing was in disrepair.

That left two adjacent bedrooms, one belonging to the absent Mavis and the other which was Mrs Offord's own.

'I don't mind if you go in, Miss,' said Mrs Offord easily, as Jenny hesitated by the door. 'And I'm sure Mavis won't mind you looking in her room either. It's not as if you're prying, is it? I knows you have to take down the particulars.'

'What a lovely room!' said Jenny impulsively as she walked in.

It really was a lovely room, bright with sunshine, looking out onto the garden. The gardens themselves, with the lawn, flower beds and a big cedar tree in the middle, would be a wonderful place to have afternoon tea.

'It is a nice room,' said Mrs Offord, with some pride. 'Mind you, we did have a problem with damp. That's a good while ago now, of course, and we haven't had any problems since. It turned out to be a leaky gutter and when the Colonel sorted it out, he said to me, as the room needed re-decorating, I could choose the wallpaper and furniture.'

'If I had this room, I'd want a window seat so I could enjoy the view,' said Jenny.

Mrs Offord laughed. 'I haven't much time for sitting and staring out the window, Miss, but it's funny you should say that. There was a window-seat here, but it had to be taken out because of the damp. Colonel Trenchard, he did talk about having it replaced, but I said as I didn't miss it, so he left it as it was.'

'It was blue,' said Jenny with complete certainty. 'Powder blue.'

Why on earth had she said that? It was weird. It was as if she'd *seen* the window seat. It wasn't as if anything else in the room was blue. There was a pinewood chest of drawers, stained to look like dark oak, a large wardrobe built into the alcove that matched the chest of drawers, a dark maroon bedspread on the bed and floral wallpaper with a pattern of red roses.

Mrs Offord's eyes widened. 'Blue? That's strange, Miss. Now you come to mention it, I think it was blue.'

'The tiles round the fireplace were blue as well,' said Jenny. How she knew she couldn't say but she knew. 'They had blue flowers on them.'

Mrs Offord stared at her. Jenny could see sudden fear in her eyes.

Without a word, Mrs Offord walked over to the fire screen and pulled it away from the empty grate.

The tiles round the fireplace were a pattern of blue cornflowers.

'You don't have second sight or anything, Miss?' asked Mrs Offord uneasily. 'Because how you knew about those tiles I do not know, as true as I'm stood here.'

'No, no, I don't have second sight,' said Jenny hastily. The idea frightened her. There must be a reasonable explanation. She smiled weakly, trying to reassure the housekeeper. 'It's a common design for Victorian tiles.'

That was rubbish. Jenny didn't have a clue if it was a common design or not. She'd never thought about tiles. On the other hand, say it *was* a common design. That must be it. She'd seen tiles like these before – they were very pretty – and, without realising it, had remembered them. Naturally, once she'd thought of the blue window seat, it was obvious there had to be blue tiles to go with it.

And why had she thought the window seat was blue? Well, that was obvious. What other colour would you have in a room like this? It was all this dark oak and gloomy maroon with the red roses that was wrong. What this room needed was a white paper with something blue and yellow as a pattern. That would bring out all the natural light in the room.

Mrs Offord relaxed. 'A common design? That must be it, Miss, but it's funny you should guess it straight off like that.'

And that was all it had been. A lucky guess, but for a moment the actual room had seemed to be overlaid with another room, a room with a powder blue window seat, a bed with a white bedspread and white wallpaper with a blue and yellow pattern. She shook herself. She had a job to do and, what's more, she didn't want the housekeeper to start any sort of gossip that might get back to Mr Lee's ears about the young lady from the house agents having funny fancies.

'I wish I was always as good at guessing,' said Jenny, starting to measure the room. 'I could win some money on the Grand National, perhaps.'

That was mundane enough. It could even pass as a joke. She was rewarded with a chuckle from Mrs Offord.

'That's thirteen foot by twelve,' said Jenny, jotting down the figures in her notebook. 'I've finished in here. I just need to look at the last bedroom and that's all the upstairs done.'

'Very good, Miss,' said Mrs Offord. 'The other bedroom, Mavis's room, is next to this,' she said, leading the way out onto the landing. 'You can, if you like, make the two rooms into a suite, as there's a connecting door, not that we ever use it. Here we are,' she said, opening the door into the bedroom.

Jenny gripped her hands together so tightly her nails dug into her palms. Mavis's room, a smaller version of Mrs Offord's bedroom, was full of natural light with the same view of the garden, but here the wallpaper wasn't a pattern of red roses; it was white with blue cornflowers tied round with a yellow ribbon.

It was the wallpaper she had imagined in Mrs Offord's room.

'This room,' she said, and was alarmed to hear her voice come out as a croak. 'This room hasn't been redecorated, has it?'

'Not in my time,' said Mrs Offord, casting Jenny a worried glance. 'Excuse me, Miss, but do you need to sit down? You don't look well. Are you all right?'

Jenny took a deep breath. She was angry with herself. She'd been given the opportunity to tackle a job that she really wanted to do and instead of getting on with it, she'd allowed herself to be rattled by a box of old toys and some wallpaper.

This was *stupid*! She must've seen the wallpaper somewhere else. That had to be the explanation and it was plain silly to allow herself to be scared. Because that's what she was; scared by the wallpaper.

'I'm fine,' she said, as firmly as she could. She had to measure the room. Measure the room and note down the features. That was what she was being paid to do. She pulled out the tape measure but had to blink hard to see the numbers on the tape.

Mrs Offord was still looking at her solicitously, but Jenny forced her hand not to tremble as she wrote down her notes. *Twelve foot by ten. Adjoining door to next room. South facing, overlooking rear garden.*

It was a small achievement but Jenny felt as if she'd won a battle when she'd completed her notes.

'Shall we,' she said, again making an effort to sound as natural as possible, 'go downstairs?'

The downstairs rooms were, mercifully, free of shocks. The dining room, the living room and the conservatory were all explored, measured and noted down. There remained one more room, running along from the conservatory, which also looked out onto the garden. It had a tiled floor and was roofed in but open along two sides, a bright, fresh space on a day like this.

The view, into the large garden with its sunlit lawn, bushes, flower beds and trees in the distance, was, in Jenny's opinion, very nearly perfect.

A man – the gardener presumably – was clipping a hedge at the far end of the lawn. Wood pigeons cooed in the cedar tree and sparrows chirped in the bushes.

Jenny drew her breath in with sheer pleasure. 'This is absolutely wonderful,' she said impulsively.

Mrs Offord was obviously pleased. 'It is nice,' she said. 'Mrs Trenchard, she liked to come out here.'

Jenny wasn't surprised. If she lived in the house, she'd never tire of looking at the garden. That feeling she'd had when she came into the house, that feeling, very deep down, that everything was safe, secure and absolutely right, came back in full force.

'Naturally, I'd see Mrs Trenchard was well wrapped up,' continued Mrs Offord, 'especially in the last year, when she was in a wheeled chair, poor soul. When the weather was warm, she liked to have her lunch here in the porch.'

The porch? That didn't sound quite a grand enough word for a house agent's brochure. A porch, to Jenny's way of thinking, was somewhere to keep macs and umbrellas, not somewhere to dine in beautiful surroundings, looking out onto the garden.

'Could it be called a veranda?' Jenny suggested. That was a better word than porch.

Mrs Offord pursed her lips. 'I suppose you could call it a veranda, Miss. Come to think of it, that's what the Colonel always called it. He'd been in India and he said that's what they called porches there. Mrs Trenchard though, she called this room the loggia.'

*Loggia.* That was the perfect word. Jenny noted it down, together with the measurements (eleven foot by twenty) and shut her notebook with a snap.

'How do I get into the garage?'

'The entrance is on the other side of the conservatory, Miss. It's this way.'

Mrs Offord stepped down from the loggia, onto the path that ran along the back of the house. 'I haven't been in here for a good while,' she said, as they came to the door set into the wall. 'I've just looked in from time to time, to see everything's as it should be. The Colonel, he used to come in here, but there's steps down and my knees aren't as good as they used to be.'

She opened the door and Jenny stepped onto the little landing at the top of the garage steps, blinking her eyes to adjust to the dim light. The garage had been built on the lower side of the slope and the floor, some twelve feet below, had obviously been dug out to make a level surface.

She was about to go down the steps, when a curious disinclination to do anything of the sort came to her.

'You need to hold onto the rail, Miss,' said Mrs Offord from behind her. 'The Colonel, he had a nasty fall on those steps.'

Jenny shook off the feeling and, holding the wooden banister, stepped down into the garage. Once in the garage, the uneasy feeling vanished. Honestly, what on earth was wrong with her? Mrs Offord was a comfortable sort of woman, but Jenny was beginning to think she had been more rattled than she cared to think about by her tales of a woman in blue. Perhaps it was because Mrs Offord was so ordinary, her story of a ghost had made such an impression.

Garage; brick built, tiled roof, with workbench and space for at least two cars, measuring fourteen foot by fourteen. Nothing to get the heebie-jeebies about.

She shut up her notebook and ran up the stairs to the waiting Mrs Offord.

'I wish I could run up stairs like you, Miss,' said Mrs Offord with a smile. 'Would you be wanting to see the garden?'

'Yes, please,' said Jenny, shutting the garage door behind her.

'Would you mind if the gardener showed you round, Miss?' asked Mrs Offord. 'I'm expecting the butcher's boy to be along soon and I don't want to miss him. The gardener is George Meredith from the village and he can show you everything you need to see. I'll just call him, shall I?'

She raised her arm to wave to the gardener, but Jenny stopped her. 'I can show myself round, Mrs Offord,' said Jenny. 'I don't want to disturb the gardener if he's working.'

That was true, but what she really wanted was some time alone, to explore this deeply peaceful place and to try and make sense of her impressions of the house.

Mrs Offord was pleased by Jenny's consideration. 'That's very thoughtful of you, Miss, not that George would mind in the least. You'll find the gardens are very well kept. The new people will probably want to keep him on, as he's a good gardener, even if he is getting on a bit. He keeps everything very nice, but you have to be careful underfoot near the stream. Follow the path round and you won't get lost.'

Mrs Offord turned back into the house as Jenny set off into the garden.

There was a flight of stone steps leading onto the lawn and a pathway off led to a vegetable garden, set to one side. Beyond the vegetable garden, the path led down, winding between the trees at the bottom of the garden.

Under the cool whispering shade of the beech trees, Jenny felt as if she was entering an enchanted wood. Under the soaring green of the beeches, she felt very small but *safe*. Safe? That was an odd word, but so exactly right.

The path led down to where a shallow stream, shifting silver in the sunlight, gurgled over rocks. There should be a bridge. A small stone bridge with a stone handrail, hiding just out of sight. A fairy bridge, she thought with a smile. That would be just perfect . . .

And there it was.

Jenny shrank back. Of course there's a bridge, she told herself. It's obvious there'd be a bridge here.

Yes, but why was the bridge so exactly as she'd imagined it? There's only so many sorts of bridges, she told herself, conscious of fighting down a feeling close to panic. Was it her imagination? Was she dreaming things, seeing stuff that wasn't there?

She stepped onto the little bridge, drawing a ridiculous amount of reassurance from the very real feeling of the rough stone of the balustrade under her hand. The bridge was real.

She looked over into the clear water, two or three feet below. There was a little sandy bank by the pile of the bridge, where the water gently rippled, as if resting before going under the bridge.

The bank was a perfect place to sail a toy boat from. A white boat with a red sail. She could see it . . .

She brought herself up with a shock. The picture of a little white boat with a red sail and a red painted anchor sprang sharply into her mind. Once again, the feeling that she'd had looking at the blue tiles and the cornflower wallpaper swept over her.

Suddenly the wood, the enchanted wood, didn't seem so safe. A fairy bridge? There was danger in fairyland.

'I must get a *grip* on myself,' she said, hardly realising she'd spoken the words out loud. She was in a Surrey garden on an ornamental Victorian bridge, the like of which she must have seen in dozens of parks and gardens. That was all it was. Nothing else, and she should have more sense. Her friends would think she was loopy if they knew how jittery she'd got about wall-paper, tiles and bridges. Either that or laugh. Betty would laugh, wouldn't she?

As a matter of fact, she probably wouldn't, thought Jenny. So what would Betty say? She'd probably tell her to calm down and have a cup of tea or something.

Well, she couldn't manage a cup of tea, but she could calm down and have a cigarette at least.

She wouldn't smoke in front of Mrs Offord – she suspected she would disapprove of girls smoking – but Mrs Offord was safely in the house.

She fumbled in her bag, pulled out her cigarette case, and lit a cigarette, willing her nerves to steady. That was better. She leaned on the bridge for a good few minutes, feeling her heart stop racing. Calm. She was calm.

She finished her cigarette and, tossing the stub into the water, watched it float away. She'd thrown sticks between the rails of a bridge just like this.

There it was again. That dreadful feeling that she'd had when she looked at the wallpaper. This time, Jenny was cross with herself. For Pete's sake, she needed to stop *imagining* things.

Shaking herself, she walked over the bridge, following the path under the trees as it climbed back up towards the lawn where the cedar tree stood, its broad, fan-shaped canopies of leaves spreading dappled patches of shade in the sunshine.

She couldn't deny it, it was something of a relief to be out from under the trees, back in the sunlight.

Thinking of trees, the cedar tree in the middle of the lawn really was magnificent. When she'd seen the cedar from the bedroom window, she'd thought how perfect it would be as a place for afternoon tea. It seemed to call out to have a table underneath it, set with a white cloth with plates of tiny sandwiches and delicious cakes. There would be men in striped blazers and straw boaters and ladies in Edwardian dresses sitting on white-painted, iron garden chairs.

Why Edwardian? It just seemed right, somehow. Women in short dresses and bobbed hair with cigarettes in long holders would have seemed strangely out of place under the tree. No; the picture she imagined – it seemed oddly real – definitely belonged to before the war.

Smiling to herself, she walked forward to stand under the shade of the branches, idly imagining herself as one of those Edwardian ladies. It wasn't actually so very long ago, she supposed. It was only twenty years or so, but a huge gulf separated then from now.

She reached out to touch the tree's thick, square-cracked bark.

And screamed.

# TWO

'**M**iss! Miss!'
The words seemed to come out of a long black tunnel. There was horror in the tunnel.

'Miss!' the voice repeated. The tunnel faded. The voice didn't belong to the horror.

Jenny fought down her panic. She took a tight grip on her senses and blinked her eyes open. There was a canopy of leaves above her, tingeing the light green. An old man's face, kindly and concerned, was close to hers.

She was lying on the grass under the cedar tree.

Hardly daring to believe where she was, she moved her head cautiously, looking for the horror.

A great wave of relief washed over her. The horror was gone.

It was gone and she was lying flat on her back. The grass was damp and she had a twig poking into her back. She stretched her hand out and grasped a handful of grass in her fingers. That was real.

She reached up and laid a hand on the man's arm, feeling the muscles of his arm under the coarse prickle of his flannel shirt. That was real.

She could see the man's worried brown eyes, the stubble on his chin. She could smell him, a mixture of earth and grass and old pipe tobacco. That was real.

The horror receded but it had been *there*.

The man – he must be George Meredith, the gardener – wiped his palm on his corduroy trousers and gingerly put his hand under her back, helping her to sit up.

Jenny tried to scramble to her feet, but the gardener stopped her. 'You just sit still for a moment, Miss. You've had a nasty turn and you need to just get your breath back.'

Jenny wasn't sorry to take his advice. She peered past him, dreading what she might see, but there was nothing but the garden, bright with sun, fringed with flowerbeds and the sound of birdsong.

It was a peaceful garden; a beautiful garden. But the horror . . .

She pushed the thought of it away. That couldn't have been real, could it? Of course it wasn't, she told herself sternly. What on earth was the matter with her? Ever since she'd set foot in the house, she'd been plagued with ridiculous imaginings. And this, too, on the first day that she'd been given real responsibility.

If Mr Lee found out, she'd be sacked. Her stomach twisted at the thought. She wanted her job. She needed her job. She mustn't get a reputation for seeing things. Especially horrible things, things that weren't human.

She drew a shuddering breath and managed a smile. 'I'm sorry,' she said weakly. She still couldn't quite believe the horror was gone.

Mrs Offord came out of the house. 'George?' she called. 'George? What is it? I thought I heard a noise.' She broke off with a little cry as she saw Jenny lying on the grass.

'The young lady fainted,' said George. 'Nothing to worry about. I expects she just needs a cup of tea and perhaps something to eat.' He turned back to Jenny. 'Do you think you could stand up now?' he asked.

Jenny nodded. 'I'm really sorry,' she said as he helped her to her feet. 'I don't know what came over me,' she added, lying valiantly. She knew exactly what she'd seen and why she'd collapsed but it wasn't something she could tell the gardener.

Mrs Offord came across the lawn and between them, Jenny got back into the house where she sat down gratefully on a chair in the kitchen.

'My word,' exclaimed the housekeeper. 'You look white as a sheet.' Jenny nodded dumbly. 'Now you just sit there,' she said, reaching for a cup and saucer. 'I'd just brewed a cup of tea and you need one, I daresay, and with plenty of sugar in it. Tea for you, George? I've got your mug here. What was it, Miss?' she asked sympathetically as she poured the tea. 'Do you suffer from dizzy spells? My aunty, she was a martyr to fainting fits, but that was years ago. Ladies, they did use to faint all the time, and it was corsets that caused it. Terrible

tight, my aunty's corsets used to be – they were in those days
– and the doctor, he said to her, "Now, you loosen your corsets,
and you'll soon feel better".'

George Meredith, mug of tea in hand, looked alarmed at the
mention of corsets and said he'd take his tea outside.

'Is it corsets?' asked Mrs Offord, once George had gone. 'I
can see you wouldn't want to say so in front of a man. Not
that,' she continued, looking at Jenny's waistline critically, 'I
would've thought that was the cause.'

Even though she still felt horribly shaken, Jenny couldn't
help smiling. 'No, it's not corsets.'

'It must be lack of a good breakfast then,' said Mrs Offord
firmly. 'I know how there's this craze for being thin – ladies
now, they're all skin and bone – but it's not right to deprive
yourself of food, especially breakfast.'

'It's not . . .' began Jenny, remembering the porridge and
toast she'd had for breakfast, then changed her mind. If she
even hinted to Mrs Offord what she had seen – what I *thought*
I saw, she corrected herself – then there would be gossip without
a doubt and it would be all over with Wilson and Lee. No one
wanted to employ anyone who saw things. Horrible things.
Things that just couldn't be there.

She had to tell the housekeeper *something* and she'd rather
be thought to have fainted from lack of food rather than seeing
things.

'I expect you're right,' she said weakly.

'There now!' said Mrs Offord with an air of triumph. 'You
young ladies are all the same. It's these magazines that do it,
always telling us what we should look like. You're as God made
you, I say, and we ought to be glad of good food with no silly
fads and fancies and I expects your mother will say the same
when she finds out.'

'My mother died five months ago,' said Jenny. 'But I think
you're right.'

Mrs Offord clucked with sympathy. 'Your mother's passed
away? You poor dear.' Her plump face drooped in concern. 'It's
grief that's put you off your food, and no wonder, but you must
eat properly. She'd want you too, I know. She wouldn't want
you to waste away now, would she? I'll just cut you a slice of

bread and butter and there's some madeira cake which I made yesterday.'

The housekeeper's concern was like balm to Jenny's spirits. In intervals of offering more food she 'just had handy, like' – Jenny thought she wouldn't have to eat for a week – she heard all about Jenny's childhood in Yorkshire – 'Now that is a fair way off, my dear' – and how much she missed her parents.

Mrs Offord was doubly sympathetic when she learned that both Jenny's parents were dead. Under the housekeeper's gentle questioning, Jenny found herself pouring out details of her family life. It had been Dad's dearest wish that Martin and Eric should be doctors, just like him, but it did mean that money was very tight.

But that, as Mrs Offord said, was the way of the world. She quite understood that Jenny really needed her job.

By the time Jenny was able to leave, Mrs Offord was completely on her side and promised faithfully not to breathe a word to anyone about Jenny's collapse in the garden.

It had been really nice, thought Jenny, as she walked back to Wilson and Lee, to talk about Mum and Dad. No one else in London had known them or knew her. Actually, that wasn't quite true, she corrected herself.

Betty had known Mum and Dad. She'd once spent two weeks of the summer holidays from school with Jenny in Yorkshire and liked them very much. Betty had been really sorry to hear about Mum and Dad. So should she tell Betty what had happened? Or would Betty think she was just imagining things? After all, to be frightened of toys and wallpaper was bad enough, but that horror in the garden . . . It sounded mental.

Mental? Jenny stopped dead. That couldn't be it, could it? But what else could you call it when you saw things that weren't there? Mental. It wasn't real, what she'd seen. It *couldn't* be real. Mental. Was she mental? She shuddered. Maybe this was just the beginning. The start of her becoming a *lunatic*.

She didn't really know how she got through that afternoon at the office. She seemed to be operating on two levels. The top level was professional and enthusiastic, the other was a cringing turmoil of emotions.

Mr Lee had, of course, wanted to know her impressions of the house, nodding with approval as Jenny enthused about its situation and amenities and, with a much longer face, agreeing with her about the number of staff needed to run the house properly. The figures she had estimated, of one pound, ten shillings a week to rent and offers around eight hundred and fifty pounds for an outright sale, were also what Mr Lee had more or less expected.

'Not that,' he said gloomily, 'there would be much chance of a sale. As a matter of fact, Mr Laidlaw' – he was the owner of Saunder's Green – 'doesn't want to sell it. The trouble is, I think there's precious little chance of letting it either. It's my idea that he's holding onto the house with a view to knocking it down and building something up to date. His firm own a number of properties around Saunder's Green. I imagine he's got ambitions for the whole area.' He glanced at her notes again. 'However, you seem to have done very well, Miss Langton,' he added with a smile. 'Let me see the particulars when you've typed them up.'

Even though part of her was silently yelling, 'Don't go near the house!' Jenny couldn't help but be pleased by Mr Lee's approbation. The figures, as he said, would have to be checked by Mr McKenzie, when he had recovered from his cold, but that would require a very brief inspection, as Jenny had done all the donkeywork of measurements and descriptions.

She typed up the particulars, resolutely thrusting to one side the urge to type, 'Don't go near the house!' – that would, she thought, with a certain amount of irony, never do – and concentrated firmly on the exterior description.

She forced herself to focus on her typing, ignoring the way her stomach twisted every time she typed 'Saunder's Green'. She could have pleaded illness, she supposed, and gone home, but sheer stubbornness made her stick at it. She was rewarded as a feeling of dull aversion to the name of Saunder's Green replaced unbearable horror as repetition deadened her senses.

And, she thought, as she completed the work, she had made the house sound great. All sunny and bright. Sunny? The stronger the sun, the darker the shadows.

There was, of course, other work to be done that afternoon; mundane, everyday work of answering the telephone, typing letters and speaking to prospective clients, all of which she welcomed as a distraction from the numbing feeling that she was keeping a dark sea of emotions firmly screwed down.

It was a struggle though. It continued to be a struggle as she put the dust cover on her typewriter and left the office. Although she'd been looking forward to seeing Betty that evening, part of her wanted to run back to her room and to hide away.

Would Betty guess anything was wrong? Not if she hid it. No; she could have a thoroughly pleasant evening with an old friend, talking of old times and the new husband (Jenny wished she could summon up her past enthusiasm) and she would never have to visit or think about Saunder's Green ever again.

Yes, she thought, as she rang the bell of Betty's house in Chandos Row, that's what she'd do. She wouldn't mention a word about the house and especially not the horror in the garden. That simply couldn't be real. It was all (as Mum would've said) a silly fancy.

She heard footsteps and voices behind the door. 'I'll get it, Kathleen. It'll be my old friend I told you about.'

Betty opened the door. She was just as she always was; kindly, freckly and with hair that simply could not be tamed into fashionable sleekness. The mere sight of her was so reassuring, Jenny felt a lump in her throat.

'Jenny!' said Betty happily. 'Come on in!' and then her expression changed. 'What on earth's wrong?'

The sympathy in her voice was too much. Jenny tried to speak, to deny anything was the matter and then – she couldn't help it – she burst into tears.

Earlier that day, in the garden, Jenny had imagined Betty telling her to calm down and have a cup of tea. It was better than that. Betty didn't tell her to keep calm but instead put a comforting arm round her, brought her into the sitting room, and poured out a stiff brandy and soda.

Sipping the unaccustomed spirit, Jenny felt a welcome warmth creep through her. Gradually the story came out, bit by bit.

'So what was it?' demanded Betty. 'What caused it, I mean?'

Jenny shook her head dismally. 'There's only one thing it can be. I never really believed in ghosts or anything like that, but I suppose the house could be haunted. It's supposed to be haunted,' she added. 'The housekeeper, Mrs Offord, said there was a lady in blue who appears in the garden.'

She held up her hand to stem Betty's protests. 'I know. I didn't believe it either, but if that's all I saw, I'd be rattled but I wouldn't be so upset. I suppose I could be seeing – well – visions of long ago, I suppose, if all that happened was a creepy feeling about the wallpaper and so on, but that thing in the garden . . .' She shuddered. 'That can't have been real. Ever.' She drained her brandy and looked at her friend. 'I must be going off my head.'

'No, you're not,' said Betty quickly.

'Can you explain it then?'

Betty shook her head. 'No, I can't. But there is an explanation, I'm sure of it.' She put her hands together in her lap, thinking. Then, obviously coming to a conclusion, she sat upright and, lighting a cigarette, looked at her friend seriously. 'Would you mind telling Jack about this?'

'Jack? Your husband?' Jenny drew back in alarm. 'Jack Haldean?' She felt panic-stricken. 'Betty, I can't! It's one thing telling you but I can't tell someone I hardly know. I know he's your husband but I've only met him once. He really will think I'm nuts.'

'Do you think you're nuts?' asked Betty acutely. 'Really?'

'I . . .' Jenny stopped. 'No, I don't,' she said with a small smile. 'I mean, I don't feel nuts, but what does that feel like? I do know it was all very real and yet it *can't* be real.'

'When I first met Jack,' said Betty, 'I'd seen something I couldn't explain. No one would believe me. Everyone said I'd had a nightmare but I knew that what I'd seen was real. You know what happened. I'd only met Jack once before, but he believed me. I can't tell you how reassuring that was.'

'But what I saw *can't* be real, Betty,' protested Jenny. 'That's the point.'

Betty put her hands wide. 'Real or not, something happened to you, something that's upset you terribly. I think there's a very good chance that Jack will be able to work out what that something was.'

'Is this wifely pride speaking?' asked Jenny with the ghost of a smile.

'Not entirely. I am proud of him, of course, but Jack's very cagey about the cases he's been caught up in. I can tell you this, though. One of his best friends is Chief Inspector Bill Rackham of Scotland Yard.'

'What, that big, ginger-haired man?' asked Jenny. 'I remember him from the wedding. I thought he was rather nice.'

'Bill is nice,' said Betty with a smile. 'What's more, he's nobody's fool, but he's told me that Jack's often been able to work out what's happened when he's been absolutely stumped.'

Jenny hesitated. 'Even so . . .'

'Come on, Jenny,' said Betty briskly. 'You're not someone to be frightened of shadows, or dream up stuff that isn't there. Jack knows that too. He's heard me talk about you. With his help, we can get to the bottom of whatever it was that happened.'

She put her cigarette case in her handbag, snapped the bag shut with a decisive click, and stood up. 'Now, why don't we have something to eat, as I planned. Jack's at the Young Services club this evening. I'll telephone him and leave a message, asking him to come home after we've had dinner. I've booked a table at Aquino's on the corner and I'm sure you'll feel better after some food.'

'You sound just like the housekeeper, Mrs Offord,' said Jenny with a valiant attempt at a smile. 'She thought food was the answer, too.'

'Well, I'm hungry,' said Betty firmly. 'Dinner is the answer to that.' She hesitated. 'Will you speak to Jack? Honestly, Jenny, he won't laugh at you. I can promise you that.'

'Let me think about it,' said Jenny after a pause. She tried to smile once more. 'But I would like some dinner, I must say.'

# THREE

D inner did help, as did Betty's complete certainty that there was a rational explanation to account for what Jenny had seen. What Betty was also completely certain of was that Jack could discover what that explanation was.

Jenny didn't agree. What's more, she felt very shy of discussing what she'd seen with a man who, despite being married to Betty, was more or less a stranger. She'd been introduced to him at the wedding, of course, but saying 'How d'you do' and 'Congratulations' hardly amounted to getting to know someone.

She'd enjoyed his books and she had a clear memory of a tall, dark-haired, good-looking man with an infectious smile who was obviously bursting with happiness. Betty had told her his mother had been a Spaniard, which accounted for his olive skin and slightly gypsy-ish looks, but although she remembered him, she didn't know him.

Dinner really had helped, though. Jenny was a little wary of the food. Betty, with her Italian honeymoon behind her, confidently ordered something called *Bucatini all' Amatriciana,* which turned out to be pork in a sauce with pasta. Jenny, with memories of the soggy macaroni served at school, tentatively tried it and, to her surprise, found it delicious.

That, naturally, bought with it an account of the honeymoon travels, but Betty was really interested in catching up with news of Jenny's family. By the time she had been brought up to date with news of Martin and Eric, with a good few memories of Jenny's parents thrown in, Jenny had relaxed to an extent that would've seemed incredible to her only an hour before. She still had to face Jack though, and re-live the whole experience of the afternoon.

They walked back to the house but, as Jenny got her key out, Jack opened the door.

'I saw you coming along the street,' he said with a friendly smile. He kissed Betty lightly on the cheek, then turned to Jenny.

'You must be Miss Langton. Betty's told me about you, of course. I'd resigned myself to spending the evening at the club, as Betty told me it was strictly girls only tonight, so this is a turn up for the books. Come on in.'

Jenny was immeasurably reassured. He was in evening dress, which suited him. Unlike some good-looking men, though, he seemed entirely unconscious of his appearance. It was nice of him to be so welcoming too. A lot of men would've resented having to change their plans for the evening, but he seemed genuinely pleased to see them.

He led the way into the hall, then hesitated. 'Would you mind coming up to my old rooms? I understand you've got a bit of a problem on your hands, Miss Langton, and I find it easier to think in familiar surroundings.'

'How tidy is it?' asked Betty suspiciously.

'It's fine,' Jack reassured her. 'Well, mainly fine, anyway.' He grinned. 'Come on.'

He took them up the stairs and showed them into his old sitting room, a comfortable room with well-worn chairs and a sofa, and a desk by the window with a typewriter, a pile of papers and a big bookcase.

The typewriter caught Jenny's interest. 'You've got a Remington, I see. I use one of those.'

'They're good machines, aren't they?' said Jack, at the sideboard. 'Can I get you a drink? I've got some coffee brewing but would you like something else as well?'

Betty looked at Jenny. 'Would you like a glass of brandy? I know I would.'

'Brandy it is,' said Jack, walking to the sideboard and reaching for the glasses.

He knew there was something wrong. Betty had always talked about Jenny as being level-headed and down to earth but she was obviously on edge with, he suspected, tears not very far away.

Money troubles? A man? No, he decided, adding soda to the brandy. If it was money, Betty could and would come to the rescue without any help from him and if it was a man, Betty was perfectly capable of doling out any sympathy and advice that was needed.

Had she witnessed a crime? Maybe; if so, it was something she was unsure about. If it was something obvious like a dead body or a burglary, Betty would have surely told him when she'd left the message for him at the club, but all she'd said was that Jenny had a problem and needed to talk to him.

He felt a tingle of excitement as he turned to the two girls. There had to be a mystery in the offing but first of all, Jenny Langton needed reassurance. So, back to talking about everyday things such as typewriters.

'Yes,' he said, putting the glasses on the table by the sofa. 'I like the Remington. Help yourself to cigarettes, by the way. The box is on the table. I had a Corona for years but it finally gave up the ghost, so I got a Remington, which is a much bigger machine.'

'Jack,' said Betty firmly, 'Jenny isn't here to talk about typewriters.' She looked at her friend. 'Shall I start or will you?'

Jenny braced herself. 'No. If you really think there's an explanation and I'm not just going nuts, I'd better tell the story.' She looked at Jack ruefully. 'Only I know how it sounds. It sounds crazy.'

'Go on,' said Jack encouragingly adding, with a smile, 'I must say you don't seem particularly crazy to me, Miss Langton.'

She gave a little sigh of relief. 'I don't feel it, either, but . . .' She shook herself. 'We mentioned typewriters. Funnily enough, my story more or less starts with typewriters.' She looked at him questioningly. 'Betty told you I work for Wilson and Lee, the house agents?' Jack nodded. 'Well, Mr Lee is an old dear. It's his family firm. There isn't a Wilson any more as the last one died about 1890 or something, but Mr Lee has been with the firm all his life and is a bit set in his views. He had to get used to the idea of lady clerks during the war, so he didn't mind giving me a job, but he was convinced that all I was really capable of was making the tea, answering the telephone and typing.'

'Was there a lot of typing?' Jack asked with a grin.

Jenny nodded vigorously. 'Tons. I did it all. None of the other clerks can type, you see. The older clerks actually refer to me as "the lady typewriter".'

Jack laughed. 'That's very sweet and old-fashioned of them.

You're better looking than a Remington, but it still sounds like an awful lot of work.'

'It is,' said Jenny with feeling. 'Anyway, I was really keen to get away from typing all day long and get to grips with something more interesting. I wanted to see round houses and so on, and this morning the great day dawned. Mr McKenzie, who should've done the visit, was taken poorly with a cold, which left old Mr Southwick, who really hasn't got a clue how to present a property to make it interesting.'

'How on earth did you manage to get Mr Lee to send you?' asked Betty. 'You've told me some of this before and I thought you had a very uphill job to convince him to trust you to visit a house.'

'I've been leaving newspapers for him to look at,' said Jenny with a slightly guilty smile. 'You know all these articles on the Modern Girl that there are in the papers? I made sure he saw them. I suppose it's a form of advertising, really.'

Jack laughed and raised his glass to her. 'Well done, you. I've written articles about the Modern Girl myself. It's nice to think they might have done some good.'

Jenny smiled in return, then her smile faded. 'I was over the moon. I didn't let Mr Lee see how happy I was, of course.'

'And then, when you got to the house, it all went wrong,' said Betty sympathetically.

'As a matter of fact, it started to go wrong before then.' Jenny twisted her cigarette nervously in her fingers. 'Do you remember at school, Betty, I sometimes talked about the Watcher?'

'No, I . . .' began Betty, then stopped. 'Yes, I do,' she said slowly. 'You didn't see him often, but I do remember that you saw him.'

'The Watcher?' asked Jack. 'Who's the Watcher?'

Jenny breathed in deeply, then started to explain. 'My mother always said it was nonsense,' she finished unhappily.

'But you don't think it is?' asked Betty gently.

'No. I honestly don't think it is, but who he is, I don't know. After what happened at the house, I suppose he might not even be real.' Her voice cracked. 'I know what I saw, but it can't be real. I don't want to see things. Things that aren't there, I mean.'

She felt a sudden surge of panic. 'Look,' she said, scrambling to her feet, 'you've both been very kind, but I really must go. I'm sorry to have troubled you. You've both got better things to do than listen to me spout a load of silly nonsense.'

With a swift movement, Jack put his hand on her shoulder, settling her back in her chair. 'No,' he said firmly. 'Miss Langton, you've obviously had a bad fright. That isn't nonsense. Won't you tell me what happened?'

'I said you'd be able to explain it, too,' put in Betty confidently.

Jack glanced at Betty with a deprecating grin. 'That's going a bit fast, perhaps.' He turned back to Jenny. His voice became very gentle. 'However, I haven't a hope of being able to explain anything, unless I know what happened.'

He saw the panic leave her eyes and she nodded slowly.

Jack took his hand from her shoulder and sat down again. 'So, let's begin. You'd seen the man you call the Watcher. That obviously unsettled you, and I'm not surprised. What happened when you arrived at the house?'

Jenny hesitated. It was so hard to know where to start.

Jack saw her floundering. 'Be a house agent,' he suggested with a smile, taking a cigarette from the box. 'Give yourself promotion and pretend I'm interested in the house. What does it look like?'

He saw her confidence return. 'I like the idea of promotion,' she said with a sudden smile. 'If you were a prospective tenant, I'd say that the property is called Saunder's Green House. It overlooks Saunder's Green on the outskirts of Stowfleet and is a spacious but manageable villa, with extensive grounds. It was built in 1882 of good-quality local brick and has mains water and gas. It has the benefit of a purpose-built garage with parking for at least two cars. The garage is a later addition, of course, but it's in keeping with the rest of the house.'

Jack grinned. 'You're doing very well. This is just like reading house particulars. To drop the house agent side of yourself for a moment, tell me what impression the house made on you when you arrived?'

'I liked it,' said Jenny impulsively. 'It's too big to be kept properly without a raft of servants, but I liked it. That's the funny thing. I said as much to the housekeeper, Mrs Offord, that it seemed to be a welcoming house.' She hesitated again. 'I hope you don't think I'm being fanciful when I talk about a house being welcoming?'

Both Jack and Betty shook their heads. 'Not in the least,' said Jack. 'I don't know why some places accrue an atmosphere, but they certainly do.'

'Well, as I say, Saunder's Green did seem welcoming and the housekeeper was a lovely old soul, who obviously enjoyed showing me round. Mind you, she did say there were tales that the place was haunted.'

'It sounds as if she was trying to put the wind up you,' said Betty.

'No, she wasn't,' said Jenny, shaking her head. 'Apparently the old lady who used to live there sometimes saw a ghost of a woman in the garden, but neither Mrs Offord or the housemaid had ever seen anything.'

'Did it worry you?' asked Jack.

'Not really. Goodness knows what the old lady had actually seen, but she couldn't have seen a ghost. There's no such things. Anyway, I started off in the kitchens, all of which were exactly as you'd expect, then Mrs Offord said we'd better go up to the attics and work down from there.' She gulped. 'That's when I got my first scare.'

With encouragement from Jack and Betty, Jenny related the experiences of the morning. 'And it was *weird*,' she finished. 'In Mrs Offord's room, it was as if I was seeing two rooms – the actual room and a sort of ghost room. Then I went into the adjoining room and the decoration and so on was exactly as I'd imagined. Absolutely exactly, I mean, right down to the tiles round the fireplace.'

She shuddered. 'It scared Mrs Offord, I could tell, but I managed to reassure her. Then I went into the garden. It was the same story in the garden. I knew the bridge was there before I came to it.'

Hesitantly, guided by Jack's questions, she took them through the details of her walk through the trees by the stream. 'And then,' she finished, 'I came to the cedar tree.'

Her voice faltered. Jack looked up sharply. 'What about the tree?'

Jenny crushed out her cigarette and lit another with shaky

fingers. 'Everything I'd seen up till then had been ordinary. I don't mean the fact that I'd seen them was ordinary. I was so on edge that I was honestly starting to wonder if there was any truth in the idea that the house was haunted, but the things themselves, the wallpaper, the tiles, the bridge and so on, were all ordinary, everyday objects.'

She pulled deeply on her cigarette. 'The cedar tree was different. It's a magnificent tree, the sort of tree you'd have afternoon tea under the shade of the branches. I thought that, and thought how nice it would be, with all the ladies in long dresses and men in blazers and straw boaters having afternoon tea in a world where the war hadn't happened and everything was peaceful, secure and *happy*.'

She said the last word with a note of wonder. 'Happy. I was thinking of being happy. And then I touched the bark of the tree.'

She lit another cigarette nervously. 'I saw a monster.'

There was complete silence.

Jack drew his breath in. He didn't know what he'd been expecting but it wasn't this.

'What sort of monster?' he asked cautiously.

Jenny put her hand to her mouth. 'I know it can't be real!' she broke out defensively. 'I know there aren't any such things as monsters.'

'Tell me what you saw,' said Jack quietly.

Jenny gulped. 'It was horrible. It was as if the world had suddenly turned upside down. Instead of looking up at the tree, I was looking down. Beneath me was a thing with a skin that looked like black leather. It glistened where the sun caught it.'

'Was it the shape of a man?'

Jenny nodded. 'More or less. It didn't have a proper face with a nose or a mouth, but had this awful blank face with awful blank eyes. They were huge, square, shining eyes and they were looking at me. There was a light like fire coming from the eyes and I knew that if the light caught me, I would die. I was terrified. I couldn't move. I knew that the monster was an utterly evil thing.'

'What happened?'

'I . . . I woke up.' She faltered to a halt. Betty reached out and squeezed her friend's hand. It was obvious Jenny was trying to hold back tears. 'I woke up in the garden. I'd fainted and the gardener was bending over me, looking worried to death. Then the housekeeper came out and she and the gardener helped me into the house.'

'Did you tell them what you saw?' asked Jack.

'Good grief, no,' said Jenny with a shudder. 'I know what it sounds like, Mr Haldean. The housekeeper put my fainting fit down to not having eaten properly, but that's rubbish. I simply couldn't tell her what I'd seen. The last thing I want to do is for Wilson and Lee to find out I see things.' She shuddered again. 'I'd lose my job, for certain. The thing is . . .' She hesitated, then shook her head.

'You wondered if you were losing your marbles,' said Betty. 'You're not.'

'Have you ever seen anything like this before?' asked Jack.

'Monsters, you mean?' asked Jenny with a nervous laugh. 'No.'

'I'm glad you don't make a habit of it.' Jack sat back thoughtfully.

What on earth could she have seen? There were a couple of explanations he could think of for the wallpaper and the tiles and so on, but monsters were definitely out of the realm of normal.

He glanced at her. The poor girl was horribly nervy. With an experience like that, it wasn't surprising that she wondered if she was going nuts. Was she? No. He was certain of that. But monsters?

It was time to clear the dead wood out of the way. Then, perhaps, he might be able to see the trees. 'Please, Miss Langton, don't worry about going off your head. I'm not a nerve specialist, but I have met men before who see things, in the common use of the term. You're not like that. You strike me as completely and utterly sane.'

He felt a twist of sympathy as he saw how relieved she looked. So that was madness cleared out of the way. She'd talked about the house being haunted, and she'd talked about seeing a room as a ghost room, so the next question was obvious.

'From what you've said, I imagine the answer to this question is "no", but do you consider yourself psychic at all?'

'Psychic?' She looked startled. 'Do I see ghosts, you mean?' She wriggled impatiently. 'After this afternoon, I'm not sure what I believe any more.' She gave an impatient sigh. 'No. That's all nonsense, isn't it? It just has to be.' She frowned. 'Until today, the only thing that's ever happened that I can't explain is when the dog howled itself stupid in its kennel when poor Dad died. Poor old Pippin loved Dad.'

Jack scratched his ear. So she wasn't prone to visions. 'I've heard of that sort of thing before, but having a psychic dog doesn't make you psychic yourself.'

Now to tackle the next obvious explanation. 'Excuse me, Miss Langton, but are you taking any medicine at the moment?'

Jenny shook her head blankly.

'And – please do excuse me asking – you haven't taken any drugs?' He saw Jenny's outraged expression and quickly amended the question. 'Something to help you sleep, perhaps? Or to help you concentrate?'

'Certainly not!'

'Jack,' said Betty reproachfully, 'I don't know how you can think such a thing.'

He held up his hands in apology. 'I'm sorry I had to ask, but it was just a thought. By the way, Miss Langton, I think you're absolutely right not to want it to come to the ears of your employers. Mum's the word until we get to the bottom of this.'

'So what was it, Jack?' asked Betty impatiently. 'I told Jenny you'd be able to explain everything.'

He shook his head. 'That's asking an awful lot, Betty.' He nodded at Jenny. 'We know that whatever it was you saw isn't real.'

'I said as much,' said Jenny, sounding rather aggrieved.

'But we know as much. If there had been anyone or anything else in the garden, the gardener would've seen them.'

'That's right. The gardener was there all the time.'

'Okey-doke. So whatever it was, it happened in your mind.'

'You mean I'm making this up?'

'Not in the least,' said Jack, calming her indignation. 'I must say that, although I'm not a great believer in ghosties and ghoulies and things that go bump in the night, I have come across things I can't explain.'

Jenny stared at him. 'But that's dreadful! I don't want to see things! Not things like that, I mean.'

'Could it not be you but the place?' suggested Betty. 'I don't know much about ghosts and so on, but in the stories I've read, it's the place that's haunted, not the person. Anyone can see a ghost if they're in a haunted house. If there are such things as ghosts,' she added doubtfully.

'Yes, but I don't *want* to believe in all that,' said Jenny impatiently. She turned to Betty. 'You met my parents. You know what sort of people they were.' She looked at Jack. 'My mother was a very down-to-earth person. She'd have thought it not only absolute nonsense but plain wrong. She had very strong views on fortune telling and all that sort of thing. She was a regular church-goer. She'd have been horrified at the thought of anything supernatural.'

'Doesn't attending church mean you believe in the supernatural?' asked Jack with an innocent expression.

Jenny stared at him.

'Jack,' said Betty warningly. She turned to Jenny. 'You'll have to excuse him. He's a Catholic and always saying things like that.'

'Oh. I see,' said Jenny cautiously. 'Or I think I do, anyway.' She shook herself impatiently. 'That can't be it. I've told you what my mother would've said and as for my father, he'd have just laughed at the idea. He was a doctor and prided himself on being a complete rationalist.'

'Yes, he was,' agreed Betty. 'I remember talking to him about science. He believed in things that could be proved. He was a very hard-headed Yorkshireman.'

'Yes, he was,' said Jenny. 'My brother Martin's just the same. I'm sure you know the type.'

'Absolutely,' said Jack. 'You mentioned your brother. Who else is in the family?'

'There's just the three of us. Martin, my elder brother, is a doctor in Leeds and Eric, my younger brother, is studying medicine at Leeds University. Dad grew up in Leeds but bought the practice in Salterbeck before I was born. That's a village about three miles outside of Huddersfield.'

'And you lived there all your life?' asked Jack.

'Yes. I went to school with Betty, of course.'

'It was your mother's old school,' said Betty. 'She enjoyed talking to us about it.' She laughed. 'Some of the mistresses who taught us had taught her.'

'She liked school,' said Jenny with the beginnings of a smile. 'I did, too.'

The mention of her family and school had obviously calmed Jenny's nerves. She looked at Jack with baffled exasperation. 'Haven't you got any other explanation, Mr Haldean? A rational explanation, I mean? As far as I can see, I really am either going nuts or seeing things. I wasn't just scared, I was terrified. If all you can tell me is that it's all in my mind, what's to stop it happening again?'

'It's not going to happen again,' said Betty confidently. 'Come on, Jack. You must be able to think of something else.'

He could, of course, but it didn't explain the monster. 'Well, the only other explanation I can think depends on a massive coincidence,' he said doubtfully. 'Can I ask you why you chose to work in Stowfleet?'

Jenny shrugged. 'I didn't, not really. Martin didn't want me to come to London at all. He wanted me to stay in Leeds, but my mother was a Londoner and I fancied a change.'

'And Stowfleet?'

'That was just how things worked out. I answered an advert in the *Evening Standard* and was lucky enough to get the job.'

'So you didn't feel any sort of affinity with Stowfleet? You'd never heard it mentioned before, perhaps?'

'No, I . . .' Jenny broke off. 'I might have done, as a matter of fact. My mother could've mentioned the place. As I said, she went to school in Surrey but Rotherdean's miles away from Stowfleet.'

'We'll take that as a tentative yes, then,' said Jack with a smile. He ignored Jenny's mutter of 'very tentative' and ploughed on. 'You see, Miss Langton, your sense of familiarity with the house may be just that. Think of the things in the house that you recognised – the toys in the toy box, the tiles round the fireplace and so on. Then there's your recognition of the bridge and your idea of sailing a toy boat in the stream and so on. Doesn't all that suggest something to you?'

She gave him a puzzled look. 'No, I can't say it does. I know the French have an expression, *déjà vu,* for when you feel you've been somewhere before. Is that what you mean?'

'Not exactly. What I'm getting at is that your feeling of

remembering the house and garden may be just that. A memory.'

'A memory? A real memory, you mean?' Jenny shook her head. 'That's impossible. Until I started work with Wilson and Lee I'd never been near Stowfleet and I've certainly never been to Saunder's Green until this morning. I told you. I grew up in Salterbeck.'

'But your mother went to school in Surrey and so did you. You said your mother was a Londoner. Don't you think it's at least possible that she had friends in Stowfleet?'

'It's possible, I suppose,' admitted Jenny. 'But my mother's memories aren't mine.'

'No, of course not. But say she did have friends in Stowfleet. Could she have visited them? And taken you with her when you were very small?'

'And those friends lived at Saunder's Green?' said Jenny sceptically.

Jack shrugged. 'Why not? They've got to live somewhere. You see, you started off by saying it's impossible that you actually remembered Saunder's Green, but I'm saying that it's not impossible. It's a coincidence, I agree, but it's not impossible.'

Jenny took a deep breath. 'All right, I agree it's possible. Just about.'

'But Jack,' broke in Betty. 'That can't be the explanation. Yes, Jenny could've visited the house when she was little.' She turned to her friend. 'I like that idea because of you remembering the toys and the little sailing boat and so on. All that adds up. But what about what happened at the cedar tree?'

Jenny put her hands to her mouth. 'What I saw by the tree wasn't human. It was a monster. An evil thing. It can't be real.'

'Can it be real, Jack?' demanded Betty.

He tapped his cigarette in the ashtray thoughtfully. 'That's an interesting question,' he said, after a pause. 'You see, if I'm right and what you experienced at Saunder's Green House wasn't you going off your head – which it obviously wasn't – *déjà vu* or something supernatural, then the only thing it really can be *is* a memory. So what were you remembering?'

# FOUR

Jenny gulped. 'It wasn't real,' she whispered. 'It can't have been real.'

'Maybe it was a nightmare,' suggested Betty. 'Not now, I mean, but a nightmare you had when you were little. Perhaps you fell asleep under the tree, years ago, and had a really bad dream and seeing the tree brought it all back, about how scared you were. Jack? Don't you agree?'

'Not really, old thing. It must have been a dickens of a nightmare to have caused Miss Langton to have fainted years later.'

'I want to *know!*' broke in Jenny fiercely. 'I want to know if my mother and I really ever did visit Saunder's Green House when I was small. I want to know if there really was anything in the garden or if I was just frightened by a bad dream. But,' she said, breaking off helplessly, 'I don't see how I can know. Mum could've told me, but she's dead. I don't see how I can ever know the truth, but if I don't find out, I'll always be worried that I really am going nuts or seeing things.'

Betty looked appealing at Jack. 'Can we help?'

'Can we help?' repeated Jack. 'We can certainly try.'

'But how?' demanded Jenny.

'We need to find out about the history of the house. I don't mean who built it and so on, but who lived there. If this really is a memory of something that happened to you when you were little, it tells us the approximate time we should look for. Say this happened to you before you were six years old. I think after you were six, you'd have a fairly clear memory of the house, at least. When does that take us back to? Are you the same age as Betty?'

Jenny nodded. 'Yes. I'm twenty-three.'

'Which means you were born in 1903. I can't believe you'd remember much when you were a babe in arms, so we're looking for whoever lived there between 1904 and 1910. If we can find who that was, you might recognise the name.'

'That's true,' said Jenny, brightening. 'If I recognised the name as belonging to one of my mother's old friends, say, that'd show us we were on the right lines.'

'They could easily still be alive,' put in Betty. 'Then all you'd have to do is to find out where they live now and ask them.'

'Ask them what?' said Jenny. She hesitated as the memory of the fear that had gripped her in the garden returned. 'We can't ask if anyone ever saw a . . . a monster.'

'That wouldn't be how I'd start the conversation, I agree,' said Jack. 'However, they might remember something odd or out of the way. The thing is, we've got hardly anything to go on at the moment, so what we need are some facts.' He stood up and stretched his shoulders. 'Betty, my darling, shall we do a little house hunting? I must admit, I'm curious to see Saunder's Green for myself.'

'I can get you an order to view,' said Jenny. 'That's easily done.'

'Thanks,' said Jack. 'There's a few other things I want to find out first, though. For instance, who owns the house? Did it belong to Mrs Trenchard? The lady who had it last, I mean?'

Jenny shook her head. 'No, she rented it. It actually belongs to a local firm, Ezra Wild and Sons. They've been going for donkey's years. They're builders who own quite a bit of property in Stowfleet and the surrounding area. We do a fair bit of business with them.'

'And should we be prospective buyers or prospective tenants?'

'You'll have to be tenants. It's for rent only. It'll be about one pound, ten shillings a week, I imagine.'

'So we'd better look modestly affluent. Do Ezra Wild and Sons have an office in Stowfleet?'

'It's nearby, in Weston Cross. Why do you want to know?'

'They'll probably have a record of who rented the house before the Trenchards. Unless Wilson and Lee have a record?'

'I can certainly have a look,' said Jenny. She looked at Jack and Betty ruefully. 'I'm putting you to an awful lot of trouble,' she said guiltily. 'After all, it could be nothing more than a bad dream.'

Jack smiled. 'You don't believe that, do you?' Jenny shook her head. 'And,' continued Jack, 'neither do I. I'm going to assume you saw something years ago that frightened you badly and that you can't explain. I want to know what it was.'

On Monday morning, Jack and Betty drove to Stowfleet and met Jenny in the Tudor Rose Café for lunch.

'I've got the names of the previous tenants of Saunder's Green House for you,' she said over her cheese and onion pie. 'They were a Mr and Mrs R. Sutton, the Misses E. and H. Holt and Mr and Mrs B. Nelson. The Nelsons had the house when it was first built, in 1882. They left in September 1895 when it was taken by the Suttons. They had it until November 1897 and in the January of 1898 the Misses Holt took it. Colonel and Mrs Trenchard arrived in April 1911.'

Jack jotted down the names and dates in his notebook. 'Do any of those names mean anything to you?'

'They don't, I'm afraid. Mind you, if any of these people really were friends of my mother, I might not have known their surname. Mum had a lot of friends in Salterbeck and I always called them Aunty Mildred and Aunty Sarah and so on when I was small. I really am sorry to put you to all this trouble,' she repeated apologetically. 'Do you actually want to see the house or are you going back to Chandos Row?'

'Of course not,' said Betty. 'I want to see the house.'

'Okay. Do you want to go after lunch?'

'Not right away,' said Jack. 'First of all, I want to visit the builders who actually own the place. They might be able to tell us something we haven't gleaned yet. If you sort out the viewing order, we'll call into Wilson and Lee's later.'

The offices of Ezra Wild and Sons (established 1853) clearly belonged to a very prosperous firm. Idyllic artists' impressions of ideal homes, all with the benefit of electricity, available from Ezra Wild's new development of Resthaven on the outskirts of London adorned the walls. A sound investment, as the posters said, for a mere £1,250.

The elderly clerk seemed disappointed that Major Haldean and his wife weren't interested in one of the splendid new houses, but instead had fixed their attentions on Saunder's Green.

'Are you sure?' asked the clerk mournfully. 'Mr Laidlaw himself has personally supervised the building and fitting out of all our Resthaven houses and I can assure you that the quality and conveniences simply cannot be matched in an older property. Resthaven, sir and madam, carries Mr Laidlaw's personal guarantee of quality.'

'Mr Laidlaw?' enquired Jack. The way the clerk said the name gave the impression that anyone who didn't instantly recognise it was hopelessly ill-informed.

'Mr Laidlaw,' repeated the clerk in shocked tones, 'owns the company.' He backed up his words by pointing to the sign where the legend '*Ezra Wild and Sons*' had, written in gold italics underneath, '*Prop. Andrew Laidlaw*'. 'He is a master builder, sir, and you can rest assured that there are no finer houses for the price to be found in the whole county.'

'Nevertheless,' said Jack, pressing his point, 'it's Saunder's Green we're interested in.'

The clerk sighed and accepted the inevitable. 'You'll have to get an order to view from Wilson and Lee in Stowfleet, I'm afraid, sir. They act as our agent in Stowfleet. Now if you were looking to buy a property, a house on our really excellent new development at Resthaven, for instance, I could arrange to have you shown round.'

'We're interested in Saunder's Green,' said Betty firmly, taking a hand in the conversation, 'because I think I used to know the house when I was little.'

Jack and Betty had decided this beforehand, to give them a reasonable excuse to ask about the former tenants of Saunder's Green House.

'I'm sure my mother's friends used to live there,' she continued. 'I don't suppose,' she added, with a winning smile, 'it would be possible for you to tell me who lived there years ago? I'd love to know if it really is the house I remember visiting.'

Betty's smile was shameless in its appeal. The clerk sighed and capitulated. A ledger of lettings was produced from the office at the back. The tenancies of the Suttons, the Holts, the Nelsons and the Trenchards were confirmed.

Betty's face was a picture of disappointment. 'I'm sure none

of those people were my mother's friends. I must be mistaken,
but I could have sworn I knew the house.'

'Did any of the tenants sub-let it?' asked Jack.

The clerk adjusted his spectacles and squinted at the ledger.
'Yes, I believe you're right, sir.' He turned the page. 'Here we
are. A Mr and Mrs M. Trevelyan. The Misses Holt sub-let the
house in 1907, but that was only for a matter of four months,
from the April.'

'Trevelyan?' said Betty musingly. 'I wonder if that was the
name? There aren't any other sub-lettings, are there?'

The clerk shook his head. 'No, Miss. That's the only sub-let
we have on record for Saunder's Green. There's a note here
about it. "Sub-let while renovations and building work carried
out." There's another note on the file . . . Ah, yes, of course.
That was a very busy time. All our properties in Stowfleet were
renovated and brought up to date in the summer of that year.
That was when Mr Arthur Wild was with us, of course. He had
some very advanced views. It was his idea to add indoor
plumbing, gas, facilities for a telephone and a garage to all his
properties.'

'A garage?' said Jack in surprise.

The clerk looked at him with an indulgent smile. 'Yes, indeed,
sir. Mr Wild was a very keen motorist. You would think the
cars of those days to be hopelessly antiquated, I know, but I
remember Mr Wild saying there would come a day when every
household would own a car. Do you own a car, sir?'

'Yes, I do, as a matter of fact.'

'All our Resthaven properties have a purpose-built garage,
complete with electric light and power.'

'It sounds as if Saunder's Green has a garage too,' said Betty,
not wanting the clerk to be diverted onto the subject of Resthaven
once more.

The clerk sighed. 'I imagine it does, madam. Mr Wild had
vision. Remarkable vision, but I imagine the building works
are the reason why the Misses Holt let the house. I remember the
Misses Holt in their latter years. They were most particular.
They were two maiden ladies and very much of the old
school. They wouldn't have cared to stay in the house while
any work was carried on.'

'I wonder if they were the people your mother knew, Betty,' said Jack.

'They could be, I suppose.' She flashed another winning smile at the clerk. 'Thank you for all your help. You've been very kind.'

'Not at all, Madam,' said the clerk gallantly. 'It's a pleasure.'

Jenny smiled brightly at them as the bell clanged above the doorway of Wilson and Lee. 'How did you get on at Ezra Wild's?' she asked in an undertone, as she passed them the order to view.

'We've got another name,' said Jack quietly. 'A Mr and Mrs Trevelyan were there in the summer of 1907. The house was sub-let to them for four months. Does that name mean anything to you?'

Jenny shook her head. 'No, I can't say it does.'

'If the dates we worked out are accurate, then the people you visited were either the Holt sisters or this Mr and Mrs Trevelyan.'

'That's something to know. You'll find,' she added in a louder voice for the benefit of Mr Southwick, who was passing the desk, 'that Saunder's Green has plenty of space and, of course, benefits from a well-established garden. The house is on the telephone. We've told Mrs Offord, the housekeeper, to expect you.'

Mrs Offord turned out to be just the sort of person they expected from Jenny's description. 'Won't you bring your car into the garage, sir?' she asked, looking at the Spyker parked on the drive.

'I'm sure it'll be fine in the open,' said Jack. 'It's not going to rain but thank you for the offer.'

The tour started. 'We saw the house when we were driving through Stowfleet,' said Betty chattily. 'I can't remember for sure, but I think my mother used to know the people who lived here.'

'Would that be Colonel and Mrs Trenchard, Miss?' asked the housekeeper.

Betty shook her head. 'No. I think the name was Trevelyan.'

'They must've been before my time,' said the housekeeper. Her brow furrowed. 'I can't recall ever hearing of any Trevelyans living here. Two maiden ladies had it before the Colonel and his wife. Now what were they called? I used to hear stories about them, about how strict they were with the staff. Hoxton, the old gardener, he used to say how easy-going the Colonel and Mrs Trenchard was in comparison. Now what were they called?'

'It doesn't matter,' said Jack easily. 'They don't sound like your mother's friends, do they, Betty?'

'No, I don't think so. Unless – were they fond of children, do you happen to know?'

'Not by the tales I've heard,' said the housekeeper with a smile. 'They liked a place for everything and everything in its place and that's difficult with children, isn't it? Now the Trenchards, they had grandchildren, and it was a treat when they came. Shall we start with the upstairs first?'

The tour progressed at a leisurely pace, starting as Jenny's had done, with the kitchens and then progressing up to the attics. Jack drew Betty to one side, ostensibly to admire the view from the dusty attic window. 'Can you get Mrs Offord out of the way for a few minutes?' he whispered.

Betty nodded. 'I'm terribly sorry,' she said, turning to the housekeeper, 'but would it be possible for me to use the . . . er . . . facilities?' adding with an embarrassed and not entirely assumed air. 'I'm afraid I really need to go.'

'Of course, Miss. Do you want me show you where it is?'

'Yes, please. I don't think I'd be able to find it by myself,' adding, completely unnecessarily in Jack's opinion, 'have you seen all you want to up here, Jack?'

'Not quite,' he said, thinking fast. 'I think one of these rooms would do nicely for my woodwork.'

'You'll find the garage much better for woodwork, sir,' said Mrs Offord, with irritating helpfulness. 'All kitted out, it is, with a bench and everything that's needed. The Colonel liked to turn his hand to a bit of carpentry. He made the bookcase on the landing and was a dab hand at all sorts of joinery. Why, there's no end of things he made, now I come to think of it.' She drew a deep breath, clearly ready to enumerate items of Colonel Trenchard's handiwork.

Jack's expression nearly made Betty giggle. 'Can we go, Mrs Offord?' she asked.

'Yes, of course, my dear. You follow me.'

They clattered off down the uncarpeted stairs, Mrs Offord listing the Colonel's carpentry achievements.

As their voices faded, Jack crossed rapidly to the ottoman which he knew from Jenny Langton's description contained the old jack-in-the-box and toys and started to quickly rummage through it.

Betty emerged from the lavatory to find Mrs Offord pointing out the Colonel's bookcase to Jack on the landing, obviously gratified by Jack's apparent absorption in mortise and tenon joints.

'Did you find anything?' she muttered, as Mrs Offord escorted them along the landing to the main bedroom.

'Yes,' he hissed. 'Tell you later. My word, Mrs Offord,' he said as she opened the door, 'this is an excellent room.'

'It'd be just right for a young couple such as yourselves,' she said indulgently. 'This used to be the Colonel and Mrs Trenchard's room. The poor mistress couldn't get upstairs for the last few years, but she used to say to me to make sure everything was kept nice and, of course, I always did.'

'You certainly have done,' said Jack, looking around the meticulously clean and tidy room. Mrs Offord looked pleased, but accepted the praise as her due.

'Are you intending to stay on as housekeeper?' asked Betty. It was the sort of thing that a prospective householder would want to know.

Mrs Offord's face fell. 'No, Ma'am. Mavis, the housemaid, might stay, but I don't think I will. You see, even if the house was to be taken by a nice young couple such as yourselves, I'd grown to be that fond of the mistress, I don't know as I could. I was used to all her little ways, you see. I know things have to change, but I don't think I could bear to see the house as I knew it gone. I'm glad to say that the mistress left me enough to be comfortable on, so I told Mr Laidlaw that although I was happy to stay on to keep the place nice while people looked round, I wouldn't want to stay once he'd found a new tenant. I hopes as how you don't mind. I'm sure you'll find someone else.'

'That's a real shame,' said Jack with such feeling that even Betty was convinced. 'Who's Mr Laidlaw, by the way?'

Betty was puzzled. After their trip to Ezra Wild and Sons, they knew who Mr Laidlaw was. He owned the place.

'He's the landlord, sir. I know as how Wilson and Lee say it's owned by Ezra Wild, the builders, but it's all Mr Laidlaw's, really.'

'I see. So there isn't a Mr Wild any longer?'

That was another thing they knew. What on earth was Jack getting at?

'Oh no, sir,' said Mrs Offord with a chuckle. 'There hasn't been a Mr Wild, or any sons, for a good number of years, for all that's what the builders are called. Mr Laidlaw's had it for as long as I've been here.'

'I suppose he bought the business, did he?' continued Jack.

Mrs Offord shook her head. 'No, he married into it, as you might say.' She smiled. 'I remember the Colonel saying that it should be called Ezra Wild and grandson-in-law or some such.'

'That hardly trips off the tongue, though, does it?' said Jack with a smile.

Connections. That had been what Jack wanted to find out. Connections. He always did want to know how things joined together.

'I suppose not, sir,' Mrs Offord agreed. She sighed. 'There's some who would envy Mr Laidlaw, because he's made the business prosper and no mistake, but he's had his troubles, same as the rest of us. His poor wife died only a few months ago but she'd been ill for years, poor lady. Very devoted, he was. Nothing but the best for her, which is how it should be, and no children to leave it all to, which must have been a sorrow to both of them.'

There didn't seem much else to be said on the topic of the devoted Mr Laidlaw. Jack and Betty allowed themselves to be led into more bedrooms and the bathroom.

Out on the landing once more, Mrs Offord paused with her hand on a door. 'This is my own room. I don't suppose you want to see in, do you?'

The answer was that Jack very much wanted to see the room. This was the room in which Jenny had been, in her own words, frightened by the tiles round the fireplace.

'Would you mind?' he asked with a smile. 'Apart from

anything else, you must have a terrific view of the garden from this side of the house.'

'Very good, sir,' she said, opening the door. 'It's a nice room and I keeps it nice, even though I say so myself.'

'It's lovely,' said Betty impulsively as they went in, which earned them a smile from Mrs Offord.

'Do you feel anything?' Jack muttered to Betty. 'Anything spooky, I mean?'

She shook her head.

'No, neither do I. Which doesn't prove anything, I know, but it's still worth noticing.'

The sunlight flooded the room. Jack went to the open window, looking out on the magnificent cedar tree on the lawn.

His attention was caught by dull squares of metal set into the brick of the window frame at regular intervals. 'This room was a nursery once,' he said, much to Mrs Offord's surprise.

'I don't think so, sir.'

'Yes, it must've been,' he said. 'Look, this is where the bars were set into the window.'

Mrs Offord peered at the window. 'Well, fancy that! You've got sharp eyes, sir. All these years I've been here, and I've never noticed.'

'You said the Trenchards had their grandchildren to visit. I suppose the bars were put up then.'

'It can't be that, sir,' said Mrs Offord. 'This has always been my room, ever since I've been here, with Mavis in the next room. Besides that, the three boys were too old to be in a nursery. Proper little scamps they were,' she added with a reminiscent smile. 'No, they slept on the other side of the house, next to the room their parents had.' Her frown deepened. 'They were too old to need bars at the window, or the Colonel would've had them put in. I never heard tell of a child living here, and that's a fact.'

'It could easily have been done before the Trenchards' time,' said Jack easily.

'Well, it wasn't the Misses Holt who had a nursery, that's for sure,' said Mrs Offord, still puzzled. She looked indulgently at Jack and Betty. 'Ah well, when you need a nursery, I dare say you could have the bars put back. I expects you're looking forward to that.'

'It's early days yet,' said Betty with a slightly embarrassed laugh. 'We've only been married a few weeks.'

'Isn't that nice?' said Mrs Offord with a sentimental sigh. 'And you after a proper family house already. Did you have a nice day for the wedding?'

'We did. Jack's aunt and uncle have a house in Sussex and we were married there. It was a wonderful day.'

Talk of the wedding carried them comfortably round the rest of the house until they got out into the garden. Here Mrs Offord left them to their own devices.

'I didn't know all those details about the bridesmaids' dresses,' asked Jack with a rather bemused air as they walked away from the house. 'And as for your wedding dress, all I could have said was that it was white and you looked an absolute corker. All that deep stuff about pin-tucks and so on totally escaped me. Are you sure Mrs Offord wanted know all about the wedding cake with four tiers and what Arthur said in his best man's speech?'

'Mrs Offord,' said Betty, slipping her hand into his, 'was gripped. Why did you want me to take her away from the attics?'

'I wanted to have a look at the toys inside the ottoman.' He glanced down, grinning at her in supressed excitement. 'And guess what I found? A teddy bear with a pink ribbon.'

Betty rolled her eyes. 'So what? A teddy bear is nothing to get excited about. Every child has a teddy bear.'

'When were teddies first sold?'

Betty thought for a moment. 'I don't know. We've always had teddy bears, haven't we?'

'Not before 1900 or thereabouts. I don't know the exact date but it's around then or later. Certainly not before. What d'you make of that?'

'What should I make of it?' asked Betty cautiously.

'The dates, old prune,' he said, squeezing her hand affectionately. 'Look, we know the Miss Holts didn't take the house until January 1898, correct?'

'I suppose so,' she said. 'I didn't write the dates down.'

'I did. And from what we've heard of the Holts, they don't seem to have put a welcome mat out for any kids, let alone keeping a box of toys for them.'

'They could have been bought by the Trenchards. They had grandchildren.'

'Yes. Three boys,' he reminded her. 'I doubt if any of them would have a teddy with a pink ribbon. I think the toys in that box belonged to a little girl and the only people a little girl could belong to are the Trevelyans, who had the house, if you recall, in the summer of 1907.'

Betty still looked unconvinced. 'I suppose you might be right. So you think the Trevelyans are the people we're looking for?' she asked.

'That's right,' said Jack, his eyes bright. 'I'm sure we're on the right lines, Betty. And that means we've gone from knowing practically nothing to having names and a date. That gives us something to get to grips with.'

Their walk had brought them under the spreading branches of the cedar tree. It really was a magnificent tree. Betty reached out and touched the ridged bark.

Jack watched her closely. 'D'you feel anything?'

'Just wood,' said Betty with an embarrassed laugh. 'I wasn't really expecting anything else. What on earth are you doing?' she added in surprise.

Jack stripped off his jacket and, catching hold of a low branch, levered himself into the tree. 'I haven't climbed a tree for ages,' he said cheerfully. 'It's odd how the urge leaves you.'

'I wish it hadn't struck you now. Jack, get down! If Mrs Offord sees you, she'll think you've gone nuts.'

'She'll put it down to my natural exuberance. Did you know the new wood has little hairs on it? All the twigs feel a bit furry. Aunt Alice has a cedar tree and I used to climb it as a kid. Here, have a pine cone,' he added, picking one off and tossing it down to her. 'They have a wonderful smell when they're burnt and the smell keeps insects away.'

'Fascinating,' said Betty tightly. 'Jack, Mrs Offord's looking!'

'And no doubt she's enjoying the spectacle.' He lay flat on the branch and ran his hand along it. 'I say, Betty, there's old nails in the wood.'

'Fascinating with knobs on,' said Betty in a strained voice. 'There must've been a swing or something up there. Jack, get down! Mrs Offord will think you're crazy.'

'It wasn't a swing,' he said thoughtfully. 'The nails aren't in the right place for that. I think someone had nailed planks up here. It must've been a tree house.'

'All right, it was a tree house! What does it matter? *Get down.*'

He didn't move. 'Betty,' he said thoughtfully, 'we know there was a family called Trevelyan, yes? And they, we're supposing, because of the bars in the nursery and the box of toys, they had a child, a little girl.'

'Yes, I suppose we are,' she said impatiently, glancing round. The housekeeper was visible through the dining-room window, placidly wielding a duster. Betty relaxed slightly. 'You worked out that Jenny must've come here when she was little. I imagine that if her mother, Mrs Langton, was friends with this Mrs Trevelyan, the fact that they both had a little girl of around the same age would give them something in common. I bet she and her mother were regular visitors. They must've been, really, for the house to have seemed so familiar years later.'

'Yes . . .' said Jack slowly, levering himself up and sitting astride the branch. 'What I was actually wondering, granted how familiar Jenny Langton found the house and the garden, was if there was only one little girl and she was it.'

Betty stared up at him. 'I beg your pardon?'

'To put it another way, I wondered if your pal Jenny Langton was actually Jenny Trevelyan. That this house was her house and those toys were her toys.'

'And the Trevelyan family was her family?'

'Yes, that's the size of it.'

Betty continued to stare up at him. 'I think there must be something about that tree,' she said eventually. 'Everyone who comes into contact with it seems to go off their rocker. Jack, Jenny *can't* be Jenny Trevelyan. She's got a perfectly good family of her own. I knew the Langtons, remember? Her mother and father and her two brothers. She even looks like her mother. And her brothers, come to that. I bet if you asked, she'd be able to produce baby photographs and all sorts of stuff.'

'Maybe I'm on the wrong lines, then,' said Jack thoughtfully. 'It was just an idea that occurred to me. By the way, what d'you mean, that everyone who comes into contact with this tree goes off their rocker? Don't you believe what Jenny Langton told us?'

Betty sighed. 'Jack, I don't know what happened but she can't have seen a monster. I certainly believe she saw something that frightened her but we know there wasn't anything actually here.'

'I said it was a memory.'

'A memory of *what,* though?' said Betty impatiently. 'Monsters don't exist and you won't ever make me believe that they do. I can't see why what I suggested can't be the truth of it. Jenny fell asleep under the tree when she was very small and had a horrible nightmare. Or, perhaps, someone – maybe an elder brother or another child who was visiting – dressed up and frightened her. You know what boys are.'

'I should do,' he murmured. 'I was one for ages.'

'And still are at times,' she said reprovingly. 'I do wish you'd come down from that tree. It seems so odd that the first thing you do when let out into the garden is to start climbing trees. Mrs Offord must think you're barmy.'

'I'll try and convince her otherwise,' he said with a laugh. 'She's on her way,' he added as the housekeeper opened the French windows and stepped down into the garden.

'Hello, Mrs Offord,' he added conversationally as she joined them under the tree. 'This would be a terrific place for a tree house.' He grinned down at the two women. 'Just peeping into chapter two, as you might say. Children an' all that.'

Betty sighed dangerously but Mrs Offord beamed warmly at him as Jack swung himself down. 'I can see you're going to have a very happy family, sir. It's nice you're thinking of children so soon and you still shaking the confetti out of your clothes, so to speak. It's funny you should think about a tree house. There was one up there, years ago.'

'Did the Colonel build it?' asked Jack, dusting off his knees.

'No, it was here when they arrived. You've got pine needles in your hair, by the way, sir. No, the Colonel didn't build it but he took it down when the boys got too big for it. Not that they ever played in it much because it was too small for them. More like a baby's tree house it was, I remember them saying. They thought it was very tame, being so close to the ground. Little monkeys for climbing, they were.'

'Boys are,' he said with a grin.

Betty sniffed. 'And some men.'

'Shall we look round the rest of the garden?' he said, ignoring the barb. He took Betty's arm and steered her away.

'And what,' she said, once they were out of earshot, 'was all that about? Whatever made you want to climb the tree?'

'I was looking for the tree house.'

'You're kidding,' said Betty with a dismissive laugh. 'You couldn't have known it was there.'

'I thought it might be. Don't you remember what Jenny Langton said? That it was as if the world had suddenly turned upside down. Instead of looking up at the tree, she was looking down. She was in the tree house, Betty.'

She gazed at him. 'You're right. She did say she was looking down.' Betty put her hands wide. 'Jack, I don't know what to think. I just can't believe she saw a monster.'

'No, of course she didn't. But she saw something, something flesh and blood that scared her witless.'

'And she remembered that as a monster, you mean?' Betty bit her lip. 'I suppose that could be the explanation but she seemed very certain about some of the details. The glistening skin and the staring eyes and so on.'

'There might be an explanation for that but I don't know what. The first thing we've got to do is find out about Mr and Mrs Trevelyan. That'll give us something to go on. But, Betty, you suggested a kid had dressed up and scared her. I think there's far more to this than a harmless prank. I think she witnessed something real and something very nasty. I want to find out what it was.'

# FIVE

For the sake of the watching housekeeper, they walked round the rest of the garden before returning to the house.

As they approached the bridge across the little stream, they saw an elderly man with a trowel and a bucket of cement fixing a loose stone on the balustrade. 'This must be George Meredith, the gardener,' muttered Jack. 'The one who came to Miss Langton's aid.'

Approaching, he smiled broadly and offered his cigarette case. 'Hello. We're just taking a look around the house. The gardens are very well kept.'

'I do my best,' said the gardener, straightening up. 'Thank 'ee very much. I won't have a cigarette, sir, I'll stick to my pipe, but thank 'ee all the same. The gardens aren't too bad if you can keep on top of it.' He paused then added, with natural politeness, 'Do you like the house?'

Betty nodded enthusiastically. 'Very much. The funny thing is, I think I used to come here when I was little. I'm sure some friends of my mother lived here. They were called Trevelyan. I don't suppose you remember them, do you?'

'Trevelyan,' repeated George Meredith thoughtfully. 'No, I can't say as I do. When did they live here, Miss?'

'It must be twenty years or so ago. I was only a little girl, of course, but I'd very much like to see them again.'

'Twenty years ago,' he said thoughtfully. 'Hold on. I do remember something now. Trevelyan. They weren't here long and there was some talk . . .' A gleam of recollection came into his eyes and he looked away.

He knows something, thought Jack with absolute conviction. 'What sort of talk? Do you remember?'

The gardener looked pointedly at Betty. 'I can't say as I do, sir. Not more than what was just gossip, I'll be bound.'

'I'd like to know,' said Betty plaintively. 'My poor mother's died, so I can't ask her, but I would like to know what happened to the Trevelyans. They had a little girl who I remember playing with. I'd love to meet her again.'

The gardener drew a deep breath. 'Perhaps you should speak to Mr Laidlaw,' he said. 'He owns the place. He would know if anyone would. But Miss – it's in the past. It's a long time ago. If I were you, I'd let it be. You can't do any good by digging up old scandals. It won't do any good.'

That was so clearly his last word on the subject that there was nothing for it but to wish him a good afternoon and continue their walk.

'Jack,' said Betty excitedly, squeezing his hand, 'there really is something there.'

'I knew that,' he said with a laugh. 'I worked it out. A pink teddy bear and a tree house, remember?'

'So what do we do next?'

'I think we should call on Mr Laidlaw. Hopefully he'll be a bit more forthcoming than George Meredith.'

Mr Laidlaw turned Jack's card over in his hands with a puzzled frown. On it Jack had written: '*Concerning Mr and Mrs Trevelyan*' and, to the clerk's obvious surprise, when it had been sent in Mr Laidlaw had agreed to see them right away.

'It's very good of you to spare the time, sir,' said Jack, pulling out a seat for Betty and drawing a chair up to the desk.

'Not at all,' said Mr Laidlaw absently.

He was a big man in his early fifties, with a friendly, open face with grey eyes, a shock of untidy grey hair and a pleasant burr of a Scottish accent. A sheaf of meticulously drawn plans for a house lay on the desk and, across the room, pinned to a board on an easel, was a half-finished architect's plan of another house drawn in blue ink. Jack noticed a smear of the same coloured ink on Mr Laidlaw's index finger.

Anyone who could draw like that obviously had very precise hands, to say nothing of a precise mind. He was, Jack reminded himself, seeing the framed scroll of the Royal Institute of British Architects on the wall, an architect. That would take a very precise mind, wouldn't it?

Plans of the layouts of the houses at Resthaven, presumably the work of Mr Laidlaw himself, adorned the walls. Pinned to a corkboard was a map showing the connections from Resthaven to London and three large prints of an artist's idyllic impression of the finished houses. Eternal sunshine, a contented husband, a smiling wife and two happy children apparently came as standard with a Resthaven house.

Betty looked at the prints with approval. 'I like those houses,' she said impulsively. 'Did you design them, Mr Laidlaw?'

He smiled at her enthusiasm. 'Yes, they're all my work and, I must say, I'm very happy with them. They look good, don't they, Mrs Haldean? I was very pleased with the artist's impressions, but they show nothing more than the truth. If you're interested, it'd be well worth your while to put your name down as soon as possible. We anticipate a ready sale to those who have to work in London and yet want to live in the fresh air of the countryside. The connections to London are first-rate.'

They'd need to be, thought Jack. To his way of thinking, looking at the map, Resthaven was practically in Woking.

'I can guarantee,' continued Mr Laidlaw, 'in fact, we will guarantee, that all the Resthaven houses are finished to the highest degree commensurate with the price.'

Jack had read too much about teething troubles with new houses to take this statement entirely at face value.

Mr Laidlaw must have sensed his cynicism, because he shook his head vigorously. 'Don't misunderstand me, Mr Haldean. I know new developments often throw up unexpected problems, but, as I say, I can guarantee that will not happen at Resthaven. I've made sure of that. After all, what could be more important than the house you live in?'

'Nothing,' agreed Betty, completely won over by his obvious sincerity.

Andrew Laidlaw beamed at her. 'Exactly. Ezra Wild, who started the firm, was a master builder and he passed those skills on to his sons. My father-in-law – I inherited the firm from him – was very keen that I should be a practical builder as well as an architect. Knowledge of the materials and the craft was his watchword. That's where good architecture starts and there's no substitute for practical knowledge. I'm glad to say,' he added, with pardonable pride, 'that I'm a practical man.'

Betty turned to Jack. 'What d'you think, Jack? The houses look lovely.'

'I'd certainly be interested in looking round,' he said. A bit of tact never hurt and Mr Laidlaw was obviously very proud of Resthaven.

'Let me give you one of our brochures,' said Mr Laidlaw, pressing the bell on his desk. 'Ah, Taylor,' he said to the clerk who opened the door, 'Mr and Mrs Haldean will require a Resthaven brochure. Please have one ready for them when they leave.'

'Very good, sir,' said the clerk.

'However,' continued Mr Laidlaw, looking at Jack's card as the clerk shut the door behind him, 'you didn't come here to talk about houses, did you?'

He picked up Jack's card and frowned at it with puzzled politeness. '"Concerning Mr and Mrs Trevelyan",' he read aloud. 'I must say, I don't know who Mr and Mrs Trevelyan are. Your name, on the other hand, Mr Haldean, seems familiar.' He looked mildly sheepish. 'As a matter of fact, the reason why I was happy to see you was because I was sure I knew your name.'

He glanced from the card to Jack then back again, before looking up, enlightenment dawning. 'Excuse me, Mr Haldean, am I addressing Major Haldean, by any chance? Were you in the Flying Corps during the war?'

Jack nodded in surprise. He'd been a perfectly decent pilot – or a lucky one, he reminded himself. There wasn't a lot of difference between the two, but he certainly hadn't been a well-known one. As the handful of pilots who had been household names were, by and large, dead, notoriety as a pilot wasn't something he'd ever aspired to. So where on earth had Mr Laidlaw come across his name?

'I've always been interested in aviation,' said Mr Laidlaw, 'but it was my brother who was really keen. I don't suppose you ever ran into him during the war? Archie Laidlaw.'

Jack thought for a moment, then shook his head. 'I'm sorry, sir, I don't think so.'

Mr Laidlaw nodded sadly. 'It was just a thought. He transferred from the infantry and was mad keen to fly, but he didn't survive for long. He was going to come into business with me after the war but it wasn't to be. He was a fine man,' he added with a sigh.

There was an awkward pause.

'I'm very sorry to hear that, sir,' said Jack quietly.

Andrew Laidlaw shook himself. 'Poor Violet, my wife, was terribly cut up over it. She was very fond of Archie.' His face twisted. 'Our son was named after him. He was carried off by the flu just after the war, poor little chap. Violet never really got over it. After little Archie went, she never really rallied. She spent too much time dwelling in the past. In the end it was quite a blessed release.'

'That's dreadful,' said Betty with shocked sympathy. 'I'm so sorry to hear that, Mr Laidlaw.'

'Thank you, Mrs Haldean,' said Mr Laidlaw quietly. 'It was a real blow. Still, life goes on, eh?' Andrew Laidlaw shook himself, as if to draw a line under the conversation. 'I'm still trying to think where I know your name from, Major Haldean. It was definitely something to do with aviation.' He looked up and snapped his fingers together.

'Got it!' he said, his face broadening in a smile. 'You were the chap who sorted out that mess at the Lassiter Aircraft company, weren't you? I remember reading about it in the newspaper. Your war record was mentioned in connection with the case. And weren't you the one who worked out exactly what was going on at Hunt Coffee?' He chuckled reminiscently. 'My word, that case made a stir, all right. You write books too, don't you? That is you, isn't it?'

'Admit it, Jack,' said Betty, beaming at Mr Laidlaw. She liked it when people recognised Jack's achievements. 'Your fame has gone before you.'

'I wouldn't call it fame, Betty,' muttered Jack deprecatingly.

If Andrew Laidlaw knew who he was, it might be awkward to use the excuse of the Trevelyans being old friends of Betty's mother. Mr Laidlaw knew him as someone who poked his nose into matters that were, strictly speaking, none of his concern, and, what's more, seemed rather impressed by his doings. He might as well trade on that fact.

'Yes, that's right, Mr Laidlaw,' he said, returning the smile.

'I've got a bit of a puzzle on my hands at the moment and my wife and I wondered if you could help. I don't suppose it's of any great importance, but a friend of my wife's asked us to look into it.'

Betty gave him a sweet smile and a slight nod. The message that the Trevelyans were no longer friends of her family was received and understood.

Andrew Laidlaw drew himself up expectantly. 'I'll do anything I can to help, Major Haldean. What do you want to know?'

'It's about one of your houses. Saunder's Green.'

'Saunder's Green?' Andrew Laidlaw looked blank for a moment, then nodded intelligently. 'Oh, yes. In Stowfleet. I know the one. It's an old house. We have quite a number of properties such as Saunder's Green on our books. That one was built by my father-in-law, Arthur Wild, back in 1880 or so. What about it?'

'Well, one of my wife's friends is certain she knew the house and the people who lived in it years ago. 1907, to be precise. There was a family called the Trevelyans who rented it from the actual tenants, the Misses Holt, for the summer. There was an incident, an unpleasantness, to call it no more than that, which happened while the Trevelyans were living there. We wondered if you knew what had actually happened?'

Andrew Laidlaw stared at them in shock. '*Those* Trevelyans,' he whispered. He looked down and pinched the bridge of his nose between his thumb and forefinger. For a long moment he said nothing, then, bracing himself, sat up and reached for the silver cigarette box that lay on the desk. 'Do you mind?' he muttered, looking at Betty. She shook her head. 'Please, help yourself,' he added, lighting a cigarette.

Jack lit Betty's cigarette and waited expectantly.

'I haven't thought about the Trevelyans in years,' said Mr Laidlaw. 'When I read the names you'd written on your card, I certainly didn't connect them with the family who lived in Saunder's Green. Tell me, Major Haldean, who wants to know about the Trevelyans? Who is your client?'

'I'm sorry,' said Jack with a smile to take away the sting of refusal. 'I promised I wouldn't say.'

Mr Laidlaw shook his head in irritation. 'I suppose you've

got to keep that sort of thing confidential. I would like to know who's interested, though. It's twenty years ago now and that seems an awfully long time to wait before dragging up old scandals.'

'So there was a scandal, then?'

Andrew Laidlaw took a deep breath then, getting up from the desk, crossed to the door and made sure it was properly shut.

'I would like you, Major Haldean, to treat this as confidential. There was indeed a scandal, a scandal that affected my own family. When you first mentioned the Trevelyans, I honestly had not made the connection but the Trevelyans of Saunder's Green . . .' He sighed and rubbed his face with his hands.

'My wife, Violet, passed away in February,' he said, returning to his desk. He gestured towards a silver-framed photograph of a middle-aged woman with a kindly, if rather vacant, face on the desk. There was a black ribbon looped round a corner of the frame. Obviously that was the late Mrs Laidlaw.

Mr Laidlaw followed Jack's gaze. 'Poor Violet.' He drummed his fingers on the desk. 'All I can say is that I'm glad she's not here to be worried about the whole sorry business once more. Caroline Trevelyan was my wife's cousin. They were very close, more like sisters than cousins. She would've been terribly upset.'

'What happened?' asked Betty softly. Mr Laidlaw looked so upset himself she felt a real stab of sympathy for him.

'I haven't thought of this for years,' he said with a sigh, 'but I remember it well enough. The Trevelyans were supposed to be moving to New Zealand. They had given up their house in London when, at the last minute, some complication arose and the move had to be postponed. As it happened, the tenants of Saunder's Green House – I forget who they were – were very unhappy about living in the house while the repairs and alterations that my father-in-law, Arthur Wild, deemed necessary, were carried out. To cut a long story short, we offered the tenants another house while the building work was underway and the Trevelyans, who had been staying in a hotel, moved into Saunder's Green until they could sail for New Zealand.'

He gave a humourless smile. 'I remember Violet was delighted. As I say, she and Caroline Trevelyan were more like sisters than cousins, and here was Caroline, close at hand. I wish they had gone to New Zealand,' he added bitterly.

He stubbed out his cigarette and lit another one. 'Caroline left her husband. One day, without a word to anyone, she simply vanished.' He breathed out a long mouthful of smoke. 'I actually saw Caroline Trevelyan that day,' he said eventually.

'You did?' asked Jack alertly. 'Did she seem upset or worried, sir?'

Mr Laidlaw shook his head. 'Not at all. That's why I was convinced, right from the start, that there was more to Caroline's disappearance than met the eye. I needed to see her in connection with some of the works. I forget exactly what now, but I know we needed to put scaffolding up and it was probably to warn her that was going to happen.'

He smiled briefly. 'She invited me in for coffee. With Caroline being so close to my wife, our relations were much more informal than is usual with my clients, you understand. There was another woman with her, an old friend. I can't remember her name, but we had quite a merry little party. That would have been about eleven o'clock or so. We chatted for a while.'

His smile faded. 'I remember enjoying the break from work.' He sat up and looked at Jack earnestly. 'The point is, Major Haldean, that Caroline Trevelyan was completely herself. Happy, even. When we got the news that she had disappeared, I, for one, wasn't at all surprised when Michael, her husband, was implicated.'

'When you say "implicated", what do you mean?' asked Jack slowly.

Andrew Laidlaw looked him squarely in the eyes. 'Do I have to spell it out for you?'

Jack gave a low whistle. 'Murder?'

Mr Laidlaw shrugged. 'The case never came to court but Michael Trevelyan made himself scarce. The implication is obvious, wouldn't you say?'

'Did you know the Trevelyans, sir?' asked Jack. 'You said Mrs Trevelyan was your wife's cousin. Were they friends of yours as well?'

Mr Laidlaw shook his head. 'Not really. Although Violet was

very close to Caroline, she never got on with her husband, so we didn't meet them socially.' He clicked his tongue. 'I must say I never had any quarrel with Trevelyan. In fact I rather liked the man at first but, as I say, Violet didn't care for him. Maybe I was unduly influenced by my wife's opinion, but possibly the best way to put it is that I came to be wary of him. Although perfectly agreeable at first, I suspected he could have an evil temper if roused. Not that I had much to do with him, you understand. I did meet him, but only for what you might call business purposes. I discussed the alterations to the house with Michael Trevelyan, but that was all. Not that, of course, he had any say in the matter. It was my wife, Violet, who suggested they live there and they got the house at a peppercorn rent. She put it to her father – Arthur Wild was Caroline Trevelyan's uncle, of course – and he agreed. It was my father-in-law who supervised most of the building work. I only called in occasionally from time to time to see how the work was progressing. Then, of course, this awful business happened and after a while it became clear that Michael Trevelyan was, as I say, implicated.'

'I'm still not sure how he was implicated,' said Jack. 'Did the police find any evidence?'

'I'm afraid I can't help you with those details,' said Mr Laidlaw. 'I believe there was some, but what I can't say. You appreciate, Major Haldean, it's a long time ago now. It was extensively reported in the press, that I do know. My wife was subject to some very unwelcome attention from journalists. Trevelyan was apprehended, as I believe, in London, but the case never came to court.'

'Why not?'

'Because he managed to give the police the slip, that's why. Goodness knows where he got to. We had the police at the house – Saunder's Green – but they couldn't find any evidence of what had happened to Caroline Trevelyan. Speaking personally, I was relieved about that. My poor wife was upset enough as it was, without having to confront any physical evidence. She was convinced for years that Caroline was still alive, but I'm afraid she was deluding herself.'

'What do you think happened, Mr Laidlaw?' asked Betty.

He stubbed out his cigarette. 'What could I think?' he

demanded. 'What could anyone think? My father in law had
no doubts upon the matter, but he held that it was a case of
least said, soonest mended. Privately speaking, he always
thought it was just as well that Trevelyan had managed to escape.
Naturally enough, he was upset about his niece's disappearance, but
she was gone and there was no bringing her back and he dreaded
the whole sorry business being dragged into court.'

'Why did he want it hushed up?' asked Betty innocently.
'After all, as you say, Mrs Trevelyan was his niece.'

Mr Laidlaw looked shocked. 'The publicity, dear lady! We are
a commercial firm and Saunder's Green House was then a
valuable property. Since then, I'm glad to say, we've expanded.'
He gestured to the plans of Resthaven on the wall. Betty still
looked puzzled.

'Would you like to live in a house where you knew a murder
had been committed?' he demanded.

Betty shook her head. 'No, I don't suppose I would,' she said
slowly. 'I don't think I'd ever feel entirely comfortable.'

'Exactly, Mrs Haldean. You've answered your own question.'

He gave an irritated sigh. 'Damn! To have this whole wretched
affair dragged up again after all these years is bad enough, but
if the story gets about again, I have no doubts that Saunder's
Green House is finished as a commercial proposition. Quite
frankly, I might as well knock it down. Even then I'd probably
have a job to sell any houses built on the site. I would be very
obliged to you both if you would refrain from starting any
unsubstantiated rumours.'

'I can promise you we won't start any unsubstantiated
rumours, sir,' said Jack sincerely. Substantiated ones, he added
to himself, were something completely different. 'One more
question. Did the Trevelyans have any children?'

'Children?' Mr Laidlaw looked surprised. 'I don't know. I
can't remember any. As I said, Caroline Trevelyan was my
wife's cousin but I hardly knew them.' He rubbed his forehead.
'I've been very frank with you, Major Haldean. Can I ask you
to drop this enquiry? No good can be served by dragging up
what happened in the past.'

He stood up and stretched his shoulders. 'Now, if you will
excuse me, I do have other matters to attend to.'

He escorted them to the door but hesitated before opening the door. He looked at them and tried to smile, obviously trying to make up for his curtness. 'It's a funny thing. When I realised who you were, Major Haldean, I felt rather pleased. I thoroughly enjoyed reading about the Lassiter affair and so on in the papers.'

He rubbed his face with his hand. 'It's quite different being actually involved, even obliquely. I must remember that in future,' he added wryly.


'Do you really fancy one of those Resthaven houses?' asked Jack, glancing down at the prismatic brochure Betty had tucked under her arm. He tilted his head to read the cover. '"Resthaven! Make this house your Home." You don't intend to, do you?'

'Of course not, silly,' said Betty with a giggle. 'Although Mr Laidlaw certainly wanted me to,' she added as they walked back to the car. 'Besides, it was you who said they wanted to look round Resthaven. You nearly convinced me.'

'That was mere persiflage, sweetheart. I thought you were sincere.'

'Well, I was really. All that fresh air and sunshine looks lovely, even if it's stretching it a bit to say Resthaven's in London. I rather liked him, Jack, and I did feel sorry for him, when he told us about losing his brother in the war and his son to the flu and then his wife as well.'

'Yes, so did I. It must've been tough for relatives during the war,' said Jack. 'I don't think it ever occurred to me when I was in the thick of things to think how the people back home were feeling. Now, in some ways, I think they had it worse than we did. Especially parents.'

He slipped his hand into Betty's and grinned. 'Perhaps it's because I can imagine being a parent myself. I'll teach the boys to climb trees.'

'I'm sure you will,' said Betty. 'Can I just say, though, that I used to climb trees when I was a child.'

'Did you?' he said in surprise.

'Yes. Girls do, you know. Some girls, anyway. But the difference, Jack, between men and women, is that girls get over wanting to. Talking of girls, I suppose we can tell Jenny that we've solved her mystery for her.'

'Have we?'

Betty looked puzzled. 'I'd say so. After all, she thought something scary had happened at Saunder's Green House and, thanks to Mr Laidlaw, we know what it was. That poor woman, Caroline, disappeared. It seems obvious, although Mr Laidlaw was a bit reluctant to say so, that her husband bumped her off, the horrible man.'

'And how is that scary?'

'Well, of course it's scary, Jack.'

'What? Just hearing that someone had disappeared? This is a little girl of about four years old we're talking about, remember. She wouldn't know anything about it. No one would spell the details out to a kid of that age.'

'No, of course they wouldn't,' said Betty thoughtfully. She clutched at his arm. 'Jack! She must've witnessed the murder!' She drew her breath in. 'Poor Jenny! That's horrible. She must've been in that little tree house and seen it all. Oh, the poor child. She must've been so scared that she remembered it as seeing a monster.'

Jack said nothing for a time but walked in silence until they reached the Spyker. 'There's a lot to be said for that idea,' he said, when they reached the car. 'As a matter of fact, it's more or less what I thought myself.'

'Mr Laidlaw said there was another woman there when he called in that morning,' said Betty. 'That must be Mrs Langton, Jenny's mother.'

'Yes . . . It's odd she never mentioned anything to Jenny about it. After all, it's the sort of thing you'd remember.'

Jenny Langton agreed. They had decided to have dinner together in Kettners in Soho, a welcome change, as Jenny said, from boarding-house fare.

However, despite an excellent steak and kidney pie, Jenny hardly noticed the food. 'I witnessed a *murder*?' she said incredulously. And then, going straight to the salient point, added, 'But how come my mother didn't say anything? I mean, you've worked out that I'd visited Saunder's Green House with my mother so she must've been there. Wouldn't she give the hue and cry? I mean, even if she didn't see anything, she would have realised her friend, this Caroline Trevelyan, had disappeared.

You don't go and visit someone for the day and have them vanish without saying a word.'

'Maybe her husband, Michael Trevelyan, made an excuse for her,' said Betty, who'd had time to think about it. 'Perhaps he said she'd gone to bed with a headache or something. Even if your mother thought it was strange at the time, she could hardly question him about it in his own house.'

'I still think it's odd,' said Jenny. 'My mother never said a word about it ever. I can't help thinking that she would've mentioned it. After all, according to Mr Laidlaw, there was quite a rumpus about it in the newspapers.'

'Would she really talk about?' asked Jack. 'I can imagine it's not something you'd want to talk about to a child.'

'Not to a child, no, but later on, when I was grown up, I'm surprised she never mentioned it.'

'Maybe she'd forgotten it,' suggested Betty.

Jenny shook her head. 'Not my mother. She wouldn't forget anything like that. Especially not if, as you say, this precious husband was involved. If she and Caroline Trevelyan were very close friends, she might have been too upset to talk about it, I suppose, but it still seems peculiar.'

She broke off and her expression became thoughtful. 'I wonder if Dad asked her not to mention it? He was very protective where I was concerned.' She smiled indulgently. 'He had some very old-fashioned ideas of what girls should and shouldn't know about. In fact . . .' She looked up sharply. 'I wonder if Dad talked to my brother, Martin, about it? Martin and Dad were very close.'

'How much older is Martin than you?' asked Jack.

'Eight years.'

'So say you did see a murder, he'd be old enough to know you were terribly upset and old enough to be warned not to talk about it.'

'That's right,' said Jenny. 'And, knowing my parents, old enough to be told the truth.' She grinned. 'Martin would want to know the truth. He's that kind of person.' Her eyes shone with sudden determination. 'I know! I'll write to him! If he knows what happened – and I bet he does – then he'll surely tell me. It can't do any harm after all this time.'

'That's a really good idea,' said Betty. 'Jack, can you find anything out? What about looking in the old newspapers?'

'I can do that, certainly, but I don't know if the press will be able to tell us much more than what we've already learned from Mr Laidlaw. Now we've got names and dates, I think Bill Rackham would be more help.'

'Of course!' said Betty. She turned to Jenny. 'I'd like you to meet Bill Rackham,' she said. 'He's an absolute dear and a chief inspector at Scotland Yard.'

'He sounds a useful sort of person,' said Jenny.

'He's been very useful on occasion,' agreed Jack with a laugh. 'I came across him ages ago when I wanted some details about the police for a story I was writing. We'd both been in the war, of course, and it turned out that we knew some of the same people and so on and really hit it off. Now I've got some details to go on, I can certainly ask Bill to look up the records. It might take him a while, though. I know he's been engaged on a case in the Lake District that's taken up all his time. How about putting an advertisement in the newspapers? Even if Bill Rackham and your brother Martin are able to fill us in, we might find out something else worth knowing.'

'You mean ask people to write to me?' asked Jenny, looking startled.

'I'll ask them to write to me, if you like,' offered Jack.

'That's very nice of you,' said Jenny in some relief. 'If you really don't mind, I'd much rather you handled it.' She paused for a moment. 'For one thing, I don't want Wilson and Lee to see my name in the papers, and . . . and . . .' She swallowed hard. 'You see, it really was very scary in the garden. If someone spelled out chapter and verse what happened . . .' She shook herself.

'You'd rather Jack dealt with it first,' put in Betty sympathetically.

Jenny nodded. 'That's exactly it.' She looked at him gratefully. 'I want to know the truth,' she said with determination, 'but,' she added, with a little break in her voice, 'I'd like some warning of it first.'

# SIX

M. Langton, MRCP
46, Boar Lane
Leeds
W. Yorkshire

Dear Jenny

I don't know how you got hold of this old story about the Trevelyans, but it would be much better if you let it drop. I think the best thing for it would be for me to have a word with this detective chap you seem to have lugged in to it and tell him to back off. Even if he is your friend's husband, we don't want an outsider poking around in our private family business and I'm surprised you ever considered it.

If you let me have a note of his address, I'll write to Major Haldean and explain the situation. I intend to call on him on Saturday afternoon and that, I hope, will be the end of it. I will be staying at the Regent's Palace hotel. If you would like to join me there for dinner, please be in the lobby at seven o'clock. Let me know about dinner.

Your affect. brother,
Martin

It was Wednesday morning. In the privacy of her own room, Jenny re-read the letter away from the prying eyes of the other boarding-house inhabitants. The outraged gasp she had given when she'd opened the letter at breakfast had drawn far too much attention and concerned – call that downright nosy – enquiries from the other guests.

She usually thought a lot of Martin. She was very fond of him as a general rule but this was just beyond a joke. She wasn't going to be pushed out of the way, no matter what Martin's opinions were, and to tell Jack Haldean to lay off was simply outrageous. Well, she thought grimly, as she scribbled a note in reply, Martin could say and do what he liked, but she was going to find out the truth whether he liked it or not.

'Bossy pig,' she commented to herself as she stuck a stamp on the envelope. 'He always did think he knows what's best.'

Jack slit open a letter with a Leeds postmark and propped it against the teapot.

> *M. Langton, MRCP*
> *46, Boar Lane*
> *Leeds*
> *W. Yorkshire*

> *Dear Sir,*
> *I understand from my sister, Jennifer Langton, that she has asked you to investigate an old scandal concerning the Trevelyans of Saunder's Green House. Can I state, in the strongest possible terms, that this investigation must cease. There is no point whatsoever in raking up old scandals which would be much better left forgotten and which can only be detrimental to the good name of my family.*
> *Jennifer has furnished me with a note of your address and I intend to call upon you at two o'clock on Saturday afternoon. Please confirm by reply that you will be able to receive me.*
> *Yrs faithfully*
> *Martin Langton (Dr)*

'What d'you think of that?' he asked, passing the letter over to Betty.

Betty's reactions, although she didn't know it, virtually mirrored those of Jenny Langton's. 'The cheeky beggar,' she said. 'I wonder what on earth's got into him? I always got on perfectly well with Martin Langton.'

'He sounds,' said Jack, 'a bit of a pompous ass.'

Betty shook her head. 'He likes his own way and he does

tend to think his way is the right way, but he's always been very nice. What on earth's he so upset about, Jack?'

Jack started to speak, then hesitated. 'I think we'd better let Dr Langton tell us that himself. At the moment, all I know is what was in the old newspapers, which was virtually what Mr Laidlaw told us. There certainly wasn't any mention of Jenny Langton or her mother. However, Bill should be back on Friday and hopefully he'll be able to dig up some solid facts.'

Bill Rackham relaxed into the familiar surroundings of Jack's rooms in Chandos Place. Running a hand through his ginger hair, he pulled the tobacco jar towards him and filled his pipe with a sigh of content. 'You're a lucky devil, Jack. I thought when you got married you'd have to give up some of your bachelor comforts, but this room's hardly changed.'

'Betty,' said Jack, 'has been very understanding. She's transformed the downstairs of the house, but she's let me keep this room more or less as I like. We've had the decorators in downstairs and this room was jolly useful to retreat to. We use it as a sort of snug, and, of course, I work up here. If I've got bookcases, a typewriter, a kettle and the absolute understanding that no one tries to tidy up when I'm working, what more do I need?'

'It's looking pretty tidy at the moment,' said Bill approvingly. He liked things to be neat and tidy.

'Betty put her foot down on the strength of this chap, Dr Langton, calling. She's out shopping at the moment, but she said she'd be back to meet Dr Langton. She knows him, of course, and she says she always liked him, but he seems a prickly sort of character.' He picked up the letter that lay on the table beside him and held it out. 'You'd better read this.'

'Dr Langton,' said Bill, reading the letter, 'seems a bit steamed up.'

It was quarter past one on Saturday afternoon. Bill had returned from Oxenholme the day before and had obligingly looked up the Trevelyan case in the records at Scotland Yard.

'It's difficult, really, to think,' he added, holding a match to his pipe, 'why he should be so excited by it all. After all, even if Miss Langton did witness a murder when she was a kid, poor little beggar, that's no reflection on her or her family, is it? I wonder,' he added significantly, 'if our Dr Langton knows more about this business than he's letting on.'

'That was my first thought,' agreed Jack, 'but he's a bit young to have been directly involved. After all, if he's eight years older than Jenny Langton, that makes him only twelve or thirteen when it happened.'

Bill pulled a face. 'That is a bit too young to be directly involved, I agree. That wasn't really my drift. I still want to hear what he's got to say, though. If he was there that day, he could've seen or heard something that might be relevant to the case. Even if he overheard his parents talking, it could put us on the right lines. After all, a murder case is never closed.'

'So you're taking it as murder?' asked Jack with an enquiring tilt of his head.

'Suspected murder, certainly,' agreed Bill, concentrating on getting his pipe to draw. 'There's nothing much else it can be.' He pulled a notebook from his pocket. 'I've jotted down the relevant facts here.'

The facts, as contained in the official report, didn't leave much room for doubt. On the 15th July 1907, Caroline Trevelyan had vanished. She had last been seen by the housemaid, a Rosanna Selgrove, at three o'clock that afternoon, who had served her mistress with afternoon tea. As it was a fine day, Caroline Trevelyan had taken tea under the shade of the cedar tree in the garden. When Rosanna Selgrove had gone to collect the tea things at just gone half three, her mistress had disappeared.

At first the police were disinclined to treat the matter seriously. It was Michael Trevelyan himself who had reported his wife's disappearance and Michael Trevelyan who insisted that the police institute a search. This they refused to do.

'Why,' asked Jack, as Bill read from his notes, 'didn't the police spring into action right away?'

Bill rubbed his nose with the stem of his pipe. 'Reading between the lines, in the first instance they believed she'd gone off of her own volition. Apparently the family were going to move to New Zealand and that, according to the servants, had caused some friction between the couple. Michael Trevelyan was all for the move. He was employed as a shipping manager by Travis and Sons of Cockspur Street, importing wool, butter, cheese and so on from New Zealand. He'd been appointed to the firm's Wellington office and the move represented considerable promotion for him. Caroline Trevelyan was dreading it. The servants had heard them arguing about it. To be honest, Jack, I think the police side of it was all very badly handled. Inspector Chartfield, who was in charge of the case, was convinced she'd turn up at some relative or friends and thought Michael Trevelyan was making a blasted nuisance of himself.'

'What made them change their minds?'

'Eight days after Mrs Trevelyan had disappeared, Michael Trevelyan turned up with a letter purporting to have come from his wife. It said that she just couldn't face the move and she was going to stay in England. The letter didn't carry an address or date but the envelope was postmarked from Norwich. Trevelyan admitted that his wife didn't have any connections in Norwich but wanted the police in Norfolk to be called in to look for her.'

'And did they?'

Bill shook his head. 'No. Right from the start the police were suspicious about that letter. I don't know if you know, but handwriting analysis had come in and was all the rage. Well, Michael Trevelyan was insisting on action, so Inspector Chartfield thought he'd start with the letter and bring modern science to bear. I don't know if he was suspicious of Trevelyan or not at this stage, but he sent the letter off for analysis. That letter's still on the file, by the way, together with an authentic sample of Mrs Trevelyan's handwriting. The upshot was that although the handwriting bore a superficial resemblance to that of Mrs Trevelyan's, it was a forgery.'

'Was it, by George?' murmured Jack.

'Well, as you can imagine, that put Caroline Trevelyan's disappearance in a very different light. It was obvious that somebody was trying to cover something up.'

'And the police thought that someone was Michael Trevelyan?'

Bill shrugged. 'It's an obvious thought, Jack, and the obvious answer is so often the truth. After all, you know perfectly well that the husband or wife is always the first suspect on the list and, to be fair to Inspector Chartfield, there didn't seem to be anyone else to suspect. Mrs Trevelyan was very well liked. There really didn't seem to be any reason for anyone to bear her any ill will. There was certainly no suspicion she'd been having an affair, went in for gambling or had got involved with any unsavoury types. On the other hand, she was known to have disagreed with her husband. Both the servants, Rosanna Selgrove and Eunice Cowick, had heard him raise his voice to her about the proposed move. He'd accused her of wanting to hold him back.'

'You can have a disagreement without resorting to murder though,' protested Jack. 'Blimey, Bill, I've not always agreed with Betty but she's still here.'

'But a disagreement about what country you're going to live in is rather more serious than where you go for dinner or what have you, isn't it? Inspector Chartfield, with the evidence of the letter, became convinced that Michael Trevelyan had made away with his wife. His theory was that, although no one was suspicious at first, it could only be a matter of time before questions were asked about Mrs Trevelyan's disappearance. His idea was that Michael Trevelyan had raised the alarm to divert the suspicion that would inevitably fall on him.'

'He's probably right at that,' commented Jack. 'Was Trevelyan able to produce an alibi?'

Bill shook his head. 'Not really. Trevelyan had returned to the house at quarter to six. By his own account he had been down at the docks on the afternoon of the fifteenth of July, but although plenty of people had seen him up to about quarter past two, he couldn't produce an alibi for the rest of the afternoon. He had returned to the Cockspur Street office just before five, but from quarter past two until five, no one had seen him. He said he had called into the Fraser Street public library to complete his paperwork and was there until about half four. Although the librarian at Fraser Street certainly recognised Trevelyan as someone who frequently used the public reading room, he couldn't say if Trevelyan had called in there on the fifteenth or not. That would, as Inspector Chartfield noted, give him ample time to get to Saunder's Green and back to Cockspur Street. He could even have time, if he really got a move on, to call in at the library to give a bit of backbone to his story.'

Jack pulled a face. 'It's hard to know what to make of an alibi like that. Did Inspector Chartfield examine the paperwork that Trevelyan had supposedly done that afternoon?'

Bill shrugged. 'If he did, there's no record of it. That's the first thing I'd have done, I must say, with such a thin alibi, but by this time Inspector Chartfield had Trevelyan firmly in his sights. You see, whoever had written that letter knew enough about Caroline Trevelyan to make a fair stab at copying her handwriting and knew she didn't want to go to New Zealand. Armed with this conviction, Inspector Chartfield got a warrant and searched the house.'

'They were looking for the body, I suppose?'

Bill nodded. 'They didn't find it, though. What they did find however, was Trevelyan's diary. Most of it was appointments and memoranda, but at the back he'd written a list of poisons together with a date; Monday, July the fifteenth.'

Jack whistled. 'That's nasty.'

'So Inspector Chartfield thought. The upshot was that the police called in on Michael Trevelyan in his office in Cockspur Street and arrested him on suspicion of murder. He seemed to come quietly. That must've put the officers off their guard, because as soon as they got into the street, he lammed a police officer and made a run for it. And that,' said Bill, tamping down the tobacco in his pipe and re-lighting it, 'is that. From that day to this, no one's had a sniff of him. What d'you think?'

Jack pursed his lips. 'I don't like the diary, I must say. You see, if Caroline Trevelyan was murdered, then obviously the murderer only had half an hour between the servant bringing out the tea tray and then returning for it. That's not long for an impulsive murderer to do the deed and hide the body. And, what's more, to hide it so well a thorough search couldn't uncover any trace of it. If it was planned though, which the list of poisons suggests it was, then he could've had a temporary hiding place arranged in a shed or so on, and disposed of it at his leisure.'

'How would you go about disposing of a body?' asked Bill curiously. 'You've disposed of dozens in fiction.'

'I'm glad you're only accusing me of fictional murders,' said Jack with a grin. 'That's interesting. It's a question that doesn't often come up in the Notes and Queries section of the news-paper. How I did it in *The Neighbours at Number 17* was to have my villain rent a house under an assumed name and talk about his dear wife who was ailing, with his willing girlfriend taking the part of the ailing wife. Then he bumped off his wife, smuggled the body into the house, called for a doctor, had her buried quite openly by a legitimate undertaker, and swanned off with the girlfriend.'

'You're too good at this,' said Bill with a grin.

Jack grinned in return. 'Thanks, but that's fiction, Bill. I can arrange the circumstances so everything falls into place.' He rolled a cigarette thoughtfully between his fingers before lighting it.

'Is there anyone else in the frame?' he asked. 'For instance, is it noted that Mrs Trevelyan had any visitors that day? When I spoke to Mr Andrew Laidlaw – his firm owns the house and they were carrying out renovations on it at the time – he told me that he'd seen Mrs Trevelyan that morning and she had a friend with her. He couldn't recall the name of the friend, but I think it must have been either a Mrs Sheila Langton or a Mrs Amelia Rotherwell.'

'There's no mention of a Mrs Langton,' said Bill. 'I'm presuming Mrs Langton is your pal, Jennifer Langton's, mother. And Dr Martin Langton's mother, come to that. Which, if you're right about Jennifer Langton having witnessed the murder, makes it odd that she's not mentioned. That other name you mentioned, though, Mrs Rotherwell, is noted as a visitor to Mrs Trevelyan on the morning of the fifteenth.'

He flicked open his notebook. 'Andrew Laidlaw made a statement to the effect that he saw Caroline Trevelyan at around eleven o'clock and they had coffee together. That was confirmed by the servants and Mrs Rotherwell, who was also there. I must say,' he commented, looking up from his notebook, 'that it all sounds very chummy. I wonder if the builders were usually invited in for morning coffee?'

'Mr Laidlaw isn't a hod-carrier,' said Jack with a grin. 'He's an architect. No, apparently his wife, Violet, and Caroline Trevelyan were cousins and great friends into the bargain.' He tapped his cigarette on the side of the ashtray. 'I must say, I rather took to him and so did Betty. It's just as well his new batch of houses aren't completed. I think Betty would have bought one on the spot. The brochure for them is on the table beside you.'

'Blimey,' said Bill, blinking at the brochure. 'They're bright, aren't they? Your Mr Laidlaw must be a whizz of a salesman.'

'No, it's not that,' said Jack with a laugh. 'She felt sorry for him. His brother was in the Flying Corps and bought it, poor devil, and his little boy died of the flu after the war. Mrs Offord, the housekeeper who showed us round Saunder's Green, told us that he'd cared devotedly for his wife who was something of an invalid. She died in February, but she'd been ill for years.'

'Poor beggar,' commented Bill. 'Still, it doesn't make his houses any better. Anyway, Mr Laidlaw left the ladies to carry on with his work at around half eleven, but Mrs Rotherwell stayed for lunch. Lunch was served at half twelve and she left Mrs Trevelyan at about half one. She did make a statement, which is on file, but as she left well before three o'clock, she couldn't say anything that was relevant to the case, apart from the fact that Mrs Trevelyan seemed in good spirits. How do you know about her?'

'She was an old friend of Mrs Trevelyan's, apparently. I knew there was at least one visitor, because Mr Laidlaw told me as much when I saw him. Mrs Rotherwell answered my advertisement. I put adverts in as many papers as I could think of, asking if anyone had any knowledge of Caroline or Michael Trevelyan, late of Saunder's Green.'

'That must've run into a bit of money.'

'At eight bob a line, yes, it did, but it got results. Mrs Rotherwell wrote to say she was great friends with Mrs Trevelyan.' Jack hesitated. 'I suppose it is certain she left the house at half one, is it?'

'That's what the servants said,' said Bill with a shrug. 'You're a suspicious devil,' he added with a laugh. 'You can rule out Mrs Rotherwell, though. At three o'clock she was in the tropical department in Harrods, being fitted out in the right togs for Ceylon. She insisted on producing the receipts to prove it. That's on file. Her husband was in Ceylon. He was a tea planter and she was due to sail out to be with him in August. I don't know if she ever got there.'

'Could I have a look at her statement, Bill?'

'You can look with pleasure, if you think it's going to do you any good.' His brow wrinkled. 'You don't honestly think she's got anything to do with Caroline Trevelyan's disappearance, do you? I told you, she was in Harrods.'

'No, it's not that,' said Jack with a laugh. 'I wouldn't waste my time suspecting impeccable memsahibs, especially if they've got impeccable alibis. According to her letter, she only got back from Ceylon a month ago. She's staying at the Royal Park Hotel in Belgravia.'

'Very nice,' muttered Bill.

'I offered to buy her lunch at the Criterion on Monday.'

'You do a posher sort of interview than Scotland Yard can run to,' said Bill with a laugh.

Jack grinned. 'I might as well get a decent lunch if I'm going to hang out with a daughter of the Empire. She sounds rather formidable, but a bit of luxury might make her more chatty. I thought that was worth a six bob lunch.'

'Six shillings for lunch?' said Bill with a laugh. 'Don't ever join the police, Jack. That would really cramp your style.'

'It's not a question of style. Well, not only a question of style,' he amended, seeing Bill's grin. 'It's that ladies of a certain age and class do tend to view any private investigator as some greasy oick of a bloke with a roll-up tucked behind his ear looking for divorce evidence.'

'Impeccable memsahibs tend to look on the police in much the same way,' said Bill mournfully. 'And the only place I can take them is the local nick.'

'Well, the Criterion was my way of reassuring her that I'm fit to be seen. Besides, I like it there. As her statement's on file, I'd like to read it before I see her. It's all such a long time ago, it'll be useful to have a few facts to check her memory against. Did anyone else call that day?'

'If they did, there's no mention of them. I presume the baker and the butcher's boy and so on called, but they're not recorded.'

'They'd call in the morning, anyway,' said Jack absently.

'There were builders in the house too, of course. They should all have been noted.'

'I agree,' said Bill. 'The trouble is, Jack, that the only information that's recorded in the files is that which is thought relevant to the investigation. As far as the builders are concerned, though, it's noted that all the workmen finished for their lunch break at twelve o'clock and then left the premises. Saunder's Green was only one of a number of houses they were working on in the area.'

Jack clicked his tongue. 'That's a ruddy nuisance. All those men could've been potential witnesses.'

'They could,' said Bill, 'but you'd have a dickens of a job tracing them after all this time. I think you can thank your lucky stars that's not on the cards. You'd drive yourself up the wall. Did you have any other responses to your advert?'

Jack nodded. 'Just one, and that was from a Mrs Shilton. She's none other than Michael Trevelyan's sister.'

'Is she, by Jove?'

'Yes. She's no happier than Dr Langton that I'm digging up the old business again. Apparently she doesn't know anything about what happened on the day Caroline Trevelyan disappeared, but she's certain that her brother was entirely innocent of the charges made. If I'd like to call round, she adds, she can reassure me in person. She only lives in Wimbledon, so it's probably worth a trip, but I don't know if she can add anything very much.'

He broke off as a snatch of voices – cross voices – sounded from the street below. 'Hello!' he said in surprise. 'That sounds like Betty.' He crossed to the window and looked down. 'Crikey, it is Betty! She's got Miss Langton with her and a bloke. He must be Martin Langton. I didn't know Jenny Langton was coming. I'd better go and show them in.'

He clattered down the stairs to return in short order with Jenny, Betty and a solidly-built, dark-haired man in his early thirties, who could only be Martin Langton.

Dr Langton was clearly put out by the presence of his sister and Betty and, although gruffly polite, not very happy to find Bill present.

'I had thought, Major Haldean,' he said, turning to Jack, 'that this was to be a private meeting.'

'Don't blame Mr Haldean,' said Jenny quickly. 'He didn't know I was coming. Betty told me about the letter you wrote to him, Martin, and if you think I'm going to let you swan in and decide what I can and can't do and what I should and shouldn't know – because I know you do know something – without telling me, then think again.'

Martin Langton bristled. 'It's a great pity,' he said, 'that you didn't follow my advice and stayed in Leeds. You could've had a perfectly good job in my practice, but no, that wasn't good enough. You insisted on coming down to London and look where it's got you. None of this upset would've happened if you'd only stayed put.'

'Don't be so half-baked, Martin,' said Jenny, suddenly sounding as northern as her brother. 'I've a perfect right to live wherever I like. What's more, Mr Rackham is an old friend of Mr Haldean's. I imagine he's just dropped in for a friendly call. You could try being a little more friendly yourself.'

'Well, er . . .' began Bill.

Jack stepped in. 'I asked Chief Inspector Rackham to be here because he knows the public facts of the case,' he said smoothly. 'That can only be helpful, surely? And, of course, you're perfectly right, Miss Langton. A little friendliness never hurt anyone. Please, everyone, do sit down. And can I get anyone a drink?'

Jenny and Betty plumped for sherry and Martin Langton went for beer.

'I didn't realise you'd tell Miss Langton her brother was calling here,' he muttered to Betty as she joined him at the sideboard.

'It's Jenny's business,' said Betty unabashed. 'Of course I told her.' She glanced behind her. 'They're very similar, aren't they? And they've both got tempers.'

There wasn't any doubt, thought Jack, as he handed Martin his beer, about the family resemblance or the temper. They were both good-looking, with dark hair, a firm chin and brown eyes.

Martin Langton glared at his sister while she radiated annoyance back at him.

'How on earth,' demanded Martin, looking at Jenny, 'did you get to hear of this old business with the Trevelyans?'

'I explained all that in my letter,' she said. 'Didn't you read it?'

'Of course I read it! And do you honestly mean to tell me that on the basis of what can only be described as a bad dream, you've had Major Haldean here, to say nothing of the police, running round after you?'

Jenny's eyes narrowed. 'It wasn't just a bad dream though, was it? And if we're talking about running around, a bad dream wouldn't bring you running down from Leeds and a bad dream won't explain the facts that Mr Haldean discovered.'

'It's a genuine case,' Jack put in. 'Bill, why don't you go through what you found out from the police records?'

Martin Langton listened to the account Bill gave with a lengthening face. 'I never wanted any of this to come out,' he said when Bill had finished. 'It's not a nice story and it's all better left in the past, where it belongs.' He reached out and squeezed Jenny's hand. 'Look, will you please drop it? It'd be so much better if you did.'

'Of course I'm not going to drop it,' said Jenny indignantly. 'What do you remember, Martin? Were you there?'

He shook his head. 'No, I wasn't. I found out the truth later – which is, more or less, what you've just told us, Mr Rackham,' he said with a nod towards Bill. 'My parents told me and, what's more, made me promise never to speak about it.'

'But why?' demanded Jenny. 'Why did they make you promise? What did Mum see that day?'

'She saw nothing,' said Martin abruptly. 'Jenny – please – I really can't tell you anything more about it.'

'Was your mother there, Dr Langton?' asked Bill.

Martin Langton looked absolutely wretched. 'No. No, she wasn't.'

'But I was,' said Jenny, staring at him. 'I know I was. They had a little girl. We must've been friends. Was I staying with the Trevelyans?'

Martin Langton flinched. 'No. That is . . .' He glanced up, caught Jack's expression and raised his hand to his mouth.

His reaction convinced Jack that what he had suspected was the truth. There was nothing for it. The truth had to be told. 'I think you'd better tell her,' said Jack quietly. 'It's bound to come out now we've gone so far.'

Jenny gazed at him. 'Tell me what?'

Before he spoke, Jack looked to Betty for approval. She looked at him in startled apprehension, then drew her breath in and nodded slowly.

'The thing is, Miss Langton,' said Jack, 'your brother's tried to protect you from the truth—'

'It was my responsibility!' broke in Martin Langton. 'Jenny . . .' he began and then broke off. 'No. I can't do it.' He glared at Jack. 'If you know so much about it, you tell her.'

Jack couldn't blame Martin Langton for funking it but he wished he didn't have to be the one to break the news. This was going to be difficult but there was nothing else for it. 'Miss Langton,' he began, his voice gentle, 'there wasn't any other little girl. There was only one. You.'

Jenny looked at him in absolute bewilderment. 'Me?'

Jack nodded.

'So I was staying with the Trevelyans?'

'Not exactly. You are a Trevelyan.'

Jenny gaped at him soundlessly then slowly turned and faced Martin Langton.

Langton buried his head in his hands. 'He's right,' he said in a voice that was nothing more than a croak. 'God knows, Jenny, I didn't want to tell you.'

She continued to stare at him, then sank back wordlessly into the chair, her face white. 'So what you're telling me,' she said eventually, 'is that my mother wasn't my mother and Dad wasn't Dad?'

Martin nodded miserably.

'And you're not my brother?'

He shook his head. 'No.' He managed the ghost of a smile. 'I always felt like your brother, though.'

'You are relatives, though,' put in Betty. 'That's obvious. Anyone can see that.'

'We're cousins,' explained Martin heavily. 'Your mother – I should say your real mother, Jenny – and mine were sisters. When the tragedy happened, Mum and Dad went and scooped you up. I remember you being brought home. I was told you were my new sister and I just accepted it.' The ghost of a smile came and went once more. 'I was only a kid myself. I was told that's how it was, so that's how it was.'

'When did you find out the truth?' asked Jenny in a whisper.

'Years later. It was after Dad had his heart attack. I suppose he could see the writing on the wall and thought it was time to clear up how things really were.'

'And no one told me?'

Martin shrugged helplessly. 'They thought it was for the best. And it *was* for the best. You must see that. If you hadn't gone to the house that day, no one would've been any the wiser. Even now . . .'

He turned to look at Jack with a curious expression. 'You knew. How?'

Jack shrugged. 'It was the obvious solution. Miss Langton felt such an overwhelming sense of familiarity with the house, I wondered right from the start if she'd actually lived there.' He lifted his head and smiled ruefully at Betty. 'But when I suggested it to Betty, she was certain that you, Miss Langton, were a Langton through and through.'

'I never doubted it,' said Betty. 'I'd met your family. Your parents were lovely, Jenny. To think they weren't your family seemed ridiculous.'

'We are her family,' said Martin quickly. 'That hasn't changed.' He glanced at Jack once more. 'Was it really nothing more than a guess?'

'More or less,' agreed Jack. 'Miss Langton certainly knew the house. That's definite. There could've been other explanations, such as your mother, Mrs Langton, was close friends with Mrs Trevelyan and had called to see her, or that Jenny had stayed with the Trevelyans for some time, but if your mother, Dr Langton, really had been there that day, she would surely have been mentioned as a possible witness in the police investigation. The fact that the Trevelyans were on the brink of moving to New Zealand made it unlikely that they'd have a child to stay who had a perfectly good family of their own, but that could've been the case.' He looked sympathetically at Martin, whose face was ashen. 'Your reaction, I may say, ruled that out.'

Martin sighed deeply and lit a cigarette. 'I blew it, didn't I?' He looked at Jenny. 'I'm sorry, Jen. If I could've come up with a good enough story, I'd have told you that, but I couldn't think what the devil I could say. All I could think of was putting my foot down and refusing to tell you anything.' He glanced at Jack. 'I would have probably told you the truth, Mr Haldean, and appealed to your better nature to have kept the secret for Jenny's sake. After all, it's a nasty thing to have in your past.'

He looked at Jenny. 'I was horrified when I got your letter.' His face twisted. 'I mean, it's a rotten thing to find out.'

'The tree,' said Jenny. 'I looked down from the tree and saw my mother. Caroline Trevelyan was my mother.'

Martin shifted uncomfortably in his seat. 'All that business with the tree and so on sounds a bit mysterious to me. Couldn't you have imagined it? You have to have imagined it, surely.'

Jenny started to speak, then stopped abruptly.

'We don't think she imagined everything,' said Betty, taking up the cudgels on her friend's behalf.

Jenny gulped. 'That monster I saw – the murderer – was that my *father*?'

Martin coughed in embarrassment and looked away.

'It can't have been,' said Jenny in a small voice. 'What I saw wasn't human. Whatever that thing was, it wasn't my father. I'd have known him, wouldn't I? I'd have known my own father.'

Martin coughed once more. 'The mind plays funny tricks sometimes, Jenny. Perhaps what you saw as – well, a monster – was just how you remembered it later.'

'He could've been dressed up?' suggested Betty.

'Whatever for?' demanded Jenny, turning on her. 'If you were going to commit a murder, you'd want to make yourself look as inconspicuous as possible, not more so.'

'You'd be surprised what people do, Miss,' put in Bill. 'I've heard of some very odd cases.'

'But this is my father,' she protested. 'I know I never knew him, but this is my father.' She sank back in her chair again, hugging her knees. 'If only I'd known him!' she broke out. 'If only there was someone who knew him, who could tell me what he was like.'

'There is,' said Jack unexpectedly.

Martin and Jenny both stared at him.

'I got a letter from a Mrs Gwyneth Shilton in answer to my advertisements. She's your father's sister. Your aunt.'

'My aunt?' repeated Jenny in bewilderment. She turned to Martin. 'Did you know about her?'

Martin looked uncomfortable. 'I do, as a matter of fact. She used to write to Mum occasionally. I found her letters after Mum died and dropped her a line to say what had happened.'

'And you never told me?'

'Tell you what?' demanded Martin. 'I don't know anything, Jenny, apart from what Dad told me that day.'

'What did he tell you, Dr Langton?' asked Bill curiously.

Martin shrugged. 'More or less what you seem to have discovered. Obviously, his first thought was for Jenny. When Mrs Trevelyan—'

'My mother,' put in Jenny in an uncertain voice.

Martin swallowed. 'All right then, your mother. When she disappeared, Trevelyan wrote to my – our – parents to ask if she'd turned up in Salterbeck.'

'Did he?' asked Jenny, looking startled. 'But that sounds as if he really didn't know what had happened to her.'

A cynical expression crossed Martin's face. If Jenny had been looking, she'd have seen exactly the same expression mirrored on the other faces in the room.

'That's not really the case, Miss Langton,' said Bill. 'If he was trying to cover his tracks, that's exactly what I'd expect him to do.'

'But . . .' began Jenny, then stopped. 'This is very difficult, isn't it?' she said in a small voice. 'Go on, Martin. What did Mum and Dad do after they got the letter?'

'Naturally Mum was concerned for her sister, but she and Dad were also concerned for you. They wrote back to Trevelyan – your father – and the upshot was that they travelled down to London and took you back with them. Dad told me it was said at the time it was supposed to be a temporary arrangement until your mother was found. That was what they told your father, but Dad believed your mother had gone for good.'

Jenny swallowed. 'You mean Dad thought my father was a – a murderer?'

Martin looked away in embarrassment. 'That's about the size of it,' he agreed reluctantly. 'He was worried for your safety, Jenny. You must see that. And so,' he added, taking a sip of beer, 'you remained in Salterbeck. As I said, I was only a kid. I do remember you arriving but everything went on more or less as it had before so it didn't really make much difference. I suppose the neighbours knew, but both Mum and Dad were well liked and respected, so everyone accepted it. No one wanted to cause any trouble.'

'I remember,' said Jenny, 'some odd conversations between the grown-ups. Women who stopped talking when they realised I was in the room.'

'Do you?' asked Martin. 'I must say I never twigged anything.'

Martin Langton, thought Jack, was the sort of person who accepted things at face value. He didn't, he thought, have a very enquiring mind. Or, to put it another way, Dr Langton wasn't, as Betty said about him, naturally nosy.

'Anyway,' continued Martin, 'it must've been a year after you arrived that Eric was born, and there we were, the three Langton children.' He took a cigarette from the box and lit it. 'I was shocked when Dad told me the truth, Jenny, but I couldn't see it mattered very much. I didn't want you to find out, of course, any more than Mum and Dad did, but only because you were my sister and Eric's sister and I didn't want you to feel upset about things.' He looked round the room helplessly. 'That's all.'

'That's a very natural reaction, Dr Langton,' said Jack.

Martin looked at him hopefully. 'You think so? Good. Then I can take it that it's over?'

'Over?' said Jenny. 'What do you mean, over?'

Martin wriggled uncomfortably. 'All this mystery business. Look, it was a brutal crime, and I'm sorry you were caught up in it, but it's all finished with, yes? You don't have to keep poking and prying. You know what happened. The best thing to do is forget about it.'

'Should I?' Jenny's voice was doubtful. She looked at her friend. 'Betty, what do you think? Do you think I should I forget about it?'

'I . . .' Betty began and hesitated. She knew that Martin Langton was willing her to say yes. And really, there were good reasons to agree. The crime, a brutal crime, as Martin had said, was tucked away safely in the past. The facts seemed clear and all the damage that could be done had been done. But that would never be satisfactory, would it? If it was her choice, she'd always want to know more, but it wasn't her decision.

'It has to be up to you,' she said.

Jenny bit her lip. 'Mr Rackham,' she said, turning to Bill. 'You told us what was in the official report. Do you think Michael Trevelyan – my father,' she added, picking her words carefully, 'was guilty of murder?'

Bill didn't answer right away. 'It seems that way,' he said eventually. 'There's some very pressing evidence against him. The letter and the diary, to say nothing of him making a run for it, all point in that direction. However, I'd like to know more. The obvious question is, what did he do with the body?'

'So you think there's questions to be answered?'

Bill nodded. 'Yes, I do, but getting answers twenty years after the event is going to be tricky, to say the least.'

'I want to know what I saw in the garden,' said Jenny. She turned to Martin. 'Don't misunderstand me. I loved Mum and Dad – and you and Eric, too, of course – but I want to know what happened. If my father really did kill my mother, I'd like to know why.' She raised her hands and then let them drop helplessly. 'I just feel there's more to be discovered.'

She turned to Jack. 'You say you had a letter from a Mrs Shilton? My aunt?' Jack nodded. 'What did she say?'

'She said she always believed in your father's innocence.'

Jenny frowned. 'I wonder if she's right?'

Martin wriggled uneasily. 'She's his sister, for heaven's sake, Jen. What do you expect her to think?' He glanced at Jack. 'Are you going to see her?'

'I am, as a matter of fact. She offered to see me if I cared to call round.'

'I'll come with you,' said Jenny with determination.

'Jenny . . .' began Martin warningly, but Jenny shook her head.

'I'm going to do it, Martin, and, what's more, I'd like to go this afternoon.' She swallowed hard. 'I don't want to lose my nerve.'

'You don't even know if she's at home,' protested Martin. 'You can't just barge in on a total stranger.'

'We can always find out if she's at home, can't we? And as for being a stranger, she is my aunt, after all.' She looked at Jack. 'Is she on the telephone? Can you ring her? Can you do it now?'

# SEVEN

Mrs Shilton's house, facing Cannon Hill Common, radiated middle-class respectability and comfort, with its double bay windows, attached garage and well-tended gardens.

Jenny hesitated before she rang the bell. She was glad that both Jack and Betty had come with her. Martin had been very dubious about the trip, but she had promised to tell him everything at dinner that evening.

Betty squeezed her arm. 'Buck up,' she said softly. 'Remember, she is your aunt.'

The door was opened by a young white-aproned maid, who clearly knew, from her look of decently restrained excitement, exactly who they were and why they had come. 'I'll tell the mistress you're here,' she said, ushering them into the hall and taking their coats. 'She's been waiting for you.'

Mrs Shilton appeared at the door to the drawing room. 'Are they here, Edith?' she called, then broke off as she saw them.

She was a small, plump, dark-eyed woman. She looked swiftly from Jenny to Betty, fixed on Jenny, then seemed to swell as she radiated happiness. She came towards them, her hands outstretched, her face crinkling in a huge smile. She looked, thought Jack, immediately charmed, like a delighted raisin.

'You're Jennifer!' she said excitedly, taking her hands. 'Little Jenny! Oh, my dear, I've thought of you so much. You look so like your poor, dear mother.' She tore her eyes away from Jenny for a moment to glance at Jack. 'Ever since you telephoned, Mr Haldean, I've been beside myself with excitement, haven't I, Edith?'

'Indeed you have, ma'am,' said the beaming maid.

Mrs Shilton's happiness was so infectious, Jack and Betty couldn't help feeling warmed by it. 'I told you it would be all right,' muttered Betty to her friend.

'All right?' questioned Mrs Shilton.

Jenny had the grace to look slightly embarrassed. 'I did wonder if you would . . .' She broke off. What had worried her, as Jack well knew, was if Mrs Shilton, aunt or no aunt, would actually care to see her, granted her brother had apparently murdered Jenny's mother. 'I wondered if you would remember me,' she finished lamely if tactfully.

'Remember you?' asked Mrs Shilton, with a laugh. 'I could hardly forget you. I used to play with you when you were little. You had a teddy bear and I used to chase you round the garden with it.'

Jack couldn't help giving Betty a smug look. He felt a proprietorial interest in that teddy bear. She snorted with laughter and nudged him in the ribs.

Both Mrs Shilton and Jenny looked at them enquiringly. 'I found that teddy bear,' he explained. 'It was in the old toy box in the attic of Saunder's Green.'

With the mention of Saunder's Green, a chill came into the atmosphere.

Mrs Shilton's face fell. 'That was all so very sad,' she said. 'Ah well, the past is the past and can't be helped. Jennifer, my dear, you must call me Aunt Gwyn.'

'Aunty Gwyn,' said Jenny suddenly. 'You're Aunty Gwyn. *Nanty.* I remember you.'

Mrs Shilton blinked away sudden tears. '*Nanty.*' She took a deep breath. 'It's years since I've heard that name. I'd forgotten that's what you used to call me.'

'Did you have tea with me in my tree house?' asked Jenny.

Mrs Shilton looked startled. 'Why, yes! You had a toy tea set and loved playing tea parties. Your daddy built you that tree house. It was very cramped but I remember squeezing in. Your mother said it was too high up for you, but it had a big wide ladder. You were perfectly safe.'

'It had a slide,' Jenny said excitedly. 'I loved it!' She turned to Jack and Betty. 'I can remember! Really remember, I mean.' Her face fell. 'I wish I could remember more. More about what happened.'

That chill came into the atmosphere once more.

Mrs Shilton took her arm, obviously sensing, if not understanding, the change in mood. 'Now, come on into the sitting room everyone and we'll have tea.' She glanced at the maid. 'It's all ready, isn't it, Edith?'

'Yes, ma'am,' said the beaming maid, who was obviously deeply touched by this reunion. 'It's all prepared, just as you asked.'

Over tea and muffins, Mrs Shilton drew out every detail Jenny could tell her about her life with the Langtons. In return they learned that Mrs Shilton was widowed. Her husband, Alan, had been killed at Passchendaele, leaving her with two sons, Robert and James.

'They're your cousins, of course, Jenny,' said Mrs Shilton proudly. 'They're away at university now, but they'll be very pleased to meet you.' These were very brief details, though. Mrs Shilton returned time and again to Jenny, hungry for information about the missing years.

'I can't tell you how much I've thought about you,' she said. 'Sheila Langton would write to me occasionally, which was good of her. I was sorry to receive a letter from Martin Langton to say she had passed away. It was kind of the Langtons to take you. To know you were well looked after was a real weight off poor Michael's mind.'

'So he cared about me?' asked Jenny nervously.

Mrs Shilton opened her eyes wide in surprise. 'Cared about you? My dear, he doted on you. You mustn't ever doubt that. And he loved your mother, no matter what wicked lies the police told. But tell me, Mr Haldean, how did you get involved? When I saw your advertisement in the newspaper I very nearly didn't respond. I thought some wretched journalist was digging the whole sorry story up again. In the end, I just couldn't bear to ignore your advertisement and I'm so glad I didn't. But how did you come to be involved?'

'You'd better tell your aunt the whole story, Miss Langton,' said Jack, then paused. 'Actually, should I call you Miss Langton? After all, we know it's not actually your name.'

'Why don't you call me Jenny?' she said after a few moment's thought. 'You've done so much to help, I'd like that. As for my surname . . . Well, I've lived with it for as long as I can remember and it seems a bit disloyal to Mum and Dad to abandon it now. Martin would hate it,' she added. 'And Eric, come to that.'

Mrs Shilton, rather to Jack's surprise, nodded in agreement. 'It's probably just as well, my dear.' She swallowed and went on. 'After all the . . . the unpleasantness with the police, it was better for you that you were brought up as a Langton.'

She sighed deeply. 'It's a shame, though. Your father – my brother, I mean – was so proud of you, I'd like to think you had his name, but it can't be helped. But what's this story that Mr Haldean was referring to? I can't understand how you found out about things after all this time.' She gave Jack a puzzled look. 'And I don't see where Mr Haldean fits into all this. Did you come across some old letters or something?'

Jenny shook her head. 'No, it's nothing like that. It was a good deal more scary.'

Helped with prompting from Jack and Betty, Jenny related what had happened to her that day at Saunder's Green.

Mrs Shilton listened to her with growing astonishment which, as Jenny recounted what she had seen from the tree house, was replaced with horror. 'You *saw* it?' she exclaimed. 'But what was this thing, this monster?'

Betty, seeing Jenny's hesitation, stepped in. 'We don't think there actually was a monster as such,' she said, ignoring Jenny's wriggle of dissent. 'We think that's how Jenny remembered it because what she actually saw was too shocking to take in.'

Mrs Shilton looked startled. 'I suppose that could be it,' she said dubiously. 'But I can't get over the idea that you were there, Jenny.' She reached out and squeezed Jenny's hand. 'No one ever knew,' she said softly. 'I remember I asked Michael about you when I heard the awful news, and he said you were fine.'

She screwed up her face in recollection. 'Now what did your nurse say? I think she said that you'd been in the garden with your mother. One of the other servants had gone to collect the tea things and neither you or your mother were anywhere to be seen.'

She looked distressed at the memory. 'Naturally everyone thought you and your mother had gone for a walk in the garden. There was a bridge over the stream that was a favourite of yours and you loved to sail little boats under the bridge. They looked there, but you were nowhere to be seen. They found you eventually safe and sound in the nursery but, of course, your poor mother had vanished.'

She looked at Jenny, puzzled. 'No one said you were particularly upset. Your nurse would've have told your daddy if you had been distressed. Are you *sure* you were there? If you really had seen something as dreadful as you say, surely you'd have been in tears.'

Jack shook his head. 'That wasn't how it was in the war, Mrs Shilton. I know men who'd seen appalling sights who would never acknowledge them. I think it's a sort of safety valve for the mind, to block out anything that is just too ghastly for words.'

He looked at Jenny. 'I imagine you'd have been very quiet and withdrawn and, of course, with everyone concerned about your mother, no one would've paid you much attention. They were probably glad you were being "good" as they'd have seen it.'

'Oh dear,' said Mrs Shilton unhappily. 'I was one of those people. Michael asked me to come and stay to look after things while he searched for Caroline. I arrived the day after she'd gone and yes, I do remember you being very quiet, Jennifer.'

She gave them a guilty look. 'It seems so dreadful now, but I remember being pleased that you were so quiet, because the house was at sixes and sevens. It was bad enough with the builders coming and going, with all the noise and dust – that had been going on all summer – and your poor father was nearly off his head with worry.'

'You were obviously very close to my father,' said Jenny.

'Indeed I was,' agreed Mrs Shilton vigorously. 'And let me say again that he would never have harmed poor Caroline. If you'd known him, you'd realise how ridiculous the idea is. Yes, he had a temper, but he was a good man. Anyone who knew my brother would've known he was utterly incapable of raising a finger to his wife. He and Caroline were a devoted couple.'

'According to the servants, they argued about the move to New Zealand, though,' said Jack.

Mrs Shilton gave a snort of disgust. 'That was said time and time again, because it was the only disagreement they ever had and the only so-called reason for her disappearance the police could find. Caroline was nervous about the move, but that was all. That's natural enough, surely?'

She looked at Jenny earnestly. 'Believe you me, she would have never have left Michael and she certainly would never have abandoned you. Michael suspected the worst right from the start but those idiots of police refused to take him seriously.'

'The evidence,' said Jack, 'if you'll excuse me saying so, seemed pretty strong.'

'Then the evidence, Mr Haldean, is nonsense. You know Michael received a letter supposedly from Caroline?'

Jack, Betty and Jenny nodded.

'It was Michael who took that letter to the police and, what's more, he told them that it wasn't from Caroline.'

'He told them?' asked Jack in surprise. That hadn't been in the official record. Bill would've mentioned it if it had been.

'Indeed, yes,' Mrs Shilton agreed vigorously. 'It was to prove his own theory, that poor Caroline had run away of her own volition, that the police inspector had the letter looked at by experts.' Her face twisted. 'You can see, Mr Haldean, why I have such a low opinion of the police.'

'What about his diary?' he asked.

Mrs Shilton's sniff threatened to rattle the windows. 'A forgery, as I believe. Yes, it was my brother's diary, but it was an old one that he hadn't seen for months. My brother was innocent. He was liked and respected by everyone who knew him.'

Jack thought of some of the respectable villains that he'd come across. Bill could add to that list. They'd all been respected until the truth was out. But if it was Michael Trevelyan who had insisted on the letter being analysed though, that really did cast a fresh light on things. The trouble was, there was no way of knowing, twenty years on, if the official record was correct or Mrs Shilton had the rights of it.

Betty thoughtfully rolled a few muffin crumbs round her plate. 'Someone must've written that letter,' she said. 'Have you any idea who it could've been?'

Mrs Shilton drew herself up, then her shoulders sagged. 'None at all,' she said sorrowfully. 'Michael discussed it with me, naturally, but he could think of no one who would either want to harm Caroline or bore him any sort of grudge.'

But there must have been someone, thought Jack. Someone who not only wished Caroline and Michael Trevelyan harm, but someone who had access to the house. On the other hand, Mrs Shilton had clearly been devoted to her brother and, as such, he had to treat her account with caution.

'I wish I'd known my parents,' said Jenny sadly. 'It's horrible to think that I'd actually forgotten them.' She turned to Mrs Shilton. 'What was my mother like, Aunty Gwyn?'

'She was a lovely woman,' said Mrs Shilton. 'She was – well – a *happy* person. She loved music and could play the piano well. She was kind, too, with lots of friends.' She smiled wistfully. 'I'm glad to say she thought the world of her sister, Sheila Langton, although they only saw each other rarely, with Sheila living so far away. She would've been happy for Shelia to have looked after you.'

'Is there anyone else who knew her?' asked Jenny. She shook herself. 'It seems so silly I can't ask Mum about my mother.'

Mrs Shilton frowned. 'I can't think of anyone. Not now, at any rate.' She looked at her apologetically. 'You see, what with the war, and then that terrible – truly terrible – Spanish flu, so many people have either moved away or passed on, it's hard to think of anyone, as a matter of fact. I did hear that poor Violet Laidlaw lost her little boy to the flu. Violet was your mother's cousin and they were very close friends into the bargain.' She shook her head sadly. 'Poor Violet's passed away too, of course, otherwise she'd be just the person to ask.'

'Laidlaw?' said Jenny. She looked at Jack. 'Is that our Mr Laidlaw, so to speak?'

Jack nodded. 'I saw him the other day,' he explained to Mrs Shilton. 'I was trying to find out who the Trevelyans were,' he explained, rather awkwardly.

'I asked Jack to find out as much as he could,' put in Jenny quickly, seeing her aunt's expression. 'This is before we knew who I really was, of course. I don't suppose,' she added, more to Jack than to her aunt, 'that he'd be able to tell me about my parents, would he?'

'Not anything more than you already know,' said Jack hastily.

With the memory of what Andrew Laidlaw had said about Michael Trevelyan fresh in his mind, he didn't want Jenny chatting over old memories with him. Mr Laidlaw might be right or might be mistaken, but his opinion wasn't something Jenny Langton would want to hear.

'I agree, dear,' said Mrs Shilton. 'He knew your mother, of course, but I don't think he knew her at all well.' She looked at Jack with interest. 'Is he still a good-looking man?'

'I suppose you could call him good-looking, yes,' agreed Jack.

Mrs Shilton's eyes twinkled. 'He'd be in his fifties now, I suppose, but he was rather dashing and very up to date in his ideas. To tell you the truth, I don't think he cared very much for the house. Saunder's Green, I mean. It was too old-fashioned for him. There were improvements, of course, but he was all for starting from scratch. He wanted to build new houses, with modern conveniences, such as electricity and a bathroom that was all plumbed in, so the servants wouldn't have to carry the water upstairs. I thought it was all very advanced. I must say I used to enjoy having a bath in my room in front of a cosy fire, but I can't deny plumbing is easier for the servants. I doubt if many girls would stay long in a place where they had to carry cans of bathwater these days.'

'You can see their point of view,' said Betty, who'd had to carry more than a few cans of water in her time. And very heavy they were, too.

'I suppose I can, my dear,' agreed Mrs Shilton. 'But I can't tell you how advanced it all sounded at the time, but that was Andrew Laidlaw. He was one of the very first men I knew to drive a motor car. You'd probably laugh at it, Mr Haldean, but we all thought it was splendid.'

Jack shook his head in polite disagreement but Mrs Shilton laughed. 'I saw you drive up to the house from the window. Your car makes the cars we had before the war look like museum pieces.' Her smile broadened. 'Not that we thought so at the time, of course.'

'The speed limit was fourteen miles an hour,' threw in Jack. 'Not terribly fast. I remember my Uncle Philip had a car before the war. I thought it was marvellous when I was a kid.'

Betty gave a gurgle of laughter at the thought of Jack being restricted to driving at fourteen miles an hour.

'Cars became terribly respectable after Queen Alexandra took to motoring,' said Mrs Shilton. 'Even if they were slow.'

'How on earth could Mr Laidlaw afford it?' asked Jack, struck by a sudden thought. 'After all, cars were a real luxury before the war. I wouldn't have thought a young architect could have run to a car.'

Mrs Shilton knowingly tapped the side of her nose. 'Ah, but he had connections, you understand. He worked for Violet Wild's father who thought the absolute world of him. Old Mr Wild was a great motoring enthusiast and used to let Andrew drive his cars.'

Jack nodded. That was, he thought, Caroline Trevelyan's Uncle Arthur who had let the Trevelyans have the house at a peppercorn rent.

'From what I could gather,' said Mrs Shilton, 'old Mr Wild had very strong views about women and the home. I remember your poor mother, Jennifer, saying that the one subject they must never mention was votes for women. He thought it simply wrong that any woman should want to move out of her proper sphere and into the hurly-burly of public life.'

She looked at them over the top of her spectacles. 'I must say, I do have some sympathy with that view.' She sighed wistfully. 'Things seemed to be so much simpler before the war.'

'How did that affect Mr Laidlaw?' asked Jack politely.

Mrs Shilton opened her eyes wide. 'It changed everything, Mr Haldean. Old Mr Wild owned the firm, you see. Violet was his only child and he was completely opposed to the idea of any girl, even if she was his daughter, inheriting the firm. When she took a shine to Andrew Laidlaw, that was old Mr Wild's problem solved. And, as I say, we all thought Andrew was very dashing. I haven't thought of him for years,' she added with a little sigh. 'They were happy days. Did he respond to your advertisement, Mr Haldean?'

'No, Betty and I went to see him because he owns Saunder's Green. A Mrs Amelia Rotherwell answered my advert, though. Did you ever come across her? I understand she had lunch with Mrs Trevelyan the day she disappeared.'

'Mrs Rotherwell?' said Mrs Shilton brightly. 'She'd remember your mother, Jenny, my dear. She slipped my mind for the moment, but I wrote to her the other day. Your advertisement was the reason for that, Mr Haldean. She wanted to see if I knew who was enquiring about the Trevelyans. I haven't actually met her since . . . well, since it all happened, but we always kept in touch with a card at Christmas and so on. I knew her years ago. She was Amelia Hawkins then. She'd been Caroline's governess, but she was only a few years older than Caroline and they became good friends. She married a man who planted sugar or tea – or was it rubber? Or indigo, perhaps. It was in Ceylon, that I do know. Her husband passed away a couple of years ago. One of her boys took over the estate and she stayed on for a time, but the climate must be very trying. Her other son lives in London, I believe, but I don't know where exactly. She only got back a few weeks ago. She was a nice woman, as I recall, if inclined to be a bit on the stiff side. I think teaching does that to people. Are you going to see her? I can't think what she'd be able to tell you about Caroline's disappearance. After all, she'd left the house before it happened.'

Yes, thought Jack, but she had been there. 'I want to see what she remembers of Mrs Trevelyan's mood that day,' he said. 'She made a statement to the police at the time, but you never know. She might be able to add to that.'

'I doubt it,' said Mrs Shilton dubiously.

'What you've got to understand, Aunty Gwyn,' said Jenny, 'is that when Mr Haldean—'

'Jack,' he corrected with a smile. 'If I'm to call you Jenny, it's only right you should call me Jack.'

'When Jack,' she said, returning the smile, 'put that advert in the newspapers, we had no idea who the Trevelyans were.' Her smile faded. 'We certainly didn't know it was my family we were enquiring about.'

Mrs Shilton nodded. 'Yes, I can see that, but now you have found out, I honestly think you've done enough. It's such a pleasure to see you again, Jennifer, but your poor mother is gone and nothing can bring her back.'

Betty cleared her throat. 'But you believe your brother was

innocent, Mrs Shilton. Wouldn't you like Jack to try and find the truth?'

'No, I wouldn't,' said Mrs Shilton sharply, her kindly face suddenly stern. 'I know the truth and anyone who knew my brother knows the truth as well. I don't require any proof, as you call it, to convince me of that.'

Jack, Betty and Jenny swapped glances, startled at Mrs Shilton's vehemence.

'Wouldn't it be better to know all of the truth, Aunty Gwyn?' asked Jenny tentatively. 'After all, I saw my mother being – well . . .' She swallowed, screwed up her eyes and said the word. '*Murdered.*' Mrs Shilton gave a little gasp of horror which Jenny ignored. 'Don't you want to know what actually happened?'

Mrs Shilton shook herself in irritation. 'No, Jennifer, I don't.' She shook herself once more. 'I don't know what you saw, but you can't have seen *that.*' She held up her hand to stifle Jenny's protests. 'I know what Mr Haldean said about why you were quiet, but, quite frankly, I don't believe it. I arrived the following day and you were as good as gold. If you really had seen what you think you saw, I would have known.'

'Nevertheless—' began Jack, but Mrs Shilton interrupted him.

'I must insist on this, Mr Haldean. Jennifer, listen to me. You have no idea how horrible it was to live with all that suspicion and talk. Once the news got out, the newspapers had a field day. We were virtually besieged with reporters and ghastly men taking photographs. I couldn't bear to look at a newspaper for weeks. It was a dreadful time. You must see how terrible it would be to have all this dragged up again. For years afterwards, if I ever mentioned my maiden name, someone was bound to make the connection to my poor brother. We would all be much better to let sleeping dogs lie. The past is the past. You must let it remain so.' She looked at them severely. 'That is my final word upon the subject.' Her voice trembled. 'Please don't stir things up again. You have no idea of the harm you could do.'

'Do you want me to let sleeping dogs lie?' asked Jack as he, Betty and Jenny walked to the car. 'Your aunt wasn't very keen on us taking this any further, to say the least.'

Jenny hesitated. 'No, she wasn't,' she said eventually. 'To be fair, I can see why. By the sound of it, it was a pretty tough time, but I want to *know*. Of course I'd like my father to be innocent, but what I'd like is neither here or there, is it?'

She looked so wretched that Betty took her arm, comfortingly. 'If your aunt was right, and it was your father who told the police that letter was a phoney, that more or less proves he's innocent.' She glanced at Jack. 'Doesn't it?'

Jack geared himself up for a reply. In his opinion, it didn't prove anything of the sort, but he was saved from saying so by Jenny.

'No, it doesn't,' she said desperately. 'Don't you see, Betty? Aunty Gwyn was in the house when that letter arrived. She's bound to have seen it. All she'd have to say is that the writing didn't look like my mother's for my father to have realised his scheme hadn't worked and the best thing for it was to tell the police. Then he could make out the letter was sent by someone else. That's at least possible, isn't it?' she added miserably. 'You think so, too, don't you?' she added, looking at Jack.

'Yes, I do,' he agreed reluctantly.

Jenny squared her shoulders. 'So there's only one thing for it. I'm sorry for Aunty Gwyn, but we have to go on. I want to know what happened to my mother.'

'So you want me to carry on?' asked Jack.

She nodded. 'Yes, I do. There's nothing else for it, now. There's something else, too. When I first talked to you, Jack, you mentioned ghosts. Well, I still don't believe in ghosts, but my mother was *there*. Somehow – and yes, it might be just a memory – my mother reached out to me when I touched the cedar tree. For her sake, we have to find the truth.' She looked at him hopefully. 'Can you do it?'

'I can try,' he said, 'but it's a pretty tall order.'

Betty smiled at him encouragingly. 'You'll do it,' she said confidently. 'I know you will.'

# EIGHT

Bill left Jack and Betty's house and turned down Chandos Row, heading for the Embankment and Scotland Yard. He needed to complete the paperwork on the Oxenholme case, but despite the knowledge that he should concentrate on the here and now, he was intrigued by Jennifer Langton and her affairs.

It was extraordinary, when he came to think about it, that this whole story of a forgotten murder – Bill had no doubts it was murder and who the murderer was – should come to light because of Jennifer Langton's dream or vision or whatever the best word to describe it might be.

He felt a rush of sympathy for Martin Langton. Maybe, as Langton obviously thought, it would've been better to let the dead bury the dead, as it said in the Bible somewhere. Leave the matter to rest in the past, where it belonged. It couldn't have been easy for Martin Langton. He hadn't wanted to be the one to tell her that the mother and father she'd always known and, obviously, loved, weren't her real parents.

He'd done his best to carry out his parents' instructions and acted in what he clearly thought were in Jennifer's best interests. Dr Langton might have been a bit heavy-handed but his heart was in the right place.

Jenny Langton though, had wanted the truth. She had no end of spirit. She clearly did think the world of her brother – it was easier to think of Martin Langton as her brother – but she wasn't going to be pushed round by him. Or by anyone else, he thought.

She had very nice eyes, Bill thought inconsequentially. They had sort of sparked when she was arguing with Martin. What would her eyes look like when she was happy? The thought gave him a warm glow.

A buzz of conversation and laughter drifted across the pavement and mingled with the sound of the traffic. He was near The Heroes of Waterloo, Jack's local, and, because of its closeness to Scotland Yard, a favourite with off-duty policemen. The door and windows, on this warm autumn afternoon, stood invitingly open.

He hesitated at the door. He had the Oxenholme paperwork to tackle but a pint of bitter would go down a treat. However, Jack and Betty had asked him to drop in for a drink that evening, so he could hear what Jenny Langton's aunt, Mrs Shilton had had to say. No. He really had better get on with some work, he regretfully decided, when he heard his name called.

'Is that young Rackham?' It was Charlie Church, standing with his elbows propped on the windowsill. 'Come in and I'll stand you a drink.'

'Hello, Mr Church!' said Bill, genuinely pleased to see him. Charlie Church was retired now, but he had been his inspector when Bill was just a sergeant. Paperwork be blowed, he thought. It was a poor show if he couldn't find time for Mr Church.

'So what brings you up to town?' asked Bill when, comfortably into the second pint, they had shared all the gossip about who was doing what from the old days. Mr Church, he knew, lived in Guildford.

'Ethel and I are staying with our Winnie and her husband, Ted, for a few days. They've got a new flat in Kensington, just off the High Street. It's a nice place. Roxborough Mansions. Do you know it?'

'No, I can't say I do. How are they?' asked Bill. He'd met Winnie and Ted Hinton a few times and liked them very much.

Charlie Church's face crinkled in pleasure. 'They're fine. But my word, the grandchildren are growing up! Ethel and I took them to the zoo yesterday. Ethel and Winnie are shopping today, and that's not something I want to get involved with.'

'Women are best left to shop alone,' said Bill with a grin. 'I bet the kids enjoyed the zoo.'

'They had a high old time and no mistake,' said Mr Church, taking a hefty swig of beer. 'They're dead keen on animals. In fact, it's animals – or at least one animal – that's brought me up to this part of town. It's probably something and nothing, but I thought I might as well have a stroll up to the Yard and report it.' He grinned. 'And, of course, with the day being warm and The Heroes on the way . . .'

'Well, I'm very glad to have bumped into you, Mr Church. What's this animal story? The one that brings you to the Yard, I mean? Has a carter been mistreating his horses?'

'No, it's nothing like that. It's one of the grandchildren, little Louise. She's got a pet cat who went missing.'

'Really?' said Bill, guardedly. Privately he thought that Charlie Church's standards of crime suitable for investigation by the police had gone seriously downhill if he thought Scotland Yard would be interested in a lost cat. 'I see.'

'No, you don't,' said Mr Church with a laugh, wiping the beer from his mouth. 'I wouldn't get the Yard out for a cat. No, what happened was that, as I said, little Louise's cat went missing and she was terribly upset. Well, for three days, we looked high and low. There was no sign of it, but Louise insisted she could hear Buttons – that's the cat – meowing in her bedroom at night. Proper took on, she did, because we couldn't find it in her bedroom. That's partly why we took the kids to the zoo, to try and take her mind off it. Anyway, last night, I went in to say goodnight, and blow me, this time I heard it, clear as day. I couldn't see anything but this morning I went into Louise's bedroom once more and there it was again.'

'So where was it?' asked Bill.

'The sound was coming from the fireplace, up the chimney from the flat below. We worked out which one was the right flat, but there was no one in. Louise called through the door, and we could hear Buttons right enough, so we went and got the porter. Anyway, to cut a long story short, although the porter had pass keys, Mrs Davenham – that's the woman who owns the flat – had changed the locks. In the end Ted and I had to force the door.'

This story could get grim, thought Bill, taking a swig of beer. However, if Mr Church had found a dead body in the flat, he'd have hardly regaled him with a tale of a lost pet cat or, for that matter, stopped off for a pint on the way to the Yard.

'You forced the door? She won't like that when she comes home,' commented Bill.

'No, I don't suppose she will. Anyway, poor Buttons shot out like a bat out of hell. Louise made a big fuss of the poor thing, of course, and I and the porter took a little look round.

What had happened was that the kitchen window had been loose. Buttons had obviously got in that way and then the window had blown shut behind it.'

'You went into the flat?' asked Bill.

Mr Church nodded. 'Yes, we did. The porter was concerned that Mrs Davenham might have been taken ill, you see, and be in the flat with no one knowing she was there. Buttons had been missing since Wednesday, so it's been the best part of four days now. Anyway, Mrs Davenham wasn't there, which, I might say was a bit of a relief, as I immediately thought the worst. That's what comes of being a copper for forty years.'

'Absolutely,' agreed Bill wryly. 'The job wears off on you. I think it's worth mentioning that forced lock at the Yard, though. You don't want to be had up for breaking and entering.'

'No, I don't,' said Mr Church with a laugh. 'The porter's had the lock replaced and he's got the key, so everything's safe and sound, but I still want to mention it in case Mrs Davenham kicks up a fuss when she gets back.'

'How long's she away for?'

'No one knows,' said Mr Church with a shrug. 'I left a note with the porter, asking her to get in touch with the Yard when she gets back, just to be on the safe side. I don't want any unpleasantness for Winnie and Ted about that lock. I want her to come to us first. It wouldn't be the first time this Mrs Davenham had gone off for a few days without mentioning it, but still . . .'

'There's probably nothing to it,' said Bill with a shrug, 'but you never know.' He grinned. 'That's the job speaking again. Always expect the worst.'

'Talking of the job,' said Mr Church, raising his glass, 'congratulations on your promotion. Chief Inspector! I remember when you first joined the force . . .'

And the conversation drifted off into remembrances.

'The cigarettes are in the box on the table,' said Jack hospitably that evening, handing Bill a whisky and soda.

They were in the newly-decorated downstairs sitting room, with the mellow September sunshine flooding the room.

Betty had, as she said, scoured the pages of *Ideal Home*

looking for exactly the right colours and the result, Wedgewood blue and dove grey picked out with white, was fresh and calm.

Bill liked it very much. What colours would Miss Langton choose if she had to decorate a room, he wondered. If it was winter, he'd want something cosy. A room where you could stretch out on the sofa with, perhaps, a dog in front of the fire and, in the armchair opposite . . .

He put a firm rein on his imagination and lit a cigarette. 'How did you get on in Wimbledon this afternoon?'

'Very well. I'm glad to say Jenny's aunt made her very welcome.'

'She was obviously thrilled to bits to see her,' said Betty. 'Mrs Shilton was really welcoming. She seems a thoroughly nice woman.'

'I'm very glad to hear it,' said Bill. 'Miss Langton had such a shock yesterday, that it's good something positive has come out of it.'

'Mrs Shilton isn't a fan of the police though,' put in Jack. 'She's convinced her brother was innocent.'

'That's understandable.'

'Yes, but she says it was Michael Trevelyan who took the forged letter to the police and told them it was phoney.'

'That's not on the file,' said Bill in surprise. 'Was she sure?'

'Yes, certain,' said Betty. 'Mrs Shilton thinks that proves her brother's innocence. I must admit, I thought it did at first, but Jack doesn't and Jenny herself saw it did nothing of the sort.'

'How come?' asked Bill. 'I must say, that'd be my first thought too, Betty.'

'Mrs Shilton,' said Jack, taking up the story, 'saw that letter. All she'd have to say is that the writing didn't look like Caroline's for Trevelyan to realise his scheme hadn't worked. The only thing he could do then was to make the best of a bad job by taking it to the police and tell them it was a forgery.'

'It's pretty sharp of Miss Langton to see that,' said Bill. 'I did wonder, after seeing her aunt, if she'd be desperate to prove her father's innocence, but it sounds as if she can still be fairly objective about it.'

'That experience in the garden really scared her, Bill,' said Betty. 'What she wants is the truth. She said as much this afternoon.'

Bill pulled a face. 'That's going to be difficult after all this time, without witnesses to interview. Take that letter, for instance. Inspector Chartfield should have noted on the file that it was Trevelyan who handed it over and told him he thought it was a fake.'

'I agree,' said Jack. 'And, of course, at this stage there's no telling whose version of events is correct. Inspector Chartfield's, or Mrs Shilton's.'

'I suppose Mrs Shilton wants you to prove Trevelyan's innocent,' said Bill.

'No, she doesn't,' said Betty. 'Apparently the scandal surrounding the case was horrible. She doesn't want it all dragged up again.'

'That must've been hard for her,' said Bill. 'I can see why she'd want it all left well alone. But Miss Langton doesn't feel like that, you say?'

Jack nodded. 'That's right. However, what I can find out is anyone's guess. I've told Jenny as much. All I can do is ask questions, I suppose. As I said this afternoon, I'm taking Mrs Rotherwell to lunch on Monday.'

Bill frowned, trying to place the name. 'She's the old friend of Caroline Trevelyan's, isn't she?'

'That's right. The woman who went to Ceylon.'

'She won't be able to tell you anything. She'd left the house hours before Mrs Trevelyan disappeared.'

Jack swirled the whisky round in his glass. 'You're probably right,' he admitted. 'When I put those adverts in the paper, I was trying to find out as much about the Trevelyans as I could and to advertise seemed an obvious first step. Now I've got the reply, I'm more or less bound to meet the woman, even if she can't tell us anything much. However, it won't hurt to have lunch with her.' He grinned. 'And I like the Criterion.'

# NINE

Beneath the gold-roofed splendour of the Criterion, Jack stood up as the waiter showed the middle-aged, severely bespectacled woman to his table. 'Mrs Rotherwell?' he said, taking her extended hand and bowing slightly over it. It seemed to be expected of him. 'It's very good of you to see me.'

Mrs Rotherwell looked him up and down imperiously. Jack felt as if he'd passed some sort of test. He knew Mrs Rotherwell had started out as a governess, and she obviously wasn't the sort who could be described as a soft touch by her pupils. That, combined with a lifetime of Empire-building in Ceylon, had obviously given her the sort of personality you could bend iron bars round. She was, thought Jack, a tough egg.

The waiter pulled out her chair. 'Can I take your coat, madam?'

'Yes, indeed,' said the tough egg, shrugging herself out of her grey wool coat. She retained her hat, though, a straw cloche with artificial cherries and grapes. Despite the tiny white chip on one of the cherries where the wax showed through, it put Jack in mind of an upturned fruit bowl.

After glaring at the chair for any possible defects, she consented to settle herself at the table.

Jack glanced at the waiter with a friendly smile. 'Thank you.'

'Not at all, m'sieur. Would you like the wine list?'

Jack looked enquiringly at Mrs Rotherwell who stiffened visibly. 'Certainly not,' she said repressively. 'I have very strong views upon the subject of alcohol. Lime juice, if you please. With ice. It was,' she added to Jack, 'a favourite of my dear husband's in Ceylon.'

'I'll have the same,' said Jack to the waiter, mentally shelfing, with some regret, the half-bottle of Chablis he'd been contemplating.

'I will,' she stated, 'come straight to the point, Mr Haldean. What is your interest in the Trevelyans?' Her eyes narrowed suspiciously. 'You assured me in your note that you were not connected with the press in any way. Now that I have met you, I will take your word upon the subject.'

'Thank you,' murmured Jack.

'However, I must say that if I thought you were attempting to rake up an old scandal for a motive I consider to be unworthy, I will decline to speak.'

Jack cranked up the charm. 'Of course, Mrs Rotherwell,' he said with wide-eyed innocence. 'That is, naturally, taken as read. It's a longish story but one which I think you'll find interesting. Can we discuss it over lunch?' he added, with what he thought of as his engaging smile. The last thing he wanted was for the prickly Mrs Rotherwell to decide to sweep out. She was far less likely to do that if she was tackling a lamb chop or whatever it was the woman wanted to eat.

'Hmm,' she said non-committedly, but, rather to Jack's relief, opened the menu. 'French,' she muttered disdainfully. '*Potage crème d'orge au vin*. Barley soup with wine. Why do foreigners always have to add alcohol to food? I insist on good plain cooking, Mr Haldean. I detest this foreign fad for disguising decent food – if it is decent, mind you – with sauces so you cannot see what is underneath.'

She must've gone down a breeze with her cook in Ceylon, thought Jack. 'The fillet of hake is very nice,' he suggested. 'And perhaps the duck with green peas to follow?'

'That would be acceptable,' she agreed reluctantly. 'As long as I can actually see what it is I am eating.'

Jack sighed inwardly. At this rate he'd have been better off taking her to the local fish and chip shop.

The waiter arrived with their drinks and took the order for lunch. Under the influence of iced lime juice, Mrs Rotherwell unbent slightly.

'Fresh lime,' she commented. 'Most refreshing. So, Mr Haldean, why are you interested in the Trevelyans?'

'I've been asked by a member of the family to find out what I can about the sad events surrounding Mrs Trevelyan's disappearance.'

'The family?' repeated Mrs Rotherwell in a puzzled voice.

'Yes, and I must say I'm very grateful to you for sparing me your time,' continued Jack, side-stepping the interruption. 'I understand you knew Mrs Trevelyan well, Mrs Rotherwell?'

She nodded. 'Yes. I was employed for a time as Caroline's governess. I am not ashamed to admit it, Mr Haldean. Some of us have had to make our own way in this world. Caroline was Miss Burbridge then, of course. She was a delightful girl, and we were actually much the same age. At least, she was only a few years younger than myself. We always kept in touch after she became too old to need instruction. I am puzzled, though, about this member of the family you mention.'

Jack nodded politely. 'Do you remember her daughter, Jennifer?'

'Little Jennifer? Of course. She was a nice, well-behaved child. What's she got to do with it?'

'She's the one who asked me to find out what I could.'

'But as I understand it, Jennifer was adopted by Caroline's sister. To the best of my knowledge, she thought it best to bring the child up in ignorance of who her real mother and father were. Did Caroline's sister tell her after all?'

'Not exactly,' said Jack. 'It's an interesting story.'

As the tale unfolded, she listened with rapt attention. He left out the part about what Jenny had seen from the tree house. Monsters, he thought, were far too difficult to explain.

'So Jennifer Trevelyan – Langton, I should say – actually visited Saunder's Green without realising her family had lived there?'

'That's right,' agreed Jack. 'And, naturally, once she had found out from her brother the truth of the matter, she wants to know what happened that day.'

The fillet of hake arrived. Mrs Rotherwell squeezed a segment of lemon over her fish and started to eat in an abstracted way.

'But surely the girl knows what happened? It's all very sad, of course, but there can be no doubt that Michael Trevelyan made away with his poor wife – she was an innocent, trusting girl – and sought to conceal his appalling crime. Women, Mr Haldean, are far too ready to trust, to dance at a man's beck and call.'

Present company excepted, thought Jack. If any man tried to

get Mrs Rotherwell to dance at his beck and call, he'd know he'd been in a fight.

'Did you know Michael Trevelyan well?' he asked.

'As well as I wanted to,' she said dryly. 'I did not care for Mr Trevelyan. He was superficially charming, but he couldn't fool me. I thought he could be a bully. He was certainly very fond of his own way and could have a savage temper if crossed.'

Jack raised his eyebrows. 'That's a different assessment of Mr Trevelyan's character from others I've heard.'

'I have a good knowledge of human nature, Mr Haldean. I suppose you've talked to Gwyneth Shilton?' Jack nodded.

Mrs Rotherwell sighed testily. 'I have known Gwyneth for years. She's a pleasant enough woman but completely unreliable on the subject of her brother. I would venture to say that you should ignore anything she says about him.'

'I'll bear that in mind, Mrs Rotherwell,' said Jack with every appearance of sincerity. Mrs Rotherwell unbent slightly and gave him a frosty smile. As a matter of fact, it wasn't so far from his own opinion. Mrs Shilton certainly wasn't an objective witness. The thing was, it didn't sound as if Mrs Rotherwell was objective either. She obviously hadn't liked Trevelyan. Ah, well . . .

'What are your recollections of that day?' he asked.

She rammed her spectacles firmly up the bridge of her nose with her forefinger, considering her reply. 'Really, it's hard to say at this distance in time,' she said, eventually, finishing her hake.

'Do you remember, for instance, the builders being in the house?' he asked hoping to stir her memory.

'Such an inconvenience,' she said with a sniff. 'Whole areas of the house were out of bounds and there was a great deal of dust and noise. I remember thinking I would not have tolerated it. Dear Caroline – such a sweet-natured girl – tried to make the best of it. The builders were not there in the afternoons but the morning of my visit was interrupted by constant noise.'

'As I understand it, the family were only living at Saunder's Green because there were building works being carried out.'

'That is the case, yes, or so I believe. The circumstances were very unusual. You know Michael Trevelyan had insisted on the family moving to New Zealand? Well, the move had been postponed at the last moment. Caroline's uncle was a builder who owned a considerable amount of property. He let Caroline and her family have the house at very short notice. They had to live round the building work, so to speak.'

'The family got on well with the builders though, didn't they?' asked Jack. 'I believe one of the builders dropped in for morning coffee.'

He had read Mrs Rotherwell's statement yesterday. Mrs Rotherwell had recounted how Andrew Laidlaw had needed to consult Caroline Trevelyan about the works and had been invited to join them for coffee, where they had had a lively discussion about how the work was progressing.

'One of the builders?' Mrs Rotherwell sat back in her chair. 'No, I . . .' she began, then stopped. 'Oh, you mean Mr Laidlaw, don't you?'

Jack nodded. 'Yes, that's right.'

'I'd completely forgotten,' she continued. 'He joined us for morning coffee. Yes, I had a slight acquaintance with him but it was actually his wife I knew. She would often join Caroline and myself for excursions and outings when I was Caroline's governess.' Her face softened. 'Dear Violet. I was terribly sorry to hear she'd passed away. I was in Ceylon when I received the news, but I understand she was never the same after the loss of her son, poor woman. He was a casualty of the flu epidemic after the war. She was completely bound up with little Archie. We used to exchange correspondence regularly. Her letters were full of his doings, but after he died, she lost all her zest for life, and she only wrote very occasionally after that.'

Poor woman, thought Jack. Virtually everyone in Britain knew someone who'd been affected by the Spanish flu. There were far more deaths from the flu than from the war, and that was saying something.

Mrs Rotherwell looked at him enquiringly. 'May I ask how you know this, Mr Haldean? You seem to be very well-informed. Indeed, I may say that you seem to know at least as much about the events of the morning as I do. Not that, as I recall, there were many events that morning. Nothing occurred to make me believe anything out of the way was going to happen.

Caroline was in good spirits although worried, as I say, about
the forthcoming move to New Zealand. I left her after lunch. I
do recall I gave a statement to the police at the time but I'm
afraid it was of very little practical use.'

'I know you were public-spirited enough to make a statement,' Jack agreed with a smile, cranking up the charm again
and adding a good dollop of flattery. 'Thanks to a good friend
of mine, Chief Inspector Rackham, I was able to read it
yesterday.'

'You did?' she said, startled. 'Is this an official enquiry?' she
demanded. 'Are the police involved?'

Jack shook his head reassuringly. 'No. All I'm trying to do
is find out the facts for Miss Langton.'

She drew her brows together in a puzzled frown. 'I wish I
could remember what I said in my statement,' she said fretfully.
'You do understand how much more accurate I could be then,
with the events fresh in my memory.' She looked up. 'I am
afraid of leading you astray. I've either forgotten times and so
on, such as the details of what was said or, what is perhaps
more misleading, confused what happened that morning with
other occasions.'

'If you'd like to refresh your memory, I made notes of the
main points of your statement,' said Jack, taking out his notebook. He found the right page and handed it over.

She took it gratefully and read his notes. 'Yes, it's coming
back to me now,' she said thoughtfully. 'I'd called on Caroline
to say goodbye before I sailed for Ceylon. I remember she was
concerned about the forthcoming move to New Zealand. I, of
course, was busy with my own arrangements for my journey
to Ceylon and we spent much of the morning discussing our
ideas about what our new lives would bring. Not that Caroline
would actually have a new life,' she added.

For a couple of minutes there was silence. Mrs Rotherwell
shuddered, then finished her hake. 'Mr Haldean,' she said in a
softer voice than she had previously used, 'I am obliged to you
for informing me why you have made this enquiry. Naturally,
once Jennifer Trevelyan – or Langton, perhaps, I should call
her – asked you to take an interest, your researches led you to
uncover some very unpalatable facts. However, although I

congratulate you on the industry you have shown in uncovering the truth, I can only wish you had not been so assiduous in your enquiries. I understand that to find out the true facts of who she is and how her mother, poor Caroline, disappeared, must have come as an awful shock to the girl.' She looked at him acutely. 'I'm right, aren't I?'

'Yes, of course you are, Mrs Rotherwell.'

'Am I also right in saying that young Jennifer harbours hopes that her father might not, in fact, be guilty of the crime he was arrested for? It would only be natural if that was the case.'

Jack looked at her ruefully. 'I think that's what she is hoping for, yes. But quite frankly, how on earth anyone can tackle trying to prove the guilt or innocence of a man who's managed to successfully vanish for the last twenty years is beyond me.'

He stopped as the waiter cleared away their plates onto his trolley. 'Was everything satisfactory, m'sieur?'

'Excellent, thank you,' said Jack. The waiter removed the silver covers from two dishes and served the duck and green peas.

'So you are not confident of success, Mr Haldean?' asked Mrs Rotherwell, prodding her knife cautiously into her duck. 'Hmm. It appears to be well cooked. I do not trust foreigners to prepare poultry properly.' She looked up. 'I understand, however, that you have had some success in the past in unravelling some knotty problems.' She favoured him with the frosty smile once more. 'After I received your letter, I made a point of enquiring into your antecedents.'

'That's very understandable, Mrs Rotherwell.' He thought of adding the hope that his antecedents bore up to scrutiny, and decided against it. Light-hearted remarks would go down with Mrs Rotherwell like a brick zeppelin. 'No, I can't say I am confident of uncovering what actually happened that day. The facts were far from clear at the time and they certainly haven't become any clearer in the intervening period.'

'Do you believe Michael Trevelyan is innocent?' asked Mrs Rotherwell sharply.

Jack looked at her wryly. 'He could be, I suppose.'

'He wasn't.'

He was surprised at her vehemence. 'Excuse me, Mrs Rotherwell, but how do you know?'

'I knew *him,* Mr Haldean. I also know that, despite appearances, his wife was afraid of him.'

Jack sat up. It was obvious she didn't like Michael Trevelyan but this went beyond what she'd said earlier.

'Caroline was loyal,' continued Mrs Rotherwell, 'but an old friend such as myself can read between the lines. You know I said she was unhappy about the forthcoming move to New Zealand? Well, one of the reasons she was worried was because she would be parted from her family. Her parents were dead but she was very close to her cousin Violet and Violet's parents, her Aunt Marie and Uncle Arthur. In New Zealand she would be thrown entirely upon her husband's society. As I said, he could be a charming man, but he hated to be crossed.' She hesitated. 'She never said as much openly, but I truly believe Caroline was afraid of him.'

Jack nodded, not letting his expression betray any scepticism. Mrs Rotherwell wasn't the easiest person to get along with. She hadn't liked Trevelyan but, by the same token, he could have disliked her. She'd probably resent that. That feeling could easily slip into outright bias.

Mrs Rotherwell toyed with her napkin. For such an assertive person, she seemed suddenly hesitant. 'There's something else, as well, Mr Haldean. This is the real reason why I was wary of responding to your advertisement.'

Jack looked at her alertly. Mrs Rotherwell clearly had something important on her mind.

'Where,' she began, picking her words carefully, 'do you think Michael Trevelyan is now?'

He hadn't expected that. The answer was that Trevelyan had vanished, just as completely as his wife, twenty years ago. Jack mentally kicked himself. Why hadn't he asked himself that question? Where had the man gone to, after escaping arrest? New Zealand? Maybe, but he could've disappeared to anywhere in the world. He didn't need a passport to travel anywhere within the Empire. As a matter of fact, he didn't need a passport to travel anywhere on earth before the war. All he needed was money and not much of that, to get a cheap passage to anywhere from Australia to Zanzibar and all points in between. A new country, a new name, and who was to say that the new man was wanted by the police? Innocent or guilty, he had certainly escaped.

Jack glanced at her expression and froze. She *knew* something. 'Do you know where he is, Mrs Rotherwell?'

She took a deep breath. 'Yes.'

Jack stared at her. 'You do?'

She nodded vigorously, so vigorously that the cherries on her hat bounced up and down. Jack waited for her to continue. 'He's in London.'

'Are you sure?'

She closed her eyes briefly, as if seeking strength to go further. 'Absolutely sure, Mr Haldean. I've seen him.'

Jack sat back. This was really unexpected. 'Where?'

'In St James' Park.' Her hands fluttered and then were still. 'I know what you must be thinking. You think I am mistaken.'

'Oh no,' Jack protested, wryly acknowledging to himself that was the first thought that had occurred to him.

'I am not,' said Mrs Rotherwell, speaking very earnestly. 'I was in the park beside the lake, enjoying the morning sunshine. The trees in their autumn colours, ducks on the water and nursemaids with their perambulators, all so very different from Ceylon. I was sitting on a bench near the pedestrian bridge that leads to Westminster. You know the one?'

Jack nodded.

'A man came over the bridge. I probably wouldn't have noticed him particularly, but he looked up and stared at me. He was shocked, Mr Haldean. I know he recognised me. I could tell. He walked on quickly, without attempting to speak and for a little while I couldn't think who he was. And then it came to me and I was . . .' Her hands twisted in the napkin. 'I was afraid,' she finished reluctantly.

'Afraid?'

She swallowed. 'With good reason, Mr Haldean. I watched him go, still puzzled, then lost sight of him but I am convinced—' she leant forward to add weight to her words – 'that he followed me back to the hotel.'

'Why, Mrs Rotherwell?'

'Because I have seen him again.' Her voice dropped to a nervous whisper. 'At least, I'm sure it was him. I was with a

friend at the time and it was nothing but a fleeting glimpse but
the day before last I am sure he was in the lobby of the hotel.
He was pretending to read a newspaper, but I'm sure – practically sure, in any event – it was Michael Trevelyan.'

Jack sat back in his chair. 'Have you been to the police?'

'The police?' She looked at him warily, then took a deep
breath and waited a few moments before speaking. 'How
can I?'

Her hands twisted in her napkin once more. 'You have done
me the courtesy of listening seriously to me, but would the
police? After all, poor Caroline disappeared a long time ago.'
She looked at him critically. 'You are a young man, Mr Haldean.
You must have been only a child at the time of Caroline's
disappearance, so probably don't realise the outcry that
surrounded those events. As someone who knew Caroline, I
was connected, albeit slightly, to the tragedy. Such events,
Mr Haldean, have a hideous glamour for a certain kind of
woman. I am not one of those women.'

'Of course not,' said Jack earnestly. He didn't doubt that for
a moment.

'Thank you,' she acknowledged briefly. 'It is good of you to
say so, but how would it strike a policeman? After all, virtually
the last thing I did before leaving for Ceylon was to talk to the
police about poor Caroline. Now I'm back in this country, I do
not want one of my first actions to once more go to the police
and talk about poor Caroline yet again. I have no desire,' she
added dryly, 'to be dismissed as a hysterical woman with too
much time on her hands and prone to fancies. After all, the man
has not attempted to approach me but the thought he is keeping
a watch is disturbing.'

To say the least, thought Jack. If it really was Michael
Trevelyan she'd seen and he wasn't a mere figment of her
imagination, then she had every reason to be worried. He did
take her point though, about not wanting to be seen as someone
who wanted to milk what she called that 'hideous glamour' for
all it was worth.

'If you're afraid of not being taken seriously, Mrs Rotherwell,
I can set your mind at rest.' He glanced at his watch. Bill should
be in the office. 'In fact, if you would like to come to Scotland

Yard with me now, I can introduce you to a good friend of mine, Chief Inspector Rackham. He will certainly listen to you.'

She shrank back. 'Now?' She shook her head. 'No, I couldn't possibly.' The wariness came back in full force. 'I thought this was a private investigation. I didn't realise you were connected with the police.'

Jack shook his head. 'I'm not, but Chief Inspector Rackham is an old friend of mine.'

'An old friend?' she repeated thoughtfully. 'That might make a difference.'

'For your own sake, if for no other reason, I really think you should see Chief Inspector Rackham,' urged Jack. 'After all, you're clearly uncomfortable about the state of affairs and I'm not surprised. The police can protect you. You'd feel much safer and you can help them to lay hands on a man they've been looking for for the last twenty years.'

She moved reluctantly in her seat. 'Let me consider the matter, Mr Haldean. I have no desire to be mixed up with the police.' She held up a hand to stem his protest. 'No, I will not be hurried.'

'You made a statement to the police after Mrs Trevelyan's disappearance,' said Jack. 'That wasn't too bad, was it?'

'I did not relish the experience, Mr Haldean,' she said sharply. 'However, that was a clear question of duty. For the sake of my old friend, I felt obliged to do so. However, this is different.'

She looked at him, obviously perplexed. 'In my own mind, I am certain it was Michael Trevelyan I saw. However, I cannot prove it. In years gone by, I would have consulted my dear husband about the matter. He would've known what to do.' Her face softened. 'Dear Reginald was always such a sensible man.'

'It would be sensible to go to the police,' said Jack.

She wriggled indecisively. 'Maybe.' She paused. 'Let me talk to my son,' she said at last. 'I have two sons. Ronnie is in Ceylon but Matthew and his wife live in Kensington.'

'I really think you should act now,' insisted Jack.

She hesitated once more. 'This man, this Inspector Rackham – are you sure he will listen to me?'

'I'm certain of it, Mrs Rotherwell.'

'In that case . . .' She took a deep breath. 'I may regret this, but yes, I will speak to the Inspector.'

'I can't believe she's seen him,' said Bill Rackham blankly.

They were in Bill's office, overlooking the Thames. Mrs Rotherwell, apprehensive but every inch the memsahib in control, had stiffly related what she had told Jack in the Criterion and then retreated, pride intact and with the assurance that steps would be taken.

Constable Horrocks, the steps in question, had been summoned, introduced to Mrs Rotherwell and despatched to the Royal Park Hotel with instructions to explain things to the hotel manager and then to keep an eye out in the lobby of the Royal Park.

'You don't mean that,' said Jack, dropping into a chair and reaching for a cigarette. 'That you don't believe her, I mean. Otherwise you wouldn't have sent Horrocks off to the hotel.'

'I believe she believes it,' said Bill. 'But damn it, Jack, why on earth didn't the damn silly woman tell us earlier? After all, she's got a man who she's convinced is a murderer tracking her down, and instead of coming to us, she leaves it for a little light conversation over lunch with you.'

'It's the usual tale, Bill,' said Jack, lighting his cigarette. 'She's nervy of being mixed up with the police.' Bill grunted in disgust. 'Add to that, she's afraid of being dismissed as hysterical.'

Bill pulled a face. 'To be fair, that's what I probably would have done, if you hadn't been digging around into the business,' he admitted with reluctance. 'Dismiss her as a bit hysterical, I mean. I'd have taken it with a pretty large pinch of salt, that's for sure. I'm still inclined to, to be honest. I wish she'd told us the name of this friend she was with when she caught what she describes as a fleeting glance. But no. She doesn't want her friends mixed up with the police. You'd think we were some sort of infectious disease. If we did know who it was, we could have gone to her for verification.'

'Verification of what?' asked Jack. 'That our Mrs R. had said she'd seen someone? That's not evidence of anything.'

'No, but it'd be nice to have another witness. Having said

that, I don't know if I would bother chasing round after old friends. I'm pretty doubtful it's Michael Trevelyan she's seen. After all, twenty years is a heck of a time ago.'

He glanced at his notes. 'The description she gave – about six foot tall, well-dressed, slim build, middle-aged with grey hair – well, that could fit about a third of the men in the British Isles.'

'To be fair, it's very difficult to describe a person, Bill. I know you haven't got a photo of Trevelyan on file, but his sister, Mrs Shilton, has a wedding photo. She showed it to us the other day.'

'Which makes it more than twenty years out of date,' said Bill grumpily. 'However, it'll be better than nothing, I suppose, if she's willing to let us see it.'

He glanced up. 'You're not going to mention this to Jennifer Langton, are you?'

Jack shook his head. 'No, I'm not. The last thing we need is her pitching up at the Royal Park, looking for dear old dad.'

Bill winced. 'That really is the last thing we want. I don't want Miss Langton getting involved.'

'Don't worry, I won't say a word.' Jack shifted unhappily. 'I feel sorry for Jenny Langton. I certainly don't want to add to her worries. All she asked me to do was to find out the truth behind what she saw in the garden that day. That sounded innocuous enough, but now the poor kid has to take on board that she probably witnessed her mother being murdered, the family who she always believed were her own are no such thing and, to wrap it all up, her father'll be arrested as soon as we lay hands on him. It's not a happy ending, Bill.'

Bill tapped his fingers on the desk. 'I feel sorry for her, too. It's not good, is it? However, if we can get hold of Trevelyan before he does any more harm, then that's a happy ending as far as I'm concerned, no matter whose father he is. Having said that, I think it's probably a false alarm. I'm not saying Mrs Rotherwell is a notoriety seeker, because I don't believe that for a minute, but I still think she might be mistaken.'

'And if she isn't?'

'All right. Say she really did see Trevelyan in St James' Park. Say, for the sake of argument, that he recognised her. Why on earth should he follow her to her hotel? As he's managed to keep his head down for twenty years, the Royal Park Hotel is the last place I'd expect to find him. His freedom depends on no one spotting him. He's hardly going to hang out in the one place where that's likely to happen.'

'I hope you're right,' said Jack uneasily. 'Because if Mrs Rotherwell isn't mistaken and Trevelyan really has been staking out the hotel, then she's in very real danger.'

All was quiet for the rest of the day. Horrocks, with the reluctant permission of Mr Wilfred Grafton, manager of the Royal Park Hotel, stationed himself in the lobby to no avail. Mrs Rotherwell came and went, but there was no indication from her she'd spotted Michael Trevelyan.

Tuesday followed the same pattern but on Wednesday morning, Bill telephoned first thing.

Jack could hear noises in the background. Bill obviously wasn't alone. 'I'm at the Royal Park Hotel,' he said quietly. 'I'm ringing from the manager's office. The hotel doesn't want any sort of fuss, but you'd better get over here. Mrs Rotherwell's disappeared.'

# TEN

**M**r Wilfred Grafton, manager of the Royal Park Hotel, was a worried man.

A plump, meticulously morning-suited man, he regarded Bill, Jack and Constable Horrocks with a sort of horror. 'I cannot believe that Mrs Rotherwell's absence calls for Scotland Yard,' he said stiffly. 'It was bad enough knowing the police were on the premises,' he said, glaring at Constable Horrocks. 'I was assured it was merely a matter of clearing up a case of identity. Surely the matter can be resolved without calling upon Scotland Yard.'

He swallowed nervously and ran a hand through his thinning hair. 'I refuse to believe that Mrs Rotherwell was involved in anything criminal. This is a most respectable hotel. Absolutely respectable.'

That, thought Jack, was exactly right. The Royal Park, although large and perfectly pleasant, wasn't glamorous. It certainly wasn't the Ritz or the Savoy. It wasn't the sort of place that was visited by millionaires, motor-racing stars, captains of industry or Indian maharajahs. No; it was firmly middle-class and exactly, from what he'd seen of her, the sort of hotel Mrs Rotherwell would choose.

'Our clientele,' continued Mr Grafton, 'are drawn exclusively from the better classes. We pride ourselves on excellent service and . . . and . . .' He struggled for a word. 'Respectability,' he finished lamely. 'We've never had any trouble of any sort that necessitated the police being called. Ever. And as for Mrs Rotherwell, I would have sworn she was a most respectable lady.'

'She is,' Bill assured him.

The manager attacked his hair again. 'There's nothing criminal involved, is there?' he asked piteously.

'We certainly don't suspect Mrs Rotherwell of anything criminal,' said Bill with what was meant to be a reassuring smile. 'We merely want to find out what has happened to her.'

'But that's exactly what I don't know!' wailed Mr Grafton.

Jack took a hand. 'The thing is, Mr Grafton, we want to reassure ourselves that Mrs Rotherwell has come to no harm.'

The manager swelled alarmingly. 'Harm? Why should she have come to any harm?'

Bill's mouth thinned. 'We think she might have come to harm,' he said, 'because she told us she was being followed by a man wanted for murder.'

In other circumstances, Jack would've enjoyed the manager's reaction. He sank back in his chair, his mouth opening and shutting wordlessly. It was like watching the air going out of a pricked balloon. '*Murder*?' he managed at last. 'Oh no. Not here.'

'Obviously not here,' Jack said dryly. 'It's the fact that Mrs Rotherwell *isn't* here that's the problem. When did you see her last?'

Mr Grafton gulped. 'Yesterday morning,' he said eventually. 'I didn't see her personally. We have a large clientele and I regret I cannot possibly be individually acquainted with all our visitors. However, at the insistence of this gentleman—' once more, he indicated Bill – 'I checked with the clerks who have been on duty at the desk since Monday. Mrs Rotherwell left her key at the desk on Tuesday morning.'

'Have you been in her room?' asked Bill.

Mr Grafton shook his head. 'Not personally, no. However, the chambermaids will have cleaned her room as usual and they certainly would have reported anything untoward.'

'Could she have left a note or something to tell us where she might be?' asked Jack. He very much wanted to see her room.

'She wouldn't have left it in her room, surely,' said Mr Grafton, reasonably enough. 'She would have told the clerk at the desk. I did have a memorandum of her absence passed to me this morning, as she had not mentioned she was planning to stay out overnight, but we had no reason to suspect any . . .' He gulped and tried for the words. 'What may be described as *foul play*.'

He looked at them pathetically. 'Surely this will prove to be nothing more than a misunderstanding. Perhaps she is staying with a friend or relative?'

'She told me she had a married son, Matthew Rotherwell, who lives in Kensington,' said Jack. He raised an enquiring eyebrow to Bill. 'We could try telephoning him. I suppose he's in the phone book.'

'Let's have a look in her room first,' suggested Bill. 'I'd rather do that first than alarm her family.'

Reluctantly, the manager agreed.

Mrs Rotherwell had been staying at the Royal Park for three weeks. The room, which obviously had been cleaned by the chambermaids, just as Mr Grafton had said, was neat and orderly. Her personal possessions consisted of clothes, toiletries, a few books and two framed photographs. One had obviously been taken in bright sunlight against a white bungalow with a veranda and was of a wiry, middle-aged man, wearing a short-sleeved shirt and shorts, together with a younger man, also in short sleeves and shorts. There was a strong resemblance between them. Mr Rotherwell and son Ronnie in Ceylon, presumably. The other was of a younger man with a woman about the same age. That must be Matthew Rotherwell and his wife, thought Jack.

'She probably had the bulk of her possessions in storage somewhere,' said Bill, picking up a handful of letters from the drawer of the dresser. 'What have we got here? Three letters from friends in Ceylon. That's to be expected. There's one with a Wimbledon postmark, too.'

Ignoring Mr Grafton's protests, he quickly read the letter through. 'It's from Mrs Shilton, Jack. That's Miss Langton's aunt, isn't it?'

'Yes, that's right. Mrs Shilton told me she'd written to Mrs Rotherwell.'

Bill put the letter back in its envelope with an impatient sigh. 'What this room hasn't got,' he said in frustration, 'is any clue to where she might be now. I'd hoped we might find an invitation or an open timetable or something of that sort, but there's nothing. I can't even see an address book or anything of that sort. She must have had one, surely.'

'If it's a small book, it's probably in her handbag,' said Jack thoughtfully. 'However, we know she didn't intend to stay out overnight. For one thing, she'd have probably said as much to the clerk on the desk, and for another, I imagine she'd take her toothbrush and face-cream and so on.' He picked up a pair of spectacles that were resting on a small book entitled *Devotional Thoughts* on the bedside table and tried them on. 'She left her reading glasses, too.'

He looked at Bill and shrugged. 'We're going to have to contact her son, Bill. I know you're reluctant to worry him, but there's nothing else for it.'

Back in the manager's office, they found the entry for Mr M. Rotherwell easily enough in the telephone directory.

Bill reached for the telephone, then hesitated. 'I think I'd better call in person,' he said. 'I've got an uneasy feeling about how this is going to turn out and I'd rather speak to them face to face.' He looked at the address. '24, Cosby Place, Kensington.'

'D'you mind if I come along?' asked Jack.

'I'd be glad if you did,' said Bill. 'I don't know if this is connected to Trevelyan, but if it is, that's your pigeon.'

'What shall I do about Mrs Rotherwell's room?' asked Mr Grafton.

'Leave it as it is for the time being,' said Bill after a few moment's thought. 'It could be that she's met with an accident and is in hospital.'

Mr Grafton seized on the suggestion with relief. 'I imagine that is the case,' he said gratefully. 'That's so much more likely than anything *criminal.*'

'My mother's disappeared?' asked Matthew Rotherwell in blank disbelief. 'She can't have done.' He turned to his wife, an intelligent-looking woman, who was clearly only a month or so off from adding to the Rotherwell family.

They were in the sitting room of the Rotherwells' flat, a pleasant sunny room, elegantly decorated in pale green and primrose.

'Could she be ill?' asked Julia Rotherwell. 'I don't like to think so, but she might have been knocked over by a car, say, and be in hospital.'

Bill shook his head. 'I'm afraid that's not the case. She was last seen at the hotel on Tuesday morning. I had the hospital reports for Tuesday onwards checked before we came here, and there's no one who's met with an accident who could be your mother.'

'But what could have happened to her?' said Matthew Rotherwell, bewildered.

Bill cleared his throat. This could be delicate. 'Forgive me for asking, sir, but has your mother ever given you cause for concern by an unexplained absence before now?'

'Has she ever done what?' asked Matthew Rotherwell, puzzled.

'Has she ever gone away without telling us,' explained his wife. 'Wandered off, in other words. No, Chief Inspector, never.'

'We don't know everything she did in Ceylon,' began Matthew, but Julia Rotherwell shook her head. 'What Mr Rackham's really asking, Matthew, is if your mother's dotty or not.' She looked at Bill. 'I'm right, aren't I? You do mean that?'

Bill reluctantly nodded.

'Certainly not,' said Matthew, affronted. 'My mother's as sane as you are.'

'She really is,' agreed Julia. 'She's a very matter-of-fact person. She copes, you know? After Matthew's father died, she stayed on in Ceylon with Matthew's brother, Ronnie, for quite a while before coming back home. We'd warned her that it was a dickens of a job to find a suitable place to live, with this terrible shortage of houses, but she said she would simply stay in a hotel so she had time to look round. She's been back for a couple of months. She only moved into the Royal Park about three weeks ago. She told me she liked it very much. I'm sure she wouldn't have left without saying anything.'

'Did she mention a Caroline Trevelyan, by any chance?' asked Jack. He and Bill had discussed how to raise the subject of Michael Trevelyan on the way to Kensington. Bill was dead against the idea of asking Matthew Rotherwell outright if his mother had talked about seeing a suspected murderer. That really would alarm any relative with an ounce of feeling, but he'd agreed to find out if Matthew would volunteer the information.

'Caroline Trevelyan?' began Matthew. The name obviously meant nothing to him, but his wife nodded vigorously.

'Yes, of course. You remember, Matthew. Caroline Trevelyan used to be one of your mother's pupils years ago. They were always very friendly and then the poor woman was bumped off by her husband. Well, she disappeared, at any rate,' she amended. 'No one knew what really happened but your mother thought it was obvious her husband had done it. It sounded all too Dr Crippen for words, but it was all very sad, when you come to think about it. There was an advertisement in the newspaper asking for information about her. Your mother was quite concerned. She wondered who on earth could be interested in Mrs Trevelyan after all this time.'

'Of course,' said Matthew. He looked at them ruefully. 'I'll be honest. I didn't really pay much attention but I know she'd written to this chap who'd advertised and was going to meet him for lunch. Perhaps he can help, if you can find out who he is.'

'That was me,' said Jack. Both the Rotherwells looked at him sharply. 'Caroline Trevelyan's daughter has asked me to find out what I can about her mother,' he explained in answer to their unspoken question. 'I lunched at the Criterion with your mother on Monday.'

'Then . . .' began Matthew uncertainly. He gave Jack a puzzled look, then rubbed his hand across his forehead. 'I was hoping whoever it was she met at the Criterion could tell us more, but if it was you, that's not much help, is it?'

'When did you last see your mother?' asked Bill.

'I went shopping with her on Saturday,' said Julia. 'We went to Heals to look at nursery furniture. She was very much looking forward to the new baby,' she said with a worried smile. 'I hope she's all right,' she added. 'I can't think what on earth could've happened to her. She's such a kind, considerate person. She'd never cause us this sort of anxiety needlessly.'

'Did she seem worried at all?' asked Bill. That was as close as he was prepared to go in asking 'had she seen a suspected murderer?'.

'She was certainly concerned that someone was asking about this Caroline Trevelyan,' said Julia. 'She'd been very fond of Mrs Trevelyan and hoped that, even after all this time, the truth would come out, but I wouldn't say she was worried, exactly.'

'It might be difficult to tell how she was feeling, Julia,' put in Matthew. 'You know what my mother is like.'

'I know she doesn't like to worry us, Matthew.'

'That's true. If she had anything on her mind, anything that was bothering her, she'd keep it to herself until she'd thought of a solution.' He nearly smiled. 'It's kindly meant, but she does like being in charge.'

'You're right,' said Julia Rotherwell. 'She'll ask for your opinion but she always has her own answer worked out. What she's really after is confirmation.'

Yes, thought Jack uneasily. That's how she'd struck him, a woman who kept things to herself. She obviously hadn't mentioned seeing Michael Trevelyan to her family, but that seemed perfectly in character. If she really had seen him, of course. Twenty years was a long time but that damned advert of his had made the whole Trevelyan business fresh in her mind. She could've recognised him.

'Does she have any friends in London?' asked Bill. 'I want to know who else we could ask, you understand.'

'She doesn't have many friends,' said Julia with a shake of her head. 'She's lived abroad for so long, you see. I know she chatted to a couple of ladies in the hotel, but they were just passing acquaintances.' She frowned in recollection. 'She did mention a couple of names, though.' She looked up brightly. 'One was in connection with this Caroline Trevelyan business. I'm trying to remember the name. Mrs Shilton? Is that it?'

Jack and Bill swapped glances. They seemed to be coming full circle. 'We know about Mrs Shilton,' said Jack. 'She was a relative of Mrs Trevelyan's.' It was best, he thought, to put it like that.

Matthew turned to his wife. 'Who did my mother used to write to? I know there was someone, a woman she'd known years ago, before she went to Ceylon.' He smiled fleetingly. 'There were a few old friends who she kept in touch with, particularly at Christmas and so on, but most of them either lived abroad or have died over the years. There was one woman though, who I know lived in London. I think they'd met up a couple of times. Julia, you know who I'm talking about. What the dickens was her name?'

Julia screwed up her face in an effort of remembrance. 'It was a Mrs Davenham,' she said slowly. 'Mrs Jane Davenham.'

Bill sat up sharply. 'Excuse me, Mrs Rotherwell, did you say Jane Davenham? Mrs Jane Davenham?'

'Yes, that's right,' said Julia Rotherwell, obviously taken aback. 'Why? Do you know her?'

Jack looked at Bill in surprise. Bill had never mentioned a Jane Davenham and yet the name clearly meant something to him. 'Who is she, Bill?'

Bill shook himself. 'It's probably something and nothing. It's just that the lady's name came up the other day.' He forced himself to smile. 'It was in connection with a lost cat.'

Although Bill's reply evidently satisfied Matthew and Julia Rotherwell, it didn't fool Jack for a moment. He knew his friend far too well to believe that a lost cat was the top and bottom of the story. Besides that, what on earth would Bill be doing chasing a lost cat? However, he obviously didn't want to say any more in front of the Rotherwells.

'It's probably another Mrs Davenham,' said Julia.

'It very well might be,' said Bill casually. 'There must be lots of Jane Davenhams in London.'

'Perhaps,' said Matthew doubtfully. 'I can't say I would've thought the name was that common.' He turned to his wife. 'Do you remember where she lived?'

'No,' said Julia. 'Your mother mentioned the address. I know it was a flat and somewhere central. What on earth was the name? Wrexham Mansions? Something like that.'

'Roxborough,' muttered Bill. 'Roxborough Mansions.'

'That's it,' said Julia with certainty. 'I remember now. It must be the same person, Mr Rackham, if the address is the same.'

'It certainly seems so,' said Bill guardedly. He cleared his throat. 'Can you tell me anything about Mrs Davenham?'

'Not really,' said Matthew with a shrug. 'All I really know is that my mother knew her years ago, before she went out to Ceylon. I'm pretty sure she's seen her since she's been back. Did Mum mention anything to you, Julia?'

'Not especially, no.'

'I don't suppose your mother would have kept letters from her by any chance?' asked Bill.

'They could be in storage,' began Matthew, but Julia shook her head.

'She had a big clear-out when she left Ceylon, Matthew. She told me so. She said it was quite dreadful how much rubbish one accumulated. She specifically mentioned old letters, theatre programmes and club menus and things of that sort.' She looked at Jack and Bill. 'If Mrs Davenham dropped her a line once she was back in London, though, that letter would be at the hotel, perhaps?'

Jack shook his head. 'There's no letter from Mrs Davenham at the hotel, I'm afraid. We looked.'

'You've searched my mother's room?' began Matthew indignantly, then stopped, suddenly worried. 'Look here, Mr Rackham, has anything happened to her?' He swallowed. 'Anything untoward, I mean?'

'We'd like to know where she is, that's all,' said Bill, trying to sound as reassuring as possible. 'After all, you say that for her to disappear like this is unusual?'

'She's certainly never done it before. I can't think where on earth she could be. If she was staying with a friend, say, surely she'd have let us know. To say nothing of letting the hotel know. She's very punctilious about that sort of thing.'

'In that case, we really need to find her. I don't suppose you've got a photograph of her I can have?'

'There's bound to be one in storage,' said Matthew. 'I know she had at least one taken with my father and I imagine she kept that. It'll only be a snapshot, though. She wasn't a great one for posing for photographs. She never had a studio portrait taken. I can hunt out the snapshot for you, if you like. Why do you want it?'

'Well, she might have suffered loss of memory, perhaps. A photo is always useful.' He paused. 'I'd be obliged if you could let me have it as soon as possible, sir. I think we ought to launch a missing person enquiry.'

'Missing person?' repeated Matthew, with an anxious look at his wife. 'I hope that's all it is. I don't mind telling you, Mr Rackham, that this is all very worrying.'

'What,' said Jack, as soon as they were safely on the pavement of Cosby Place and out of earshot of the Rotherwells, 'was all that about Mrs Davenham and a lost cat? Were you just making it up? About the cat, I mean?'

'No, I wasn't. After I left you on Saturday, I bumped into Mr Church. You've heard me talk about Charlie Church, my old inspector?'

'Yes, of course.'

'Well, the thing is, Jack,' said Bill, after he'd run through the story, 'that Mr Church said he was going to leave a note with the porter asking this Mrs Davenham to contact the Yard when she returned. The way he saw it, Mrs Davenham would probably be a bit shirty about having her flat broken into and her locks changed. He thought she might very well blame Winnie and Ted Hinton and wanted to deflect any ill-feeling towards the Yard. There's nothing like a bit of official involvement to take the steam out of a complaint and keep things peaceful between neighbours.'

'And has she? Has she been in touch, I mean?'

'Not as far as I know.' Bill hesitated for a moment, then made up his mind. 'Let's go to Roxborough Mansions, Jack. If Mrs Davenham has returned, then we could do with asking her about Mrs Rotherwell. If not . . .'

'If not, we might have another missing person on our hands,' completed Jack softly.

Roxborough Mansions, South Nyland Street, Kensington, proved to be a prosperous-looking, large, brick-built building. Jack walked up the steps and ran his finger down the list of residents. 'Here we are, Bill. Mrs J. Davenham, number four.'

They pushed open the street door and went into the hall.

The porter put down his *Racing Post* and looked up from his desk. 'Can I help you, gentlemen?'

'I hope so. We're looking for a Mrs Jane Davenham,' said Bill.

The porter shook his head. 'I'm sorry, sir, but she's away.'

Bill swapped glances with Jack. This was what they had been afraid of. 'Has Mrs Davenham left an address where we could get in touch with her?'

'No, she didn't, sir, but you can leave a message with me, if you like.'

Bill shook his head. 'Thanks, but we need to see Mrs Davenham herself. I'm Chief Inspector Rackham of Scotland Yard and this is Major Haldean.'

The porter's eyebrows shot up in alarm. 'If this is about Mr Hinton having to force the door . . .'

'We know all about that,' said Jack with a smile. 'This is nothing to do with the Hintons, the door, or the lost cat.'

The porter spread his hands wide. 'I'm sorry, gents, I can't help you. Mrs Davenham went away about a week ago, it would be now, and I haven't seen or heard from her since.'

'Could we have a look inside the flat?' asked Bill. 'I understand the lock was changed and you have the key.'

'Yes, I have sir. I suppose it's all right, with you being from Scotland Yard, an' all.' The porter took a key from a drawer and led the way along the corridor. 'Has anything happened to Mrs Davenham, sir?'

'We just don't know,' said Jack easily. 'We hope not but it's unusual for her to be away for this long without letting you know, isn't it?'

'Well, it is, sir. A couple of nights, yes, and no harm done, but I'll have to have a word when she returns.'

They arrived at number four and the porter opened the door. Although neat, the flat was dusty after a week's neglect. The flat was of a fairly standard construction, with a sitting room, dining room, bedroom, bathroom and kitchen, all very much lived-in, with ornaments on the mantelpiece, pictures on the walls and clothes in the wardrobe.

The clothes were good quality and fashionable. A favourite shop seemed to be Debenhams and Freebody's, but, Jack observed with raised eyebrows, there were two dresses from Callot Soeurs and one from Vionnet.

To shop in Paris argued a woman with some money behind her. If she had shopped in Paris, she must have a passport, but there was no passport, address book or bank book or, indeed, any private documents at all. The waste-paper bin was empty, with no receipts or bills to show where she might have gone for a meal or out for the evening. Nothing, in fact, much to Bill's disgust, to show where Mrs Davenham had been, where she might be now, or how she could be contacted.

Was this deliberate? It was difficult to tell. After all, for all they knew, Mrs Davenham might be in Paris at the moment. That would explain her absence and the lack of a passport and bank book but why hadn't she informed the porter? Maybe he was making a mystery out of a perfectly ordinary occurrence, but he didn't like the way Mrs Davenham had simply vanished. There was one thing for sure; judging from the things she had left in the flat, she obviously had every intention of coming back.

Leaving Bill to question the porter, Jack sat down in an armchair and started to flick through the papers and magazines in the paper-rack.

Mrs Davenham took the *Herald,* but there was an odd copy of the *Daily Mail* and the *Sketch* as well. The latest paper, which didn't look as if it'd been read, was dated Tuesday the 20th. Last week. The magazines were superior ladies' magazines, all for the previous month. *Vogue, Beau Monde, The Windsor.*

'She obviously didn't have a servant,' said Bill.

The porter shook his head. 'Not in these flats, no. The larger flats upstairs, the family flats, some of them keep a maid, but these flats are really only for one person or a couple.'

Mrs Davenham, it turned out, had lived in Roxborough Mansions for the best part of a year. Although pleasant, she kept herself to herself. She certainly liked her privacy, thought Jack. The fact she'd changed the locks testified to that.

'Did Mrs Davenham live alone?' continued Bill. 'Or was there a Mr Davenham?'

The porter grinned. 'I don't know about a Mr Davenham, but the lady wasn't alone, as often as not, if you get my meaning. Oh, nothing rowdy. The management wouldn't stand for that, but she certainly had a visitor.' He frowned. 'I did hear the name but I can't call it to mind.'

Jack knew Bill was still speaking but his voice seemed to fade as he gazed in astonishment at the magazine he'd taken from the rack. 'Blimey, Bill!'

Bill spun round. 'What is it?'

Jack held out the brightly coloured magazine. It wasn't really a magazine, it was a brochure with an idyllic family outside an idyllic house. *Resthaven – Make this house your Home.*

'Good grief!' said Bill, taking the brochure. 'I've seen this before! You've got a copy, Jack.'

'Yes, we have,' said Jack, sitting back in the armchair. He cocked an eyebrow at the porter, who was obviously bewildered by the excitement the Resthaven brochure had created. 'This visitor Mrs Davenham had. Can you describe him?'

'I dunno,' said the porter. 'Tallish chap, well-built, grey-haired . . .'

'Spoke with a Scottish accent?' asked Jack.

'Why, yes he did, now you come to mention it.'

'Was his name Laidlaw, by any chance?'

The porter gazed at him. 'Why, yes it is! How did you know that?'

Jack replaced the brochure in the rack and stood up. 'I've met him before. Bill, shall we go and meet him again?'

'That,' said Bill, 'sounds like a very good idea.'

The clerk who answered the telephone of Ezra Wild and Sons regretted that Mr Laidlaw had been out all morning at Resthaven and wasn't expected back in the office. However, if Chief Inspector Rackham would care to get in touch with Mr Laidlaw at home, the address was 1, Cossington Terrace. The telephone number was Chelsea 260.

'Thanks,' said Bill, scribbling down the address and number. 'You've been very helpful. No, there isn't anything wrong. It's just a routine enquiry in connection with another matter.'

He hung up the receiver and grinned ruefully at Jack. 'People do think the worst when they hear it's the police on the telephone.' He picked up the phone again. 'Now for Mr Laidlaw.'

A richly fruity voice answered the phone. Mr Laidlaw wasn't at home but was expected shortly. If Chief Inspector Rackham would care to leave a message?

'I'll be round right away,' said Bill, cutting off the butler's protests and hanging up the receiver. 'Come on, Jack. Get your hat and let's go.'

# ELEVEN

Cossington Terrace was a row of Victorian houses with imposing doors, high windows and – yes – the odd turret poking out of the roof. The builder had obviously taken on board the Victorian craze for Gothic architecture with keen, if perhaps misplaced, enthusiasm. Number 1, the largest house in the terrace, was a bit like a castle crossed with a cathedral.

A monumental butler answered the door. 'Chief Inspector Rackham and Major Haldean to see Mr Laidlaw,' said Bill. 'I telephoned earlier.'

The butler, who appeared to be the same vintage as the house, regarded them doubtfully. 'Indeed, sir.'

Jack knew what the man was thinking as clearly as if he'd shouted it. Policemen, of whatever rank, shouldn't be admitted by the front door but belonged round the back, at the tradesman's entrance.

'I gave Mr Laidlaw your message and he left instructions to admit you,' said the butler, in a tone of some regret.

'Well, show us in, man,' said Bill with some asperity. The look had not been lost on him.

The butler bore up manfully. 'If you would come this way, sir,' he murmured in sepulchral tones. 'I will inform Mr Laidlaw you have arrived.'

He led them through the wide hall and showed them into the drawing room. The drawing room, with its high ceilings, elaborate plasterwork and gigantic fireplace, wasn't, in any sense, a cosy room, but it was light and airy and painted, Jack was glad to see, not in Victorian deep reds and cabbage greens, but in modern sky blue and terracotta.

An enormous oak sideboard held, together with usual decanters and syphons, an array of silver-framed photographs – a young man in Royal Flying Corps uniform was there, together with a few of a little boy and, prominent amongst these, a middle-aged, rather lost-looking woman with a black ribbon on one corner of the frame.

'That must be Laidlaw's brother,' said Jack quietly, looking at the pilot in the photograph. 'This poor little chap must be the son who died of flu, and I imagine that's Violet, his late wife.'

Bill looked at the sad display and winced.

'Poor beggar,' he murmured. 'Judging from the house, he's obviously well-off, but money isn't everything, not by a long chalk.'

The door opened and, with a slight feeling of guilt, they stepped away from the sideboard as Andrew Laidlaw came into the room.

'Chief Inspector?' he said, as he strode across the room, hand outstretched. 'Major Haldean, I must say I was surprised when Ellicott, my butler, said to expect you.'

He glanced down to the sideboard and smiled faintly. 'I see you've been looking at the family photographs.' He indicated the lost-looking woman. 'That's my poor wife, Violet. She passed away earlier this year, in February.'

'I'm sorry for your loss, sir,' said Bill sincerely.

Laidlaw looked solemn for a moment, then shook himself with a sigh. 'I can't imagine you came here to hear about my family. Please sit down, won't you?' he added, indicating the sofa. 'There's cigarettes in the box beside you. Please help yourself. And can I offer you a drink? Sherry, perhaps?'

'That's very kind of you, sir, but not at the moment,' said Bill, sitting down.

Laidlaw looked at Jack with a puzzled frown. 'Major Haldean, you're not still investigating the Trevelyans, are you?'

'Not precisely,' said Jack, 'although Michael Trevelyan might have a bearing on the matter we're looking into.'

Laidlaw's puzzlement increased. 'I told you everything I could recollect of the business when you and your wife called to see me earlier, Major. I don't know if I can add anything to what I've already told you.'

'As a matter of fact,' said Bill, 'it's another person we would like to ask you about. A Mrs Jane Davenham.'

There was no mistaking Andrew Laidlaw's shock. He had taken a cigarette from the box. He froze, the match unlighted in his hand. 'Jane?' he repeated in a whisper. 'Jane? What's happened? Has anything happened?'

'We hoped you might tell us that, sir,' said Bill. 'You obviously know the lady.'

Laidlaw brushed his hair back impatiently. 'Yes, of course I know her.' He shook himself and stared at them. 'How do you know about Jane?'

'It's a fairly complicated story, sir,' said Bill, 'but to cut a long story short, we had reason to call in at her flat in Roxborough Mansions earlier today.'

'Why?' demanded Laidlaw.

'Nothing to be concerned about, sir,' said Bill with a smile.

Jack appreciated Bill's tact. To say they were on the trail of one missing woman and thought that Jane Davenham might make number two on the list wasn't something Bill wanted to thresh out with a man as obviously concerned as Andrew Laidlaw. 'The thing is, Mr Laidlaw,' he said as easily as possible, taking a cigarette from the box, 'we didn't find Mrs Davenham but we did find one of your Resthaven brochures in her flat.'

'But anyone could have one of those brochures!' exploded Laidlaw. 'You've got one, Major!'

'Indeed I have, sir,' said Jack with a smile. 'And, of course, you're quite right. However, the porter at Roxborough Mansions remembered you as a visitor to Mrs Davenham.'

Laidlaw let out a deep breath and lit his cigarette with a shaky hand. 'All right. I admit it. I was hoping none of this would come out, but I admit it.' He passed a hand over his forehead. 'Why do you want to see Mrs Davenham?'

'I understand she was a friend of a lady called Mrs Rotherwell, sir,' said Bill. 'We merely wanted to ask Mrs Davenham about Mrs Rotherwell.'

'Mrs Rotherwell?' repeated Andrew Laidlaw blankly.

'Yes, sir. Have you heard of her?'

Laidlaw shook his head in irritation. 'I might have heard Jane mention her. The name sounds vaguely familiar. What about her?'

'We merely want to ask her a few questions. We hoped Mrs Davenham would be able to tell us something about her. However, I gather Mrs Davenham's been away for a few days.'

'She has,' said Andrew Laidlaw grimly. 'And, I might say, if you find her, I'd be glad to know where she is myself.' He looked at Bill with sudden worry. 'Mr Rackham, you're not saying anything's happened to Jane, are you?' He swallowed. 'Anything untoward, I mean?'

'I certainly hope not, sir,' said Bill with assumed cheerfulness. 'It's just that we'd like to speak to the lady.'

Laidlaw put his hands wide. 'I only wish I could help you. I . . . I wouldn't want anything to have happened to Jane.'

Jack reached for the ashtray. 'Could you tell us something about her, Mr Laidlaw? How long had she known Mrs Rotherwell, for instance?'

He didn't have a clue if anything Andrew Laidlaw said would be relevant to the hunt for Mrs Rotherwell, but any clue, however slight, was worth following up.

Laidlaw looked blank. 'I'm awfully sorry. As I said, I've only got a vague recollection of the name.'

That was a blow, but there might be some information worth gathering, all the same. 'How did you come to know Mrs Davenham, sir?' asked Jack quietly.

Andrew Laidlaw sat very still for a few moments then, getting up, walked to the door and checked it was firmly shut.

'I've said too much to pretend Jane is merely a friend. However, I would take it as a great favour if none of what I am about to say was made public.'

'You can have my assurance on that, sir,' said Bill. 'Unless it's absolutely necessary that it should be otherwise, your private affairs are your own.'

Laidlaw walked to the sideboard and, almost absently, laid a hand on the photograph of his wife. 'Thank you for that.'

He pinched the bridge of his nose between his fingers, then with a sigh, looked up and squared his shoulders, bracing himself. 'What you have to understand, gentlemen, is that I'm very fond of Mrs Davenham. Very fond indeed. You've probably gathered that, but,' he added, with an unconscious glance at the photograph of Violet Laidlaw, 'I had hoped that, in the course of time, if circumstances permitted, Jane would do me the honour of becoming my wife.'

Jack swapped a surprised glance with Bill. Laidlaw's

relationship with Jane Davenham was obviously much more than a mere passing affair.

'I see, sir,' said Bill gravely. 'How long have you known Mrs Davenham?'

Laidlaw took a deep breath and plunged in. 'I've known Mrs Davenham for over a year now.' He held up his hand, as if to forestall criticism. 'I know how it sounds. I probably shouldn't have let myself be drawn into a . . . a friendship with Mrs Davenham while my poor wife was still alive.'

Neither Jack or Bill said anything. For one thing, it wasn't their place to comment and, for another, it was the best way of getting Laidlaw to carry on talking.

'I'd like you to understand,' said Laidlaw with a hint of desperation. 'I cared deeply for Violet. I always have done. We'd been married for years, and happily married at that. However, after little Archie died, Violet was never the same again.'

'I'm very sorry to hear that, sir,' said Bill sincerely.

Laidlaw relaxed, reassured by Bill's sympathy. 'I did what I could for her, but Violet seemed to retreat into a world of her own. Eventually she was diagnosed with a heart condition, but the real trouble was that she couldn't seem to put her feelings for little Archie to one side and get on with life. She became virtually an invalid. I did my best,' he added quietly.

'I'm sure you did,' said Bill awkwardly.

Jack nodded. He'd been told that Laidlaw was reputed to be a devoted husband, but he could well understand how Andrew Laidlaw, a fit and vigorous man, would be tempted to stray from the straight and narrow, with a wife who had been an invalid for years.

'I miss Violet terribly,' continued Laidlaw. 'You mustn't doubt me.' He waved a hand at the room. 'This house was her grandfather's, one of the first he built. She grew up here. I've stayed on because she loved the house so much. Sometimes I can virtually feel her presence. I know she would want me to be happy. Violet always wanted that.'

Which was, of course, all very convenient, thought Jack, but really, there was no reason to doubt it. Andrew Laidlaw was a widower, after all, and free to marry whoever he liked, no matter when the relationship started. If he wanted to believe his late wife was cheering him on from beyond the veil, then why shouldn't he? It didn't do any harm and probably made him feel better. He did wonder, however, exactly how convenient Violet Laidlaw's death had been. He made a mental note to find out who Mrs Laidlaw's doctor had been.

Bill cleared his throat. 'I'm sure your wife would have wanted you to be happy, sir. It sounds a very difficult situation. However, if I could ask you about Mrs Davenham?'

The facts, although they took some time in the telling, could be summed up readily enough.

Jane Davenham was, Andrew supposed, in her forties. He didn't know her exact age. He didn't have a photograph of her but she was about five foot five inches tall, with fair hair, hazel eyes and no obvious, as Bill would have said, distinguishing features.

'I only wish I did have a photograph,' Laidlaw said helplessly. 'It would help to find her and I do want to find her. I . . . I miss her. I could talk to Jane about anything. She was very well-read and took a keen interest in politics and current affairs.'

All of which, thought Jack, must have been a welcome change from the semi-invalided Mrs Laidlaw.

They had first met about a year and a half ago at Gloucester Road tube station. She had missed her footing alighting from a train and Andrew had gallantly come to her rescue. He had helped her up, picked up her bags and then taken her for a restorative cup of tea. Or rather, in her case, coffee, for which she had a very un-English preference.

Although English, she had lived for a good few years in America. And that was part of the problem. She had married an American, a seemingly successful businessman. For a time everything went well, then she began to suspect some of his deals were distinctly shady. Prohibition had opened up a raft of undercover dealings for men who weren't too punctilious about breaking the law. He'd always managed to get alcohol but now he drank too much and had a string of affairs. The last straw had come when he had raised a hand to her.

Laidlaw was horrified. That anyone could treat any woman, let alone an educated, cultured woman, in this way seemed abhorrent to him. She knew no one in London and was wary of meeting anyone in case news got back to her husband. She did, however, agree to see him again and they began to meet up occasionally and then, as the relationship deepened, more frequently.

Naturally enough, after poor Violet had died, Andrew had raised the topic of marriage, but Mrs Davenham was still married and wary of approaching her husband.

'The trouble was,' said Laidlaw, 'is that Jane was very unsure if a divorce would be granted, even if her husband was agreeable, which wasn't at all certain. As I said, her husband had had a string of affairs, but they have some very odd laws in the States. Apparently as long as Jane could maintain she was the innocent party, then a lawyer could argue the case on her behalf as a wronged woman. However, if it became known that I was involved, then both Jane and her husband would be counted as transgressors against the institution of matrimony, and neither would be allowed to divorce the other.'

Bill pulled a face. 'That's a very awkward situation, sir.'

'You're telling me,' said Laidlaw glumly. 'I must say, it led to some tension between us. And . . . And when I said I cared for my wife, I meant it. Poor Violet needed me, and although in many ways, her end was a blessed release, I missed her terribly when she was gone. Violet depended on me and I missed her.'

He smiled faintly. 'Perhaps I said too much about Violet to Jane. I don't know, but perhaps she resented how I felt.' A slightly exasperated note crept into his voice. 'It's hard to be sure with women, isn't it? They never seem to say exactly how they feel or what's bothering them, but leave you to work it out.'

'So you're saying that relations between you had deteriorated recently?' asked Bill.

'Yes, I suppose I am.' He gave an irritated sigh. 'There's no point in being anything but completely honest. It must've been about six weeks or so ago when things started to go downhill. Jane didn't want to meet as frequently as before, and was often cold and a bit off-hand when we did.'

He looked at them helplessly. 'I might be wrong, but I wondered if she had met someone else. She seemed to become more and more impatient when I talked about investigating the possibility of a divorce. There's something else, too. I know that on at least one occasion a man had been in her flat. I found a cigar stub that wasn't mine but when I asked her about it, she told me it was none of my business. I called to see her the Saturday before last.'

His face twisted. 'We quarrelled. I'd read in the paper that it was easy to get a divorce in some parts of the States and wanted her to try. They call the process a Reno Quickie, as I understand. I must admit I find the whole idea pretty distasteful, but I was willing to try anything to sort out this mess.'

'But Mrs Davenham refused?' asked Jack.

'Yes, she did, Major Haldean. Apparently it's not as easy as you might think. Jane said I didn't understand the difficulties involved.' He shrugged his shoulders expressively. 'That was the last time I saw her. On the Monday evening I called round to try and patch things up, but she wasn't there.' His face hardened. 'Since then, I haven't heard a word.'

'Did she leave a forwarding address?'

'No, she didn't. I assumed that she'd telephone or write to me at least.'

Bill thought for a moment, then tried to phrase the question as delicately as he could. 'You'll excuse me for asking, Mr Laidlaw, but do you think she wants you to find her?'

Laidlaw made an impatient gesture. 'I don't know. A few weeks ago, the question would've been absurd, but now I simply don't know. However, I do feel I'm owed an explanation.' His face grew grim. 'If Jane wants to call it off, then that's her decision, but the least she can do is tell me. I must say, I would never have expected her to simply go off in this way.'

He lit another cigarette and took a deep, worried breath. 'You might think I'm being unduly melodramatic, but as time's gone on, I can't help worrying that something's happened to her.'

Jack didn't think he was being remotely melodramatic. If Jane Davenham wanted to break off the relationship, then surely she could've written the man a note?

Bill cupped his chin in his hand, thinking. 'What do you think happened, sir?'

Laidlaw swung his fist in an exasperated gesture. 'I don't know but I do know there's another man involved! That cigar stub I found proves it. What if that other man is her husband? From all I've heard, he's a nasty piece of work who wouldn't think twice about forcing Jane to do as he wants.'

'Surely she'd have told you if she had seen her husband?'

'I would've have thought so but quite honestly, Chief Inspector, I don't know what to think.'

'Would you like to formally request we treat Mrs Davenham as a missing person, sir?' asked Bill.

Andrew Laidlaw made an exasperated noise. 'I don't know, Chief Inspector! What if this is nothing but a storm in a teacup? The last thing I want is for Jane to turn up with some completely innocent explanation of where she's been and what she's been doing and to find I've set the police on her trail. That really would put the cat among the pigeons,' he added with a grimace. 'I could whistle for any chance of a reconciliation then. I can't help worrying though. Where the dickens is she?'

He shook his head, puzzled, then looked at Jack. 'Excuse me, Major Haldean, but did you say Michael Trevelyan had a bearing on a matter you're looking into?'

'That's probably a bit of a wild goose chase,' said Jack with a smile.

Laidlaw didn't smile back. 'Really?' He shrugged. 'I can't get that cigar stub out of my mind.'

'I doubt very much if Michael Trevelyan left it there, sir,' said Bill.

Laidlaw shot him a quick glance of acknowledgement. 'To be honest, that did occur to me, after what Major Haldean said.' He shrugged. 'That idea's crazy, I know. Forget it.'

There didn't seem much to add. With a nod to Jack, Bill stood up. 'Thank you for your time, sir. If, by any chance, Mrs Davenham does get in touch, could you let me know?'

'I certainly will, Mr Rackham.' He looked wretched. 'The Jane I know wouldn't just vanish. I'm sure something's happened to her.'

Betty plumped up the cushions and relaxed into the sofa, watching Jack light the spirit lamp under the coffee percolator on the hearth.

'That'll be done soon,' he said, standing up. 'And in the

meantime . . .' he said, sitting beside her. He slipped an arm round her waist and pulled her close.

'And in the meantime,' she said, a few minutes later, stroking the hair back behind his ear, 'you can tell me what on earth you think has happened to these poor women who've vanished.'

Jack hesitated. 'The thing is,' he said, catching hold of her hand and kissing it absently, 'I realise you're bosom buddies with Jenny Langton, but some of this stuff is a bit sensitive, you know? I mean, now Mrs Rotherwell's vanished and Mrs Davenham is God knows where, Bill's involved officially. There's far more to it than Jenny trying to find out the truth of what happened years ago.'

Betty looked at him reproachfully. 'Jack, I wouldn't tell her anything I shouldn't.'

'You told her Martin Langton was coming to see me.'

'That's different,' said Betty firmly. 'He's Jenny's brother and he was here to talk about Jenny. She had every right to hear what he had to say. That's a million miles away from me telling her anything you've learnt as part of an official investigation.'

'As a matter of fact, there's hardly anything Bill and I have learned as part of an official investigation,' said Jack ruefully. 'We know two women have disappeared. Where they've gone to is anyone's guess.'

'It couldn't be some sort of lunatic, could it?' asked Betty, frowning. 'Someone who goes round kidnapping middle-aged women?'

Jack laughed. 'Hardly. To be honest, we don't actually know Mrs Davenham really has disappeared. By the sound of things, she might have a new boyfriend. I suppose she could've jumped ship to avoid breaking the news to Andrew Laidlaw.'

'That seems quite a drastic solution,' said Betty. 'It can't be pleasant telling someone that you're not interested in them any more, but it seems a bit extreme to up and vanish, leaving everything you own. Especially if what you own are Parisian dresses.'

'You liked the sound of those, didn't you?' said Jack affectionately. 'Betty, you don't need anything from Paris to make yourself look lovely.'

'I'd still like to have them though,' she said with a laugh. 'I suppose if Mrs Davenham really has got a new boyfriend, she might have simply gone off for a few days but that explanation doesn't account for Mrs Rotherwell's disappearance.'

The plopping from the percolator subsided into a gentle bubbling noise. Jack got up to pour the coffee.

'Milk in mine, darling,' she said, lighting a cigarette. 'Jack, Mrs Rotherwell told you she was being watched by Michael Trevelyan. I don't like it.'

'Neither do I,' he said, handing her a cup of coffee. 'But you don't like it because he's Jenny's father.'

'Of course it's because he's Jenny's father!'

'How does Jenny feel about it?'

Betty started to speak, then hesitated. 'As a matter of fact, I don't really know. I know she very much wants to find the truth about her mother but I don't know how she feels about her father. Uncomfortable, I think is the best description.' She frowned. 'I know how I'd feel. I'd be horrified.'

'Yes, but this is Jenny Langton we're talking about, sweetheart, not you.'

'I still think it'd be a rotten thing for her to find out.'

'That's not really relevant to the facts, is it?'

'No, but you might think of another explanation. To start with, Mrs Rotherwell could've been mistaken. After all, she only *thought* she saw him. Why was she so certain?'

'She'd answered my advert in the paper,' said Jack, with that uneasy sense of guilt returning. If he hadn't placed that advert, Mrs Rotherwell might still be living happily at the Royal Park Hotel. 'That would've brought it all back to her mind.'

Betty squeezed his hand. 'That's probably true,' she said uncertainly. 'She would've been thinking of the Trevelyans. It all seemed so innocent at the time, didn't it? You were doing a favour for Jenny. You weren't to know what would happen.' She sighed in exasperation. 'I hate the idea that Jenny's father is to blame.'

'The father who wrote a list of poisons in a diary, together with the date of his wife's disappearance? The father who produced a forged letter, supposedly from his wife?'

'That might have been sent by somebody else.'

'Who?'

Betty pulled on her cigarette again. 'What about Andrew Laidlaw?' she said after a few moments. 'I must say, I rather liked him, but he could've had it in for Michael Trevelyan.'

'Why?'

'Oh, I don't know. He could've been madly in love with Caroline, I suppose. She could've been having an affair with Mr Laidlaw. He's rather attractive in an older sort of way. Not that he would've been older then, if you see what I mean.'

'I think I can follow that,' said Jack.

'We know Jenny's mother didn't want to go to New Zealand. That could have made her turn to Andrew Laidlaw.'

'But Laidlaw was married to Violet, old Wild's daughter.'

Betty grinned. 'That's very sweet of you, Jack, to have such strong views about men and marriage.'

'I'm pure in heart,' muttered Jack. 'I can produce certificates to prove it.'

'Besides that,' said Betty, giggling, 'we know he started the affair with Jane Davenham while Violet Laidlaw was still alive.'

'To be fair to him, while I'm not saying it's okay he should be seeing Jane Davenham while his wife was still alive, I think it's very understandable. After years spent dancing round an invalid, he meets this woman and obviously fell for her like a ton of bricks. That's not the case twenty years ago. The objection to him having an affair with Caroline Trevelyan is that he'd benefited hugely from being married to Violet. Don't you remember, Mrs Shilton told us he was absolutely old Mr Wild's blue-eyed boy?'

'So?'

'So he had a lot to lose if he was caught playing around. And, to be fair to him, everyone says he really was devoted to Violet.'

'Until he skidded off the rails and met Jane Davenham.'

'Fair enough,' acknowledged Jack. 'All right, Miss Cynic, despite him having everything to lose, let's grant he had an affair with Caroline Trevelyan. What then?'

'Well, he murders her, of course. Maybe he didn't actually have an affair but wanted to. She rejected him and threatened to tell her cousin, Violet.' Betty looked rather pleased with herself. 'That'd make it awkward for him, especially as he was the blue-eyed boy, as you said. Then he shoved the blame onto Michael Trevelyan.'

'That's possible, I suppose.'

'It's more than possible,' she said warming to her theme. 'After all, we know he was around at the time. Didn't he have coffee with Caroline Trevelyan and Mrs Rotherwell the morning Caroline vanished?'

'Well, yes, so he did. He told us as much.'

'Actually, Jack,' she said, catching hold of his arm excitedly, 'that proves Mr Laidlaw knows Mrs Rotherwell!'

'If you can describe meeting someone for coffee twenty years ago as knowing them, yes, I suppose so.'

'Well, don't you see? Mr Laidlaw runs into Mrs Rotherwell and bumps her off!'

'But why?'

'Because Mrs Rotherwell knew Jane Davenham and knew Andrew Laidlaw was having an affair with her!'

Jack hid his head in his hands. 'Betty,' he said in a muffled voice, 'stop talking complete mashed potatoes, will you?'

'Well, I like that . . .' Betty began indignantly.

Jack looked up. 'Darling. Sweetheart. Follow me here. By the time Mrs Rotherwell came back to England, Violet Laidlaw was dead. What's more, dead from natural causes. When we got back to the Yard, Bill telephoned the doctor who attended Mrs Laidlaw.'

'How did you find out who the doctor was?'

'Bill dug up the death certificate. The doctor was shocked that there should be any doubt whatsoever about Violet Laidlaw's death. He's the family doctor and knew both Mr and Mrs Laidlaw well. Bill had to tell him it was a routine enquiry, checking up on death statistics, as it seemed a bit rich to cast suspicion on Laidlaw without any cause. Apparently Mrs Laidlaw had a heart condition, exacerbated by her mental state, for years. The doctor said that in his opinion, it was only Laidlaw's care that kept her going as long as she did. If there was anything that could be done for her, Laidlaw did it without question.'

'I must say that sounds rather nice of him,' said Betty.

'Yes, it does, doesn't it? There's also the minor point that if you are going to bump off your wife so you can marry your girlfriend, you might as well wait until your girlfriend has sorted out her own matrimonial tangles. By the time Mrs Rotherwell came back to England, Andrew Laidlaw could have been having affairs with fifty Jane Davenhams without anyone giving a tinker's curse.'

'He might not have wanted it to get about, though. Especially as he was supposed to have been so very devoted to his wife.' She clicked her tongue in irritation. 'I just wish Jenny's father wasn't involved. Look, say it is Mr Laidlaw . . .'

'Here we go again,' said Jack with a smile. 'What did he do, apart from bump off Mrs Rotherwell?'

'Well, he bumped off Mrs Davenham as well. To cover it up, he pretended he'd been madly in love with her.'

'It seems a bit wholesale, but all right,' said Jack grinning. 'For the sake of argument, we'll say he did. What's his motive?'

'Perhaps Jane Davenham found out somehow that he murdered Caroline Trevelyan years ago. Actually, he might not have murdered Mrs Davenham. She might have been suspicious of him and fled. But in the meantime, she's told her old friend, Mrs Rotherwell, all about him. Then Andrew Laidlaw discovers that Mrs Rotherwell knows all about it.'

'How? Does she confront him, saying, "I Know All"?'

'Beast,' said Betty punching him in the side. 'You're laughing at me.'

'That's because it's a goofy idea. If Mrs Rotherwell had any idea Laidlaw was responsible for Caroline Trevelyan's disappearance, surely she'd have mentioned it to me when we had lunch. She also came with me to Scotland Yard, where she had Bill's undivided attention. She could've told him. And then, just to cap it off, she had Detective Constable Horrocks sitting in the lobby at her beck and call. She could've told him anytime she wanted.'

'That is a problem,' said Betty in a small voice. 'I just don't want it to be Jenny's father who's to blame.'

'Unfortunately, as I said before, that's neither here nor there. Just think what Mrs Rotherwell *did* tell me. And Bill, for that matter. And that was that she'd seen Trevelyan and that he'd seen her. Don't forget, he's wanted for murder. Mrs Rotherwell is a threat to him, all right. A serious threat.'

'Oh, I suppose so,' said Betty impatiently. 'Where does this Mrs Davenham fit in, then? What's the connection between Jenny's father and her? I suppose she could've just have happened to have known Mrs Rotherwell by coincidence and then gone off with a new boyfriend, but it's much neater if there's a proper connection.'

'There might not be any connection,' said Jack with a shrug. 'It really could be just a coincidence but here's a guess, if you want one. Matthew Rotherwell told us that his mother had met Jane Davenham. Mrs Rotherwell told us that Trevelyan was keeping an eye on her. That's pretty scary. She could've easily have said something to her old friend . . .'

His voice trailed away. 'That's it!' He sat upright and snapped his fingers together. 'Blimey, Betty, that really is it! Mrs Rotherwell *told* us, both me and Bill, that she'd caught a fleeting glance of Trevelyan when she was with "a friend". Mrs Rotherwell hardly had any friends, not now. Not after having lived in Ceylon for years. She hardly knew anyone in England. What's the betting that old friend is Jane Davenham?'

Betty gulped. 'That's horribly convincing, Jack. But why didn't she tell her son?'

'I don't know,' said Jack thoughtfully. 'Maybe she felt protective towards him. As I said, it must've been scary. However, if the two women were actually together when Mrs Rotherwell spotted Trevelyan, she could have easily pointed him out.'

Betty stared at him. 'That's right,' she said quietly. She gripped his arm. 'Jack! The new boyfriend, Mrs Davenham's new boyfriend. Could he be Trevelyan?'

'What? But surely Mrs Rotherwell would've said so.'

'Would she? She might not know. Say it really was a fleeting glance. Mrs Rotherwell tells her friend all about him and the friend – Jane Davenham – listens horrified, but without really believing it. She says nothing at the time, but then determines to have it out with him when they're alone.'

Jack shook himself and let out a deep breath. 'It could be. I hope not. However, this is nothing but speculation.'

'If I'm right,' began Betty hesitantly, 'why's it all happening now? Say it is Jenny's father who's behind everything. Why's he suddenly reappeared now?'

'Because we've been digging into it,' said Jack bitterly. 'We've poked a stick into the hornet's nest.'

'Maybe he hasn't reappeared,' said Betty, continuing her chain of thought. 'Maybe he's always been here. After all, it was Mrs Rotherwell who's newly arrived. Jenny's always said that she thought someone was watching her. She's thought that on and off for years. Maybe it's him.'

A search of Mrs Rotherwell's effects in storage turned up, as Julia Rotherwell had predicted, no old letters but a handful of snapshots. With a photograph provided by Matthew Rotherwell and help from the hotel, an increasingly worried Matthew and Julia Rotherwell agreed to a description being issued to the press and a missing persons enquiry being sent out to all the police authorities in the British Isles.

'I don't think much of the description in the papers,' said Jack, who had called in on Bill in his office in Scotland Yard. 'Forty-eight years old, medium height, grey-haired, spare build, wears gold, wire-rimmed, round spectacles and gold wedding ring, speaks with a firm, clear voice. Last seen wearing mid-calf-length, double-breasted, grey wool coat, fastened with three large carved buttons, with inset sleeves and deep cuffs and natural straw cloche hat trimmed with wax fruit, etcetera, etcetera. That could describe a whole raft of middle-aged women. I can't say I think much of the photo, either. It's a good description of her coat. She was wearing that outfit when I met her at the Criterion. The hat was unforgettable. It's a pity that the description of the woman herself isn't as detailed.'

'Well, can you add anything to it?' demanded Bill.

Jack hesitated. 'I don't know that I can,' he admitted, rubbing his nose.

'That's the trouble,' said Bill. 'It's blinkin' hard to describe someone so that they're instantly recognisable. In fact, I don't think it's possible. We only got the clothes she was wearing because the clerk on the desk remembered the hat. He had the impression she was wearing grey and Julia Rotherwell supplied the description of it. That's where the photo comes in.'

'A picture's worth a thousand words, as they say in the adverts,' murmured Jack. 'Only in this instance, I wouldn't agree.'

'It's the best there is,' said Bill with a shrug. 'Matthew Rotherwell chose it. The trouble is, it's obviously taken in tropical sunlight and she's wearing a hat. However, as Mr Rotherwell said, we wouldn't even have that, if they didn't have a neighbour who owned a Box Brownie.'

Jack put down the newspaper. 'Has anyone seen her?'

'A good few people *think* they've seen her,' said Bill with a grimace. 'I don't know how many middle-aged women of medium height and build with grey coats and straw hats with wax fruit on them there are in England, but I'm beginning to think that we'll shortly have a record of every one of them. The Chief,' he added with feeling, 'is beginning to get a bit shirty about the amount of police time this is taking up.'

'He does know about the Michael Trevelyan connection?' asked Jack.

Bill nodded. 'He does. In fact, he suggested that I call round and see Mrs Shilton. If Michael Trevelyan really is alive and kicking, then it's at least possible that his sister knows something about it. From what you've told me she was absolutely certain that he was innocent, so he may very well turn to her. After all, he's got to live somewhere.'

'Mrs Shilton's got at least one servant,' Jack said thoughtfully. 'I doubt if Trevelyan would risk coming to the house.'

'Nevertheless, it's the only connection we've got.' He raised an inquisitive eyebrow. 'I did ask the Chief if I could ask you to come with me. After all, Mrs Shilton has met you. She might be a bit more forthcoming, as she knows you as a friend of her niece's. In fact, if you're free this afternoon, you could give her a ring and arrange to see her.'

It was on the morning of the same day that the doorbell rang at number 34, Catton Street. Mrs Muscliff wiped her hands on a tea towel and went to open the door.

At first sight she thought the man standing on the doorstep was a foreigner. He had a bushy dark beard and very brown skin, but his voice, when he spoke, was reassuringly cockney. 'Mornin' Missus. Delivery for a party name of . . .' He turned his head to look at the label on the box. 'Langton. Miss J. Langton.'

Mrs Muscliff unconsciously took in the van outside, the man's khaki overalls and then, her eyes widening, the size of the box. 'Whatever's in there?'

The man shrugged. 'Dunno. It could be a chair or somfink.'

'You'd better bring it in,' said Mrs Muscliff, standing to one side. She glanced at the stairs leading off the hall. 'Miss Langton's room is on the second floor.'

'I'll take it up to her, shall I?' asked the delivery man, hefting the box. 'It's not too heavy but it's awkward.'

'Thanks,' said Mrs Muscliff. 'That's very good of you.' She doubted if Miss Langton would be able to manage it and she certainly didn't want a box that size cluttering up her hall. 'She's out at work at the moment, so I'll just get the key.'

She took the key from the board, then led the way up the stairs at a stately plod, the delivery man grunting behind her.

As she opened the door to Jenny's room, the delivery man paused, his head to one side. 'Was that the doorbell?'

'I didn't hear nothing.'

'I'm sure I heard the bell.'

'Drat the thing,' she grumbled, setting off down the stairs. 'I'd better see who it is.'

The door to Mrs Shilton's house was opened, as before, by Edith, the maid, who greeted Jack and Bill with a worried smile. 'It's nice to see you again, sir,' she said to Jack as she took their coats. She cast an anxious glance behind her, down the hallway. 'There's something up. I don't know what, but the mistress is upset.'

'About us coming to see her?' asked Jack.

Edith shook her head. 'No, it's not that. I don't know what's wrong and that's the truth. If you could come this way, though, the mistress is expecting you. Miss Langton's here as well.'

She showed them into the sitting room. Jenny Langton stood up and greeted them with a look of relief. 'Mr Rackham! I'm really pleased to see you. And you too, of course, Jack. Come in and sit down. Aunty told me you were on your way. I didn't think you'd mind if I was here as well. I'd have to tell you what's happened, anyway.'

Jack looked at Mrs Shilton's face. She sat pale-faced, with a hand to her mouth. 'Whatever's wrong?' he asked, pulling up a chair.

Mrs Shilton glanced from him to Bill and shook her head.

'We can tell Jack, Aunty,' urged Jenny. 'And I've met Mr Rackham before.' She glanced at Bill with a shy smile. 'I told Aunty that I'd met you.'

Mrs Shilton gathered herself to speak, then stopped.

'Please tell us what's wrong,' asked Jack.

Mrs Shilton blinked gratefully at him, reassured by his tone. 'I can't understand it!' she said with a sniff, her voice wavering. She looked at Jenny. 'I can't think why your father would do such a thing.'

Jack blinked as the significance of the words struck him. '*Your father?*'

Jenny nodded.

Bill drew his breath in. 'Are we talking about Michael Trevelyan?' he said quietly. Mrs Shilton nodded miserably. 'I think,' said Bill grimly, 'you'd better tell me all about it.'

Mrs Shilton shrank back.

Jenny saw her aunt's hesitation, and plunged in. 'It happened this morning,' she said in a rush, silencing her aunt's protests. 'A delivery man arrived at my house with a big box for me. I live in a boarding house on Catton Street, off Southampton Row,' she explained to Bill. 'There's four other lodgers and the landlady lives there as well, of course. I was at work, but the landlady opened the door to the man. Well, usually the landlady would simply tell him to leave the box in the hall, but, as I say, it was a big box, so he offered to carry it upstairs. That seemed very nice of him, so she took him upstairs and opened my door. I usually keep it locked, but she has a key, of course. When I got home, the landlady mentioned it. I wasn't expecting a parcel so I was curious, naturally enough, so I went straight upstairs and opened the box.'

She paused.

'Well?' demanded Jack. 'What was in the box?'

'Nothing. It was empty, apart from this. This was inside.'

She reached into her handbag and took out a small jeweller's case and passed it to Jack. He opened it with a puzzled frown, then gave a silent whistle.

Inside, set on cotton wool, was a square silver brooch made of twisted silver wire, with a tassel of fine silver links. It was set with a square-cut sapphire with tiny sapphires inset into the silver filigree. Although striking, it looked heavy and old-fashioned. Jack could imagine Mrs Shilton wearing it, but not Jenny. 'It's Edwardian, I think,' he said, turning it over in his hand.

Jenny nodded. 'That's what I thought.' She swallowed. 'It came with a note.' She held out a folded piece of paper to Jack, who opened it.

There was one typewritten line on the note. '"This was your mother's",' he read. '"She would have wanted you to have it. She always loved you".'

He stared at Jenny.

'Can I see that?' asked Bill, urgently.

At a nod from Jenny, Jack passed it over. 'And you think this is from your father?' Bill demanded.

'Who else can it be from?' she said. 'Who else would have my mother's brooch?'

Mrs Shilton gave a sniff. 'I don't understand it,' she said once more. 'Your father said it was best for you if he disappeared . . .' She stopped as she saw the intense look Bill gave her. She gave a little cry and turned to Jack.

'When did he tell you that?' asked Jack, his voice very gentle.

She gave a little sob, dabbed her eyes, then screwed her handkerchief into a ball. 'I know it was wrong of me,' she said desperately. 'I know that, but he was my brother and I *knew* he was innocent. After he escaped from the police, he came here at the dead of night.' She glanced at Jenny. 'Your Uncle Alan was alive then. He told Michael that the best thing he could do was to give himself up, but Michael said that someone wanted him dead and he had to get away.'

She gave a little wriggle of dissent. 'I couldn't believe that. I mean, who would want to harm Michael? He never did any wrong to anyone.'

'There was the letter,' said Jenny uncertainly. 'The letter my mother supposedly wrote. Whoever wrote that obviously wished him harm.'

'It must've been some sort of misunderstanding,' said Mrs

Shilton helplessly. 'Anything else would be . . .' She sought for a word. '*Wicked*. I just don't believe it.'

Mrs Shilton, thought Jack, probably didn't believe it. She was the sort of person who, kindly herself, had been brought up with the axiom that if you didn't have anything nice to say about anyone, then don't say it. What's more, you mustn't think it, either. If that meant ignoring the obvious, then the obvious would be ignored.

'What did your brother do?' asked Bill.

Mrs Shilton sniffed. 'He went to Australia. Alan didn't like it, but I persuaded him to help with money and clothes and so on. I *knew* he was innocent,' she repeated, correctly interpreting Bill's look. 'We had to help. Once Michael was safely on the ship, Alan washed his hands of him. He said he never wanted to hear from him again. He was very firm about it,' she added with a petulant note.

'And did you?' asked Bill. 'Did you hear from him?'

Mrs Shilton hesitated, then looked away. 'I had a postcard from Sydney. It just said, "Arrived. M.". That's the last I ever heard from him,' she said in a muffled voice, the handkerchief pressed to her mouth.

Jack glanced at Bill and silently shook his head. He might be a cynic, but he just didn't believe her.

'I think you did hear from him again though, didn't you, Mrs Shilton?' said Bill.

She gave him a quick, frightened glance and shook her head. 'No. That's not true.'

'Really, Mrs Shilton?' asked Jack persuasively. 'Surely you've seen him recently?'

'No!' She sat upright in her chair, obviously summoning up courage. 'How dare you suggest such a thing?' She gathered herself together. 'I would remind you that this is my house and you are here by my invitation,' she said, her voice trembling. 'I am not accustomed to having my word doubted.' She reached out her hand to the bell. 'I think it is about time you left.'

Bill hesitated for a long moment, then getting up, bowed slightly. 'Very well, Mrs Shilton,' he said with as much good grace as he could muster. 'As you say, this is your house and I'm sure neither of us have any desire to upset you.'

Jack stood up. There was nothing else for it. He caught Jenny's apologetic expression and smiled. 'There's something I'd like to know though, before we push off.' He looked at the brooch on the table. 'It's such a little case. You said the box it came in, the box the delivery man carried upstairs, was large.'

'It was. I thought at first it must be a chair or a small table, although I hadn't ordered anything of the sort.'

'So whoever sent the brooch went to a lot of trouble putting it in a much bigger box. Why?'

Jenny blinked at him. 'I don't know. I was so bowled over by the brooch and the note, I didn't think of that. I just snatched up the case and came here, to show it to Aunty. It's all very peculiar, I must say.' She frowned. 'It seems pointless.'

'Unless the delivery man had a particular reason for wanting to see where you lived,' said Jack. 'A personal reason, perhaps?'

Jenny looked bewildered. 'What do you mean?'

'Maybe the delivery man wanted to see your room.'

Jenny stared at him, then realisation struck her. 'Of course! It's obvious! If my father had just wanted to give me my mother's brooch, he could have posted it. This way he could bring it himself.' She turned to her aunt. 'The man – the delivery man – he *must* have been my father! He didn't just send the brooch, he was the delivery man who brought it.' She drew her breath in. 'He would want to see where I lived, wouldn't he? No one else would want to.'

'Jennifer,' said her aunt with desperate warning.

Jennifer turned an anxious face to her. 'Don't you see? It has to be him.'

Mrs Shilton blanched. Much as she clearly disliked the idea, that was obviously the conclusion she had come to as well. 'There is,' she said repressively, 'no need to speculate on the matter.'

Jenny's eyes widened. 'He knows where I live.' She looked at Bill anxiously. 'That's a bit scary.'

Bill instinctively started forward, then stopped. 'Miss Langton,' he said seriously, 'you will be careful, won't you? Please, can I ask you not to answer any unexpected invitations? At least not without telling either myself or Major Haldean?'

Mrs Shilton gave a squeal of outrage. 'Mr Rackham, what

are you implying? If this man, this delivery man, is my brother, which I do not for one moment believe, he would never harm Jennifer. The idea is utterly ridiculous.'

Jenny Langton obviously didn't think it was ridiculous. She had gone rather white. 'I'll be careful, Mr Rackham.' She shot a glance at Mrs Shilton and added quietly, 'I can't forget what I saw in the garden.'

'Enough!' said Mrs Shilton imperiously. 'Gentlemen, please leave.'

'Just one more thing,' said Jack, as Edith came into the room in answer to the bell. 'You might care to check your belongings when you get back to your room, Jenny. You might find something's missing.'

Jenny stared at him. 'All right. I will. But he couldn't have taken anything, not with the landlady there.'

'That's enough,' said Mrs Shilton stiffly. 'These gentlemen are leaving, Edith. Please show them out.'

'Well,' said Bill, as they walked away down Cannon Hill Lane towards the car, 'talk about being sent away with a flea in your ear. I hope to God that Miss Langton does take my advice.'

'Don't worry, Bill. The poor girl was really rattled, despite having Mrs Shilton tell her how wonderful her father is.'

Bill gave a snort of disgust. 'Mrs Shilton knows a damn sight more than she should if you ask me. Jack, that delivery man has to have been Trevelyan, doesn't he?'

'It's hard to think who else it could've been.'

Bill shook his head in disbelief. 'But Jack, Trevelyan's been hidden for twenty years! What the devil's he playing at? Why on earth has he turned up now?'

'Because Jenny's turned up,' said Jack. 'He's bound to be curious about her.'

Bill swore under his breath. 'He's taking a hell of a risk.'

'Was he? Why should Jennifer Langton's landlady think he was anything other than a helpful delivery man?'

'Yes, dammit, you're right. Speaking of the landlady, I'd better interview her before I'm much older.'

'Are you going to see her now?'

'I might as well. I want to get all the details she can

remember while they're still fresh in her mind. Do you want to come?'

Jack hesitated. 'I think I'd better go home. Drop in this evening and let me know how you got on.'

'Thanks. I will.' Bill gave an irritated sigh. 'Not that I imagine she'll be able to tell us much we don't already know. I hate this business, Jack. If you're right, and Trevelyan really is Jane Davenham's new boyfriend, God only knows what's happened to her. Nothing good, at a guess.' He swallowed hard. 'I hope Miss Langton remembers what she promised about being careful. But I say again, why's he reappeared now? He's kept his head down for years.'

'It has to be because of Jenny Langton. After all, she's only just found out who she really is. Despite what Mrs Shilton said, like you, I'm sure she's in contact with him. She'd be certain to tell him all about it. It probably awoke all sorts of feelings in him. He could easily find out from her where Jennifer lived and when she would be at work.'

'That's not a nice thought. I wish we had proof, Jack,' he added in exasperation. 'I've guessed that Mrs Shilton is in touch with her brother, but I can't prove it.'

They reached the car. Bill paused with his hand on the door. 'Why do you think Mrs Shilton knows where her brother is?'

'For the same reasons as you do. I thought her reactions were very telling to this delivery man stunt for a start. He might have gone to Australia years ago but he's back now and no mistake. She knows. I'll tell you something else, too. When Betty, Jennifer Langton and I saw Mrs Shilton for the first time, although Mrs Shilton was very keen to tell us Trevelyan was innocent, she was dead against Jenny's idea that we should investigate. She said she didn't want to stir up the unwelcome publicity that she had suffered from years ago. That might be true, but I think it's at least as likely that she wanted to keep her brother safely out of sight.'

'That's a dangerous game she's playing. I'm going to recommend that we keep an eye on Mrs Shilton's house.'

Jack pulled a face. 'It's an obvious precaution, but it'd be risky for Trevelyan to turn up as himself. That girl Edith would be bound to gossip.'

'He doesn't seem to mind risk,' grunted Bill. 'To be honest, I'm doubtful it'll come to anything, but it's something I can do. I can't question Mrs Shilton without proof, as much as I'd like to. There's such a thing as Judges' Rules, but if he does show up, we've got him.'

# TWELVE

'That's probably Bill,' said Jack as the doorbell rang. 'I told you I'd asked him to drop in.'

'So you did, darling,' said Betty, putting down her coffee cup.

The door opened and Kathleen, the maid, showed in not just Bill but Jenny Langton as well.

'We met on the doorstep,' explained Bill cheerfully. 'My word, that coffee smells good.'

'Can we have two more cups, please, Kathleen,' said Betty. 'It's nice to see you, Jenny.' She looked at her quizzically. 'Is everything all right? You look a bit flustered.'

'There's nothing much wrong, but I wanted to talk to Jack. I hope you don't mind me dropping in unannounced.'

'Of course not. Come and sit down and you can talk to Jack as much as you like. He doesn't charge for it,' she added with a smile. 'Is coffee all right or would you like something stronger?'

'Coffee for me, please,' said Jenny.

Jack gestured to Bill to follow him to the sideboard. 'I'm sure you can manage a whisky and splash as well as a coffee,' he said, then added quietly, 'you saw the landlady?'

Bill nodded.

'Is it okay to talk? With Jenny here?'

'Yes, there's nothing much we didn't already know.'

Kathleen brought in the two extra cups and Betty poured the coffee. 'What is it, Jenny?' she asked. 'Has anything happened?'

Jenny shook her head. 'Not really, but it was something Jack said this afternoon. You know about the delivery man, Betty?'

'Yes, Jack told me.'

'Well, it was quite a shock when Jack pointed out that the delivery man more or less had to be my father.' She looked at Jack ruefully. 'Aunty Gwyn thought so too. She hadn't worked it out until you said so. She thinks, though, that it was actually very sweet of him, to want to see where I lived and to give me my mother's brooch.'

'Do you think it's sweet of him?' asked Betty.

Jenny hesitated. 'Not really. I'm glad to have the brooch but I wish he hadn't done it. I don't like it. I hate this feeling of being followed. It's . . . it's unsettling.'

'I'll say so,' said Bill with feeling.

'I wouldn't mind so much if he had posted the brooch to me,' she continued, lighting a cigarette. 'I'd have liked that, but the thought of him being in my room . . . Anyway,' she said, sitting up straight. 'I remembered what you said, Jack, to have a look and see if anything was missing. I couldn't see anything at first, but you were absolutely right. I had a framed photo of Martin, Eric and me in the garden at home. It's gone. It was on my bookcase but it's gone. It has to be him who's taken it. No one else would want it.'

'But how could he have taken it?' asked Betty. 'Surely your landlady didn't leave him alone in your room? He could've looted the place.'

'I asked her that,' said Jenny. 'Apparently the doorbell rang and she had to go and answer it.'

'That was very convenient,' said Jack slowly. He looked at Bill. 'Do you know about this?'

Bill nodded. 'Yes, I do. And guess what, there was no one at the door.'

'She just imagined a ring at the doorbell, you mean?'

'Apparently the delivery man imagined it. It took a bit of doing to get the story out of her, as she thought it was completely unimportant. It was the delivery man who said he'd heard a ring at the door and she went to check it. She didn't think anything much of it, because by the time she'd got to the front door and opened it, the delivery man was coming down the stairs.'

'That doesn't seem to get us very far,' said Jack. 'Can she describe him?'

'She said he seemed very cheerful and obliging, but with very dark skin and hair. She wondered if he was foreign, at first, but he spoke like a cockney. He had a beard, apparently.'

'I bet he did,' said Jack.

Jenny looked puzzled. 'He was wearing a false beard,' translated Betty. 'That's what you mean, isn't it, Jack?'

Jack nodded. 'It doesn't add up to much, does it, Bill? Dark skin, dark hair – both out of a bottle, I bet – and a beard which could be bought at any tuppenny ha'penny joke shop.'

'Add a cockney accent – assumed, I suppose – brown overalls and a black cap, and there you have it. It's not much but it's a good disguise. I had a look at the box, but it's just an ordinary packing case. I've got the box but I don't think it can tell us anything. Miss Langton's name and address was typed on a pasted slip, but that was all.'

'How was the parcel carried?' asked Jack. 'Was it brought in a van or on a bicycle or what?'

'There was a van,' said Bill. 'That's the only thing that might amount to a possible lead, if you can call it that. We've checked the local hire companies and no one hired out a van to any but a regular customer. We haven't had any reports of a van stolen or missing, so it looks as if he might own it. The landlady saw the van but didn't notice if there was any name written on it.'

Jenny shuddered. 'I don't like it. I know what Aunt Gwyn says, but I hate the thought he's been in my room.'

She pulled deeply on her cigarette. 'Jack, there's something I want to ask you. I read in the newspaper about this poor woman, this Mrs Rotherwell, who's disappeared. Is she the same Mrs Rotherwell who wrote to Aunt Gwyn? The Mrs Rotherwell you met?'

Jack exchanged glances with Bill and nodded reluctantly. 'Yes, she is. As a matter of fact, both Bill and I met her.'

'And she's disappeared?' said Jenny sharply. She looked at the two men with sudden apprehension. 'You met her because you were trying to help me. Did she have anything to do with my father?'

Jack hesitated before answering. He had warned Betty about saying too much to Jenny Langton. The connection with Michael Trevelyan had not been made in the press and he didn't want to give away anything the police would rather keep to themselves.

'It's all right, Jack,' said Bill. 'I think Miss Langton should know the whole story.' He looked at Jenny. 'I'm going to tell you everything we know. It's not just Mrs Rotherwell, there's a Mrs Davenham as well. Especially after this incident with the brooch, I think it's too dangerous for you not to know. I want you to be on your guard.'

'But that's horrible!' said Jenny, who had listened in mounting horror to Bill's account. 'Both of those women had people who cared about them. Mrs Rotherwell had a family. Her son and his wife are expecting a baby. They sound really nice people.' She gulped. 'I only hope they're both found soon.'

'So do I,' agreed Bill fervently. 'We're doing as much as we can. We've had a big response from the missing persons appeal concerning Mrs Rotherwell in the newspapers. You never know. One of those reports might turn up trumps yet.'

It was two days later. Mr Harold Royston-Jones, of 5, Summer's Court off Wigmore Street, contentedly enjoying his evening pipe and whisky, skimmed through the *Evening Standard*. He glanced at the picture of Mrs Amelia Rotherwell, tutted sympathetically, and, with a contented sigh, turned to the racing results.

It had been his wife's idea to rent a pied-à-terre in London. It was actually, to his way of thinking, Westminster, but it could, with only a small stretch of his wife's imagination, count as Mayfair.

A splash of water fell on the report from Alexandra Park. He stared at it, puzzled. Water? What the dickens . . .? Another larger splash fell.

Pipe in mouth, he glanced up, then, with a cry of alarm, pushed his chair over and staggered backwards, out from under the bulging ceiling.

'Evelyn!' he bellowed.

His wife appeared at the sitting-room door, then gazed in horror as, with a deafening noise, the entire ceiling collapsed in a ferocious deluge of water, wood and plaster.

Then came a creaking and grinding as more planks splintered, collapsed and fell. Time seemed to slow down as part of a bath crunched through the ceiling and hung crazily through the plaster.

With a stifled yelp, Evelyn Royston-Jones put her hand to her mouth.

A sodden grey mass flung out its arms and fell from the bath onto the debris below.

And then she saw the face and screamed.

'I think,' said Bill over the telephone, 'that we've found Mrs Rotherwell. 'It's 5, Summer's Court, off Wigmore Street.'

Jack hardly liked to ask, but he did so anyway. 'Is she dead?'

'Very.'

Bill met Jack at the door to Summer's Court. 'It was actually the tenants of the flat below that gave the alarm,' he explained, as they walked up the stairs. 'That's a Mr and Mrs Royston-Jones. He was reading the paper, poor bloke, when the ceiling collapsed in a flood above him.'

'A flood?'

'Yep. Water everywhere, to say nothing of wood, plaster, you name it. The mess is incredible and it stinks to high heaven. What also came through the ceiling was the bath – and in the bath there was the body.'

Jack winced. 'Was she drowned?'

'That's something only the post-mortem can discover, but she'd certainly been in the bath for days, poor woman.'

'Was she dressed?'

Bill nodded. 'Yes. Fully dressed.'

No one would get into a bath fully clothed, thought Jack. That made it murder.

They reached the door of number 5. 'Prepare yourself,' warned Bill. 'It's nasty.'

It was.

The first thing that struck him was the smell, a stink of wet plaster and rotten wood. Hand to his mouth, he eased himself into the crowded room.

Among the policemen and the attendants from the morgue, Jack recognised Dr Roude, the police surgeon, arms crossed, bag at his side, waiting for the photographer to finish.

Jack looked at the body sprawled on the rubble with a sinking heart. He'd seen men drowned in shell holes in the war, but this was the first time he'd ever seen a drowned woman. The sight turned his stomach. The swollen, bloated flesh was beyond recognition, but the grey coat was Mrs Rotherwell's, sure enough.

The photographer crouched on the floor and the flash gun blazed. 'I think that's all we need, sir,' he said, getting to his feet and looking at Bill.

Dr Roude skirted the debris and nodded to Jack. 'Hello, Haldean. The Chief Inspector said this was one of yours.'

'I wish it wasn't,' said Jack tightly. 'The poor woman's got a family. I feel sorry for them.'

'Poor beggars,' said Dr Roude. 'Unfortunately, we'll have to ask them to formally identify the body.'

Jack winced. 'It seems rotten to put someone through that for no good reason. I can't see how anyone could identify her, just by looking.'

'No, neither can I, but it's the law.'

'Is there any way to say for certain who she is?'

Dr Roude shrugged. 'The relatives could identify her belongings, perhaps. If she had a dentist, his records would confirm who she was. You met her, I understand?'

'Yes, and so did Bill Rackham, but I couldn't swear to her.'

'I don't think anyone could.' He raised his voice. 'Can we remove the body, Chief Inspector?'

'Yes, I think we've finished here for the moment.'

Dr Roude waved the mortuary men forward. They rolled the body onto a stretcher and covered it with a canvas sheet. With a sense of relief, Jack watched them leave. 'Shall we have a look at the flat upstairs?' he asked quietly.

'Give me a moment,' begged Bill. 'After seeing that, I could do with a breather and a cigarette.'

'I could do with a stiff drink,' muttered Jack. 'But that'll have to wait.'

Number 8, the flat – or, rather, the pied-à-terre – upstairs had, according to Mr Cullin, the porter, been taken a fortnight ago by, 'A gent of the name of Smith. Posh-like,' continued the porter, 'but that's what you'd expect. Very nice, it is, here. As I say, posh. They rents them ready-furnished. No, there weren't no servant. None of the residents have servants, with only having the one bedroom, you see, though most have a char come in daily. No, Mr Smith didn't have no char. I 'spects he would have made arrangements sooner or later. Very nice people we get, very nice. He seemed very nice too, but at first sight, I thought he was foreign. He had very dark hair and brown skin, like he might be an Indian or some such, but he was English, right enough.'

'Did he have a beard?' asked Jack, swapping glances with Bill.

'Yes, he did. There was a lady too. I saw her a couple of times. Well, it's no business of mine what the residents do, as long as they don't cause annoyance, but she stayed over, that I do know. Describe her?' Mr Cullin puffed out his cheeks. 'Ordinary. Nicely dressed. Round about forty, I suppose. There's nothing much to describe. I haven't seen either of them for at least a week. Not that I see everyone who comes and goes, of course. All the residents have their own keys and see to themselves, unless they need help with bags and so on.'

'Were there any visitors?' asked Bill.

The porter shook his head, then hesitated. 'No, wait, I tell a lie. There was one, a lady. She came in with the lady I spoke about, chatting away they were, very friendly, and didn't need any help from me. That was just after Mr Smith had moved in. I can't swear to the day, so don't ask me. And don't ask me to describe her, either, cos I can't. I only seed her in passing.'

'Isn't there anything you can remember?' demanded Bill.

Jack picked up the newspaper on the porter's desk and flicked through it until he came to the picture of Mrs Rotherwell. 'I don't suppose that rings a bell, does it?' he asked, showing the man the photograph.

Mr Cullin gaped at the picture. 'That's her! True as I'm stood here, that's her! She had a different hat, one of these that's all over with wax fruit, but that's her.'

'I thought it might be,' said Bill grimly. The picture in the newspapers had, if not come up trumps, proved its worth after all.

A telephone call to Brook and Bailey, the landlords, established that the rent was four guineas a week and Mr Smith had paid a month in advance.

'It did cross my mind,' said Jack, as they walked up the stairs, 'that our Mr Smith was lucky to get a place like this, with flats being so hard to come by, but I suppose if you wave enough money around, that problem disappears.'

'It certainly helps,' said Bill. 'He paid cash, naturally. He would. And, of course, it was banked a fortnight ago, so there's no hope of getting the numbers of the bank notes. So what about it, Jack? Our Mr Smith sounds a dead ringer for Miss Langton's delivery man, doesn't he?'

'Apart from the accent, of course, but that's easily assumed.'

Bill unlocked the door of number 8 and led the way from the tiny hall and into the living room.

The first thing that struck Jack was the stale smell of old tobacco. He could see at a glance there were three ashtrays in the room, but they were all empty. He looked into the waste-paper basket by the hearth. It was nearly a quarter full with the crushed-out stubs of untipped cigarettes and slim cigars. Jack looked at the old cigarette ends.

'I'd say a man smoked at least some of these cigarettes, Bill,' he said, picking out a couple. 'There's no trace of lipstick on them.'

'Could it be a woman? She'd use a holder.'

Jack clicked his tongue. 'Maybe, but some of these ends have been bitten.'

He looked round the room. 'It's a very blokey room, isn't it?'

The room was divided into two parts, a sitting room and a dining area. The sitting room was smartly furnished with fashionable square-shaped easy chairs and a sofa in a primrose and black jazz pattern. A wireless set on a mahogany stand stood by the large window. The furniture, Jack reminded himself, had come with the flat. It wasn't any sort of clue to the elusive Mr Smith's personality. From the crumpled cushions and general untidiness, it was only too obvious that, as the porter said, he hadn't employed a cleaner.

A typewriter, its cover to one side, stood on the dining table. 'Any clue from the typewriter, Jack?' asked Bill. 'That's much more your line of country than mine.'

'It's an Underwood number five,' said Jack. 'There's thousands of them about.' He stopped suddenly. 'I say, Bill! You said the note on the packing case that was delivered to Jenny Langton was typewritten. I wonder if that note was written on this machine?'

'Wait a moment,' said Bill. 'Let me check it for prints.' He opened his case and took out a bottle of grey mercury powder and an insufflator. He puffed the grey powder over the machine.

'Nothing,' he said in disgust. 'That machine's been wiped clean. Jack, can you type Miss Langton's name and address?' He tore out a sheet from his notebook and handed it to Jack. 'We can compare it with the note on the packing case.'

'Right-oh,' said Jack.

Bill wandered round the room, unimpressed. 'I must say that for four guineas a week, I'd expect more room.'

'It's a pied-à-terre,' said Jack, concentrating on his typing. 'You aren't meant to live here, just use it for visiting.'

'I wonder if this can tell us anything?' said Bill, picking up a man's tweed jacket that was slung across the arm of the sofa. 'Good God!'

'What is it?' asked Jack, taking the paper from the machine and looking up.

Bill pointed down to the sofa. 'This was under the jacket.'

It was a straw hat ornamented with wax fruit. 'It's Mrs Rotherwell's,' he said, under his breath. 'Jack, it has to be her hat.'

Jack picked up the hat and looked at it, remembering Mrs Rotherwell's earnest face which had peered out from under that hat. 'It is,' he said, pointing to a tiny little white chip on one of the cherries. 'I didn't think of it until I saw it, but I remember this cherry was damaged. It bounced up and down as she spoke. She was fairly worked up. It was when she told me that Michael Trevelyan was in London.'

'And we've just found out where he was,' said Bill heavily. He breathed deeply, then shook himself. 'Come on. Let's see what we can find out.'

The flat, in addition to the sitting room with the dining area, consisted of a kitchen, a cloakroom and toilet and, of course, the bathroom.

The door to the bathroom was shut. Bill tried to open it but it was jammed part way by the broken planks of the floor. He managed to put his head round the door and inspected the devastation within. Light shone up through the floor from the flat below.

'I bet there's nothing to find out in there, even if we could get in the room,' he said, shutting the door. 'That room's a write-off. Let's have a look at the rest of the place.'

It didn't take them long.

It seemed obvious that the flat had been left in a hurry. In the bedroom the wardrobes gaped open. In one there were some men's clothes, two lounge suits, some shirts and a couple of jerseys. In the drawers were men's underwear and socks but none of the clothes were labelled with a name.

In the other wardrobe and drawers were three dresses, two hats, some underwear and a coat.

'The coat and these dresses are from Debenhams and Freebody's,' said Bill.

'Mrs Davenham shopped at Debenhams and Freebody's,' said Jack quietly.

'I know.' Bill raised an eyebrow to Jack. 'And so do many hundreds of other women but it looks as if your idea about Jane Davenham's new boyfriend may be correct.'

The usual clutter that would lie on a dressing table – hairbrushes, mirrors and so on – had obviously been swept away. If there were any toiletries, presumably they were in the devastated bathroom.

In the newspaper rack in the living room there were some magazines, *Radiogram and Wireless Answers, Sports Pictorial* and the *Radio Times,* all the latest editions, and a few copies of the *Daily Express.*

Bill looked through the newspapers. 'The last one is dated Wednesday 21st,' he said. 'It's Saturday today, so that's three days ago.'

'And the day that Mrs Rotherwell disappeared from the Royal Park,' said Jack.

'Exactly,' agreed Bill. 'Well, there's something,' he said, putting down the newspaper. He frowned at the undisturbed layer of dust that coated every surface. 'The whole flat looks as if it's been wiped clean to me, Jack. Damn! I'll get the fingerprint boys in here, but I don't know if we'll find anything.'

'You haven't actually got Trevelyan's fingerprints on file though, have you?' asked Jack.

Bill shook his head. 'No, but you never know. He might turn up under another name.' He looked around. 'Well, it's obvious that four guineas a week or no four guineas a week, they didn't intend to return.'

'Not having left a dead body in the bath, no,' said Jack. 'That would dampen any householder's spirits. You could ask your fingerprint lads to look round the hearth.' He looked at the cinders in the grate. 'They obviously had a fire burning. There might be something on the coal scuttle or fire tongs.'

'I'll ask,' said Bill, 'but I bet it's all been cleaned.' He broke off. 'Hello! What's that?'

He stooped down and fished out a charred scrunched-up piece of paper from the back of the grate. He opened it out on his knee. It was part of a photograph, cut down along one side. Two boys in a garden looked out of the picture. One of the boys, a solid youth of about fifteen, looked familiar.

'That's Martin Langton, surely,' said Bill. 'This must be the photo Trevelyan took from Miss Langton's room. Or part of it, anyway.'

'It looks as if he's kept the piece with Jenny Langton in and thrown away the rest,' said Jack.

'He wouldn't want a picture of the boys,' said Bill. He took an envelope from his pocket and put the photograph in it. 'After hearing the porter's description of Mr Smith, I didn't have many doubts who we were looking for, but this confirms it.'

Jack walked over to the kneehole desk. The lid of the desk was down and a leather-bound blotter lay on the top. Jack slipped the top sheet out and held it so the light from the window shone across the surface. 'Bill! There's marks on the blotter. Someone's written a letter.'

'Let me see that.' Bill tilted the sheet towards the light. '"*Dear . . .*" Does that say *Amelia?*'

'Yes, it does,' said Jack, with such a note of supressed excitement in his voice that Bill looked round sharply.

Jack had taken the blotter off the desk and was looking at a piece of paper underneath. 'This is the letter! It's not finished, but listen to this.'

*Dear Amelia,*

*It was lovely to see you yesterday. Would it be possible for you to call on Tuesday? I'm looking forward to showing you the new place. We'll have it all to ourselves. It's small but I like it very much.*

*I'm sure you're wrong about Mike. He can't be the man you thought*

Jack looked up. 'It breaks off there and, as it was shoved under the blotter, my guess is that "Mike" came into the room and the writer hid it.'

Bill strode across the room and looked down at the letter. 'Bingo!' he breathed. 'Mike. He'll have another surname, but this is Trevelyan or I'm a Dutchman.' He glanced at Jack. 'You were right. The new boyfriend *was* Michael Trevelyan. Well done.'

'Thanks,' said Jack in satisfaction. 'It fits, doesn't it? Unless . . .' He stopped, his smile fading.

'Unless what?'

Jack shook himself in irritation. 'Don't mind me. You know I always like to make things more complicated than they are. I just wondered if we were *meant* to find that letter.'

'Meant to find it?' repeated Bill. 'But you said yourself that Jane Davenham must've shoved it under the blotter when Mike came into the room.'

'I know,' said Jack ruefully. 'And that probably is what happened. It just seems a bit neat. I mean, we were looking for Michael Trevelyan and Jane Davenham, and here they are.'

'They're not actually here, Jack,' corrected Bill. 'As far as that goes, we're no closer to finding either of them than we were. Knowing where they were isn't the same as knowing where they are. And as for neat – well, take a look in the bathroom.'

'Okay. You're right. So what do we think happened?'

Bill sat down on the sofa. 'Well, we know that Mrs Rotherwell and Jane Davenham have known each other for years. Matthew and Julia Rotherwell told us that. Naturally, when Mrs Rotherwell returned from Ceylon, she got in touch with her old friend. You worked out that the two women were together when they saw Michael Trevelyan.'

Bill nodded towards the desk. 'I think that letter was written as a result of that chance encounter. I don't know why it wasn't sent, but it seems to me that, despite what she wrote, Jane Davenham was actually a bit uneasy about Trevelyan. Otherwise she wouldn't have, as you said, broken off and shoved it under the blotter when Trevelyan came into the room. Presumably, as we know from the porter that the two women came into the building together, Mrs Davenham must've seen Mrs Rotherwell on a subsequent occasion and invited her here. We know from the letter that's what she intended to do. What's more, Jane Davenham didn't intend Trevelyan to be around.'

'No. You'd hardly invite a guest who's going to accuse the host of murder. That would be awkward.'

'Very,' said Bill with the ghost of a smile. 'Now this is guess-work, but I'll be surprised if it's too far off the truth. I think Trevelyan came in unexpectedly, saw Mrs Rotherwell, and, knowing what she knew, killed her.'

He gestured round the room. 'And then the pair of them ran for it.'

'D'you think Jane Davenham was a willing partner?'

Bill shrugged. 'That's something we can only find out when we find her. If Trevelyan's holding her against her will, she might manage to escape.'

'Or she could end up dead,' said Jack soberly. He stood silently for a few moments. 'Look, I know Dr Roude is a first-rate man, but one thing we really need to prove, beyond all doubt, is that the dead woman, poor soul, really is Mrs Rotherwell.'

'Of course it's Mrs Rotherwell, you idiot. Who else could it be?'

'We know there was another woman here. There could be a substitution going on.'

Bill stared at him speechlessly. 'Don't be daft. Whatever gave you that idea?'

'I met Mrs Rotherwell,' said Jack. 'So did you. Could you say that woman we saw downstairs is Mrs Rotherwell?'

'No, of course I couldn't, but who else could it be?'

'Jane Davenham, of course.'

'But . . .' Bill sighed in exasperation. 'Jack, are you making difficulties for fun?'

Jack grinned. 'No. I'm honestly not, Bill, but I want to know why the body was put in the bath. After all, she could have been left in this room, say, and no one would be any the wiser.'

'You're right,' said Bill thoughtfully. 'Damn it, Jack, you are. As you said, this flat is a pied-à-terre. The fact that the occupant hadn't been seen for a while wouldn't raise any alarm bells with anyone. As long as the rent was paid, there'd be no reason for the porter or anyone else to come in here. The rent was paid for a month,' he added thoughtfully. 'If it had been a month before we discovered the body, we wouldn't be any the wiser in any event. We both saw enough in the war to know what a month's decay looks like. We wouldn't be able to recognise her, that's for sure.'

He drummed his fingers on the arm of the sofa. 'How about this? Trevelyan comes in, sees Mrs Rotherwell, they have a set-to and he wallops her. However, he's not sure she's dead – she might not have been – so he sticks her in the bath while she's unconscious, so she'll drown. How about that?'

'That's very convincing,' said Jack. 'And it's the most likely explanation of what happened. However, if you *could* make a point of making sure we've got the right corpse, it really would help me to think about what actually happened instead of what might have happened.'

'All right, Jack. I don't have any doubts at all that it really is Mrs Rotherwell who's been murdered, but if it can be proved, it will be proved.'

# THIRTEEN

'Right, Doubting Thomas, we've got proof,' said Bill Rackham over the telephone. It was eleven o'clock on Monday morning. 'Can you call round this afternoon?'

'Yes, of course. I'm meeting my editor for lunch but I'll drop in afterwards. What proof have you got? The newspapers restricted themselves to saying that the body was believed to be that of Amelia Rotherwell.'

'I know they did, but since then, that poor beggar, Matthew Rotherwell, has identified her.'

'How did he do that?' asked Jack. 'Second sight?'

There was a tut down the telephone. 'You know what I mean. Of course he couldn't say it was his mother just by looking at her, but he had to go through the formalities all the same. He was fairly sure it was her, because of the clothes and the shape and so on.'

'That's not very definite.'

'No, I'm coming to that. What he did tell us, and this is definite, was that his mother had broken her leg, years ago, and, moreover, he gave us the name of her dentist.'

'Ah.'

'As you say, ah. Dr Roude found the old fracture and the dental records match, so that's it. Oh, and by the way, it looks as if I was right about how she was killed. There's signs of a blow on the skull, but she was drowned, all right. There was water in the lungs.'

'Well done you,' said Jack.

'So you can safely put all your wilder ideas to rest. We've issued an arrest warrant for Michael Trevelyan. God only knows what's happened to Jane Davenham. I just hope we don't find her corpse next.'

'So do I. By the way, did you compare the typing from the Underwood we found at the flat with the typing on the packing case Jenny Langton received?'

'We did. They're a match. It's the same typewriter sure enough. There's another thing. We've managed to get a photo of Trevelyan out of Mrs Shilton.'

'Good grief! I bet that took some effort.'

'It certainly did,' said Bill with feeling.

'I can't imagine she'll be very happy about you using it.'

'Happy or not, we've got it. I'm going to nail this bloke, Jack. Think of the Rotherwells and the misery he's caused. Matthew Rotherwell was really cut up about his mother. He was delighted that she had come back to England and she was really looking forward to her first grandchild. She'll never see that baby.'

Jack paused. That was a shockingly sad thought. 'That's pretty tough,' he said quietly.

'I'll say.' It was Bill's turn to hesitate. 'And he knows where Miss Langton lives. That's not nice. He's got away with murder for too long.'


'Aunty's terribly upset,' said Jenny, crushing out her cigarette. 'The police have been round and more or less forced her to give them the photograph of my father.'

'Forced?' asked Betty, her nose wrinkling.

'I don't mean physically forced, of course, but asked her in a way she couldn't really refuse. They talked about hindering the police in the execution of their duties and all that sort of thing, and Aunty just isn't the sort of person to stand up to it.' Jenny sighed and shook herself impatiently. 'Having said that, she was so upset, she was gearing herself up to go and beard poor Mr Rackham in his den, so to speak.'

'She's going to Scotland Yard?' said Betty in surprise.

'That's what she said. She spent all yesterday afternoon talking about it.'

It was Jenny's afternoon off and the two girls had met for lunch in the Lyon's tea room on Tottenham Court Road. Jenny wanted to do some shopping and then there was dinner tonight with Jack and Betty. And Mr Rackham. Was that a problem?

Betty had been really lucky, Jenny thought to herself with a touch of envy. After a lifetime of never having enough, Betty suddenly had a lovely home, enough money not to be worried and a man who really cared about her. A man who cared. At this point her mind conjured up a picture, not of Jack, but of a square-shouldered, untidy, ginger-haired man with thoughtful eyes and an engaging grin. She thrust the image forcibly away. Mr Rackham was the police and the police, according to Aunty Gwyn, were the enemy.

Aunty Gwyn had so taken it for granted that Jenny shared her views, it was difficult not to be swayed, and yet . . .

'It's so hard,' she broke out. 'I remember coming to see you that day I'd been to Saunder's Green. You were an absolute brick. You were so kind, Betty.'

Betty couldn't help but feel pleased.

Jenny half-smiled at her expression. 'You really were. You listened and didn't laugh at me. I wanted to know what I'd seen and why I'd seen it. And yet if I'd had any idea what I was stirring up, I would never have asked Jack to . . .' She broke off. She had nearly said *interfere* but that was unfair.

'Help?' suggested Betty.

'Help,' repeated Jenny ironically. She rubbed her face with her hands. 'It never crossed my mind that anything like this would come out. About my poor mother and what sort of man my father was, I mean. I thought my father was Dad.'

'Dr Langton?'

'Yes. Dad. I really cared about Dad. Dad *was* my father in every respect apart from the actual biological one, and that's the bit that hurts. Who the hell is this man – my father? I must have something in common with him and that's an awful thought. It's frightening.'

Betty reached across the table and squeezed her hand encouragingly. 'You're not your father. You're you. After all, no one's a carbon copy of their parents. There's loads of other stuff that matters. In your case, it's who brought you up, to say nothing of your own self.'

'Thanks,' said Jenny softly. 'D'you know, part of why I'm feeling so wretched, is that I almost wanted to find him? Then, as things have gone on, I've just become more and more scared that the police *will* find him. I'll have to face him, Betty, and I don't want to.' She shuddered. 'I wish I could feel like Aunty Gwyn. She's convinced my father is innocent.'

'What? Even after poor Mrs Rotherwell?' said Betty. 'Surely that must've shaken her.'

'Oh, it did, but she doesn't really believe it. She refused point blank to read the accounts in the Sunday newspapers.'

'Well, they were pretty lurid.'

Jenny tossed her head impatiently. 'She's just hiding her head in the sand. I do care for her, Betty. She's such a kind person, but she believes that everyone is good at heart and they're not, are they?'

'Is she really certain he's innocent?' asked Betty sceptically.

'Absolutely. The police are telling wicked lies and that's the end of that.'

Betty hesitated. 'Jack thinks she might be in touch with him. I know Bill Rackham thinks the same.'

Jenny winced. 'She might be. After all, how did he know about me if she didn't tell him? He sent me that brooch and took my photo from my room. Aunty Gwyn thinks I should be *pleased* he took my photograph,' she burst out. 'She thinks it was clever of him. She thinks it showed he cared.'

'How do you feel?' asked Betty.

'Honestly?' Jenny lit another cigarette. 'Scared. You know what happened to Mrs Rotherwell. I don't *want* him to care. I don't want anything to do with him.'

'That's understandable,' said Betty. 'I don't see how anyone could enjoy being in your shoes.' She looked at her friend's expression. 'Try not to worry too much, Jenny. I know it's easy to say, but Jack's doing all he can.'

'And Mr Rackham,' added Jenny. 'Yes, I know.' There was a little lift in her voice as she said his name.

Betty felt a little glow of triumph. She'd guessed Jenny liked Bill Rackham. Liked him very much. That was partly why she'd arranged a dinner party for the four of them.

Jenny glanced at the clock and picked up her bag. 'I must be off.'

'Well, don't forget, dinner tonight.'

'No, I won't. Seven o'clock. I'm looking forward to it. I really must be going, but I'll see you then.'

\*    \*    \*

After placating Archie Keyne, his editor, with the promise of two short stories and an article, Jack left the Cheshire Cheese and walked from Fleet Street to the Embankment.

The afternoon was glorious, with the autumn sunshine turning the Thames into a glittering carpet of light. He usually enjoyed this stretch of London, with the barges on the busy river and the trees lining the pavement. However, he was so absorbed in his thoughts that he scarcely took in the scene. It was one thing discussing fictional murders with Archie, and quite another contemplating poor Mrs Rotherwell.

He had been moved that morning when Bill had reminded him of the baby that she would never see. Matthew and Julia Rotherwell had really cared about her. What sort of grandmother would she have made? It was an interesting question. In fact, it was a fascinating question. What sort of woman was she?

He was so absorbed in his train of thought, that he nearly walked into a woman who was striding determinedly along the pavement.

He veered off abruptly to one side, when he realised who the woman was.

'Mrs Shilton?' he said, raising his hat. 'I do apologise. What brings you to town?'

'Good afternoon, Mr Haldean.' She glanced along the road to the bulk of Scotland Yard. 'I intend to call on the police. Do you know they have issued a warrant for my brother's arrest? I am going to tell them that this must be stopped. They insist that my brother murdered – *murdered*, I say – Amelia Rotherwell. He would never harm a hair of her head. He would never harm anyone. It is quite outrageous that they should blacken his character in this way.'

'It must be very upsetting for you,' said Jack diplomatically.

'Indeed it is, Mr Haldean.' She gripped the handle of the furled umbrella she was carrying as if she was going to use it as a weapon. 'I understand from Jennifer that the officer in charge of the case is the man who accompanied you to my house. Rackham, I believe his name is,' she added with a sniff. 'I intend to give him a piece of my mind. I will not,' she said fiercely, nearly jabbing Jack with the umbrella, 'allow this to continue a moment longer.'

Poor Bill had quite enough on his plate without Mrs Shilton descending on him like an avenging fury, thought Jack. 'I'm terribly sorry, Mrs Shilton, but I don't think you'll be able to see him. I happen to know he's engaged for the afternoon.'

'Engaged?' Her voice trembled. 'But I must speak to him! It's . . . It's . . .'

Jack felt a stab of sudden sympathy, mingled, he realised, with a twist of embarrassment, as her lip quivered and she blinked away tears.

'Don't, Mrs Shilton,' he said, reaching out his hand to hers. 'Please don't upset yourself so.'

She took a handkerchief from her handbag and dabbed her eyes. 'I'm sorry,' she said, between sniffs. 'I just can't bear anyone thinking such horrible things about Michael.'

There was a bench a few yards away, under the shade of a plane tree. 'Let's sit down until you feel a bit more yourself, shall we?' he suggested, taking her arm and gently escorting her to the bench.

'You're very kind,' she managed as they sat down. She took a deep breath and, dabbing her eyes again, scrunched up her handkerchief in her hand.

'I wish I could convince the police how impossible it is that Michael has done the things they say he's done. It's just *wrong,*' she added with a resurgence of her old ferocity. 'Michael is a good, kind man. He was distraught when Caroline went missing. He did everything he could to try and find her. No one who knew him could credit for an instant that he was responsible for her disappearance. Violet Laidlaw was deeply attached to her cousin and she never believed Michael was guilty. She even persuaded her father, old Mr Wild, to put up the money for Michael's defence.'

'The case never came to court though,' said Jack.

'No, it didn't. But if it had, old Mr Wild was prepared to foot the bill.' She heaved a deep sigh. 'You'd have to have known Mr Wild to realise how remarkable that was. He was very careful with his money. I must say I never cared overly much for Mr Wild. He ruled the household with a rod of iron, but I was grateful to him for promising to help Michael. I like to think that if it had come to court, the truth would have come out and Michael would have been proved innocent. After all, someone must know the truth about what really happened that day.'

'Whoever wrote the forged letter from Caroline Trevelyan must do,' said Jack thoughtfully.

She turned to him eagerly. 'You're right, Mr Haldean.'

'Tell me, Mrs Shilton, were you there when that letter arrived?'

'Indeed I was. Michael was excited at first, but very puzzled. He showed it to me and asked what I thought. I was relieved at first, to think we had some news, however peculiar, of Caroline, and then we both became convinced that Caroline simply could not have written that letter.'

And that was probably as near to an accurate account as they would ever get. It was as they had thought. Trevelyan could have easily written the letter.

'I feel so helpless,' she said, her voice cracking. 'Even Jennifer seems to believe the worst. She actually thought I'd read the awful things that were in the newspapers. I refused, of course.'

'Of course you did, Mrs Shilton.'

'But even so, I can't help knowing what's been said. How can anyone think that Michael – *Michael!* – not only murdered Caroline and Mrs Rotherwell but is also thought to have done away with this Mrs Davenham as well? That is simply not possible, Mr Haldean.'

She glared at him so fiercely that he sat back in surprise.

'Not possible?'

'Absolutely not possible.' She flushed with indignation. 'Don't you see? I believe the newspapers are saying that this woman, this Mrs Davenham, was associated with my brother.'

'Well, er . . .'

'In an immoral relationship!' she added, her voice rising. 'The idea is utterly incredible!' She shuddered in disgust. 'As if my brother would have anything to do with a woman like that!'

'An immoral relationship,' repeated Jack slowly. He had no urge to laugh. They might be living in the Jazz Age, as the newspapers called it, but Mrs Shilton's outlook was formed long before the war.

Vague ideas were starting to form a pattern in his mind. Yes, if Jane Davenham had been murdered, then that was certainly immoral, but Mrs Shilton, he knew, meant the phrase in its conventional sense.

'Tell me, Mrs Shilton – and I apologise if the question seems odd – but would you befriend a woman who was in an immoral relationship?'

'Certainly not!' she exclaimed in near horror. 'I don't know how you can ask such a thing.'

'Well, such relationships are known,' he said with a smile.

'I have no truck with this modern post-war laxity,' she said severely.

Jack nodded. Not that illicit relationships were unheard of before the war, of course, but they were certainly talked about a great deal more nowadays.

'No, of course you don't,' he said thoughtfully. 'I wouldn't expect a lady such as yourself to have any other views on the matter. What if – and once again, I apologise if the question seems odd – an old friend, someone you had known for many years, found herself caught up in such a relationship?'

She looked at him quizzically, as well she might. 'I would, I hope, try to convince her of the error of her ways. I may say this has never actually happened, Mr Haldean, but if it came to my attention that one of my friends was indeed in such a situation, I would probably write to them, informing them that our friendship was at an end until the situation was resolved. I would feel it was my duty, however painful, to do so. I wouldn't enjoy it,' she added.

'No, I don't think you would enjoy it. You knew Mrs Rotherwell, didn't you?'

She blinked. 'Are you implying that *Amelia Rotherwell* was caught up in such a relationship? Because let me tell you, young man, that such a suggestion is utterly outrageous.'

'No, I—'

'I was horrified when I heard what had happened to poor Amelia. The idea that my brother was responsible in any way is completely ridiculous, of course.'

'Yes, but—'

'And for you to imply that Amelia Rotherwell, a most respectable woman and a widow to boot, should . . . Well! Words fail me.'

It was just as well words had failed her, thought Jack. He couldn't see how he was going to get a word in otherwise. 'No, I wasn't suggesting anything of the sort, Mrs Shilton. All I was trying to do was gauge if Mrs Rotherwell's opinions on such matters were similar to yours.'

'Rather stricter, if anything,' she snapped, only partially mollified.

And that was interesting. Mrs Rotherwell had told both him and Bill she had been with a friend when she had glimpsed Michael Trevelyan. That friend, they believed, was Jane Davenham.

Matthew Rotherwell knew Jane Davenham as an old friend of his mother's, but Mrs Rotherwell had been in Ceylon for the last twenty years. They had exchanged letters, certainly, but Mrs Davenham could have had any number of affairs without Mrs Rotherwell being any the wiser, if all Mrs Rotherwell knew was what Jane Davenham chose to tell her in her letters.

So far, so good, but that state of affairs would change abruptly as soon as Mrs Rotherwell visited Jane Davenham in Summer's Court.

They had obviously been friendly enough when they came in. They had the porter's word for that. But it was obvious, once inside the flat, that a man lived there. However, according to Mrs Shilton – and he believed her absolutely – if Mrs Rotherwell had known Jane Davenham was in an illicit relationship, she would have cut the friendship dead.

*I'm looking forward to showing you the new place. We'll have it all to ourselves . . .* That was a phrase from the unsent letter. That surely implied that Jane Davenham usually didn't have it to herself? And, what's more, that Mrs Rotherwell knew it. Maybe that's why the letter wasn't sent, but even so, it was odd.

'Amelia Rotherwell,' said Mrs Shilton, still bristling with indignation, 'was the soul of respectability.'

'I'm sure she was,' agreed Jack. 'I was actually thinking of Jane Davenham.'

'Jane Davenham!' repeated Mrs Shilton with a snort. 'If there is such a person. For my part, I believe she's nothing but a figment of the police's imagination.'

'No, she's real enough,' said Jack.

'Then . . .' She paused. 'I just don't understand it,' she said, her voice close to breaking.

'Are you sure you never came across her or heard the name, Mrs Shilton?'

She shook her head blankly. 'No, not as far as I know. One cannot remember every name one's ever heard, of course, but, to the best of my knowledge, I've never heard of her before this latest outrage. An outrage, I may say, that Michael is completely innocent of.'

Her voice was very definite. She was so certain that it made him pause. She'd been proclaiming her brother's innocence for years, but could she actually *know* anything? He decided to probe a bit further.

'You're sure of that, aren't you, Mrs Shilton?'

'Of course. I have hardly made a secret of my beliefs.'

He didn't want belief, he wanted knowledge. 'I think this is rather more than belief though, isn't it?'

Her eyes widened. Flustered, she started to stammer a reply, when a barge on the river hooted in a deafening blast of steam, drowning out her words. With a sense of boiling frustration, Jack knew the noise had given her a chance to think and startled her into wariness.

'I don't know what you mean,' she said defensively.

Dammit, thought Jack, the blasted woman was on the point of actually telling me something. 'Mrs Shilton,' he pleaded, 'if you do know anything, tell me.'

For a fleeting few seconds, he thought she was going to tell him and then she drew herself up. 'Naturally I believe in my brother's innocence. I always have done. My late husband, Alan, was of the same opinion.'

They were back to belief and yet, she *knew*. What did she know?

She tilted her chin upright and glared at him. 'I suppose you're about to tell me that Alan and I shouldn't have helped him.'

'No,' said Jack sincerely. Even now, there was a chance. 'You're his sister and you believed in him. It's only natural that you should help him.' He paused. 'You're helping him now, aren't you?'

She stared at him wordlessly. As the noise of the traffic on the Embankment rumbled behind them, she looked at him for what seemed a long while. Then, with a great effort, she spoke. 'Mr Haldean, I do not tell lies. When I tell you my brother is innocent, please do me the courtesy of believing what I say.'

They were back to where they had started. 'I certainly believe you are telling the truth as you see it.'

'Then act upon it, young man!'

'I need facts, Mrs Shilton.'

She gave a disdainful sniff. 'They are bound to be there if you choose to look for them.'

She adjusted her coat and scarf and stood up. 'You say that Mr Rackham is engaged this afternoon?'

What did she know? What he wanted to do was see Bill, tell him that he was convinced that Mrs Shilton really did know something and see if official persuasion could get her to speak. 'Why don't you give him an hour or so?' he said with a smile. 'I'm sure he'll make every effort to see you if it's at all possible.'

'An hour, you say?' She looked thoughtful. 'Very well. Thank you for your advice, Mr Haldean. I will act upon it. I trust the next time we meet, it will be in happier circumstances.'

# FOURTEEN

Jack pulled out a chair and reached for a cigarette from the box on the desk. 'I bumped into Mrs Shilton on the Embankment, Bill.'

'Blimey, did you?'

'I'm afraid so, yes. She intends to descend on you this afternoon. She's breathing fire and fury because you've issued a warrant for Trevelyan.'

'What does the blasted woman expect us to do?' He looked at his friend. 'Couldn't you put her off? Say I'd left the country or something?'

'Not really,' said Jack with a grin. 'The thing is, Bill, I'm sure she knows something.'

'Well, that's not new.'

'Yes, but I'm certain of it. I hoped you might be able to get it out of her.'

Bill gave an irritated sigh. 'I can't force her to tell us, Jack, much as I'd like to. Besides that, what we really want to know is where we can lay our hands on him. He's far too wily a bird to let slip information like that, sister or no sister.'

He flicked open the file on the desk in front of him and slewed it round so Jack could see. There was a photograph of a good-looking, broad-shouldered man in the doorway of a church. Beside him a pretty woman in an elaborate wedding dress smiled towards the camera. She had a distinct resemblance to Jennifer Langton.

'She made a dickens of a fuss about us having this photo and, to be honest, I don't know if it was really worth the trouble to get it. Not only is it years old, Trevelyan seems to be able to walk around London at will, without anyone noticing.'

'Mrs Rotherwell noticed him,' murmured Jack.

'Yes, poor beggar. The flat was clean as a whistle, by the way. I thought as much, when we saw how the dust was undisturbed, but the fingerprint boys confirmed it.'

He paused, running his finger round the photograph. 'It's funny to think these are Miss Langton's parents.' He looked up. 'I'm glad she stuck to the name of Langton. If she was called Trevelyan, she'd get saddled with all sorts of publicity. That would be rotten for her.'

'It's pretty rotten as it is. She's scared, Bill.'

'She's quite right to be scared. We need to get hold of this man and get him safely behind bars.'

His voice was so vehement, Jack raised his eyebrows in surprise. 'Calm down, Bill,' he said, stubbing out his cigarette. 'I can't blame Jenny Langton for being rattled, but we don't know he intends her any harm. After all, all he's actually done is give her a brooch and pinch a photo from her room.'

'We know perfectly well he's capable of harm, though.'

'But she's his daughter.'

'So what?' Bill hesitated, trying to marshal his thoughts. 'I don't think we're dealing with what I'd call a good, straight-forward, crook.'

Jack raised his eyebrows. 'Straightforward?'

'Yes, straightforward. I know it sounds strange, but just think about it. Why do crooks commit crimes?'

Jack pursed his lips. 'Because they want something, I suppose. Money, perhaps, is the obvious one.'

'Exactly. A straightforward crook, to use that word, is a man who, if he wants money, will commit a robbery. There's nothing wrong with wanting money. It's a perfectly understandable ambition, but you know as well as I do that there are other types of crooks. Men with a kink, with a twist, somewhere in their characters. Now, take Trevelyan. Why did he murder Mrs Rotherwell?'

'You know the answer as well as I do,' said Jack with a shrug. 'Amelia Rotherwell knew who he was. She was a danger to him.'

'Was she?' Bill got up and walked to the window. 'Think about it, Jack. Yes, she told us she'd seen him. The first time, in St James' Park, happened by complete chance. The second time, when she was with Jane Davenham, might have been chance as well, but I'm not so sure about that. And what does Trevelyan do? We know he can disguise himself, but does he do it? No. Does he disappear, as he managed to disappear years ago?' He whirled round. 'No. He tracks her to her hotel.'

Jack stared at him. 'I see what you mean.'

'Exactly,' said Bill grimly. 'He didn't try and hide, but deliberately put himself in the one place where he knew she would be. Now d'you see what I mean about him not being straightforward? I think he's got a kink or a twist that makes him toy with danger for the sheer satisfaction of getting away with it. He didn't have to go to his daughter's rooms in person. He could've easily have posted that brooch, but he didn't. I know he took Miss Langton's photograph and that idiot sister of his seems to find that rather touching. I don't.'

Bill stretched his shoulders. 'If all he had wanted was a photograph, then he could've got one another way, maybe from Mrs Shilton. She could've arranged that easily enough.' He glanced at his friend. 'Perhaps you'll think I'm being overly dramatic, but I think he was marking possession, staking out territory.'

Jack shook his head. 'Bill, this is nothing but a nightmare.'

'Is it? I tell you, Jack, he's twisted.'

He walked back to the desk and, leaning on his arms, shook his head. He stared down at the files wearily. 'I've gone over those damn things until I can hardly see them any longer.' He glanced at Jack. 'Haven't you got any ideas? You're usually full of them.'

The answer was that yes, he was beginning to have some ideas. They had come to him on the Embankment, before he had met Mrs Shilton, but his thoughts were so vague that even he hardly knew what they were. He needed to think, to fit them into a coherent shape, to find evidence, for heaven's sake.

'I'm not a magician,' he said soberly. 'I haven't got a magic wand. I can't rustle up theories out of thin air. I need some facts to work on.'

The telephone on the desk rang. Bill picked it up. 'Oh, is she?' he said. 'All right, I'll come down.' He hung up the receiver with a grimace. 'Guess who's downstairs, wanting to see me.'

'Mrs Shilton?' He glanced at his watch. 'I asked her to give you an hour. She's early.'

'I might as well get it over with,' said Bill with a sigh. 'Look, I don't want to hold you up, but could you go through the files again? I know you've seen them all before but something might strike you.'

'All right,' said Jack obligingly. He took another cigarette from the box and, lighting it, pulled the files towards him.

'Thanks,' said Bill softly. 'I'll leave you to it.'

He was gone for nearly half an hour. When he returned, he was surprised to see Jack sitting on the desk, telephone in hand. He waggled his eyebrows interrogatively. Jack made a silent shushing gesture.

'Yes, Chief Inspector Rackham's office,' he said into the phone. 'Now, if you can manage it. I'm very much obliged.' He hung up the receiver and punched the air in satisfaction. 'Yes!'

'What the devil's all that about?' asked Bill. 'Who were you speaking to?'

Jack opened his mouth to speak and then stopped. 'Actually, would you mind waiting a couple of ticks? I might not have a magic wand, but I've just asked for a magician. In a manner of speaking, that is. I don't want to spoil the show. Did you get anything out of Mrs Shilton?'

'No, but like you, I'm convinced she really does know something. What d'you mean, a magician?'

'Wait and see,' said Jack with a smile.

'Just as you say,' said Bill. He took his pipe from his pocket and filled it with an air of highly put-upon patience.

A few minutes later, a knock came at the door and Jack, getting swiftly to his feet, opened it to admit a rather severe-looking, grey-haired lady in an old-fashioned dress and a pince-nez.

'Miss Hollander?' said Jack, pulling out a chair for her. 'It's good of you to come.'

'Not at all, Mr Haldean,' said Miss Hollander, settling herself stiffly on the chair. She bestowed a quick, if wintery, smile upon Bill. 'And you are, I take it, Chief Inspector Rackham?'

'I am, Miss Hollander. Pleased to meet you.' He frowned. 'I'm sure I've come across your name before.'

'I have, on occasion, given evidence in court as an expert witness,' said Miss Hollander.

Bill looked at Jack. 'Is this your magician?' he asked.

Jack nodded with a smile.

'Magician?' repeated Miss Hollander with a frown. 'I'm afraid you're under a misapprehension, sir.'

'Miss Hollander,' interjected Jack, 'is attached to the British Museum and is an authority on medieval palimpsests.'

Bill blinked. 'Good grief, Jack, I know this case goes back a few years, but not to the Middle Ages.'

'She is also,' continued Jack, 'one of the country's leading experts – in fact, I might say, *the* leading expert – on hand-writing, who has often advised Scotland Yard.'

'I knew I knew the name,' said Bill.

'And to be an expert on handwriting, Miss Hollander,' said Jack, 'is, to us mere mortals, something akin to magic.'

'Too kind,' she murmured, accepting the praise as her due. 'It was indeed fortunate that I was in the building when you telephoned. May I see the documents in question?'

Jack gave her two sheets of paper. Bill recognised one as the letter they'd found under the blotter in Trevelyan's flat. The other sheet of paper was evidently older. It was, he realised with surprise, the forged letter, supposedly from Caroline Trevelyan, that had been filed in the original documents in the Trevelyan case.

Miss Hollander adjusted her pince-nez and examined the letters. 'Oh, yes,' she said after a brief examination. 'This is very clear.' She put down the letters and, opening her bag, took out a magnifying glass. 'I can immediately identify fifteen distinguishing characteristics. I would expect to find more on closer examination. You can see for yourself the similarity of the cursive *a* and the way the *t* is formed.'

She looked up at Jack in approval. 'I'm not surprised you spotted it, Mr Haldean. It really is quite unmistakable.'

'Excuse me, but what's unmistakable?' asked Bill.

Miss Hollander looked at him over the top of her pince-nez. 'Why, the fact that the letters were written by the same person, of course.'

'*What?*'

'There's no doubt about it,' said Miss Hollander, obviously taken aback by Bill's tone. 'This letter,' she said, tapping the one signed by Caroline, 'bears signs that the writer has attempted to either conceal their identity or imitate another's handwriting. However, as you can see for yourself,' she said, handing Bill the letters and the magnifying glass, 'the dimensions and proportions of the letters, the spacing both between and within words, and the way in which words and letters are connected are obvious indications that the same hand penned both letters.'

'Michael Trevelyan,' said Bill in a whisper. 'He did forge the letter from his wife.'

Jack cleared his throat. 'Excuse me, Miss Hollander, but did a man write this?'

'It is impossible to say, Mr Haldean.'

'Are you sure?' he said in surprise. 'After all, in detective stories, everyone seems to be able to tell right away if a letter's written by a man or a woman.'

'Then detective novelists, Mr Haldean – including yourself, I may say – should consult the facts before helping to promulgate a widely-held error. Other indications, such as scent, coloured ink or the smell of strong pipe tobacco may lead to a presumption of the writer's sex, but to make a judgement from the handwriting alone? No.'

She retrieved the magnifying glass from the table and stood up. 'Is that all? If you want me to give evidence to the court, Chief Inspector, I will, of course, examine the documents again and draw up a list of identifying characteristics.'

'I just wanted to know if they were written by the same person,' said Jack.

'The answer is a very definite yes.'

Jack opened the door for her and turned back to Bill, eyes shining. 'What d'you think of that? Magic, eh?'

'It's incredible,' said Bill, pulling the letters towards him. 'What on earth made you spot it?'

'Pure chance. I'd had both letters out of the file and on the desk. Then, without looking properly, I picked up what I thought was the Caroline letter but was actually the one from Jane Davenham. I wondered why on earth I'd made that mistake, and that made me look not at the words, but the actual writing.

It was what Miss Hollander called the dimensions and proportions of the letters that really struck me. The more I looked, the more similar they seemed, so I thought I'd better get an expert on the job.'

'I'm very glad you did,' said Bill, sitting back. He re-lit his pipe and flicked the match into the ashtray. 'So that's it. We look for the common thread between Caroline Trevelyan's murder – I'm going to assume she was murdered – and Mrs Rotherwell's murder and the common thread is, surprise, surprise, Michael Trevelyan.'

'All right,' said Jack. 'It's obvious why Trevelyan should write the first letter. He wanted to convince the police that his wife had run away. But why should he write the second?'

'Because . . .' Bill paused. 'I don't know. That's really odd. There doesn't seem to be any reason. We know he didn't send it. Do you think we were meant to find it?'

'If we were, what's it told us?'

Bill pulled the partly-finished letter towards him and read through it again. 'Nothing we didn't know already.' He looked up. 'What's the point of it, Jack?'

'If Michael Trevelyan wrote it? I really don't know. It could be a rough draft of a letter to entice Mrs Rotherwell to the flat, I suppose. But say Jane Davenham wrote it.'

'But she . . .'

Jack held up a hand to quell Bill's protests. 'We know from the porter at the flats that Mrs Rotherwell and Jane Davenham came in to the building together, so it looks as if Jane Davenham was instrumental in getting Mrs Rotherwell to visit the flat that day. I was beginning to wonder about her, you know.'

Bill gave him a sceptical look.

'Honestly, I really was. Think about it. Mrs Rotherwell was a highly respectable lady, yes? Now just think what a highly respectable lady would do on finding out that an old friend was in an irregular relationship. Take a line through any maiden aunts you happen to have.'

Bill put his head on one side thoughtfully. 'She'd probably have forty fits and break off the friendship,' he said slowly.

'Exactly. I asked Mrs Shilton and she said the same.'

'That seems a rum sort of conversation,' commented Bill. 'Do you usually ask middle-aged ladies what their views are on couples living over the brush?'

'Not as a general rule,' said Jack with a laugh. 'It all came up very naturally. Trust me. I didn't give anything away, but she was certain that would be Mrs Rotherwell's reaction. You saw the flat. It was obvious that a man lived there. As soon as Mrs Rotherwell walked in, she'd be scandalised. Her reaction would probably be to exclaim in horror and then walk out – unless she was prevented.'

'But Jane Davenham *can't* have written the letter we found,' said Bill. 'I understand everything you've said about Mrs Rotherwell's reactions on walking into the flat. I think you're dead right there, but she can't have written it. Your Miss Hollander's just told us that both letters, the forged one from Caroline Trevelyan and the one we found in the flat, were written by the same person.'

'And?'

'Jane Davenham can't have written the Caroline letter. She wasn't around at the time.'

'Are you sure? Is there any reason why she couldn't have been around?'

Bill puffed on his pipe for a long moment. 'As a matter of fact, there isn't any reason,' he admitted. 'It's just that she's never been mentioned in connection with the Caroline Trevelyan case.'

He chewed thoughtfully on the stem of his pipe, then looked up in sudden apprehension. 'Jack! Do you realise what this is? It's a motive! It's a copper-bottomed motive for Trevelyan murdering his wife!'

'It is, isn't it?'

'Good grief.' Bill leaned back in his chair. 'Say Trevelyan and Jane Davenham were having an affair years ago. Trevelyan murders his wife and gets Jane Davenham to write a letter in an attempt to cover up what he's done. Then he has to make a break for it and goes where? We don't know. What we do know is that years later, they obviously met up with one another again and decided to take up where they left off.'

'With another murder thrown in,' added Jack in distaste.

'Blimey, what a pair. If I'm right, Trevelyan's not the only one with a twist in his character. They seem very well-suited.'

'Too right,' agreed Bill grimly. He gathered the papers together. 'I'd better go and let Sir Douglas know about this right away. Do you want to come? After all, it's your discovery.'

Jack glanced at his watch. 'I'll let you break the news, Bill. I can't add anything to the bare facts Miss Hollander told us and Betty wanted me to be home sooner rather than later. Are you still all right for dinner?'

'Absolutely,' said Bill, standing up. 'Seven o'clock this evening. And Jack – well done.'

# FIFTEEN

Jack came out onto the Embankment and, leaning on the barrier by the side of the road, idly watched the traffic stream past. He had promised Betty he would call at the fishmongers and pick up some oysters for tonight, but first of all he wanted to give himself a few minutes to put his thoughts in order. That was the real reason why he had left it to Bill to tell Sir Douglas about the letters. He didn't want to go through the facts again. He knew what those facts were, but he wanted some time to make sense of them.

Jane Davenham: not an innocent victim, but party to a murder; party to two murders, in fact. Where was she now?

The cars and lorries rumbled on down the Embankment in a constant stream, the sunlight flashing off the windscreens and polished metal in a rapid succession of brief, blinding glares.

Almost mesmerised, Jack watched them go past and then jerked his head up suddenly. He'd nearly had it! Somehow, somewhere, there was a connection, a link, between the traffic on the Strand and a monster seen from a tree.

He knew better than to try and cudgel the fleeting thought into coherent shape. It would come to him if he left it well alone. It was a bit like doing a jigsaw puzzle whilst wearing a blindfold. He couldn't see the pieces but he knew they were there. He could *feel* them.

Somehow the traffic on the Strand was one piece and Jenny Langton's monster was another. He could feel the pieces nudging closer together.

He threw the stub of his cigarette onto the road, the oysters and the dinner party completely forgotten. He had to go back to Saunder's Green.

Mrs Offord opened the front door of Saunder's Green. She looked at him inquiringly, then, as recognition dawned, her face creased in a welcoming smile. 'Why, it's Mr Haldean, isn't it? How nice to see you again, sir.'

'And it's a pleasure to see you, Mrs Offord,' said Jack, raising his hat.

'Is Mrs Haldean with you, sir?' she said looking down the drive as if Betty had decided to playfully hide in the shrubbery.

'No, she's not,' said Jack, drawing nearer and lowering his voice confidentially. 'But as a matter of fact, it's because of my wife that I'm here. She wanted me to take another look at the house before we made a final decision.'

Mrs Offord's face fell in disappointment. 'I'm ever so sorry, Mr Haldean, but the house has been taken. That's such a pity, but it's gone. The agents wrote to me to say that there's a new tenant all signed up and ready to move in tomorrow. You're lucky to catch me. Mavis has already left and I'm off tomorrow morning.'

This was a complete pain. He'd hoped to get into the house on the pretext of taking a second look, but that idea had been kicked into touch.

'I'm really sorry to hear that,' he said, with complete sincerity.

She looked at him in honest distress. 'It's such a shame, sir. A Mr Raglan has taken it. He's bringing his own servants with him. Not that I'm sorry to go, because I only stayed on to oblige, like, but I'm sorry you and your young lady won't be living here. I'd like the house to go to someone who cared for it, I would indeed.'

Well, at least there was one good thing. As there was no danger of being harried by Wilson and Lee who wanted to saddle him with an inconveniently large Victorian house, he could be as complimentary as he liked. 'It's a real shame, Mrs Offord. Both my wife and I liked the house very much.'

It was the right thing to say. Mrs Offord beamed at him. 'It's good to hear you say so, sir. I've been here so long, I'd like it to go to someone who appreciates it. I just hope as how the new tenant does.'

Now this was all very nice and friendly, but he needed to get inside. 'So do I, Mrs Offord,' said Jack with a simulated sigh of disappointment. 'Would you mind awfully if I did come in for a look round, though? The thing is, my wife gave me a silver cigarette case and I've lost it. Thinking back, I'm sure I must've mislaid it here. Poor Betty was terribly disappointed as she'd gone to some trouble to get it specially made. And,' he added, playing for sympathy, 'I'm what you might call in the doghouse, until I do find it.'

'Come in and welcome, sir,' said Mrs Offord, opening the door wide. 'I must say, though, I haven't seen any such thing.'

As his cigarette case (which was, indeed, a present from Betty) was in his pocket at that moment, that was hardly surprising.

'Maybe,' said Mrs Offord with a smile, 'it slipped out of your pocket when you were climbing the tree. It cheered me up, that did, to see such high spirits and to hear you both talking about children. Mind you, if you had lost it then, I'd have expected the gardener to have found it.'

'He might have overlooked it,' said Jack, stepping into the hall. 'That's a very good idea of yours, Mrs Offord. Would you mind if I took a look in the garden?'

'Feel free, sir. George Meredith, the gardener, isn't here today, or I'm sure he'd have helped you.'

This was all to the good. The last thing he wanted was someone tracking his footsteps. 'And please don't bother yourself helping me to look for it, Mrs Offord,' he said as she led him down the hall and out onto the veranda. 'It's my own silly fault for losing it.'

'Now don't you talk like that, sir. I'm sure as how it's easily done. If none of us ever lost anything, it'd be an odd thing.'

She gazed at him indulgently as he walked down the stone steps into the garden, then turned away, back into the kitchen.

For form's sake, he hunted round by the cedar tree for a few minutes, then set off along past the vegetable garden to where the path wound down between the beech trees.

He wanted to find the parameters. Where were the boundaries of the garden? He plunged down between the trees, past the little stone bridge and then, leaving the path, walked on in as straight a line as he could manage.

In about twenty yards or so, he came to a stone wall. It was about ten feet high and overgrown with moss and ivy. Following the wall, he picked his way over boggy ground and through the nettles, cow parsley and brambles until he had made a complete circuit of the copse. No one, he thought, untangling a strand of rampant blackberry thorn from his trousers, had come along here for years.

What was on the other side of the wall? He sized up the ivy, then, grasping a thick stem, he scrambled up and looked over. More trees; at a guess they belonged to another garden backing onto this.

He dropped down, smacking his hands together to get rid of the dirt. So, there was no practical way out of the garden through the trees.

He went back through the wood and back onto the lawn. Here the garden wall was lower, but it was bordered by dense shrubs and flower beds.

He looked at the veranda. It was central to the house. On one side was the kitchen and on the other was the garage.

At one side of the veranda a short path led to a door at the back of the garage. At the other side, the path ran past the kitchens. Jack walked past the kitchens, round the side of the house, to where the way was barred by a high back gate.

The gate, a sturdy construction, was obviously as old as the house. He opened the gate, with its neatly lettered sign of *Tradesmen* affixed to the front, and saw how the path opened out onto the drive. The drive, he knew, was a big semi-circular sweep of gravel that fronted the entire front of the house.

Retracing his steps, he walked back along the path, down the stone steps and stood by the cedar tree, feeling the rough, ridged bark under his hand.

Caroline Trevelyan had sat under this tree while her daughter played in the tree house above. And under this tree, Caroline Trevelyan had died. Frozen with terror, the little girl had watched until the monster had gone.

When it was over, little Jenny had escaped, terrified, to the safety of the nursery. What she had seen was so horrific, she had buried the memory for years until chance led her back to this house, to this tree.

Jack pressed his hand into the bark of the cedar. *Show me,* he whispered to himself and let his imagination have free rein.

Jenny's disappearance was accounted for; she had run away

and no one had seen her go. But what had happened to Caroline Trevelyan?

He was certain Jennifer had seen her killed. Nothing else, he thought, would account for her reactions.

So what had happened to the body?

Could the poor woman's body have been hidden in the woods? That was a possibility. If that was the case, presumably the body would be moved under cover of darkness, but . . .

Jack clicked his tongue in irritation. That meant either climbing the wall at the bottom of the garden or bringing the body out of the woods and back across the lawn.

It was possible, he supposed, that the killer could've moved the body after dark, but it was horribly risky. It would be a matter of sheer luck whether he was seen or not. And, of course, there was the question of where would he move it to?

Out of the back gate and where? And how? A car was out of the question; cars in 1907 were noisy, temperamental machines that invariably drew a crowd of onlookers. The sound of a car at night would certainly draw the attention of the neighbours. Stick a dead woman in the back seat and those neighbours would be certain to see something *and* talk about it.

That wasn't a good idea for someone wanting to move a body. A handcart or a pony and trap was a possibility, but the body would have to be got out of the gate first. Saunder's Green wasn't some isolated mansion but a house in a suburban street. A cart or a pony and trap wouldn't draw the same attention as a car, but there were still the neighbours who could easily be looking out of the windows. There might even be a passer-by. Sneaking the body out of the back gate wasn't impossible but, Jack thought, it was improbable.

The wall could be climbed but that was unlikely, particularly if a man was burdened with a dead body. Even if the under-growth and brambles hadn't achieved such a vigorous growth twenty years ago as they had now – Jack ruefully picked a tiny blackberry thorn out of the heel of his hand – it would be a difficult climb. And really, it was hard to see the point of doing such a thing. The garden led onto more gardens so that didn't so much as solve the problem but create more.

The other point against hiding the body in the woods was

that the woods had been searched on the day of Caroline's disappearance. The killer might have been lucky but he couldn't count on being lucky.

No; leaving aside going back into the house, there were only two practical ways out of the garden, and that was through the back gate or through the garage.

It had been, thought Jack, an impulsive murder. After all, the tree, with the tea table beside it, had been in full view of the house. Even if the builders had knocked off for the afternoon, there were still the servants to deal with. That the only witness had been an unseen, terrified child was a matter of sheer luck.

So what would I do? he asked himself. I've just committed a murder. I'm scared. I might be seen. I need to hide the body. I need to work fast. Where can I hide it?

He looked round urgently. The garage!

Yes, the garage. Get out from the garden, get under cover and *fast*.

Pick up the body. It's heavy but I'm strong and I'm a killer, yes? No one stops me. No one crosses me. I've got the power of death in my hands. I am invincible.

Carrying an imaginary body over his shoulder – Jack could almost feel the weight of it – he walked to the garage door and opened it.

There was a small landing, surrounded by a wooden rail with a brick-built staircase leading down to the concrete floor some twelve feet below.

Blinking his eyes to adjust to the dim light, he went down the stairs and stepped down onto the concrete floor. He placed his imaginary burden on the floor, panting with the effort.

What now? Hide the damn thing, of course. And he'd better move fast.

The garage was a large, high, dimly lit room with space for at least two cars.

There hadn't been a car in here for years, but say there was, the two big wooden doors would be opened onto the drive.

No. Hang on. The garage was being built when Caroline – he could virtually see her body on the floor – was murdered. Were the doors in place on the 15th of July all those years ago? There was no possible way of knowing but he was going to guess they were. Because if the doors were there and closed, that would give him what he so desperately needed, a space away from prying eyes.

And the plan had worked. He had succeeded. So what had he done next?

He ran up the staircase. There was a rusty old bolt on the door that, with a grunt, he managed to ease into position. The last thing he wanted was Mrs Offord wandering into the garage. Fair enough, there wasn't actually a body on the floor, but he didn't want her to see what he was doing, all the same.

Back down the staircase to the imaginary corpse. It was strange how easy it was to imagine her there. The woman's face was turned away from him but he could almost see details of her fair hair and blue dress. It was odd how certain he was that her dress was blue.

He shuddered. Although he was safe in here for the moment, he needed to get cracking before Caroline . . . No. Don't think of her – it – as Caroline. It was a body and that body would start to stiffen soon. What to do next?

Building works. There were building works going on. There was bound to be sand and cement and bricks.

Slowly Jack put aside the mantle of the killer and consciously stepped back into his own personality. It was quite a relief.

So where was the body hidden? Could it be under the concrete floor? It could, he supposed. Damn! If, on that day in July, the floor hadn't been laid but was still the bare earth, then it would be simple enough to dig a grave.

Hold on. Jack had seen men at work on building sites before now. Concrete wasn't just poured onto bare earth. It was actually a fairly laborious process. First of all the earth was dug out, then a thick layer of crushed stone was laid on top and levelled out. Sand went on top of that, compacted down, and only then the concrete was laid.

If the floor really had been bare earth, then a grave would be discovered as soon as the men started work. If the floor was a work in progress, would the killer really start digging into layers of crushed stone and sand?

That was some job he was taking on. To say nothing of the physical effort of digging, he'd have to make sure the floor, whatever stage it was at, looked completely undisturbed after-wards. Then he'd have to get rid of the surplus soil, spadefull by spadefull. That was a huge amount of work.

What if the concrete had actually been laid? Well, that would rule the floor out. So what other options were there?

Jack stepped out into the middle of the garage. Along one wall ran a wooden shelf with a litter of old tools. There was no hiding place there, but the staircase? That was another matter altogether. Bricks; it was built of bricks, the steps sideways onto the wall, with a wooden rail at the top and a wooden bannister. Was that staircase hollow?

Time to find out. He searched amongst the old tools on the bench and found a heavy chisel and a hammer. Picking up the chisel, and fervently hoping Mrs Offord was too far away to hear any noise, he set to work, chipping the mortar out from around a brick at the corner. The mortar came away in strips. Taking a long-bladed screwdriver, Jack wriggled it into the gap he had made and eased the brick away from its neighbours.

The rush of foul air told him he'd found what he was looking for. Hand to his mouth, he staggered back, leaning against the wall of the garage.

After a few minutes, he approached the shelf again. Kneeling down, he struck a match, holding it so the light shone into the cavity made by the missing brick. The first thing he saw was crumpled cloth. Blue crumpled cloth. He swallowed hard, remembered how clearly he had seen the imagined corpse, dressed in blue. The match went out and he struck another, this time seeing the gleam of white bone amongst the blue.

Poor Caroline. Wearily he picked up the brick and put it back into the hole. He went back up the staircase and, going into the garden, picked up a handful of damp earth. He put it into the gap left by the missing mortar. It wouldn't deceive anyone who was looking especially at the bricks, but it was good enough to escape immediate attention.

Betty had obviously heard him come in. She met him at the door with a resigned expression. 'Jack! You really are the limit. Where have you been? We had to start dinner without you.'

'Dinner?' His eyes widened as the memory flooded back. 'Crikey, I'm ever so sorry, Betty. I forgot all about dinner.'

'I suppose you forgot all about the oysters, too?'

Jack hung up his coat and hat. 'Darling, I'm so sorry. I'm afraid it didn't cross my mind.' He hesitated. 'You see, I've been to Saunder's Green.'

'Saunder's Green?' Betty looked at his expression then put a concerned hand on his arm. 'What happened?'

'Is Bill here?'

Betty nodded. 'Yes, and Jenny Langton too.'

He took a deep breath and squared his shoulders. 'It's probably for the best. I'm glad you're here and Bill come to that. I think poor Jenny Langton is going to need her friends.'

He walked along the hall and into the dining room. Bill and Jenny had finished their dessert and were chatting animatedly to one another.

'Hello, stranger,' said Bill cheerfully, then stopped as he saw Jack's expression. 'Whatever's the matter, old man?'

Jenny looked at him anxiously. 'Would you like us to leave?'

Jack shook his head. 'No. Please don't. I'd have to tell you anyway.' He sank into a chair and looked at Betty. 'I don't want any food but I'd love a whisky.'

She poured him a drink. He took a deep draught, then looked at them apologetically. 'I'm sorry about the dinner party.' He took another drink and braced himself. 'I've just come from Saunder's Green.' He stopped abruptly, looking at Jenny.

'Go on,' said Bill warily.

'The fact is – I'm desperately sorry, Jenny – but I've found the body.'

Jenny gave a little cry and clapped her hand to her mouth.

'*What?*' Bill nearly shouted, then turned instinctively to Jenny.

Jenny didn't speak but gazed at Jack in horror.

Starting up, Bill came round the table swiftly and, sitting beside her, took her hand. 'Miss Langton, are you all right?' he asked gently.

Jenny took a deep breath. 'I . . . I will be,' she said shakily. 'It's just a bit of a shock, you know?' She swallowed hard. 'I'm sorry. It's a bit silly of me, really. After all, I can't remember her.'

'But she was your mother,' said Betty. 'It's only natural you should feel upset. It's horrible.'

Jenny didn't speak for a moment 'Yes, it is,' she agreed eventually. She breathed deeply for a few seconds, then looked up. 'Where was she?'

'In the garage, under the steps up into the garden.'

Jenny stared at him. 'The garage? When I was there, at Saunder's Green, I opened the door into the garage and I could hardly bring myself to go in. I had to force myself to go down the stairs. Are you sure she's there?'

'Quite sure.' Jack finished his drink and, getting up, poured himself another.

Bill cast a sideways glance at Jenny. 'What did you – er – do with it?'

'Nothing much,' said Jack, rubbing his face with his hands. 'The staircase makes a kind of brick-built box. After I'd worked out that under the stairs was the most likely place, I knocked a brick out with a chisel. Once I'd seen what was inside, I put the brick back and replaced the missing mortar with earth. It's all so dusty and dark in there, I doubt anyone would see where the brick had been taken out, unless they were looking for it.'

'So no one knows what you found? You didn't give the alarm at all?'

'No. The only person in the house is Mrs Offord, the house-keeper, and she's such a kindly old soul, I couldn't possibly tell her what I'd found.' He gave a humourless laugh. 'I got into the house on the pretence of looking for my cigarette case which I said I'd lost. She was concerned enough about that, bless her. She was so pleased when I said I'd found it. She saw how grubby I was after rooting round in the garden and insisted I have a wash. I made a point of mentioning the garden. I didn't want her to know there was anything untoward in the garage.'

'She'll have to know tomorrow, though.'

Jack shook his head. 'She won't be there tomorrow. She told me I was lucky to catch her, as this was her last day. A new tenant, with his own servants, moves in tomorrow.'

'Poor beggar,' commented Bill. 'It's hardly the welcome to a new home anyone would want.'

'No, it isn't.' He looked at Jenny. 'This is awful news for you. If you want to stay here tonight, please do. I really don't think you ought to be alone.' He glanced at Betty. 'That's all right, isn't it?'

'Of course it is,' she said warmly. 'I think you should stay, Jenny. I can lend you night things and everything you need.'

'That's very kind of you,' Jenny said. 'I'd like to stay but it's a rule at my boarding house that we have to say if we're going to be out overnight.'

'I'll tell them, Miss Langton, don't you worry,' said Bill, getting to his feet. 'I know the address and can easily call on my way home.' He glanced at the clock. 'It's about time I was going anyway.'

'I'll see you to the door, Bill,' said Jack, standing up.

The two men walked into the hall. 'Thanks for looking after Miss Langton,' said Bill quietly, as Jack helped him on with his coat. 'It's good to know she's safely with you for tonight, at least.' He looked at his friend. 'Are you okay? It must've been a dickens of a shock. Whatever sent you hunting round Saunder's Green?'

'It was a train of thought, an idea I had. As far as that goes, I'm no further forward. It's all a bit nebulous at the moment, but I wouldn't mind talking it over with you, after I've had time to sleep on it.' He hesitated. 'Look, about this body . . .'

'Yes?'

'Would you mind keeping it to yourself for the moment?'

'I can't do that!' said Bill, aghast. 'I'll have to report it, first thing. I can't withhold information. The Chief would have my head on a plate.'

'In that case . . .' Jack hesitated. 'Look, let me see Sir Douglas first thing tomorrow. If you could be there as well, that would make things easier.' He nearly smiled. 'If nothing else, it'll stop me having to repeat myself.'

'All right,' said Bill after a moment's thought. 'See me at the Yard at ten tomorrow.'

# SIXTEEN

'You found the *body*?' said Sir Douglas Lynton in disbelief. 'Good grief, Major Haldean, I can hardly credit it. Whatever led you to the garage?'

'I looked at the traffic on the Strand and it made me think of cars. That's one reason. I went back to Saunder's Green to try and establish once and for all, if Caroline Trevelyan had been murdered, what had happened to her body. I did some hunting round and proved, to my own satisfaction, that it would be very difficult indeed for the killer to get her corpse off the premises without being seen. That meant it was hidden somewhere, and the garage seemed the obvious place to look. Once I'd worked that out, there was only one place where it could be, and that was bricked up in the staircase.'

'It's a damn good piece of work, all the same,' said Sir Douglas. He took a cigarette from the silver box beside him, then pushed the box across the desk. 'Help yourself, Major. And you, Chief Inspector.' He looked at Jack with respect. 'Dash it, I can hardly credit it. The Trevelyan case was a real cause célèbre. The police were swarming all over that house without uncovering a damn thing, apart from Trevelyan's diary, and then, twenty years later, you turn up and go straight to the body. Why the dickens wasn't she found at the time?'

'I think I can answer that, sir,' said Bill. 'Inspector Chartfield, who was in charge of the case, put a lot of store by the fact that the servants had overheard Trevelyan and his wife quarrelling about the proposed move to New Zealand. He thought Mrs Trevelyan had simply taken herself off and Trevelyan was making a huge fuss about nothing. Then, of course, when the letter arrived and was proved to be a forgery, everything changed. He realised that it was a case of murder and Trevelyan had tried to cover his tracks. By then, so much time had been wasted, that it seemed obvious that Trevelyan would have had ample time to dispose of the body. The initial searches hadn't turned anything up, so I can't imagine the house and grounds were searched with anything like the thoroughness they should've been.'

'It seems to have been very lax, all the same,' grunted Sir Douglas.

'It must've been difficult to spot at the time,' said Jack. 'After all, the house was being renovated and the garage must've been full of building materials.'

'Come off it,' said Bill. 'If it was a competition for brains between you and Inspector Chartfield, I know who'd I'd back.'

'Spare my blushes,' murmured Jack.

'Well, I'd like to endorse Rackham's opinion,' asserted Sir Douglas. 'Incidentally, Major, not only do I have to congratulate you on finding Caroline Trevelyan's remains, I understand that congratulations are in order for spotting that the forged letter in the original case and the unfinished letter found at Summer's Court were written by the same person.'

'That,' said Jack, 'really was nothing more than good luck. I picked up the wrong letter by mistake, and it struck me how similar they looked.'

'I can only wish that the rest of us had as much good luck,' said Sir Douglas. 'Now Miss Hollander's confirmed it, there isn't any doubt that Trevelyan really did forge the letter from his wife. I gather from Rackham that you had some other ideas on the subject, but to my mind, it's an open-and-shut case. As I see it, Trevelyan was hatching up a scheme with the unfinished letter to entice Mrs Rotherwell into the flat, and didn't want Jane Davenham to know about it.'

'You mean that Trevelyan was writing the letter when he was interrupted by Jane Davenham, sir?' asked Bill.

'That's about the size of it, yes,' said Sir Douglas.

'As a matter of fact,' said Jack, 'I don't agree.'

Sir Douglas looked at Jack. 'Go on,' he said guardedly. 'What don't you agree with?'

'That Michael Trevelyan wrote the letters. Miss Hollander told us that it was impossible to determine from the handwriting alone if a letter was written by a man or a woman. I think Jane Davenham wrote both.'

Sir Douglas shook his head in disagreement. 'Nonsense. Jane Davenham wasn't around twenty years ago.'

'Wasn't she, sir?'

'There's never been any mention of the fact.'

'That doesn't rule it out though, does it?' Jack tapped his cigarette on the ashtray. 'Just because she never came to the attention of the police, it doesn't mean she wasn't there.'

Sir Douglas chewed this over. 'As a matter of fact, you're quite right,' he grudgingly admitted. 'Inspector Chartfield,' he added, tapping the file, 'doesn't seem to have covered himself with glory over this case. I suppose he could've missed spotting Mrs Davenham.'

'There's another thing, too,' continued Jack. 'Mrs Davenham and Mrs Rotherwell had been in correspondence for years. We know that from Matthew and Julia Rotherwell.'

'Well, so we do,' said Sir Douglas, then stopped. 'Dash it, Major, I see what you mean. Mrs Rotherwell must've known Jane Davenham's handwriting well. If she got a letter in a hand she didn't recognise, she would've smelt a rat.'

'That could be why Trevelyan didn't send the letter,' ventured Bill. 'The unfinished one, I mean. He could've started it and then realised it wasn't working. Then, as you say, sir,' he added with a nod to Sir Douglas, 'Jane Davenham came into the room and he hid the letter in a hurry.'

'Exactly,' agreed Sir Douglas. Jack shook his head. 'Well, Major? What's wrong with that?'

'Nothing,' admitted Jack. 'It's perfectly valid reasoning and does explain the Summer's Court letter. However, I bumped into Mrs Shilton yesterday—' both Sir Douglas and Bill groaned—' and she told me that Amelia Rotherwell was a very moral, very upright woman, who held strong views on anyone living in an irregular relationship. She had no hesitation in telling me she would cut them dead until the situation was rectified.'

'What's the point, Major?' asked Sir Douglas impatiently. 'I may say that I wouldn't expect a lady such as Mrs Rotherwell to hold any other opinion.'

'The point, Sir Douglas, is this. We know from the porter at the flats that Mrs Davenham and Mrs Rotherwell came in together, the best of friends. That happy atmosphere would be wiped out immediately Mrs Rotherwell walked into the flat. What else could Jane Davenham expect?'

'It sounds a bit thin to me, Jack,' said Bill. 'Jane Davenham might not have realised how strict Mrs Rotherwell's views were.'

'After having been in correspondence for years? I doubt it.'

'All right then, for all I know Jane Davenham might have hoped that she could persuade her friend to make an exception in her case. You know how some people are. Rules, even rules they expect other people to stick to, don't apply in their case. Yes, she might've known that Mrs Rotherwell was fairly strict, but she could've hoped to have changed her mind.'

Jack put his hands wide. 'Fair enough. Once you start arguing about human nature, anything goes, I suppose. I thought it was worth pointing out, though. Because, you see, that makes Jane Davenham not a victim but very much a villain.'

'A villain?' Sir Douglas shifted uneasily. 'I don't think so. In my opinion, she's likely to have been murdered herself. Unless she's being held under duress, there must be some reason why she hasn't made herself known to us. I suppose she could be in thrall to this Trevelyan feller, even knowing what happened to Mrs Rotherwell.'

Bill nodded. 'She could be scared witless of speaking to us. If he's managed to persuade her that's she's up to her neck in murder, she might believe that she'll be arrested and tried for murder as soon as she speaks out.' His face grew grave. 'I agree with Sir Douglas, though. I think her most likely fate is that she's been murdered herself. Don't you agree, Jack?'

'You could be right,' he admitted. 'You very well might be right. But wouldn't it be nice to be proved right?'

'Of course it would, man,' said Sir Douglas. 'But how do you propose to do that?'

'I do have a couple of ideas,' said Jack, 'but they involve looking at the case in quite a different way. First of all, Sir Douglas, how difficult is it to trace a record of marriage?'

Sir Douglas blinked. 'Easy enough, I suppose, as long as you know who you're looking for. Somerset House have the registers.'

'I'm looking for Jane Davenham.'

Bill gave a whistle. 'This is all about the letter, isn't it, Jack? The forged Caroline letter. You said you thought Jane Davenham had written it. If Trevelyan and Jane Davenham were married, then that would explain a lot. They'd have to be married after Caroline Trevelyan was dead, of course.'

'Let me get this straight,' said Sir Douglas. 'You think, Major, that Jane Davenham was privy to Caroline Trevelyan's murder. Is that right?'

'Yes, sir. I think it's possible.'

'I see.' Sir Douglas smoothed out his moustache. 'It is possible, I suppose. And,' he added, brightening, 'it gives a motive for Mrs Trevelyan's murder. A fairly compelling motive. Do you think they would have actually got married, though? After all, Trevelyan was on the run for murder. He could have gone anywhere on earth.'

'Yes, he could,' agreed Jack. 'I still think it's worth checking the register, though. And I do have some more ideas. At the moment they're questions, really, but, for instance, I would like to know why the tap was left dripping in the bath in Summer's Court.'

'Why the tap was dripping?' repeated Bill in astonishment. 'Why shouldn't it be dripping? How d'you know it was dripping, anyway? All the pipework was wrenched out.' He stopped. 'Hold on. Of course it was dripping. Otherwise the bath wouldn't have filled up and overflowed.' He shrugged. 'Maybe there was a dodgy washer.'

'And maybe that's all it is,' agreed Jack. 'But, you see, if it was left dripping on purpose, that more or less guaranteed that the bath would overflow and we'd be led to the body.'

Sir Douglas stared at him. 'I think you're barking up the wrong tree there, Major. We'd have found the body in the course of time in any event, tap or no tap.'

'True,' conceded Jack. 'This made it sooner rather than later, though.'

Bill was looking at him quizzically. 'You had the idea that the body in the bath wasn't really Mrs Rotherwell's. You're not still harping on about that, are you?'

'No, I'm not. The dental evidence and the old fracture Dr Roude found prove that the woman we found was Mrs Rotherwell. There's no doubt about that.'

'Then what are you going on about?' asked Bill in frustration.

Jack hesitated. 'Look, everything's a bit vague at the moment.

If I can find that marriage certificate, it'll all become a lot clearer.'

'Good luck with that,' commented Bill ironically.

'Good luck indeed,' echoed Sir Douglas, completely missing the sarcasm. 'I must say I doubt if you'll find any such thing, but it'd be very strong evidence to show that Trevelyan had a motive to dispose of his wife.' He shuffled his papers together. 'Well, Major Haldean, congratulations once more on finding Caroline Trevelyan. I'll get some men down to Saunder's Green right away.'

'Would you mind not doing that, sir?' asked Jack.

'Not doing that?' Sir Douglas repeated blankly. 'Of course I've got to do that, Major. Dash it, never mind that the house-keeper at Saunder's Green seemed to take a real shine to you. I know it'll be a real blow for the poor woman, to find out there's been a dead body on the premises, but we don't have any choice in the matter. We can't be swayed by sentiment.'

'No, of course not,' said Jack. 'That's not why I'm asking. It's just that when the body is disinterred, there won't be any chance of hiding the fact. The balloon will go up good and proper and, just for the moment, I'd rather let sleeping dogs lie.'

'I'm sorry, Major, it's out of the question.'

'Give me three days,' asked Jack. 'After all, the poor woman's body has been there for twenty years. Three days won't make that much difference.'

'I can't possibly agree,' said Sir Douglas.

'Three days,' repeated Jack. 'Three days to find the marriage certificate.'

'If there is one,' commented Bill.

'Oh, I think there is,' said Jack absently. He looked at Sir Douglas with a smile. 'It really could make all the difference.'

Sir Douglas looked at him thoughtfully. 'You've got something in mind.' He stubbed out his cigarette. 'Tell me. Does this apper-tain to the Rotherwell enquiry?'

'Yes, it does, sir.'

'Dammed if I see how,' he grunted. He drummed his fingers on the desk, then came to a decision. 'Very well, Major. This is all very irregular, but as you actually found the body, you have a right to ask.' He cocked an eyebrow at Bill. 'Granted it's part of the Rotherwell case, you'd better help him, Rackham. You can add some official weight to the enquiry. And then, when you've found what you're looking for, maybe you'll be kind enough to tell me what it's all about.'

It was at ten past eleven on the second day that Jack looked up from the leather-bound register in Somerset House. 'I say, Bill,' he said with supressed excitement, 'I've found it.'

The next day, an advertisement appeared in the classified column of all the daily newspapers.

> Mrs Jane Davenham – did you really think my mother didn't talk about marriage? Times are hard, but I'm sure we can come to an arrangement. M.R. Reply to P.O. Box 64, Harley Street.

The following morning Jack presented his card for box number 64 at Harley Street post office. He was rewarded with a letter. He quickly ripped it open and read it, then stuffing the letter in his pocket and, trying to smother a broad grin, he walked down Harley Street to the Embankment and Scotland Yard. Bait taken.

'I'm surprised Sir Douglas agreed to the scheme,' said Betty that evening.

Jack pulled her closer to him on the sofa. 'He's a sporting old bird,' he said. 'He wants to get hold of Jane Davenham as much as I do. Besides, what we're doing might be unconventional, but it isn't illegal. He wouldn't agree to anything against the law.' His arm tightened round her. 'No, my sweetheart, now we've got Matthew and Julia Rotherwell safely out of the way, my main concern is you.'

'I'll be fine,' said Betty. 'After all, all I have to do is meet the woman.'

Bracing herself, Betty walked over the footbridge in St James' Park and, shoulders squared, made for the left-hand bench, looking out onto the lake. Taking a copy of *On The Town* from her bag, she left it unopened on her knee. She hadn't bought it to read; it was a signal.

It was about ten minutes later when a middle-aged woman walked past the bench. She had a coat with big patch pockets and was fingering something in the pocket. She seemed to be taking a very keen interest in the landscape, looking around her constantly.

Her eyes went first to the magazine and then to Betty. She walked on a few steps then stood for a moment, as if contemplating the pelicans and ducks on the lake. Turning back, she looked suspiciously at her surroundings once more, then sat down beside Betty.

'Mrs Julia Rotherwell?' she said without preamble.

'Yes,' said Betty. 'And you are Mrs Davenham, I presume. My mother-in-law spoke about you. And marriage.'

'She was mistaken.'

Betty shook her head with a knowing smile. 'No. I've got the marriage certificate.'

Jane Davenham drew her breath in with a hiss.

'It took me some time to find it,' continued Betty, 'but I wanted proof positive before I wrote to you. Marriages, Mrs Davenham, are a matter of public record and Somerset House is open to everyone.'

'Have you got the certificate with you?'

'Of course not,' said Betty with a dismissive laugh. 'It's in a safe place with, I may say, instructions to send it to the police with a full explanation, should anything untoward happen to me. So, Mrs Davenham, you can stop playing with that gun or knife or whatever it is in your pocket and listen to me.'

Mrs Davenham gave her a startled glance and, withdrawing her hand from her pocket, sat back on the bench.

'I want to see the certificate,' she said after a few moments.

'Fair enough,' agreed Betty. 'I can easily get another copy. I'll give you that copy in return for two hundred pounds.'

'Two hundred pounds?'

'In the first instance, yes. There will be further instalments.'

Jane Davenham's eyes narrowed. 'I would advise you not to be too greedy, Mrs Rotherwell. I know where you live.'

'You probably know where we *did* live, Mrs Davenham. I have no illusions about what you are capable of. And, I may say, that you are in no position to make threats. I am going to give you a letter. It contains instructions as to where you will leave the money. If those instructions are not followed, then I will go to the police.'

'You won't make any money like that,' said Jane Davenham with a sneer.

'No, but you will suffer the consequences. That was actually what my husband wanted to do. It was I who persuaded him that there could be another way.' She smiled. 'Think of it as a mutually beneficent arrangement.'

She didn't miss the cold, angry gleam in Jane Davenham's eyes. Suddenly Betty wanted to be as far away from this woman as possible. She stood up and, taking an envelope from inside the magazine, paused before giving it to her.

'Wait ten minutes before you open this. Don't forget, if anything happens to me, the police will know the truth. Matthew wants to tell them. If I think I've been followed, I will let him have his way.' She handed her the letter. 'Goodbye, Mrs Davenham.'

Boiling with anger, Jane Davenham watched her walk away. She glanced at her watch. She'd better keep to the instructions. For the moment, that woman had the upper hand. She smiled slowly. For the moment.

The minutes ticked by. Jane Davenham looked at her watch again. Nearly ten minutes. She took the knife from her pocket and slit open the envelope. She gazed in utter astonishment at the single word on the sheet of paper it contained.

The word was, *Boo!*

What the *hell?* She thrust the letter angrily into her pocket as a man sat down on the bench beside her. 'Good morning, Mrs Davenham,' he said politely.

She gazed at him in horrified recognition. It was Chief Inspector Rackham.

Another man sat down on the other side. Her stomach turned over as she recognised Jack Haldean. She looked at him wildly as he tipped his hat and smiled.

'Or should that be *Mrs Rotherwell?*'

His hand shot out and gripped her wrist, forcing her to let go of the knife. It clattered to the ground as she struggled in his grip.

'Let me go!' she screamed. She hit out frantically as three more men hurried across the path to the bench. 'Help me!'

With some difficulty, Rackham snapped the handcuffs round her wrist. 'I'm sorry, Mrs Davenham, but these are my men and you are under arrest.'

'What an absolute wild cat,' said Rackham. He and Jack were in Rackham's office at Scotland Yard. 'I feel better now she's safely under lock and key.'

He glanced up as a knock sounded on the door and Betty walked in.

Jack leapt to his feet and hugged her close. 'Betty, you complete star,' he said, pulling out a chair for her. 'We couldn't have pulled it off without you. You were brilliant. I was so relieved when I saw you walk away from that woman.'

'I was pretty relieved myself,' said Betty, unbuttoning her coat. 'She was so angry that I honestly thought she might try and murder me on the spot. I'm sure she had a weapon.'

'She had a knife,' said Jack. 'And yes, I think she was prepared to use it.' He squeezed her shoulders, conscious of the sudden lump in his throat. 'I'm just glad to have you back.'

'I'll drink to that,' said Bill, raising his cup of tea. He put the cup down and stood up. 'Let me take your coat, Betty. You carried it off magnificently. She never suspected a thing.'

'Thanks,' said Betty, sinking into the chair. 'It made such a difference, knowing you were close at hand. I couldn't have done it otherwise. Is that tea?' she asked, looking at the tray on the desk. 'Can I have some?'

'Certainly,' said Bill. He hung up Betty's coat and, returning to the desk, poured her out a cup. 'I think it should be champagne,' he added with a grin, 'but tea will have to do.'

'It's all I want,' she said, taking the cup. 'She was a horrible woman,' she added, shuddering. 'She frightened me stiff. Goodness knows what Mrs Rotherwell – the real Mrs Rotherwell, I mean – ever saw in her.'

'Well, to be fair, I don't suppose the real Mrs Rotherwell

ever tried to blackmail her,' said Jack with a grin. 'That must affect how you feel about a person.'

'Where is she now?' asked Betty.

'In one of the cells downstairs,' said Bill. 'She's refused to say anything without a lawyer present, which is, of course, her perfect right, so she can cool her heels for the time being. I'm waiting for him to turn up before I go near her.'

He opened the box of cigarettes on his desk. 'Help yourself,' he said. He lit a cigarette and leaning back, stretched out his legs luxuriantly. 'Whatever put you onto it, Jack? That she was Mrs Rotherwell, I mean?'

'It was Matthew and Julia Rotherwell who set me thinking,' said Jack. 'The woman they described, the real Mrs Rotherwell, Matthew's mother, sounded superficially like the woman we'd met. The clothes were perfect, of course, because they were actually Mrs Rotherwell's own. The two women were similar enough in height and build for the deception to work and the woman we met certainly knew enough about the real Mrs Rotherwell to give a very convincing performance. No, it was the Rotherwells' mention of how kindly a woman Matthew's mother had been and how she was looking forward to the new baby. It occurred to me to wonder what sort of grandmother she would make, and I just couldn't get the picture to gel in my head. Now, admittedly I had spent longer with her than you did, Bill, but I didn't get any impression of maternal feeling or kindliness from her.'

'Kindliness isn't how I'd describe Jane Davenham, that's for sure,' said Bill.

'Certainly not,' echoed Betty with feeling.

'It was really nothing more than a niggle, but it worried me,' said Jack. 'At the same time, Mrs Rotherwell was certainly a real person. Her son and daughter-in-law vouched for that, and there was the fact that she had come forward of her own volition. She answered my advertisement and, what's more, had written to Mrs Shilton about it. And, if anything was certain, it was that the poor woman had indeed been murdered. As you know, I was a bit doubtful that the body we found in Summer's Court was her, but I couldn't argue with the evidence.'

'You weren't happy though, were you, darling?' said Betty.

'No, I wasn't, but it was meeting Mrs Shilton on the Embankment that finally made me think about Mrs Rotherwell properly. Yes, there was a real Mrs Rotherwell, but was she the woman that Bill and I met?'

Bill blew out a long mouthful of smoke. 'Well done,' he said. 'I met her and I didn't have any doubts whatsoever.'

'Yes, but don't forget I had the dubious pleasure of taking her to lunch. I had longer with her than you did.'

Betty drank the rest of her tea. 'When was the poor thing – the real Mrs Rotherwell, I mean – actually killed?'

'The day before I met her at the Criterion, if you know what I mean. That's a guess, but I bet I'm right. There was some faked evidence to make us think otherwise. There was a newspaper left in Summer's Court dated Wednesday 21st, the day that Mrs Rotherwell was supposed to have disappeared, but what I think happened is this. Jane Davenham took Mrs Rotherwell to Summer's Court on Sunday the 18th. She never left the flat. Then Mrs Davenham, wearing Mrs Rotherwell's clothes, went back to the Royal Park Hotel and stayed there overnight. She met me for lunch on the Monday, stayed another night at the hotel, and then disappeared the following day.'

'Wasn't that terribly risky?' asked Betty. 'To stay at the hotel, I mean?'

'It obviously came off,' said Jack. 'And although I haven't got a down on middle-aged ladies, I've noticed before how similar ladies of a certain age and class can appear. And,' he added with a smile, 'the desk clerk was a man.'

'What's that got to do with it?' asked Betty.

'Think about it, sweetheart. If a young, attractive woman was staying at the hotel, the desk clerk would notice. If it was you, say, he couldn't help but take notice.' Betty looked understandably pleased. 'But an older woman? Not so much. It's really mannerisms and clothes that he'd go on. The chambermaid who brought the morning tea would probably have noticed, but I bet our Mrs Davenham made sure she was covered up with bedclothes when the woman was in the room.'

'What about the dripping tap in Summer's Court?' asked Bill. 'Do you really think that was left dripping on purpose?'

Jack nodded. 'I can't prove it, but that's my guess. If it was deliberately left dripping, I think it was fairly carefully calculated as to the time it would take to fill the bath and flood the flat.'

'It sounds like a macabre version of a school maths problem,' said Bill. 'I still don't get the point.'

'I think the point was to force the issue, to make us act sooner rather than later. The idea of putting her in the bath was to make Mrs Rotherwell unrecognisable. I'd met Jane Davenham and so had you. If we'd seen the poor woman before the bath had filled, we'd know she wasn't the woman we'd met, no matter how many dentists testified that she was the real Mrs Rotherwell. Incidentally, when I met Jane Davenham in the Criterion, she was rattled when she discovered I'd read the original statement and was fairly chummy with the police. She was taken aback when I suggested she should come here and talk to you, Bill. Then, after she'd thought about it for a few moments, she probably realised how that would make her case stronger.'

'And what is that case?' asked Bill.

'To convince us that there's such a person as Michael Trevelyan. There isn't.'

Bill snorted in disagreement. 'Yes, there is. Of course there is.' He broke off in irritation as the phone rang. 'Excuse me,' he said, and pulled the telephone towards him. 'Chief Inspector Rackham speaking.'

They saw his face alter as a voice crackled down the telephone. They could only hear his part of the conversation, but his words and the urgency of his voice brought Jack to his feet. 'She said what? . . . No, no! Don't do that! . . . I'll be there as quickly as I can.'

Bill hung up the receiver and looked at them, his face white. 'Jack, you're wrong. You're very wrong. Michael Trevelyan's real all right. That was Miss Langton. She's had her aunt on the phone in a terrible state. Michael Trevelyan's at Saunder's Green and he's planning something desperate.' His face twisted. 'Jennifer Langton's going to Saunder's Green. She's determined to face her father.'

# SEVENTEEN

Betty started up. 'Jenny mustn't do that! He's dangerous!'
'I know!' Bill almost ran towards the door, then stopped and knocked his knuckles against his forehead, as if forcing himself to think. Then, striding back to the desk, he snatched up the telephone and rang Sir Douglas.

After a few brief words, Bill jammed the receiver back on the rest. 'I'm to get to Saunder's Green as quickly as possible. Sir Douglas is organising more men to follow.'

'Come on!' said Jack urgently. 'Can we take a police car, Bill?' he asked as they clattered down the stairs. 'I'll drive.'

'Yes, that's for the best,' said Bill, who was obviously trying desperately to get his fears under control. 'I can't believe Jenny's going there. I couldn't stop her.'

They ran out into the car park and towards the garage. 'Sergeant!' snapped Bill to the man in charge. 'I need your fastest car right away.'

'Very good, sir,' said the sergeant and turned away into the depths of the garage.

Jack put his hand on Betty's shoulder. 'Will you go home? You'll be safer at home.'

She swallowed and shook her head. 'Let me come with you, Jack. I can't bear the thought of staying behind, not knowing what's happening. Besides, Jenny might need me.'

He squeezed her hand. 'All right.'

A black Wolseley, the sergeant at the wheel, drove out of the garage and came to a halt. 'Here you are, sir,' he said, dismounting.

Jack, Bill and Betty scrambled into the car.

'Can't you go any faster?' said Bill tersely as they drove down the Embankment.

'Not in this bus and not in this traffic,' said Jack. 'If we have an accident, that'll really tear things.'

The traffic thinned as they got out of central London, but as

Jack wrestled the heavy, sluggish Wolseley along the suburban roads, he ached for the quick responses of his Spyker. How the devil did the cops ever catch anyone in these old crates?

'What shall we do when we get to the house? It's probably better not to go up the drive. We need to find out what's going on without giving the alarm.'

'Good idea,' said Bill. 'Park on the road a little way from the house.'

In the event it took them twenty-two minutes of agonisingly slow, if skilful, driving to get to Saunder's Green.

Jack drew to a halt in front of the tall hedges that shielded the front of the house. There was no one around.

They walked quickly up to the house. A racing-green, open-topped Bentley was parked in the drive. Jack put his hand on the bonnet. 'It's still warm,' he said quietly.

There was no sign of life from the house, no movement behind those blank windows. Bill reached out to ring the door-bell and hesitated. 'Did you say there's an entrance round the back?' he asked. 'I'll try there first.'

'No, wait,' said Jack. He pushed the heavy front door. It swung open noiselessly. They stepped into the hall. Silence.

'There must be somebody here,' said Betty quietly. 'That Bentley didn't come by itself.'

It didn't take them long to explore the downstairs of the house. Everything was neat and clean but silent.

'Where the devil is everyone?' said Bill in a low voice as they came back into the hall.

'Hold on!' said Betty. 'There's someone upstairs.'

There was a creak on the upper landing.

'Hello!' called Jack cautiously.

There was a noise like half a sob in reply.

'Who's there?' called Bill. 'This is the police!'

Jenny put her head over the bannisters, gave another half-choked sob and came down the stairs. Bill stepped forward and held out his arms to her.

'Thank God you're all right,' he muttered. 'Miss Langton, you shouldn't be here.'

She gave a shuddering breath. 'I had to come. Aunty Gwyn was beside herself. She rang me at work. I don't know what my father's got planned, but I had to stop it. I rang you, then snatched up the keys and came straight away.'

'You opened the door?' asked Jack.

She nodded.

Bill sighed in exasperation and relief. 'You should've waited for us.' He squeezed her hand. 'I'm only glad you didn't come to any harm.'

'But there's no one here,' said Jenny. 'I've been over the entire house and there's no one here.'

'Have you looked in the garden?' began Jack, when Betty waved him silent. 'Shush! I heard something.'

There was a very faint noise from along the hallway. Startled, they looked at each other in bewilderment. They had looked in every room that led off the hall.

Jack suddenly slapped his hand against the wall. 'The sound's on the other side of this wall! It's the garage! It's on the other side of this wall. Come on!'

Leading the way, he raced into the morning room, pulled open the French windows and out onto the veranda. 'The garage door's along here,' he called.

Together, they opened the garage door, and crowded onto the small landing on top of the steps. The steps, thought Jack, with a twist of his stomach, where Caroline Trevelyan was buried.

He reached for the rail surrounding the landing and looked down. Then for a fleeting fraction of a second, he saw a monster.

Its skin was black leather, its face was blank and black, and it had huge, blank, square eyes. It was suspended like a ghastly puppet with a noose around its neck with a rope attached to one of the roof beams of the garage.

Jenny's terrified scream snapped him back to his senses.

He grabbed her by the shoulders. 'Jenny! It's not a monster! It's a man!' He turned her round, forcing her to look down.

He had worked this out when he'd stood looking at the traffic on the Embankment, the day he had discovered Caroline Trevelyan's body. He'd seen the drivers, in their motoring coats, helmets and goggles.

He'd thought then what it would look like, looking down as a terrified child from above, to see a man in a motoring coat and helmet with his goggles pushed back, the sunlight dazzling off the glass to make two staring eyes.

He knew what the monster was. 'It's a man in a helmet and goggles. It's a man!'

Jenny's scream turned to a terrified whimper. 'It's a man?'

The man, his hands tied behind his back, tilted his face up towards them. He was standing on a wooden kitchen chair, a noose around his neck. If he stepped off the chair, he would be hanged.

'Help!' he croaked. 'Help!'

'For God's sake,' muttered Bill under his breath and, leading the way, clattered down the stairs to the man on the chair.

'Jack, hold him up!' he commanded. 'We've got to get him down.'

Jack wrapped his arms round the man's thighs as Bill, taking a penknife from his pocket, climbed gingerly up the chair beside him.

Jack felt the weight shift dangerously as Bill sawed through the rope.

Then the last threads were cut. Jack staggered as he took the man's whole weight. Bill jumped down, his arm supporting the man as he slumped onto the kitchen chair.

Bill cut through the ropes that bound the man's hands. He gave a little whimper and buried his head in his hands, his breath coming in heaving gasps. Jack reached out and, tilting the man's head back, ripped open his collar.

'Mr Laidlaw?' said Jenny in a terrified whisper, as she saw the man's face. 'Mr Laidlaw?' He turned a terrified face, drained of colour, towards her. 'What happened?'

'I was attacked. Attacked by a lunatic,' he gasped. 'He got me here with some cock-and-bull story and hit me with something.' His eyes flicked upwards to where the rope still hung. 'When I came to, I was up there.'

A shaft of sunlight shot across the garage floor as the door to the garden opened. A man, black against the sunlight, stepped onto the landing.

There was a frozen moment, then the black silhouette raised a gun and fired, the sound deafening in the enclosed space.

Chips of concrete zinged off the floor as they all dived away.

Jack, his back to the wooden shelf, closed his hand round the shaft of a hammer.

'Stand back,' commanded the man on the landing. 'Stand back or, by God, I'll shoot you all.'

'Trevelyan!' yelled Jack. 'Drop the gun!'

Jenny gave a little choking sob. 'Trevelyan? You're my father?' Like someone in a dream, she started forward towards the stairs.

'No, Jenny!' yelled Bill, lunging towards her and catching her in his arms.

Another bullet exploded, sending more chips of concrete off the floor. 'Stay where you are!' Trevelyan yelled.

Jenny looked up to the landing. 'You're my father.' Her voice broke. 'You're my *father*?'

Trevelyan caught his breath. 'Jenny?' he said in bewilderment, staring downwards. 'Jenny?' His hand holding the gun dropped to his side. He pushed his hair back and gazed down at her. 'Jenny?' His voice cracked. 'Jenny, sweetheart, you shouldn't be here.'

With a stifled cry, Jenny broke away from Bill and started up the stairs.

'No, Jenny!' called Bill but she ignored him.

She continued up the stairs towards her father. He held out his hand to her, then pulled her close.

Bill took his chance. Taking the stairs two at a time, he leapt up the stairs after Jenny. He stopped short as the muzzle of the gun came up.

'Stay there.'

Bill stopped warily. 'Michael Trevelyan, I am a police officer.' He spared a glance for Andrew Laidlaw. 'I arrest you on a charge of false imprisonment and attempted murder. Put down the gun, man, and come quietly. There's a squad of police arriving. You can't get away.'

Trevelyan's hand tightened on Jenny's shoulder, then pushed her gently away. 'Off you go,' he said, softly, his gaze fixed on Bill. 'I'm not running any longer. I came here to do one thing, and that's to get even with Laidlaw. You can't stop me.'

Even in the dim light, Jack could see Trevelyan's eyes narrow as the gun came up, pointed at the man in the chair. With all the strength in his arm, he flung the heavy hammer. It caught Trevelyan in the chest as the gun went off, flinging him backwards. The gun skittered out of his hand.

Bill leapt forward and forced Trevelyan to the ground. Jack raced up the stairs, adding his weight to Bill's struggles with the frantic Trevelyan.

With both Jack and Bill holding onto him, Trevelyan was firmly pinned to the floor. Struggling furiously, he tried to escape as a thunderous knocking sounded at the garage doors.

'Open up in there!' shouted a voice from outside. 'It's the police!'

'Betty!' shouted Jack. 'Open the doors!' he gasped, then renewed his strength to contain the struggling man. 'Give up, man! It's over!'

Betty fumbled with the catch and then light flooded into the room as the doors swung open and four policemen burst in, a sergeant at their head. Sir Douglas Lynton brought up the rear.

'What the blazes?' he exclaimed incredulously. He spun round to the sergeant and pointed up the stairs. 'Help them, man!'

The sergeant, with the constables behind him, charged up the stairs. With Jack and Bill's help, he managed to snap a pair of handcuffs onto Trevelyan's wrists.

Sir Douglas looked at Andrew Laidlaw, still slumped on the chair. 'What the devil's been going on here? Who are you, sir?'

Trevelyan levered himself up on his elbow. 'His name's Laidlaw,' he said in a gasp. 'He murdered my wife.'

'Absolute nonsense,' said Laidlaw in a croak. 'The man's mad. He got me down here with some crazy story and attacked me.'

'He murdered my wife,' said Trevelyan again.

Laidlaw seemed to recognise Jack for the first time. 'Haldean! Tell them what he did! Tell them the truth.'

'I know the truth,' said Jack, his voice steely. He picked up the hammer and walked down the stairs. 'He's speaking the truth. You murdered Caroline Trevelyan, Laidlaw.' He hefted the hammer. 'And you hid her body here.'

He brought the heavy hammer crashing down on the bricks of the steps. A chunk of brickwork round the loose brick came away, revealing a mass of blue fabric.

Laidlaw gazed in horror at the hole in the bricks. 'It's not true,' he whimpered. 'I couldn't help it. It wasn't really murder. Not really.'

'Arrest him,' said Sir Douglas curtly, to his sergeant.

'On what charge, sir?' asked the sergeant, walking to stand beside Laidlaw.

'The murder of Caroline Trevelyan.'

'And Amelia Rotherwell,' put in Jack.

Andrew Laidlaw crumpled. 'You know about that?'

'Yes,' said Jack. 'I know about that.' He turned to Michael Trevelyan, who was gazing at him, thunderstruck, and dropped a hand on his shoulder. 'I'm sorry I had to hit you, sir, but you don't have to run any longer. You're a free man. Or,' he added, with the beginnings of a smile, 'you will be once we get the handcuffs off.'

Sir Douglas nodded to one of the constables. 'Release him.'

Michael Trevelyan stood up slowly as the handcuffs were removed. Staring at Jack, he tried to speak, then buried his face in his hands. Jenny tentatively put her hand on his arm. 'Father? Dad? It's over.'

It was early evening. Andrew Laidlaw, without an ounce of fight left in him, was safely behind bars.

Michael Trevelyan had joined Bill, Jenny, Betty and Jack in the house in Chandos Row, in the upstairs sitting room where, Jack thought, as he poured out the whisky, Jenny had first told him about the monster in the garden at Saunder's Green.

'Help yourself to cigarettes, sir,' he said hospitably to the man on the sofa.

'Thanks.' Trevelyan smiled. It was a cautious smile, the smile of a man who had had very little to smile about. 'I can't believe it's all over. This morning all I wanted to do was get the truth out of Andrew Laidlaw.'

Jenny reached out and squeezed his hand. 'Would you have really killed him?'

Trevelyan hesitated. 'I don't know.' He looked at her shyly. 'I really don't know. I certainly wanted to. I wanted to hear the truth from his own lips and then . . .' He shook his head. 'It seemed right, in a way. If justice had been done, years ago, he would've been hanged. But when it actually came to it? I just don't know.' He glanced at Jack. 'All I can say is that I'm very grateful to you for stopping me.' He nodded at Bill. 'And to you. To all of you, in fact.'

'What happened, Dad?' asked Jenny.

'Dad!' Trevelyan smiled, a genuine smile this time. 'I can't tell you the times I've wanted to hear you call me that.' He paused. 'I can't believe you're here with me!' he broke out. 'I've dreamed of this, Jenny.' There was a catch in his voice. 'I never thought it would happen. I used to watch out for you, you know? I think you nearly saw me at least once.'

Jenny gripped his hand tighter. 'More than once.'

'Gwyn, my sister, sent me news of you occasionally. Sheila Langton used to write to her. I knew you were well looked after, but sometimes I just had to actually see you. I saw you at school and sometimes I went up to Yorkshire, just to try and catch a glimpse of you, but the last time I saw you, that was pure chance.'

'Was that in Stowfleet?' asked Jenny.

'Yes, that's right. I knew Saunder's Green was vacant and I was toying with the idea of renting it, to try and see if, even after all this time, I could find out what happened to poor Caroline. I knew Wilson and Lee were the house agents. I stood on the street, telling myself I was a fool for even thinking of the idea but tempted, all the same.'

He glanced at Jack, Betty and Bill. 'You can imagine how I felt when Jenny, of all people, came out of the house agents. I was so shocked for a moment I couldn't budge.' He turned to Jenny. 'I didn't know you worked there. You saw me, didn't you?' Jenny nodded. 'You came marching across the road to me. I hardly got away in time.'

'That was the morning it all started,' said Jenny. 'When I had that horrible experience by the tree, I mean. But Dad, what did happen years ago?'

Trevelyan shrugged. 'That's what I wanted to get out of Laidlaw. I always had my suspicions of him, but until this recent business, with poor Amelia Rotherwell, I couldn't be sure. But after she was killed and I was blamed, I *knew* I wasn't guilty.

I didn't know how and I didn't know why, but I knew Laidlaw was the man.'

'So what happened that day?' repeated Jenny.

Michael Trevelyan shrugged. 'As far as I was concerned, I came home from work that day on the 15th of July to find Caroline, your mother, gone. And that really was it. I tried to raise the alarm, but the police inspector obviously thought that your mother would come home in her own good time. Gwyn came to stay, to look after you, because I was beside myself.'

'Then the forged letter arrived,' said Jack.

'Yes, it did,' agreed Trevelyan. 'I knew Caroline hadn't written it. Until then I'd hoped she'd come back, but after I saw that letter, I knew something very sinister was going on.'

He swallowed hard and took a gulp of whisky. 'I'd been worried to death about Caroline, but that's when I started to worry for myself. Gwyn thought there had to be an innocent explanation, but I knew there couldn't be. Someone was trying to cover things up and, if that failed, it was obvious the police inspector, Chartfield, had me in his sights. I wrote to Sheila and John Langton to take care of you, Jenny, because I thought things would turn nasty very soon.' He took another gulp of whisky. 'And, as we know, they did.'

'There was a diary found in your room, sir,' said Jack, standing up and, taking Trevelyan's glass, re-filling it.

'That bloody diary!' said Trevelyan. 'Excuse the language, but honestly! I'd always been interested in chemistry at school. Caroline and I both loved detective stories, but we used to joke about how the poison used in them was always so wildly improbable. It was always a "little known Asiatic poison" and never anything real.'

'I know that type of story,' said Jack with a grin.

'I made a list of real poisons, that's all. I didn't add the date, though. Someone else did that and, later on, after I'd made a run for it, I was pretty sure that someone was Andrew Laidlaw. It had to have been done by someone who could get into the house. He could, of course, because of the building work. But,' he added with a shrug, 'why he did what he did I don't know.'

'I think,' said Bill, 'that Jack can probably enlighten us as to that.'

'Don't worry, I will, but to go back to your story, Mr Trevelyan. Your sister told us she helped you get away to Australia.'

'So she did. When the war broke out, I joined the Australian army, calling myself Raglan, my mother's name. I served first in Gallipoli and then in France. After the war was over, I had a perfectly decent name that was mine, with a war record to prove it. So I came home, and I've been here ever since. When I saw the advert in the papers, asking for news of the Trevelyans late of Saunder's Green House, I was worried. However, Gwyn wrote to me to say you were behind the enquiries, Jenny, so I breathed again. Gwyn was over the moon to have you back as a niece.'

'I know she was,' said Jenny. 'That was the only good thing to come out of it, as far as I could see. I've told you what I saw in the garden. I was terrified.'

'And you thought that was me,' said Trevelyan softly. 'A monster.' He looked at Jack. 'Why did Laidlaw do it?'

Jack sipped his whisky and lit a cigarette. 'When Jenny told us what she'd seen, one of my first thoughts was that she'd lived in Saunder's Green as a child. Although on the face of it, that seemed unlikely, it proved to be true. Once we had the name Trevelyan, I was able to advertise and that led us to Mrs Shilton. Mrs Rotherwell, recently returned from Ceylon, had also seen the advert.'

'I know,' agreed Trevelyan. 'Gwyn told me she'd written to her.'

'However, another old friend of Mrs Rotherwell's, a Mrs Jane Davenham, had also seen the advert. And Mrs Jane Davenham, who really had, in all probability, met up with Mrs Rotherwell since her return from Ceylon, realised that if Mrs Rotherwell met me, she and Andrew Laidlaw would be in real danger.'

'But why?' asked Trevelyan.

Jack ran his finger round the top of his glass. 'Because Jane Davenham and Laidlaw were married. What's more, Mrs Rotherwell knew it. She didn't know about his marriage to Violet Wild but she knew he was married to Jane Davenham.'

'They were *married*?' said Trevelyan incredulously.

'That's right,' said Jack, leaning forward in his chair. 'And, although Laidlaw deserves everything that's coming to him, in a way, I can feel sorry for him.'

'I can't,' ground out Trevelyan. 'He murdered Caroline and ruined my life.'

'So he did. But in the beginning, it mustn't have seemed as if he'd done anything that was so very wrong. He'd married Jane Davenham in secret and they obviously stayed together. I spoke to your sister earlier on, Mr Trevelyan, and she told me that Mr Wild would have sacked him on the spot if he knew Laidlaw had married without his permission.'

'That's probably true,' admitted Trevelyan grudgingly. 'Arthur Wild was a real old tyrant. That sort of attitude was fairly common before the war. I had to ask permission from Travis and Sons before I married Caroline. But dammit, Haldean, if he was married to this Davenham woman, why on earth did he marry Violet?'

'Because he had a huge amount to gain. Again, I owe this to your sister, Mr Trevelyan. She told me how old Mr Wild wouldn't leave his business – his very successful business – to his daughter but would to his son-in-law. Jane Davenham obviously went along with the plan.'

Trevelyan ran a bewildered hand across his forehead. 'Do you actually know this, or are you just guessing?'

'We know, all right,' said Jack. 'We've got the marriage certificate. We've got the certificates for both marriages, as a matter of fact.' He grinned at Bill. 'It took some hunting, but we found them.'

'So how did that lead to him killing poor Caroline?'

Jack lit a cigarette. 'This is supposition, but something like it must've happened that morning of the 15th of July in 1907. We know Amelia Rotherwell had called to see your wife, Mr Trevelyan. Andrew Laidlaw joined the ladies for coffee. And Mrs Rotherwell, who was acquainted with Jane Davenham, was bound to remark, once they'd been introduced, that she knew his wife.'

Trevelyan looked at him sharply. 'Are you sure? Caroline was very close to Violet. She'd have thrown Laidlaw out of the house.'

Jack shook his head. 'Would she? Andrew Laidlaw was a

quick thinker. It would be easy enough for him to say that Mrs
Rotherwell had made a mistake and to cover it up that way.
It's difficult to disagree with a guest, especially when that guest
is such a smooth talker as Andrew Laidlaw. However, that only
bought him a couple of hours at the most. Caroline Trevelyan
was bound to mention what Mrs Rotherwell said to Violet the
next time they met.'

Trevelyan whistled. 'The fat would've really been in
the fire then. Old Arthur Wild was a very hard-headed man.
If there were facts to be uncovered, he'd uncover them.'

'And bang would go Andrew Laidlaw's chance of inheriting
the firm,' said Jack. 'Yes, that was the motive. Laidlaw had to
act fast. He knew the builders weren't at the house that afternoon, so he took a chance and came back. He must've let
himself in at the side gate because none of the servants saw
him. As he was dressed in motoring things, he could've intended
to ask your wife to come for a drive, Mr Trevelyan. Maybe he
did and she refused.'

'And he killed her,' said Trevelyan bitterly. He squeezed
Jenny's hand. 'And you, you poor little mite, saw him.'

Jenny swallowed hard. 'Whatever put you onto it, Jack?'

'There were a few pointers,' said Jack. 'One of them was
your Aunt Gwyn, Jenny. She told me how much Laidlaw had
gained from his marriage to Violet Wild. That was one thing.'

He tapped his cigarette on the ashtray. 'Now when I realised
that the Mrs Rotherwell who I'd met at the Criterion was a
phoney, I went back over what she'd told me. Most of it was
about you, Mr Trevelyan, about how she'd met you and so on.'

'That's a pack of lies,' said Trevelyan. 'I never clapped eyes
on the woman.'

'No, of course you hadn't. What's more, I don't think either
Andrew Laidlaw or Jane Davenham ever imagined that you,
the real Michael Trevelyan, was around. What they did know
though, was that I had placed an advertisement in the papers,
asking for information about the Trevelyans. Jane Davenham
knew Mrs Rotherwell. She'd have known Mrs Rotherwell had
arranged to meet me and that meeting simply must not happen.
Laidlaw murdered your wife, Trevelyan, to keep his marriage
a secret. Mrs Rotherwell was murdered for exactly the same

reason. If she was allowed to talk to me, the truth would've come out and it would be curtains for the pair of them.'

'That's right,' agreed Bill. 'If Jack had met the real Mrs Rotherwell and learned that Laidlaw was married, not to Violet Wild but to Jane Davenham, then not only would he be guilty of bigamy, which is a very serious offence, but it wouldn't take us long to look at Caroline Trevelyan's murder in a very different light.'

'Absolutely,' agreed Jack. 'Although they didn't believe in you, Mr Trevelyan, they wanted us to believe that there *was* a Michael Trevelyan, who had murdered his wife twenty years ago and was now setting out to murder Mrs Rotherwell.'

'That's horrible, Jack!' said Betty.

'Yes, it is, but they needed a scapegoat. Now, so far, so good. But it didn't tell me the reason why the false Mrs Rotherwell should be doing any such thing. Had she said anything else? Well, yes, she had. She talked about Violet, Andrew Laidlaw's wife. She spoke quite a bit about her. Add to that, Laidlaw and Jane Davenham had a bad break. Bill's old inspector had, quite by chance, gone into Jane Davenham's flat. She had mysteriously disappeared. We made the connection between Jane Davenham and Laidlaw, and called to see him.'

'He was fairly rattled when we turned up, Jack,' said Bill.

'Yes, he was, but he rallied. Again, his wife, Violet, seemed to come into the conversation quite a lot.'

'Why did Jane Davenham disappear, Jack?' asked Betty.

'I don't think that was the original idea,' said Jack. 'I think what should have happened is that Jane Davenham should meet me for lunch at the Criterion, chat about Andrew Laidlaw and Violet, then feed me a tale about being followed by Michael Trevelyan. After a couple of nights at the Royal Park Hotel, I imagine she intended to go back to her own flat. However, once she realised how closely I was working with the police, and, what's more, knew about her as Jane Davenham, she had to disappear.'

'Is that when she moved into the flat at Summer's Court?' asked Betty.

'She moved in before then. I think Laidlaw took that flat for the sole purpose of getting Mrs Rotherwell – the real Amelia

Rotherwell – to come and be killed. The pair of them, Jane Davenham and Laidlaw, faked some evidence to show that you, Mr Trevelyan, had lived in the flat. One of them must've slipped back into the flat to leave the newspaper with the date of Wednesday the 21st on it, the date the fake Mrs Rotherwell apparently vanished.'

'That was risky,' said Bill.

'Not really. Laidlaw had taken the flat in disguise. He could stroll in as himself – he probably did try and avoid the porter – but even if he'd been seen, why should anyone recognise him or think anything of it?'

'And Laidlaw made out he was me?' growled Trevelyan.

Jack nodded. 'That's right. As I said, I don't think either of them believed you were actually here. They could shovel the blame onto you with impunity, while the police chased a totally mythical Michael Trevelyan. I'm pretty sure they left the tap dripping so that the bath would overflow and the discovery made sooner rather than later. They wanted things to come to a head. It must have been tense waiting for the discovery to be made. They'd put the poor woman in the bath so that by the time she was found, neither Bill or myself would be able to say she wasn't the woman we'd met.'

'What did you know about it, Mr Trevelyan?' asked Bill curiously.

'What I'd read in the papers,' he said grimly. 'Gwyn and I exchanged the occasional letter through a post office box number. She wrote to me, about the brooch I'd apparently delivered to Jenny. Naturally, I knew I'd done no such thing. I knew something beastly was being planned and I was certain Laidlaw was behind it. I didn't know anything about Jane Davenham but I was certain Laidlaw was the man. Then, when the news about Amelia Rotherwell broke and I was blamed, I was certain. More than anything else, I wanted to get my hands on him, to make him tell me the truth. I couldn't think how to go about it, when my old idea about taking Saunder's Green came back to me.'

He looked at Jenny and smiled. 'Naturally, I couldn't turn up at Wilson and Lee, so I wrote to them as Michael Raglan and arranged it all through the post. It was strange being back there.'

He entwined his fingers together, looking down at his hands. 'I've thought about Caroline an awful lot over the years, but she seemed to be *there*. You'll think I'm crazy, but I could've sworn I even caught a glimpse of her once or twice.'

Jenny looked at him sharply. 'Was it in the garden? Was she wearing a blue dress?'

Jack felt the hairs on the back of his neck prickle. He too had seen – virtually seen – the woman in the blue dress.

Trevelyan stared at his daughter. 'That's right. How do you know?'

'The lady who last had the house, a Mrs Trenchard, saw her too. The housekeeper, Mrs Offord, told me so.' Jenny took a deep breath. 'When I was there, when I saw the monster, I'm sure it was my mother, trying to show me what had happened.'

Trevelyan drew in on his cigarette. 'You may be right,' he said eventually. 'There's no two ways about it, I became convinced that Caroline was still there. That's what gave me the idea. I telephoned Laidlaw, giving my name as Raglan. I told him that I was the new tenant and had discovered what looked like human remains.'

'What did he do?' asked Bill.

'He had the wind up, that's for sure. He told me to keep it to myself and he'd be there as soon as possible. I telephoned Gwyn, with the idea of saying goodbye.'

He looked at them and shook his head. 'You have to remember I was absolutely desperate. I'd long since given up hope of convincing anyone I was innocent, so I decided to have justice in my own way. Laidlaw didn't recognise me. I think he was too on edge about the body I'd apparently discovered.'

He glanced at Jack. 'I had no idea poor Caroline was actually there, but all I can say is, I'm not surprised. I had the rope ready in the garage. Laidlaw went into the garage and I coshed him. I strung him up, then, as he was still unconscious, went into the garden to clear my head.'

He shrugged. 'Then you arrived. Thank God,' he added, under his breath.

It was the following morning. The mortal remains of Caroline Trevelyan had been taken away by the police.

Jack, Betty, Bill, Jenny and Michael Trevelyan stood under the cedar tree, its leaves turning to burnished copper in the autumn sunlight. Jenny reached out and tentatively touched the rough, ridged bark. 'She's not here,' she said quietly. 'She's at peace.'

'It's a nice old house,' said Bill to Jenny as they walked back to the car. 'I'd prefer something a bit smaller, though.'

She looked up at him with a smile. 'So would I. I think we've got quite a lot in common, don't you?'

Bill felt his heart lift. 'I'm looking forward to finding out.'